C000145937

TH
CROWD

THREE'S A
CROWD

RICHARD GARNER

UMBRIA PRESS

Umbria Press
London SW15 5DP
www.umbriapress.co.uk

Printed in Poland by Totem
www.totem.com.pl

Paperback ISBN: 978 1 910074 26 8
E book ISBN: 978 1 910074 27 5

CHAPTER ONE

Rivers leant across the table in the Italian restaurant – and his outstretched hand touched Jo's arm. "It's good to see you again," he said.

"Good to be back," said Jo – a smile forming on his lips. "Not much to do on Calicos." It was the tiny island in the Bahamas where Jo had been born and worked as a boatman for several years. "But you do need me to help you, don't you?" he asked – a trace of anxiety in his voice. Jo did not want charity from Rivers. He wanted to know he was fulfilling a useful purpose in working with the private detective.

At first Rivers did not respond. His eyes seemed to be fixing their gaze on something behind Jo. Momentarily distracted, he soon took on board what the former boatman was saying. "Oh, yes," he said. "Nikki and I have decided we're not good working together and she wants to go back to her old career as an events' organiser. I need an assistant." He smiled. The two had been close friends for years – meeting when Rivers had been staying with his sister on holiday in the Bahamas and became involved in investigating a murder. Jo had saved his life but had to serve a prison sentence when he killed a man who was about to kill Rivers. Jo had worked for Rivers for a brief spell in the UK but gone home to look after his dying mother. It would be good to work with Jo again, he thought. He put past memories behind him, though, and awaited a response from Jo. Suddenly, though, he became distracted again. Jo thought it must have been by something that was going on behind him. "What is it?" asked Jo.

Rivers smiled apologetically. "Sorry," he said, "but there's a right ding-dong going on in the alleyway beside the pub across the road."

Jo turned around. He could see a man – possibly in his sixties – looking all done in. The woman appeared to be sobbing. At that stage a waiter approached their table. "Are you ready to order, sir?" he asked Rivers.

"No," replied the private detective. "Give us a couple more minutes." He blushed. "I've been distracted by that row going on across the road." He pointed at the two people in the alleyway.

The waiter smiled. "Of course, sir," he said and moved away from the table. The couple across the road appeared to have finished their argument. Maybe they had just run out of insults to throw at each other, thought Rivers. The woman walked away and went back into the pub. The man sat on his haunches – his head in his hands. Moments later the woman flounced out of the pub carrying a handbag and marched straight past him without a word and continued to walk towards the centre of town. It didn't augur well for their relationship, thought Rivers.

"Why did you bring me here tonight?" asked Jo. "It's a few miles from Finchley – where you live."

"Yes," said Rivers, still watching as the man got to his feet again, emitting a huge sigh. "I'm thinking of moving out here. Buying a new house. I'm tired of living on top of the job. Hertford's a much nicer place to live and relax."

"Unless you're a curly haired white man in his sixties," remarked Jo.

"Yes," thought Rivers. The man seemed to be making no effort either to move back into the pub or walk away. He was, however, standing up again when another woman came out of the pub. This one was more smartly dressed and nearer the curly headed man in age, thought Rivers. While the previous woman had had the look of someone who had either been dragged through a hedge backwards or had been on a long walk in blustery conditions, his new companion looked as if she was just about to go to a cocktail party with a few middle-class friends. She, too, exhibited antagonism towards the man. She jabbed him in the chest with her forefinger as she made a point forcefully to him. He shrugged his shoulders as if he did not know how to respond to her. It was at that moment that she slapped him on the cheek. The waiter then approached their table again and this time Rivers managed to concentrate enough on ordering some food. "Just one course," he said to Jo. "I'd like to find out a bit more about what's going on across the road."

"Is that just your inquisitive nature talking?" he asked.

"No," said Rivers quickly. "I just have a gut feeling that somebody over there may be in need of the services of a private detective soon." The waiter had finished taking the order by now and Rivers looked up to focus his gaze on the alleyway again. "I don't believe it," he exclaimed.

"What?" said Jo.

"There's a third woman there now," he said. Jo turned around again. Rivers was right. This woman, again, was a younger model – not sophisticatedly dressed like the second woman or to take part in a ramblers' outing like the first woman. Jo detected this woman was somewhere between the other two in terms of her elegance. She wore a smart pair of jeans that were neither scuffed nor muddy and a casual sweater. She was not angry or aggressive like the previous woman, nor sobbing like the first one. If anything, she looked a little hurt. The man with the curly hair moved to comfort her by placing a hand on her shoulder. She recoiled, though. She said something to him that made him look sorrowful rather than angry. Then she, too, went on her way without making a detour back to the pub – going in the direction of the town centre like the other two women. Rivers chuckled to himself. "I wonder what would happen if they all three met up in town," he said. The food arrived just as he finished speaking. "Come on, Jo," he said. "We'd better eat up. We must get across the road and mingle. One thing you have to learn about the job of a private detective – you're never off duty."

"I could have told you that," came the reply. "I have worked with you before."

• • ● • •

"I need a pint," said the curly headed man as he made his way back into the pub after his altercations with the three women. "A pint of your strongest ale, Derek," he said as he arrived at the bar.

"Not your day, Rob," said one of a group of six drinkers standing at the left hand side of the bar.

Rob took a sip from his pint of bitter before responding. "No," he said thoughtfully. "I'd never have thought .... " His voice tailed off.

"Never have thought what?" said the man who had just spoken to him.

"The coincidence of it all," he said. "I seem to remember there was a famous essay question asking students to explain the use of coincidence in Shakespeare's plays. Well, perhaps that could be rewritten to read: explain the use of coincidence in Rob Corcoran's life. What do you think, Colin?" he said to the man who had been speaking to him.

"Perhaps you shouldn't go around dating three women who live in the same town?" the other man replied.

"Maybe it doesn't stop at three," quipped one of the others in the group of drinkers.

Rob fixed him with a stare. "What do you take me for?" he asked – a hint of aggression in his tone.

"A womaniser?" said the third man.

Rob scowled. "More like Billy-no-mates – going out with no-one now," he said.

"Have they all ditched you?" asked Colin sincerely. He

at least amongst the six drinkers seemed to appreciate that what had happened was not in the least bit funny, thought Rob. "I wouldn't quite say that," he said. "Sue seemed upset by discovering I had another woman, Jackie was just – well, angry. Miranda was hurt, I think," he said. He paused. "All Miranda saw, though, was me being hit by another woman. She may have thought I was finishing with her – the other woman, I mean. There's something to work on there."

"Which one would you most like to be with?" persisted Colin.

Rob looked at him. "I've never had to make that choice," he said.

"You may have to now," said Colin.

It was at that juncture that Rivers and Jo made their way into the bar. "I'll get these," said Jo, "seeing as you got the meal."

"But you're not drinking?"

"Yes, I am."

Rivers look at him disapprovingly. "I thought you were driving," he said sternly.

"I am," said Jo, "but I can still have a coke." Then he added: "It is a drink."

"Of course," said Rivers.

"So I can buy the round?"

"Okay."

"What are you having?"

"A pint of their home brew."

Jo walked up to the bar – aware that one or two eyes were upon him as he ordered their drinks. He took them to the table in the corner where Rivers was now sitting. "I don't think they've had too many black people drinking in here," he said. "I feel distinctly unwelcome."

"I've been in here before," said Rivers. "They're not racist. They're conservative with a small 'c' – set in their ways. If I walked into a bar in Calicos, there would be one or two people looking at me – wondering what I was doing there."

Jo nodded. "Point taken," he said. "Perhaps I'm just too sensitive."

"Yes," said Rivers. "Don't look for racism where it isn't. There will sadly be plenty of occasions where it is there." He took another sip from his pint. "Now, listening mode, let's see what we can pick up," he said. It was not that large a pub so it was quite easy to pick up conversations from nearby tables and Rob and Colin – who had broken away from the group of six drinkers by the bar – were now sitting at a table adjacent to the one that Rivers and Jo were occupying.

"Seriously, though, Rob," said Colin. "Have you thought what you are going to do?"

Rob thought for a moment before responding. "Sleep on it," he said. Then he added dolefully: "Alone."

"You don't feel you should try to make amends with one of them?"

"No," said Rob. "Ever since Trish and I split up, I haven't wanted to settle down with any one person. Safety in numbers."

"Except when they all three turn up at the same place."

Rob emitted a half laugh, half grimace. "You may be right there," he said. He paused again to take a sip from his pint of ale. "If I were to pick one of the three, it would be Sue. She's warm, understanding – and she's got no ties. Miranda's married – so that's a bit awkward. That may be the reason she wasn't as annoyed as the other two. She doesn't believe, maybe, that she's got the right to monopolise me."

"So Jackie is the easiest one to ditch?"

"Especially in view of the ferocious right hook that she has." He gingerly felt his cheekbone. "I don't think there's much point in chasing after her."

"If you don't mind me asking," began Colin tentatively. Rob appeared to wave him on to continue. "Is one of the reasons that you haven't been able to settle down since the break-up with Trish because you secretly hope to get back together again?"

"I don't see much of her now," he said. "She's moved out of Hertford now."

"Is your daughter still living with her?"

"She's at university now."

"You've never told me – did you break up with her or she with you?"

"Six of one and half a dozen of the other," said Rob.

"Except that it never really works like that," said Colin. "One or other of a partnership has to be the instigator of a break-up."

"I was having an affair."

"With any of the three?"

"No," said Rob, "She's long departed from the scene."

"So the upshot of all this is that you can't keep it in your trousers?"

Rob did not take offence. He guffawed slightly. "Something like that, I suppose," he said. "Another pint?"

"Yes," said Colin.

Rob nodded and got up from his seat, smiling at Rivers and Jo as he went past them on his way to the bar.

• • ● • •

"Fucking Rob," shouted Sue Plummer as she returned home that night. "I'll kill him. I'll kill him." With that she slammed the door behind her with such force that it brought her startled flatmate, Debra Paget, into the hallway.

"What's wrong?" Debra asked, worried.

"He's been two-timing me," she said. She took a bottle of wine from the fridge and poured herself a large glass. She lifted it in Debra's direction but her flatmate shook her head, declining the offer of a drink. "I'll kill him," she said again. "I went to the pub for a nice, quiet drink with him and there was this other woman." She had almost finished the drink by now and went

11

back into the kitchen to fetch the bottle. "We were sitting there, holding hands, and this woman came up to us and said 'and what, prey, are you two doing?' Sounded as if she'd got a plum in her throat. All lah de dah. His bit of posh, I suppose."

"So what happened?"

Sue looked at Debra. Her flatmate worked with her in the school meals department of a nearby primary school. Sue was the supervisor. She had taken Debra on out of pity. She had found her selling copies of *The Big Issue* on the corner of the market place on Hertford. She was living in a hostel in a neighbouring town. Couldn't read, couldn't write and her parents had chucked her out of their home at the age of 16 – saying she was a burden on them. She couldn't get a job because of her lack of qualifications and her mother said she couldn't afford to feed another hungry mouth who wasn't contributing at all to the family budget. Her father was almost perpetually drunk and the only contribution he had made to the family in recent years was saddling her mother with two children – twins – that were both unexpected and unwanted. Debra had adored the twins and was, she thought, helping the family out by playing her part in looking after them – allowing her mother to join her father for a drink whilst she babysat. It appeared, though, that her father didn't want that. Sue offered her a place in her flat and then took her on as a school meals assistant. Debra, who seemed unscarred by her whole home experience and just eternally grateful when anyone showed her the remotest act of kindness, realised how much she owed to Sue. She was determined to show her appreciation by doing anything Sue suggested or wanted done. She had learnt to read and write on Sue's instigation. Sue had originally intended her offer of a flat-share to be a short-term solution while she attempted to try and find something suitable for Debra. She now realised it was a more long term commitment – and possibly got in the way of allowing her and Rob to progress their relationship. "I shouldn't be saddling you with this," said Sue as she poured herself a third glass of wine.

"No," said Debra, coming to sit on the sofa beside Sue. "I want to help."

"I know you do," said Sue patting her flatmate on the knee, "but you can't. Nobody can."

"Did you mean it when you said you wanted to kill Rob?"

The comment, softly spoken, alarmed Sue.

"No," she said, patting her reassuringly on the knee. "We sometimes say things we don't mean when we get angry. You must know that."

In truth, Debra did not. In her world, you took the things that people said at face value. She couldn't conceive of the range of emotions that Sue was feeling as a result of being confronted by the fact her Rob had another lover. She nodded, though, as if agreeing with Sue. "Do you think you'll be seeing him again?" she asked.

"At the moment I never want to lay eyes on him again," she said. But things might change, she thought to herself, especially if... Then she checked herself. It was almost as if she dared not think about it. What she had meant was that she might change her mind if Rob gave her any proof that he had ceased to see this other woman. She did not, of course, know anything about the third woman – having departed from the pub long before she had arrived on the scene.

"So if he comes round?"

"Just say I'm not in," she said. "That would be best." She took another swirl from her wine glass and finished off the third glass. She looked at her watch. It was gone 10 o'clock. "Got to get up for work tomorrow," said Sue, "and so have you."

"Yes," said Debra.

Sue got up from the sofa. She staggered a bit as she did so and steadied herself by touching its arm. "I'm sorry," she said. "I'm sorry you've seen me like this."

Debra smiled as if to say it made no difference to her. She looked after Sue as she staggered her way back to the hallway and then to her bedroom, muttering under her breath: "Fucking Rob Corcoran – I'll kill him. I'll kill him."

• • ● • •

The doorbell rang soon after Jackie returned home that evening. For a moment she felt herself go cold. If it was Rob, how should she react? It was difficult enough seeing him with another woman – but when you added on top of that the fact that he nearly had his tongue down her throat, well, it spelt out the prospect that the relationship she had with him was all but over.

"Who is it?" she asked.

"It's Pauline. I just wanted to find out whether you were all right."

Ah, Pauline, thought Jackie. The woman she had gone out for a quiet drink with that evening. In all the emotion of seeing Rob with Sue, she had forgotten about her and left the pub on her own – leaving Pauline to gather up her belongings and try to guess what had happened. "Hold on a moment, I'll open the door," she said. She went into the hallway – walking past one or two pictures on the wall that denoted happier times in her past. One was of a family gathering which also featured her former husband from whom she had secured a divorce just 18 months ago on the grounds of her affair with Rob. You'd be smiling now, she thought to herself. You always said no good would come of it. Well, maybe you were right. She walked past him quickly. It wasn't as if he could offer her the hope of a route out of the dilemma she now found herself in – whether to finish with Rob or try and patch things up. He was living in a blissful relationship with a rather matronly woman whom Jackie could not conceive of ever having an illicit relationship with anyone. "Pauline," she said on finally reaching the front door and opening it. "Come in."

"You left your coat in the pub," said Pauline on being invited into the living room by Jackie, "although that wasn't the only reason I came round."

"No, I'm sorry," said Jackie. "You must think me incredibly rude."

"That wasn't the predominant emotion that I had," said Pauline. "I could see from your reaction to Rob and that woman that you were in a state of shock."

"I know. Silly. You'd think with my past I'd have taken the fact that Rob was seeing somebody else a bit more in my stride."

"Depends where you thought the relationship was going."

"Yes," she said. She thought for a moment before continuing. "I suppose – to be fair to Rob – he never promised me anything after I broke up with Ray. We just kind of continued like we had done before – seeing each other once a week."

"But?"

"I never suspected he was two-timing me." She gave a snort of laughter. "Like Ray never suspected I was two-timing him."

"Did you want more of a commitment from Rob?"

"I'm not sure that I did. I've got my work to see me through. The shop keeps the wolves from the door and allows me to keep this place on. I suppose I told myself that I couldn't manage a closer commitment than the relationship I had with Rob."

"But?" said Pauline again, prompting.

"But I thought Rob felt the same way as me and was happy with the way things were going rather than pack his life with as much nookie as possible."

"Ouch, you really are bitter."

"You didn't see what I did. Just as I was leaving, Rob was accosted by another woman who just happened to be walking along the street. She had seen the argument with me. I think she must have thought that meant Rob was having an affair with me – although, to all intents and purposes, by the manner that I left him she should have come to the conclusion that –

if there was another affair – it was highly likely to be over."

"So he was three-timing you?"

"You could say that."

"So what do you plan on doing now?"

"I don't know," said Jackie. She paused as if for reflection but then changed tack. "I say, I've been an awful host. Can I offer you a drink?"

Pauline looked at her watch. It was 10.30pm. "Well, just a quick one," she said.

Jackie nodded. "I think I could do with at least one too."

• • ● • •

Miranda tried to compose herself as she got back home that night. Aaron, her husband, had been staying in catching up on some work before the new week started. It was just after 10pm when she got back. He had finished his work and was watching television.

"Good evening?" he asked as Miranda entered the living room.

"Yes," she said quietly. "I've just got to go to the bathroom."

Aaron looked up. "Okay, love," he said. He stared intently at her. "You've been crying," he said. Miranda made no response. "What's wrong?" he persisted. "Is it your sister?"

"No, no, nothing like that," she said. She had been round to her sister's that evening. It would have been better, thought Miranda with hindsight, if she had invented some problem with her sister. Instead, it all came gushing out. "I've been seeing somebody else," she said.

"What?" said Aaron incredulously. "So you weren't with your sister tonight?"

"No, no, I was."

"But he was there, too?"

"No, no, she knows nothing about it. It's just that I saw him on the way home tonight."

"I thought you were a bit late. After all, your sister's got to get the kids off to school tomorrow morning."

"I saw him with somebody else. Oh, Aaron, I've been such a fool."

"Who is this guy?"

"I think it may be all over now. I just wanted to make a clean breast of it – and start again with you."

"Whoa," said Aaron. "I haven't come to terms with stopping being with you yet – if indeed that's what's happened. How long has this been going on?"

Miranda sat down on a chair opposite her husband. "About five or six months," she said. "I'm sorry."

"Jesus Christ," said Aaron. "I never suspected a thing. Who is it?"

"It wouldn't do any good telling you, Aaron."

"Was it that guy we met at that party we went to last year? The curly headed guy? I thought he took a shine to you." Miranda remained silent. "It was him, wasn't it? What was his name?" Miranda failed to respond again. "I'll find out and – when I do – I'll give him a piece of my mind."

"There's no point in laying all the blame on him. Blame me, too."

"Don't worry, I do. So there's no need to play your famous role of martyr."

"Famous role?"

"You are always quick to take the blame when anything goes wrong. Only this time you're quite right to."

"I'm sorry," she said.

"So you keep on saying." Aaron was deep in thought again. "Rob – that was his name. Rob – I can't remember his surname but he worked in the planning department at the town hall."

Miranda became a little bit apprehensive. "Don't do anything silly," she counselled.

"No, you've already done that," said Aaron.

Miranda was worried, though. Rob would be no match for

Aaron if it came to a fight between the two of them. Aaron was a former rugby player – and still kept himself fit in the gym every week. Rob was almost weedy by comparison – painfully thin except for the emergence of a slight beer gut as a result of spending too much time in the pub. "I told him you and I no longer...." her voice tailed off.

"Had sex, you mean" said Aaron. "Well, he might be in that boat when I've finished with him." He walked over to the drinks cabinet and poured himself a large scotch.

"What about us?" said Miranda tentatively.

"Us?" shrieked Aaron. "Us? There is no us now. Get out of my sight."

"But you can't just throw me out at this time of night."

"Why not? You could go to your sister's."

"Aaron, please."

"All right. You can get out of my sight by staying in the spare room tonight. Then we'll see."

"Thank you," said Miranda as she gingerly got up from her seat. She walked over to the door to make her way to the spare room. Once at the door, she turned around to face him again.

"I know," he said pre-empting what she was going to say. "You're sorry but I'm not going to come near you now. I'm afraid I might hit you. Good night."

"Good night, Aaron." With that, she disappeared into the hallway and into the spare bedroom. It was not all her fault she reasoned. Aaron had shown scant interest in her in recent months – preferring to spend much of his spare time at the rugby club. She had not thought to defend herself, though. Firstly, she thought Aaron would not listen in his present mood and secondly what he had done paled in comparison to what she had been guilty of.

Once in the bedroom, she undressed and got into bed. Sleep was a long time coming. She began to wonder if she had done the right thing by confessing but she was not the sort of person who could live a lie. Come to think of it, she mused, it was amazing how she had managed to keep the whole thing secret for six months. What did she want, she thought to herself? A reunion with Aaron or a continued relationship with Rob – or perhaps neither of the above. It would depend on how Aaron behaved over the next few weeks but at present she was thinking that none of the above really suited her.

Aaron, for his part, poured himself another glass of scotch. He downed it quite quickly and then started going over the events of the evening. Tears welled in the rugby player's eyes. He knew he had neglected Miranda during the past few months – longer even. It was, perhaps, not surprising that she had sought comfort elsewhere. It seemed, though, that she had been led astray by a womaniser. He focussed on Rob now. Anger welled up inside him and he flung the now empty glass into which he had poured his scotch over to the other side of the room. Whatever else happened, he thought to himself, he would make Rob pay for what he had done.

● ● ● ● ●

The telephone rang late in Trish's home that evening. Her daughter, Sally, just back from university, had already gone to bed. Trish was convinced the caller would be for her daughter. After all, she never got late night calls. Since splitting up with Rob, she had led an almost monastic existence – spending her time worrying about Sally and working at a charity shop in the centre of Hertford. She picked up the telephone. "Yes?" she said.

"Trish," said a voice on the other end of the 'phone. "It's Colin."

"Colin?"

"Colin Standen – from the Dog and Partridge." It was the easiest way in which to identify himself. When Rob and Trish had been together, they had often met him there.

"Oh, yes," said Trish, recognition flooding back to her.

"You'll never guess what's happened tonight," continued Colin, Quite right, thought Trish, and why should I? I'm not part of your crowd any more.

"It's Rob," said Colin. "He's been caught out womanising. Apparently, he was dating three different women – and they all turned up at the pub at the same time tonight."

Trish was beginning to think she wasn't really interested in the contents of this telephone call.

"Colin, I was just going to bed," she began.

"He was hit by one of them. I thought you might like to know."

"I'm rivetted by what you've been saying," she said sarcastically. "Why should I be interested in anything that shower does now?"

"Because as the way things are at the moment you still stand to inherit anything he has when he dies. He hasn't got his act together to make a will and – I suspect – nor will he. But, talking to him tonight, he is keen on one of them so that may change."

"So what do you expect me to do about it?"

"I just thought you ought to know," said Colin. "By the way he's putting it about that your splitting up was a case of six of one and half a dozen of the other."

"The lying bullshitter."

"I just thought you ought to know," said Colin repeating himself.

"So you keep saying."

"I could keep tabs on him for you."

"Eh?"

"We could meet for a drink. Discuss things."

Trish thought she began to see where the conversation was leading. Colin, who had been single for most of his adult life, wanted a date. She was not keen. Colin was a boring man with a substantial pot belly as a result of his nightly drinking habit at the Dog and Partridge. He had been a salesman at the local car showrooms and some people – quite frankly – were baffled as to how he retained the job for so long as he always seemed to still stink of booze in the morning. Now, though, he had been made redundant. She switched to thinking about her ex-husband. Perhaps she should keep closer tabs on him – after all, he was relatively well off as a result of earning a decent wage working for the planning department. She, on the other hand, had the upkeep of an albeit ramshackle old house to pay for out of her modest earnings working for a charity shop. "Okay," she said. "I'll meet you for a drink."

"Where do you fancy?"

"Anywhere but the Dog and Partridge," came the reply. "It's hardly exclusive and we don't want our business known."

"All right," said Colin. "I'll come over to your village. Will tomorrow night do?"

"That's fine. Come to my house and we'll go to the pub down the road."

Colin replaced the receiver and smiled to himself. It was the first time he had organised a date for himself in a couple of years. He had always fancied Trish from afar. Tomorrow could open up a new chapter in both of their lives, he thought.

As Trish replaced the receiver and made her way upstairs, Sally appeared on the landing. "Was that for me?" she asked.

"Not every telephone call in this house is for you," said Trish. "It was about your father. Apparently he's squandering our inheritance on three separate women."

"Oh," said Sally, sounding not the least bit worried.

Trish, though, for her part, was beginning to feel a bit concerned. She wasn't coming at the situation from the same standpoint as Colin. She was not worried about the possibility of Rob remarrying and passing on all his worldly goods to a new wife. No, she was worried about the here and now. Perhaps she should have tried to get a settlement out of him when the two of them had split up. She wasn't the type to think of trying to take her ex for all he was worth, though. On the other hand, if he was leading an extravagant social life on the back of finances she had contributed to when they had been together, perhaps she deserved a share of his fortune,

• • ● • •

Rob had shown no signs of leaving the pub after his drinking companion, Colin, had gone. In fact, just the opposite. He had immediately bought himself another pint. He ignored the party drinking in the corner – aware of the fact that they had been cracking jokes at his expense during the course of the evening. He returned to sit at the table next to Rivers and Jo. He sipped his pint and then turned to them. "You're new here, aren't you?" he said. He offered his hand to shake first with Jo and then with Rivers. "Rob Corcoran," he said introducing himself.

"Philip Rivers," said the private detective, "and this is my associate Jo."

"Jo?"

"Just Jo," said the former boatman.

"Your associate?" said Rob, querying the term Rivers had used.

"Yes, I'm a private detective," said Rivers. "Jo has just come back to the UK to work for me."

"Good," said Rob. "Pleased to meet you both." He seemed to be going out of his way to be friendly to Jo, Rivers thought, possibly in view of the frosty reception his companion had got from a certain section in the bar on arrival.

"You don't seem to get many non-whites in this pub," said Jo.

"That's an understatement," said Rob. "You're the first in a long time. Not many ethnic minorities in Hertford. Not many lefties, either. I subscribe to representing the second group but obviously not the first."

Jo smiled. "Maybe I should try and get some brothers and sisters to come down here," he said.

"Maybe," said Rob. He ruminated a bit before continuing.

"You're a private detective. What sort of things do you take on?"

"Most of our work is boring," Rivers said. "Tailing errant husbands to give their wives ammunition for divorce – and vice versa."

Rob smiled. "I'm surprised you haven't been tailing me," he said. Then a note of suspicion entered his voice. "Or perhaps you are?"

Rivers laughed. "No," he said. "Do you deserve to be tailed?"

"You must have seen the shenanaghins earlier on this evening. I was caught out by the three women I've been dating. One of them is married, one divorced. The third one is single."

"You may need me," said Rivers.

"Why?"

"Well, hell hath no fury like a woman scorned. You could be at risk – either from one of the women or – you did say – one of them had a husband."

"I doubt it," he said. "They're not violent types." He began to feel his cheekbone. "One of them did land a rather telling blow on my cheekbone, though. No, I'm more at risk because of my day job."

"What's that?" asked Rivers.

"I work in the planning department at the town hall. There's a lot of corruption about. You'd do well to escape it if you were working there."

"Have you?" interjected Jo.

"Yes, in fact I'm thinking of doing something about it. Employees of the state shouldn't be greasing their palms with bribes."

"Would you like me to help you with that?" asked Rivers.

Rob remained silent for a moment. "I'd like to think about it," he said – adopting a tone which indicated to Rivers that he was being serious about contemplating help.

"Well, in that case, here's my card," said Rivers fishing one from out of his pocket. "We'd be glad to be of service."

Rob scrutinised the card. "Finchley?" he said looking at the address on it. "What are you doing here?"

"Contemplating buying a house here," said Rivers. "It's such a lovely place."

"Compared with Finchley?"

"I have had murders to deal with in Finchley," said the private detective.

"Well, let's hope you don't get any here," said Rob. He finished his pint. "Well, I think I'll be on my way now," he said. "Nice to meet the two of you," he added offering them a handshake as he departed.

He turned left on going out of the pub, making his way towards the town centre but cut off towards the village of Bengeo once he reached the traffic lights. Rivers and Jo followed him out of the pub. They became aware of a man in a hood following him as he went up the road towards the village.

"In view of what he said, I don't like that," said Rivers. "He could be in danger. Come on."

They reached the traffic lights but could not see him. Then they heard a groaning noise from an alleyway. They ran to where it had come from. Rob was lying on the ground with blood spurting from his head. He was still conscious. "This guy came up behind me and hit me with – it must have been with something like a club," he said. "He said 'this'll teach you a lesson' and then he was gone."

"Did you see who it was?"

"No, he had a hood on and a scarf covering his mouth."

"We'd better get you to hospital."

"It's not that serious," said Rob. "It looks worse than it is."

"Nevertheless, we'd better get it checked out." Rivers paused for a moment. "Would you like to reconsider that offer for me to look after you," he added.

"I'll think about it."

CHAPTER TWO

"The police are here, Rob," said Rivers as he handed the wounded planning official a cup of coffee.

Rob sighed. "I don't know that I want all the fuss," he said. "I probably deserved what I got but I don't know who delivered it."

"It's their job to find that out – or mine if you ask me to," said Rivers. He thought for a moment. It was no use badgering Rob into seeking his help.

As he hesitated, a couple of uniformed police constables approached Rob as he sat on a chair in the accident and emergency department of the hospital. "How do you feel, sir?" one of them asked Rob.

"Not too bad," he said.

"We've come to try and find out who did this to you," said the constable. "Have you any idea who would want to harm you? I take it this was a deliberate attack on you and not just some random attack or mugging?"

"They didn't take anything," said Rivers.

"Thank you, sir, but if you'd leave me to question the victim, I'd appreciate it." Rivers nodded. The last thing he wanted to do was to get into the police's bad books. Especially if he was coming to live and possibly work in Hertford. "I repeat – do you know who might want to harm you?"

"How long have you got?" asked Rob. He sighed. "No, I don't want to go down that road. I've caused enough trouble without wanting to see anyone in court. Besides, he could have hurt me much more. He obviously didn't want to kill me or anything like that."

"He?" questioned the PC.

"It was obviously a man. A woman couldn't have hit me with that force. Besides, I did see the shape of the attacker even though he was wearing a hood and some kind of a mask."

"Why do you think you deserved what happened to you?" asked the PC. "Surely no-one actually deserves to be assaulted like that."

"I'd been rumbled earlier on in the evening. I've been dating three women and they all found out about it earlier this evening."

"So why would that lead you to the conclusion it must have been a man?"

"Well, one of them was married," said Paul. "And the gruff voice. It was a man's voice."

"You told me this evening you had more to fear from your work in the planning department than from your womanising," intervened Rivers.

The PC turned on him. "I've told you, sir, this is my case and if you persist in interrupting me I shall have to have you forcibly removed from here," he said. Having set the cat among the pigeons, Rivers held his hands up as if to say sorry.

"Also, I'm not sure if I want to get into that can of worms," said Rob. "I've got enough on my plate dealing with the three women."

"Could you tell me who they all are, sir?" said the PC. "Their names and addresses."

"No," he said quite firmly.

"Well, at least give me your address," he said. Rob relented and complied with the PC's wishes. The PC then turned to Rivers. "Now it's your turn," he said. "Are you a friend?"

"No, I only met Rob for the first time in the pub tonight," said Rivers. "I was with my colleague Jo," he said pointing to the former boatman – who had been standing quietly by the side of Rob's chair through this conversation. "We followed Rob out of the pub and saw that he was being followed."

"Did you catch a sight of his attacker?"

"No, by the time we caught up after he had gone round a corner Rob had been attacked and the assailant had gone away."

"And the same goes for you?" the PC asked Jo.

"Yes."

"Are you sure?"

"Yes, I got to the scene after my friend Rivers. I got even less of a look at Rob's attacker than Rivers here. Why do you ask me if I'm sure?"

"Well, I know your lot sometimes are reluctant to help the police." The second police constable frowned at his colleague over this remark but said nothing.

"My lot? Who are my lot? You couldn't possibly be lumping all black people together, could you?"

"Just checking, sir."

"No, you weren't."

"Okay, okay," said Rivers intervening. "This isn't getting us anywhere." He turned to the PC. "I'm sure if you said you were sorry if you caused offence, we could move on from here."

"This is my enquiry, Sir, I'll conduct it in the way that I wish. I'm just trying to get at the facts."

"If you stick to that, we'll be fine," said Rivers – speaking through clenched teeth.

"May I ask who you are, sir?"

Rivers reached into his pocket and brought out a card. "Philip Rivers, private detective," he said pressing the card into the PC's hand. "This is my assistant Jo," he said.

"Jo who?"

Rivers faltered. "I can't remember," he confessed.

"You mean they're all the same to you so you don't bother to remember their names or is it that you can't tell them apart, sir?"

"Oh, for Christ's sake," said Rivers muttering through clenched teeth again.

"No, come on, tell me. What were you meaning?" Rivers declined to answer. "I've got your name and address," said the PC after a moment's pause. "That'll do for now. I shall have to make a report on this incident. We may need to talk to you again – or it could be a case for our CID."

"Let's hope it is," said Rivers as the two PC's departed from the waiting area. As they disappeared, a nurse approached Rob and informed him they were ready to patch up his wound but an X-ray had shown there were no bones broken. "We can give you a lift home when they've finished," said Rivers.

"Thank you," said Rob, "but I've taken up enough of your time already. I can get a taxi home."

Rivers decided not to press the point.

• • ● • •

Roger Broadbent looked up as the secretary ushered his visitor into his office. "That'll be all, Janine," he said. "Jerry," he said. "What can I do for you?"

"I think you know," said the visitor as he perched himself on Broadbent's desk. The two men could not have been more different than chalk and cheese. Jerry Vincent was dressed – well, Broadbent could only think of one way to describe it – flamboyantly. He wore an open neck patterned shirt and a brown ankle length flowing coat. His brown corduroy trousers were the only conservative part of his attire but they were held up with a broad belt which had the motif of a lion attached to its buckle. His shoes were high heeled – Chelsea boots they would have called them in an earlier era, thought Broadbent. Also, he obviously could not see Vincent's car but he knew he drove an Aston Martin which was probably even now taking up two spaces in the municipal car park. Precision parking was not one of Vincent's specialities.

"Couldn't you have sent someone to see me who didn't draw so much attention to himself?" asked Broadbent. He was wearing a sober grey suit and white shirt. The only distinguishing feature was an old cricketing tie which looked as if it had seen better days – probably a throwback to his playing days. He wore spectacles and had a receding hair line. What hair that was left was grey while Vincent had flowing brown locks long enough to rest on his shoulders.

"Dear boy," he said. Despite their looks, Broadbent was five years his junior. "You should be flattered I pay you so much attention. I wanted to check on the progress of my planning application?"

"I've drawn up a report for the committee recommending its approval."

"That's good – but is it enough?"

"You know you want to build these homes in an area where we want to retain as much of the rural nature of the countryside as possible."

"Yes, but the farmer who owns the land is begging for a sale. The farm is too big for him now and he wants to retire. You'll be doing him a favour."

"There will be objections from the civic society."

"How much would it take to bribe them?"

Broadbent looked horrified. "You can't be suggesting?"

"I'm not. I was only joking," came the reply. "Gosh, Darling, you'd better lighten up. You'll have a heart attack."

"I have argued that the government's priority is to build more housing and this would help us fulfil our target towards that end."

"Bravo," said Vincent, clapping as he responded to the planning official. "Will it be enough to convince the committee?"

"I'll need to get the chief planning officer on side."

"I wouldn't anticipate any trouble there," said Vincent. "By the way, did you enjoy Wimbledon?"

"Er, yes," said Broadbent, blushing.

"Great – and was the float I gave you enough to secure some strawberries and champagne?"

"Yes, thank you." Then he added in a whisper: "Keep your voice down."

"Darling, nobody can hear us. Your colleague doesn't seem to be in and the secretaries are out of earshot. Just think on this, Roger dear. If you deliver on this there'll be Lords' test match tickets in the post to you – and a hamper from Harrods that you can pick up on the day. If, on the other hand, you fail, oh Roger – I wouldn't want you to go down that road." He made a gesture as if he was slitting his own throat.

"I can't guarantee how the elected councillors will vote – especially the guy that represents that area."

"I can, dear boy. I can."

"He's in your pocket, too?" Roger asked incredulously.

"Nobody's in my pocket, dear boy. We're all just individuals doing what we think is right to deliver a better tomorrow. Let's just say that once the homes get built, we'll have an opening ceremony to which the householders who buy them will be invited and he will be asked to cut the ribbon. He seemed flattered. And he didn't want to miss up an opportunity to impress so many potential new voters. He's cheaper than you, Roge, me old mucker." With that, he got up from the desk. "Maybe there's a lesson in that."

It was at that juncture that Rob Corcoran walked into the office that he shared with Roger Broadbent. "Good morning," he said on spotting Vincent.

"Good morning, old fruit," said the property developer. He looked closely at the bandage on Rob's forehead. "My goodness," he said, "better be a bit careful in future. Go easy on the sauce."

"I'll see you out," said Broadbent to Vincent. When they were out of Rob's earshot, he turned earnestly to him. "Don't give Rob the flamboyant routine," he said. "He's already suspicious of you – and he's straight."

"Never suggested he was bent, old boy. Just warned him

to be careful." He tickled Broadbent under the chin. "After all, we all ought to be careful," he added. "I'll just pay my respects to your boss before I go."

"Not everyone's corrupt," sighed Broadbent. "I wish you'd remember that."

Vincent was gone, though, to the oak-panelled doorway across the hall where Douglas Roulay, the chief planning officer, worked. He knocked on the door and smiled sweetly back at Broadbent as he heard the word "enter!" and opened it, "I've been discussing a planning application with one of your staff," he said as Roulay invited him to sit down. "It's for homes on farmer Hedger's site. Could be a real money spinner."

"Yes, I know about it. It's against past council policy, though," said Roulay.

"Times change and council policy should change with it. I think I've convinced your staff to back it."

"I'm sure you have."

"You'll be presenting Broadbent's report to the committee?"

"I should imagine so. I'll have to read it, of course, before I pass judgement on it."

"Of course." He lowered his voice. "You won't find anything to disagree with in it," he said.

"I. er ...."

"I said you won't find anything to disagree with in it." His voice sounded menacing. He looked at a photograph on Roulay's desk. "Is that your house?" he asked.

"Yes."

"And your wife and kids?" Vincent mulled over the photograph for a moment. "Nice place. Quite spacious. Could do with a swimming pool. Would you like one?"

"I . er...."

"Of course you would but you're too polite to mention it. On the other hand, it would be a tragedy if something happened

31

in it." With that, he got up from his chair. "Toodle pip," he said. "I'm sure nothing can go wrong."

• • ● • •

"I want to thank you for coming over and helping us out," said the chief superintendent as Detective Chief Inspector Francesca Manners walked into the room. "What with illness and staff shortages we'd be in a pickle if you hadn't."

"That's all right, sir," she said. To be honest, she thought, I'd far rather be working under you than Chief Superintendent "Pratt by name Pratt by nature" – as her former boss Larry Green had called him – back in Finchley. Rory Gleeson was a different kettle of fish. He did not have the pomposity of Pratt, he did not talk down to his officers but if you let him down he would let you know it. Also, he wasn't overweight or precious like previous bosses she had known. A keep fit fanatic, he could be found at the gym three days a week and would often go for a jog before coming to work. To anybody who bothered to ask, he said it was a good way of clearing his mind. Solutions often came to problems when he was jogging along Waterford Common and immersed in spotting the wildlife – in that large expanse of open space just outside Hertford. "I don't know whether it's my place to say it, sir," she added, "but should a suitable vacancy occur in Hertfordshire, I would be happy to be considered for it."

"You never know," said Gleeson. "The job you're covering at the moment could become vacant. It's not much of an advert for the post but Detective Chief Inspector Brett who you're covering for has had a nervous breakdown after tackling an armed robber and being shot at. He may not be coming back."

"He was a good detective," said Francesca. She wanted to say she was sorry to hear that but her protestations may have seemed false in view of her earlier comment, she thought.

"To business, Manners," said Gleeson. "There's a new recruit arriving today. Detective Constable Gary Clarke. I want you to take him under your wing. I've met him. There are one or two rough edges that need to be ironed out but he should make a good detective."

"Rough edges?"

"Over zealous. Likely to jump in with both feet without considering all the options but I'm sure you can cope with that. I think he'd prefer to be working with the Met rather than out here in Hertfordshire."

"Right sir."

"Well, I think that's all, Manners. You may find he's already arrived when you go to your office."

Sure enough, he had. Gary Clarke was 25 and looked going on 17. He had short closely cropped hair but with sideburns going down to his earlobe. He wore glasses and, to Francesca's mind, looked a bit like a younger version of the pop singer Elvis Costello. She mustn't jump to conclusions too quickly, though.

"Welcome on board," she said, proffering her hand. "I hope we'll make a good team."

"Yes, ma'am."

"You can call me Francesca and I'll call you Gary – unless we're interviewing somebody and then it's Detective Chief Inspector Manners." She still liked referring to herself by her new title. She had been recommended for the job by her retiring boss Larry Green on the back of some sterling work the two of them had done in tracking down the murderer of a couple of prostitutes' punters the previous year. The Pratt had been impressed by her, too.

"Yes, ma'am – er – Francesca."

Francesca smiled. Gary Clarke didn't seem overbearing at first sight. Judgement, though, would have to be suspended. "Let's see what we've got here," she said, taking some paperwork out of her in-tray. It had been placed there this morning. She came across the note the two PCs had made about the assault on Rob Corcoran.

It said that he was reluctant to press charges but one fact caught her eye. The only witness to the incident was named as private detective Philip Rivers. She had worked well with Rivers in the past and doubted whether he would just have been innocently passing by. There may, she thought, just may be more to this incident than met the eye. "We'll take this one on," she said. "I know Philip Rivers. He's been helpful in the past." She also liked him. At one stage they had come within an ace of having a fling with each other but that was in the past – and they had remained good friends. It would be good to see Philip Rivers again.

● ● ● ● ●

"More toast, Jo?" asked Nikki as he finished the first two slices that she had offered him with obvious relish.

"No, I don't think so, Nikki," he said. "I should imagine Rivers would like me to start work soon."

Nikki nodded but added: "He's not the best at getting up in the morning. By the way, why do you always call him Rivers? His name's Philip."

"I think he likes to be called by his surname. I did when I first met him in the Bahamas and it's kind of gone on from there."

"He does," said Rivers entering the room at this juncture, "and – whilst we're on the subject of names – what's your surname? I keep getting asked it and I can't go on stalling everybody."

"It's debatable," said Jo.

"Go on," said Rivers, intrigued.

"My Dad's surname was Rawlins and he insisted I should be known by that name. But my mother brought me up and her name was Eddison-Clifford so, by rights, I thought I should take her name. I couldn't be known as Rawlins-Eddison-Clifford. You have to draw the line somewhere."

"And where did you draw the line – on your passport, for instance?"

"I pretended Eddison was a Christian name – so I'm Jo Eddison Rawlins-Clifford. For my bank account, I'm Jo Eddison Clifford-Rawlins, just to even things up. I'd prefer to be known as just Jo, though."

"Then I think we should respect your wishes," said Rivers. "I shall try stalling on the name of your surname for as long as possible. Anyway, it's too complicated. Goodness knows what will happen when it comes to the next generation."

"Thank you," said Jo.

"Right," said Rivers. "I've got to go and get my car serviced this morning so I wonder if you could open the office up. I'll probably be with you about lunchtime." He chucked the keys across the table to Jo.

"I might as well get going," said Jo. It was about 15 minutes' walk to Rivers' office from the flat he and Nikki shared. Upon arrival, he noticed an elderly man waiting outside the door. "Have you come to see a detective?" Jo asked him as he put the key in the lock and opened up.

"Yes."

"Come in," said Jo. He offered the man, who looked as if he was in his 60's but had not really taken care of himself, a seat. He was overweight with a pot belly protruding from some jeans which had long since ceased to fit him. His open necked shirt looked as if it was still harbouring milk stains from his breakfast. "How can I help you?"

"I want to see a detective."

"You're looking at one," said Jo pleasantly. "How can I help?"

"No, I'll wait."

"What for?"

"I want a real detective. No offence, mate, but you're not. I've walked past this office several times and there's another guy who works here."

Jo nodded. "Yes, there is. Mr Rivers."

"That's him," said the man. "I'll wait for him."

"We're both detectives. He's going to be out for some time. I repeat – can I help?"

"No."

"No? Why?"

"Well.....!"

"I'm not white?"

"Well, yes, I mean, you're not going to clear the darkies out from next door."

Probably not, thought Jo. "Tell me about the problem."

"No, you'll only go and take their side."

"That depends on what they've done – or whether they've done anything."

"There you are, you see. Taking their side."

"I'm not taking anyone's side." Inside, Jo was thinking to himself. Give it a rest. You're never going to convince this guy to let you help him. He's as racist as they come. He doesn't deserve my help. Outside, he felt he owed it to Rivers to try and find a way round the problem. He doubted whether there was.

"They make noises all night long. And they take drugs. I want pictures of what they're doing so we can take them to the council and get them thrown out."

"I'm not sure we can take pictures of noises. Anyhow, what kind of noises do you mean? Do they fart, have loud sex? What?"

"You're not taking me seriously."

"If you have a problem with noisy neighbours, contact the environmental health department at the town hall."

"Mr Rivers shouldn't have given a job to someone like you."

"Well, he has."

"We didn't vote for people like you to be allowed into the country. In the referendum. I'm not sure I want a firm like this to help me."

"Well, rest assured, if you don't want us to help you, we'll be glad not to."

"That's racism," said the man. "You only said that to me

because I'm white."

"No, I said it to you because you're you. Please go."

"I will. I'll go somewhere else."

"Good."

With that, the man shuffled out of the door. Jo watched him go. He picked up a pen from the desk and then flung it on the floor in exasperation. "Bloody hell," he said. He reflected. It had not been a good start for him in the UK. First, the frosty reception in the pub, then the police officer who seemed to have a problem with people like him and now this punter who only wanted white men to help him out with his so called problem. He didn't remember it being like this when he had been previously over in the UK helping Rivers out a few years back.

· · ● · ·

"Who was that guy?" Rob asked Roger Broadbent when Vincent had long gone from the room.

"Oh, just some guy consulting me about a planning application," said Broadbent non-commitally.

"I'd be careful if I was you."

"About what?"

"Well, he seemed to me to be a bit threatening," said Paul. "You've had dealings with him in the past, haven't you?"

"He's a property developer. He often puts in planning applications. I have to deal with him."

"How come I've never dealt with him? Why do all his applications go through you?"

"There's such a thing as asking too many questions, Rob?"

"I don't think I have. Not nearly enough questions, I would say."

"Where are you taking this, Rob?"

"To be honest with you, Roger, I don't know. I just think you have a kind of unhealthy relationship with him. Most of his applications go against council policy. Using green belt land for housing, for instance. I wonder how he gets them through."

"You don't know that, Rob. You're just speculating."

"And would I be speculating about the wonderful life-style you have? Doing things way above what your earnings would deliver. Wimbledon every year. Lords, too. And I seem to remember there's a chalet in the Channel Islands that you disappear to every summer."

"I earn a decent wage."

"And I bet if the police looked into your bank account they'd find most of it is still in there or invested in something."

"That's not a crime."

"No, but it would be if they were to find he had made payments to you."

"You've got no evidence," Roger cut in.

"No," said Rob slowly and deliberately. "Not yet." He paused for a moment. "There are, of course, other ways to tease out what's going on."

"Such as?"

"Present the evidence of how council policy has been subverted to one of our local councillors. They'd find it interesting. Especially if one showed them evidence of how it was always the same developer who benefitted from it and the same planning official who drew up reports recommending his schemes got the go ahead." He looked at his colleague. Roger seemed to be shaking. "You're worried," observed Rob, "And then there's always the press."

"Now you're wrong. There isn't. The local papers have hardly got any reporting staff left. They wouldn't be able to sustain an investigation like this."

"You're sounding relieved about that, Roger. As if you have got something to hide. Anyhow, I wasn't necessarily thinking about the local press. I was thinking of something like *Private Eye*. They keep a watch on corruption in town halls."

Roger remained silent. "Not so smug now, Roger," Rob continued. "What's the matter? Have I got to you?"

"You're just jealous," said Roger, trying another tack. "Why don't you come on board? There's plenty of money to be made."

"I wish I had a tape recorder recording this," said Rob, "I might try that next time. Talk about shooting yourself in the foot."

"Seriously, though, Rob, what are you going to do?"

"I haven't decided yet," came the reply. "I suppose as a first off I ought to tell Roulay what I know. I just wanted to tell you I was on to it so you could stop it if you wanted to."

"It's not as simple as that," said Roger looking crestfallen. He held on to one fact, though. He was sure that Roulay was sufficiently in thrall to Vincent to brush it all under the carpet. The question was: what would Rob do if that happened

"Anyhow," said Rob. "I have a site meeting to go to now. I'll sleep on it and tell you what I plan to do in the morning."

Roger nodded and watched as Rob left the room. After he had gone, he took his mobile phone out of his pocket and rang Jerry Vincent. "Jerry, I think we have a problem," he began.

"I don't want to hear about problems," came the reply. "You can sort it, can't you?"

"I think this one may need your persuasive techniques," he said. "You know Rob who I share an office with?"

"Yes?"

"He's doing some research which, he says, will expose the relationship between you and me."

"And you think he can do that?"

"He's going to look through past planning applications and see how many you've submitted and got the go ahead despite them breaching council policy. Then he'll try and find out whether the reports on them were all written by me. He's then going to have a look at my supposed lavish lifestyle. We could end up in *Private Eye*."

"It'll take him a while to do all that," said Vincent.

"Yes," said Roger. "I suppose it will."

"We can dissuade him from going down that road."

• • ● • •

"How are you this morning?" said Debra – concerned as she sat across the table from Sue at breakfast time.

"I've felt better," said Sue. Her answer was an understatement. She had a splitting headache – probably from all the wine she had drunk the night before. She had also gone without much sleep.

"Have you been thinking about Rob?"

What a naive question, thought Sue. Of course I have. She decided not to adopt a brusque response to it, though. Debra didn't really know any better. She probably had no idea of the impact that Rob's unfaithfulness had had on her. "I've been thinking of little else," she said.

"You shouldn't kill him," said Debra.

Sue relaxed and allowed a smile to form on her lips. "I'm not going to kill him," she said. "That was just something I said in the heat of the moment."

"No," said Debra. "You said it several times."

"In the heat of several moments, then."

"People might expect you to kill him," she said. "You'd be caught."

"Debra, I don't want to have this conversation. I don't want to kill him."

Debra looked thoughtful. "It should be somebody who no-one would suspect," she said.

"It shouldn't be anybody, Debra."

With that, Debra got up from the table. "He's hurt you, hasn't he?" she said.

"Yes, but lots of people get hurt by people every day. They don't go around killing them, though." Sue was beginning to feel exasperated by the conversation. It was bad enough trying to deal with her own emotions following the exposure of Rob's love life the previous evening without having to sort Debra's mind out about it, too.

"A hurt to you is a hurt to me," said Debra.

"It's very sweet of you to say so, Debra, but you're not any more hurt than me – and I'm not feeling vengeful towards Rob in any way." She was lying, of course. She would have liked nothing better than to get her own back on Rob that morning but she couldn't see a way of doing that – and she didn't want to dwell on the subject any more with Debra. "Come on, Darling, let's get to work," she said. "Take our minds off nasty things like getting hurt and hurting people." Chance would be a fine thing, though, she thought to herself.

• • • • •

"Never really expected to find you in," said Jerry Vincent as he arrived at Jackie Quesling's house that afternoon. "Just happened to be passing so thought I'd knock on the door on the off chance."

"It's a bad hair day," said Jackie. "I was feeling under the weather so I thought I'd take a day off."

"Oh, would you rather I didn't stay, Darling?" asked Jerry.

"No, no," she said. "You might be able to cheer me up."

"I can try. What's the problem?"

"Oh, men," said Jackie grimacing.

"All of them?"

"No, one in particular."

"And his name would be?"

"Rob Corcoran."

"Funny," said Jerry, "I seem to have heard that name quite a lot today. What's he done?"

"Oh, I was having an affair with him."

"Was?"

"That seems to be the case now."

"Good," said Jerry. "That means you can start having an affair with me."

Jackie sighed. "That's a nice attempt to try and boost my morale."

"It was supposed to be a nice attempt to get into your knickers." He paused to see what effect his words would have on her. On perceiving that she was lost for something to say, he decided to break the silence himself. "But, seeing as your involvement with him has only just come to an end, we must give you time to recover before making any serious advances." He kissed her on the cheek. "That'll have to do for now," he said.

"Thanks," she said. "You are a tonic."

"I'd like to think I was perhaps something stronger. A gin and tonic, perhaps? Anyway, tell Uncle Jerry – if he's not going to be lover Jerry – what happened."

"He's been two timing me. Well, even that's not strictly true. He's been three timing me."

"And how did you find this out?"

"I saw him sitting with his arms around another woman in the pub last night. He made no attempt to deny it."

"Have you spoken to him after discovering this?"

"Other than calling him a shit-house and thumping him, no."

"Good for you," said Jerry. "Do you intend to contact him?"

"What's the point? I can't trust him anymore. Oh, I know that sounds rich from someone who two-timed her husband – but this seems different somehow."

"So it's over, finished. You don't want to see him anymore."

"Something like that."

"His loss." Jerry tut-tutted. "He should be taught a lesson."

"Oh, no, Jerry. Just leave it."

"I can't. He's crossed me in another way today."

"Oh?"

"Yes, you know that housing development that I'm planning for farmer Hedger's land?"

"Yes."

"Everything going swimmingly. Planning department rooting for it, local councillor in favour. Then up pops Corcoran, cries 'corruption' and threatens to make an issue of it in the media. Can't have that."

"Oh, dear."

"Precisely. Oh dear. You're thinking what I'm thinking, I'll be bound."

"Our plan?"

"Yes. Modest by comparison. You want to build on land at the back here. A second home you can sell. Rakes in about £750,000. Everything hunky-dory. Said planning official writing positive report despite the fact it breaches existing council policy to protect conservation areas from development. Bit of gold-dust going his way. Day at the races for the chief planning officer, too. Costs, say, £20,000 out of the £750,000. £100,000 to build the new house. Enough for several holidays in the Bahamas, Thailand wherever you want. We could go together once you've recovered your equilibrium and regained your desire to take your knickers off – sorry, couldn't help it, don't mean it, platonic holidays a speciality. Can't do it, though, if we're splashed all over the pages of *Private Eye* and facing a possible criminal investigation over the planning application."

"What? Me, too."

"Yes, sorry, Darling, it is your planning application."

"Had we better drop it?"

"The planning application?" he said with a twinkle in his eye.

"This is a serious matter, Jerry," she said insistently.

"Yes, I know it is and no, we shouldn't have to drop it. We should stop said Corcoran in his tracks. I know a few people who can be quite persuasive."

Jackie looked shocked. "Wouldn't that get us into more trouble?"

"Not if they're persuasive enough."

"And if they're not?"

"Negativity. I can't deal with negativity. The guys I'm thinking of haven't failed with anybody yet. Besides, Corcoran's got so much to worry about he'd probably be quite happy to drop something that could get him into deep water from his in-tray. Somebody took a pop at him yesterday. Wasn't you, was it?"

"Took a pop? How do you mean?"

"I was in his office today. He had a bandage on his head."

"No, that wasn't me. I slapped him on the cheek but it wouldn't have required a bandage."

"This was on the side of his head. Anyhow, it doesn't matter who did it. The fact is that someone did and I'll bet he doesn't want to continue getting pastings from a load of different people. He'll see sense and drop his campaign."

"He's a stubborn man," said Jackie. She looked wistfully ahead of her. "Principled even – in some ways," she added. It sounded as if it was a quality in him that she admired.

"My guys are stubborn," said Jerry. "Not principled, though. Perhaps I should have a word with them about that."

"And our planning application?"

"It's with the department. As soon as I know how Corcoran's going to go on this issue, I'll make an unassailable pitch to the planners to let it go through."

"Thanks."

"No worries." He paused. "Well, I'll be on my way then," he said eventually. He kissed her on the cheek. "You know, Darling, you ought to make room in your life some time to have some fun with someone like Uncle Jerry."

Jackie smiled but pushed him away. "Maybe some time," she said.

• • ● • •

Rob sighed as he made his way home from work that afternoon. Do you ever think you may have bitten off more than you can chew? he thought to himself. His dilemma over his love life was enough to cope with without taking on the establishment of the planning department as well. Perhaps he ought to put that on the back burner. On the other hand, it would give him some purpose in life now he seemed to have burnt his bridges with his three lovers. What to do about that, he thought. If he were to make amends with one of them, who would it be? He smiled. It reminded him of the question asked the end of every edition of the BBC's Desert Island Discs: if you had to take just one of these records, which one would it be? He always failed that test when he was devising his own best eight records. He tried to concentrate a bit harder. Instantly, he ruled out Jackie. She wasn't cut from the same hue as him with her ultra-smart clothes and the upper middle-class Tory circles that she moved in. Miranda was sweet, he thought, but did he really want to bust up another marriage. It all pointed to Sue – that dragged through a hedge backwards look plus the fact that she was, like him, a public servant. A leech on society, as some of Jackie's friends might suggest. Perhaps he would try going round to Sue's later that evening.

By this time he had reached his block of flats and became aware of a figure he recognised standing outside the doorway. It was Debra Paget, Sue's lodger. He remembered her from parties at Sue's place. Not quite the full shilling but loyal and devoted to Sue. He had warmed to her, too. There didn't seem to be an ounce of malice in her from what he had seen. He was about to get a rude awakening.

"You bastard," she shouted as he approached the door.

"I'm sorry?" said Rob.

"Bastard."

"Oh," said Rob. "You know, then?"

"How could I not know? I live with her."

"How is she?"

"She wants to kill you. She said so last night."

"I'm sorry to hear that," he said. "Did she send you here to tell me that?"

Debra eyed him as though he were the one whose faculties were impaired. "No, I've come of my own accord," she said. "I just wanted you to realise what you'd done."

"I do realise what I've done and I want to put it right. Can you tell her that when you go home?"

"She won't listen," said Debra. "It's gone too far."

"I'd like to call round and see her later on tonight. Explain what happened. Can you tell her that?"

"She won't want to hear that – or see you," said Debra. She shook her head. "Bastard. Why did you do it?"

"We all do things we didn't mean sometime. I never meant Sue to be confronted like that last night."

"You mean you never meant her to find out about the other woman." It was quite sharp for Debra to have deduced that, thought Rob. She was spot on, he realised. "I'm going now," said Debra. "If you've got any sense, you won't come round tonight," she added. "She said she wanted to kill you."

Rob nodded. "Maybe I'll ring instead," he said. Debra glared at him and went on her way.

• • ● • •

Francesca Manners knocked on the door of Philip Rivers' detective agency. "Anyone at home?" she asked.

Jo came to open it. "Can I help?" he asked.

"Yes, my name's Detective Chief Inspector Francesca Manners. I'm a friend of Philip's but I'm also here on business. Is he in?"

"I'm expecting him back soon," said Jo.

"This is my assistant; Detective Constable Gary Clarke," she added, introducing Jo to the man by her side.

"Welcome," said Jo. "Do you want to come in and wait for him?"

"Yes," said Francesca, "if you don't think he's going to be that long."

"No."

She and Gary sat down in seats offered to them by Jo. "You must be Jo, then," said Francesca.

"You've heard of me?" Jo seemed quite surprised.

"Yes, Philip talks a lot about you. He told me Nikki, his wife, wanted out of the agency to pursue her own career and he was going to take somebody else on. You've worked for him before, I gather?"

"Yes, both here and in the Bahamas when he was investigating a case. This is my first day of my second spell over here."

"And how's it going?"

"I wish I could say smoothly, My first client was a racist. Didn't want a black person helping him. I haven't had anybody since."

"That's a shame," said Francesca. "We're not all racists. Things are bound to get better. Actually, I wanted to speak to Philip about an incident last night."

"The assault on Rob Corcoran?" asked Jo.

"Yes, were you there?" Jo nodded. "What happened?"

"He'd had a bit of woman trouble." Francesca looked surprised. Jo smiled apologetically. "Corcoran not Rivers," he explained. "He'd got into arguments with three women he was dating who found out about each other. As he left the pub we were in, we noticed he was being followed but – by the time we caught up with him – he'd been bashed about the head with something and the assailant was gone."

"You didn't see who it was?"

"No, but Rob said it was a man."

"Why were you there?"

"We went up to Hertford for the day. Rivers and Nikki are thinking of moving out there."

"How did you get talking to Mr Corcoran?"

"We went to an Italian for a meal. It was opposite a pub and Rivers could see this guy arguing with three women during the course of the evening. He thought he might be in need of some professional help so he decided to strike up a conversation with him in the pub. He didn't want help, though."

"So Philip – er, Rivers – is not investigating this case?"

"No. No-one's paying him to."

At this juncture the door opened and Rivers came in. He smiled on seeing Francesca. "Francesca," he said, leaning over to kiss her on the cheek. "What brings you here?"

"Following up a crime you witnessed – or rather nearly witnessed last night? By the way, this is Detective Constable Gary Clarke. He's learning the ropes."

"He couldn't have a better teacher."

"He does talk," said Gary. "You don't have to address me in the third person."

"Sorry," said Rivers. He looked at Francesca. He hadn't seen her for several months, in fact not since the "Jill the Ripper" case –as the press had daubed it – had come to a successful conclusion. He had come very near to having a fling with her during that case – but both had shied away from it, Rivers because of Nikki and Francesca because she had not quite got over the end of a relationship some three years ago. The circumstances in which it had ended made her abhorrent at the thought of getting involved with someone already in another relationship. She had found out the man was two-timing her. To Rivers, though, it was good to see her again even though it evoked a small feeling of what might have been. "How are you?" he asked.

"I'm helping out in Hertford at the moment. Small case of staff shortages. Hence following up this case. I must say when I saw your name connected to it I thought there might have been more to it than met the eye."

"Afraid not."

"By the way, I've been promoted to Detective Chief Inspector. I applied for the post after Larry Green retired. I was qualified to do it and I got it."

"Congratulations," said Rivers. He himself had been in the police force until he had become disillusioned with it. It had seemed to him that you had to grease too many palms if you wanted promotion. From what he had seen of Francesca's career, though, she hadn't and had got her promotions entirely on merit. Good on her, he thought.

"Thank you," she said. "Back to the case, though. What do you think would happen if I went to interview Rob Corcoran?"

"He'd be very polite but he wouldn't tell you anything."

"What about his three girl friends?"

"He won't tell you who they are."

"We could probably find out their names from the pub you were in."

Rivers smiled. "That would be exactly what I would do if somebody had been paying me to investigate the case," he said.

Francesca nodded. "Well, it's good to see you again, Philip," she said – getting up from her seat, "but we'd better be off now." She and Gary Clarke got up to go. Rivers and Jo rose to their feet, too. "Goodbye, Jo," said Francesca. "I hope things get better."

"Thanks," he said.

Once outside, Francesca turned to Gary Clarke. "You were very quiet in there, I thought," she said.

"I didn't want to spoil the reunion," he said.

"Oh." Gary did not seem to her on first sight like the overzealous young recruit that Chief Superintendent Gleeson had made him out to be.

"Actually," said Gary, "I don't really like fraternising with private detectives. They cut corners. You can't trust them."

"They can sometimes do things that we can't because they're not hidebound by rules. Philip Rivers has done that for us in the past and been very helpful to me in my career. You'd do well to make a friend of him."

"Yes, ma'am," said Gary without conviction.

Francesca frowned. "Remember it's Francesca when we're on our own together and Detective Chief Inspector Francesca Manners in more formal settings."

"Sorry, ma – er – Francesca," he said. "I can't overcome the habits of a lifetime," he added.

"Don't worry, you'll get used to it."

• • ● • •

Trish dressed soberly for her meeting with her solicitor that afternoon. She did not want to give him the impression that she was too well off. That, she thought, could count against her if she was seeking a financial settlement from Rob.

"I have an appointment with Mr Raina," she said to the receptionist on her arrival at his swanky offices in the centre of Hertford.

"Come through," said the secretary. She knocked on a door just adjacent to the reception desk. "Come in," said a voice and Trish was ushered into the presence of Amit Raina, her solicitor. He got up from the desk and shook hands with her. He was a small man, smaller than her, she reflected. She had not met him before but had got his name from the Yellow Pages. She had not wanted to consult with anyone who might have had dealings with her and Rob during the years they had been together. "How can I help you?" asked the solicitor.

"It's my husband," she said.

Raina nodded. It often was with clients who came to see him. Much of his time seemed to be taken up with advising and helping clients with marriage break-ups. "You are separated, then?" he asked.

"Yes, for over a year. I should have come sooner but I'm

looking for some kind of financial settlement."

"What are your circumstances?"

"How do you mean?"

"Is either of you still in the family home? Do you have any dependants? That sort of thing."

"No. We sold the family home – and shared the proceeds. He took the lion's share because he had contributed more towards the mortgage. I went along with that." She cleared her throat. "I haven't been thinking straight over the last year or so – otherwise I'd have come to you sooner. I do have a dependent. Our daughter, Sally. She's at university. Paying fees. She's got a loan but I have to subsidise her for her everyday needs."

"I'm sure we can work something out there," said Raina. "One thought, have either of you married again?"

"No, we're still married to each other."

"That could be to your benefit. Do you know if your husband's made another will?"

"I don't know. I don't think he has."

"You're probably his beneficiary, then."

"By the time he dies I probably won't be."

"What makes you say that?"

"He doesn't have any difficulty in attracting women," she said. "In fact, that's one of the reasons I contacted you. He broke up with three of them last night."

"Three?" queried Raina incredulously.

"Yes, that's one of the reasons I've come to you today. He appears to have a quite lavish lifestyle. He earns more than me."

"That's the sort of thing we ought to work on. If you can tell me details of your earnings and – as far as you know them – his plus details of your expenditure on your daughter, I'm sure we can put together a package for him to give you financial support. He may cough up if you sound determined to take the matter to court if he doesn't."

"Thank you, Mr Raina."

"It won't be a treasure trove but hopefully we can get something for you."

"Thank you again. I should be able to get details of his earnings. He works in the public services – in the planning department at the town council."

"Good," said Mr Raina. "Get it all together and the come back to me. Pleasure to be of service."

Trish smiled. As she left the buildings, Raina's revelation that she was still probably the beneficiary in his will were ringing in her ears – so long as he didn't marry again or make a new will. I hope he dies before he gets old, she said – remembering the lyrics of the old Who record, My Generation.

· · ● · ·

Francesca decided she would wait until she estimated Rob Corcoran would have returned from work before she and Gary Clarke confronted him about the assault. He looked less than pleased, though, when he opened his front door to find the two of them showing their warrant cards. "Could we come in?" asked Francesca.

"If you must," he said. He walked to the living room but did not give them an invitation to sit down.

"It's about the assault on you last night," Francesca began.

"Really, it was nothing," said Rob. "Forget about it. I have."

"I don't think you should," said Gary. "We can't condone that sort of thing going on."

"But what you going to be able to do about it? I didn't see who it was."

"We gather you had rather an eventful night last night," Gary continued – given leeway to continue his questioning by Francesca. "Three girlfriends found out about each other."

"I'm not proud of it," said Rob.

"Could you tell us who they were?"

"No."

Francesca intervened. "We can find out who they were by questioning people at the pub," she said. "You could make our job a lot easier."

"But I'm not going to."

"You can't be sure whoever it was doesn't take another pot shot at you," said Gary Clarke.

"I'd hardly call it a pot shot."

"A thumping, then."

"I can take care of myself," said Rob.

"Like you did last night?"

"When are you going to realise, Detective Inspector that I'm not going to co-operate with any police enquiry."

Francesca decided not to stand on ceremony and insist on being called detective chief inspector. It was not her style. "Now," she said. "Come on, Detective Constable Clarke. I think we're wasting our time here."

They turned on their heels to go – only to be confronted by someone else knocking on the door just as they were about to leave. Francesca opened the door – being nearest to it. Outside stood a woman – Trish.

"Is this one of them?" asked Gary, looking back in Rob's direction.

"One of what?" asked Trish.

"The three women who caught him out last night."

"No, I caught him out some time ago," she said. "I'm the ex-wife."

Rob looked puzzled. "What are you doing here?" he asked.

"Do you really want us to air our dirty linen in front of the police? You should probably let them go first."

Rob nodded. "Would you?" he said to Francesca and Gary. "Go, I mean."

Gary observed the look on Trish's face. "I think you could be in for a little more trouble and strife," he said.

"Why? What's happened?"

"Your ex was attacked last night – but it seems as if he doesn't want to prefer charges."

Trish looked at Rob quizzically. "Was it one of them?" she asked.

"I didn't see who it was," he said, "but I'm pretty sure it was a man."

"That Miranda Headley's got a husband," said Trish.

"How did you know about Miranda?" asked Rob.

"The gossip factory is all around town."

"Thanks," said Gary noting the name down. "Do you know who the other two were?"

"Yes," said Trish. "There was Sue."

"Stop it, Trish. I don't want them bothered."

"As if your wants carried any ice with me," she said.

"Well then?" asked Gary after a sufficient pause.

"Well then what?" asked Trish.

"The names of the other two."

"I'd better not. Otherwise you might be investigating another assault come tomorrow morning."

"Your husband a violent man?"

"Steady on," said Rob. He looked at Trish beseechingly – as if to plead with her to take the matter no further.

"Only it would be nice to pin something on him seeing as he's wasted so much police time," said Gary.

Neither Rob nor Trish spoke. "I think we're done here," said Francesca. "Good-day, Mr Corcoran." She produced a card from her pocket. "If you change your mind or find that you do need police help at any time, all you have to do is call on this number," she said handing it to him as she got up to go.

Rob took the card from her and the two detectives left. "So, who's been a naughty boy, then?" said Trish. "On second thoughts, no need to answer that. I think I've always known."

"What do you want?" asked Rob in a surly manner without

inviting Trish into the house further than the hallway – where she was already standing.

"To tell you you've got away lightly," she said. "That I've been to see a solicitor and want some form of settlement to cover our daughter's university costs and to keep me in the style of living to which I was accustomed when I was with you." She noticed the cut on his head. "Ouch," she said. "Who did that? You can tell me."

"I honestly don't know." Rob sighed. "Look, if you need more money, you won't find me unreasonable."

"Good," said Trish. "My solicitor will be in touch." She turned on her heels – relishing the fact that he seemed now to be in some physical danger as a result of the developments in his private life. That – coupled with the fact that her solicitor had told her she was still the beneficiary of his will – made it seem like a good day. "You look after yourself," she said. "You're mixing with some dangerous people."

"Yes," he said, "more dangerous than you think."

Trish looked at him. "What do you mean?" she asked.

"No," he said. "I've probably said too much already."

• • ● • •

Miranda heard Aaron's key in the door. Her heart fluttered. What kind of mood would he be in? Would he be ready to forgive her – or, if that was not possible, at least allow her to stay in the house?

"Darling," she said tentatively.

"Not an appropriate term," said Aaron gruffly.

Her heart sank. "So, how do you feel?"

Aaron sighed. "Have you really put this affair behind you?" he asked.

"Yes," she said.

"But only because you've caught him out with someone else?"

"No," said Miranda, "although I must admit that helped to bring me to my senses."

Aaron walked to the drinks cabinet in their living room and poured himself a whisky. He savoured the drink before swallowing it. "I have a confession to make myself," he said.

"Not you as well?"

Aaron gave her a stern look. "Nothing like that," he said. He took another swig of whisky. "After you told me about Rob Corcoran and you'd gone to bed, I went out," he said. "I caught up with him as he was leaving the pub and I assaulted him."

Miranda was about to respond – but decided that if she asked if Rob was all right it would be construed by Aaron as evidence that she still cared about him. "You shouldn't have," she confined herself to saying. "You could get into trouble."

"And you shouldn't have gone to bed with him," he shouted.

"How are we going to resolve this?" said Miranda. "Are you going to ask me to leave?"

"I've been giving that some thought," came the reply slowly – as if he was still thinking about it. "I think not. You can stay. We'll try and pick up the pieces. It won't be easy but if you ever give me cause to think you've gone back to him." He swallowed hard. He had been going to say "I don't know what I'll do" but thought the better of it. Instead he confined himself to saying: "It'll be the end for you and me."

"Yes," she said. "I accept that. Thank you."

$$\bullet \ \bullet \ \bullet \ \bullet \ \bullet$$

"I've done the deed," said Trish as she sipped a glass of wine with Colin at their pre-arranged meeting place in the pub. "My solicitor reckons I've got a good case for a settlement and, what's more, I'm still the main beneficiary of his will as I'm still married to him. Not that that's going to come into play for some time, he's still fit and well. Witness the three women he's been leading on a string." Colin smiled. "He's in a dicey situation, though," she said allowing herself another sip of wine. "He's already been beaten up by someone – he won't say who – over this stuff with his three mistresses. He also said something rather odd to me as I was leaving," she added.

"Oh? What?"

"The gist of it was that he was in greater danger from somebody else than anyone connected to his three women friends. Do you know what he could have meant?"

"No," said Colin, taking a swig from his beer glass. He looked at Trish. She would be a good catch if she got her settlement and – heaven forbid – if something dreadful happened to Rob. He could do with a partner who could offer him financial support. He had lost his job at the car showrooms – something he did not dwell on too much. He would ask Trish out, he thought. Not tonight – that might be a bit obvious. It would be some time soon, though.

• • • • •

Just as Rob was about to relax and start making himself something to eat, there was another knock at the door. He sighed, put his cooking implements down and went to answer it.

"Dear boy," said Jerry Vincent as the door opened. He did not wait to be invited in but brushed Rob aside and walked into the living room – where he sat down on an armchair. Rob hovered by the doorway. "Oh, do come in and sit down," said Jerry sarcastically.

"What do you want?" Rob asked suspiciously.

"A private word in your shell-like," said the property developer. "I understand you could be about to stir up a bit of shit and throw it in my direction." Rob remained silent. "I'll take that as a yes, then, old boy." Rob still made no response. "Well, don't," said Jerry.

57

"I have a public duty," Rob began.

"Fuck that," said Jerry. "I'm not going to sit back and let you ruin my business operations. I've got a nice little thing going on down in the planning department."

"Thanks to the corrupt behaviour of one of my colleagues," said Rob.

Jerry fixed him with a stare. "Language, dear boy, language," he said. "Let's not bandy accusations around when there's no need to. Why not join in our little arrangement? I'm sure we could agree on something that's mutually beneficial."

"I'm not interested in anything like that," said Rob stiffly. "Now, I don't remember inviting you into my house."

"There's no need to adopt that kind of tone," said Jerry.

"There's every need," replied Rob.

"In which case I shall have to adopt a similar tone," he said. "I have some friends in very low places and they won't like the type of arrangements that I have being threatened. They are people in very low places, I would stress."

"Are you threatening me?"

"Got it in one, dear boy," said Jerry smiling. "Now these friends of mine, they're not as sophisticated as I am. They only know one way of communicating – and that's with their fists. Do you get my drift?"

"Do you really expect me to answer that?"

"If they think you've been acting unreasonably, then I don't know if I'm going to be able to restrain them. I really don't." He eyed Rob's head. "It looks as though you've been in the wars already," he said.

"That's no business of yours."

"A spot of woman trouble, I believe – and there were you getting all haughty and holier than thou about your morality. Seems that kind of stance won't wash." Rob made as if to interrupt him – but Jerry waived him aside with a dismissive gesture. "That really isn't in the least bit of interest to me," he said, "but I just might observe that my friends are unlikely to be as restrained as the jealous husband or whoever it was that attacked you has been. Pity."

"Would you kindly leave? Now?" said Rob.

Jerry ignored his intervention. "I was saying it would be a pity," he continued. "A pity because you have good looks for your age. Doubtless that helped you attract all these women in the first place. It would be a pity because after my friends have spent some time with you, I doubt whether you will be able to attract good-looking women for some time to come – if ever."

"Leave," insisted Rob.

"Well, I've said my piece," said Jerry. "Drop any idea of interfering with my business plans. If I find out that you are still continuing with that idea, I shall have no alternative but to console myself by telling my friends about what you are doing." He pursed his lips and took a sharp intake of breath. "And that would not be nice for you." At that he got up from the armchair. "Well, I must go," he said. He raised his hand. "No," he said, "I'm going to have to resist your exhortations for me to stay." He opened the front door and walked outside, turning whilst still on the top step. "Oh, and should you decide to report this conversation to anyone, you'll find I wasn't here," he said. "I have a cast-iron alibi putting myself in another place. Toodle-pip." With that, he was gone.

Rob was left shaking. If only he had just three jealous women to cope with, he thought.

CHAPTER THREE

"Could I have a word, Mr Roulay, sir?" asked Rob as he tentatively approached the director of planning's office the next morning. He knew it was the right thing to do – to report his suspicions to his superior. Jerry Vincent's threats to set his low life friends on him still weighed heavily on his mind, though.

"By all means, Rob," beamed Douglas Roulay from behind his desk. "What's the problem?"

Rob fidgeted before accepting the offer of a seat from his boss. "I have suspicions about corruption in the planning department. I thought I ought to voice them to you."

"You are quite right to, Rob. I like to think my staff can raise any questions of that sort with me." He paused for a moment and then lent forward across the desk in a manner designed to display confidentiality. "You say you have suspicions, Rob," he said. "Not chapter and verse."

"I think it's a question of interpretation," Rob began. "I know a colleague is accepting gifts from a property developer who has had numerous planning applications approved by us – some of which have been blatantly against council policy at the time."

"Are you prepared to name this colleague?"

"It's a question of whether it's just a form of hospitality – or whether there's something more sinister behind it."

"And your feeling is?"

"There's something more sinister. It includes Wimbledon tickets, Lords tickets, lavish lunches. In exchange building applications in conservation areas have been approved."

"You know I am ultimately responsible for each planning application that goes before the committee?"

Rob stopped in his tracks. He had not expected this response. "Yes, sir," he said, "but you will be heavily influenced by the recommendation of your senior officers."

"I asked you earlier if you were prepared to name this colleague. You sidestepped the question."

"I don't think I need to. There's only one person I share an office with and whose working arrangements I have first-hand knowledge of."

"Roger Broadbent?" Rob nodded. "You need to furnish me with more information than you have done. It's just a suspicion at the moment."

"I can furnish you with details of planning applications put in by the property developer Jerry Vincent, how they were approved despite being contrary to council conservation guidelines. I can list the benefits I have heard Roger Broadbent taking advantage of. I don't think there would be anything as blatant as cheques being paid into his bank account by Vincent. You might find on digging that various works done on his property have been paid for by Vincent or supplied free of charge by Vincent's company."

"I might find on digging?" queried Roulay "Not enough for me to open an investigation yet, I feel. Don't get me wrong, Rob, I'm grateful that you've brought your concerns to me but we have to tread carefully here. We can't just adopt a scattergun approach."

Rob sighed. "No, sir," he said. Well, he thought to himself, at least he had followed the dictates of his own conscience. It was not his fault if his allegations did not lead anywhere.

"I'll tell you what, Rob," said Roulay. "You draw up your list of the planning applications you believe have been wrongly approved. And the list of what you know Roger Broadbent to have received and we'll take it from there." He got up from his desk and went over to the door and opened it for Rob. He was signifying to his junior that it was time to go. He shook Rob's hand as he left the office. "Once again, Rob," he said, "let me stress to me how much I value the fact that you feel free to come to me and share your suspicions with me."

"Thank you, sir," mumbled Rob as he left the office. In truth, he did not know whether he had done the right thing by confiding in Roulay. Perhaps he would have done better by going to the police in the first place. That Detective Chief Inspector – what was her name? – Manners, Francesca Manners. She seemed a straight sort. He put his hand in his pocket and took out her card. He looked at it as he walked back to his office. If Roulay did not come up trumps, that was always one option he had up his sleeve. He wondered if he should have mentioned Vincent's threats but thought – on balance – he should wait and bring the police in to investigate them. Roulay would have undoubtedly pointed out it would be just his word against Vincent's.

Roulay, meanwhile, returned to his desk. He sat down and took a mobile phone out of his desk. He called up Jerry Vincent's number and rang it. "Dear boy," came the response when the call was answered. "What a delightful surprise. To what do I owe the honour of this telephone call?"

"I've just had Rob Corcoran in here complaining of corruption in the planning department."

"How scandalous," came the reply, "We must move heaven and earth to put a stop to it."

"This is no joking matter, Jerry."

"And I wasn't joking. I know a way of putting a stop to this sniff of corruption – or should I say someone who will make sure the allegations go no further. What have you decided to do?"

"I've asked Rob to give me chapter and verse – or at least go as far as he can go."

"Which is the right thing to do in the circumstances. I think I can reassure you that you will never be receiving that information."

"Jerry, I don't want you doing anything illegal." A note of terror had entered into Roulay's voice.

"Don't worry yourself, Darling," he said. "I merely mean to use the power of persuasion. Or should I say my friends merely mean to use it – and they can be more persuasive than me."

"All right, but don't tell anyone about this phone call."

Jerry screwed up his face in puzzlement. "That would be stupid, dear boy," he said. "No, just relax. And do nothing. Everything will be all right." With that, he put the phone down. Spineless idiot, he thought to himself. Can't he take care of matters himself? Just tell Rob he has no evidence on which to take forward an investigation. "Honestly," he said speaking aloud to himself. "Do I have to take care of everything?" He thought for a moment. "Yes," he said as he dialled another number on his mobile. "Ah, is that the delightful Bruiser?" he asked when a gruff voice answered at the other end of the line.

"Who wants to know?" came the response.

"Ah, it is." Jerry gave a slight chuckle. "I always know when it's you, Bruiser, because you always answer that question in precisely the same way. It's Jerry Vincent here." There was no point in wasting small talk on Bruiser, reflected Jerry He did not understand the concept. "I have a friend who needs to be persuaded there's no point in pursuing an allegation of corruption in the planning department," he said. "Can you help?"

"Yes," came the response.

"Good," said Jerry. "His name's Rob Corcoran." Jerry went on to give Bruiser Rob's home address. "He'll be at work now but pay him a visit early evening. It needs to be done today. Take Eel with you. It'll be more persuasive if there are two of you."

"Eel's not good at the rough stuff."

"And he doesn't have to be. Not with you there, Bruiser, does he?" Jerry smiled. He had dealt with Bruiser and Eel for years. They ran a legitimate scrap metal business (McCarthy and Higgs) but – behind the façade – were known amongst the criminal fraternity to be available to recover debts, make sure people never spilled the beans on their clients to the police and sundry other jobs which might require Bruiser to use his fists to achieve his client's wishes. They would soon sort Rob Corcoran out, thought Jerry.

• • ● • •

"To the Dog and Partridge," said Francesca Manners as she and Gary Clarke got into his car that morning. "It does a mean pint, or so I hear."

"I didn't know you were a pub connoisseur, ma'am," said Gary.

"The name's Francesca – remember?" she said.

"Francesca," he corrected himself. It still did not seem right to him, though, calling his boss by her first name.

"And, in answer to your question, no, I'm not," she said, "but I googled it earlier this morning and it's won awards for its beers. It's as well to know these things when you go to interview people, Gary. Forewarned is forearmed – or something like that." Gary appeared uninterested in what she was saying. She looked at her young colleague. She would have identified him as a lager man rather than a connoisseur of the finest ales as brewed in the Dog and Partridge's cellars. Not that she held that against him. She was more into fine wines but it was only 10 o'clock in the morning and thoughts of sampling the Dog and Partridge's wares were far from her mind. They parked in the street and Francesca went straight to the door and used the brass knocker to draw attention to their arrival. A bespectacled man – probably in his late 50's – answered her knock.

"I'm looking for Jed Coulson," she said – showing him her warrant card.

"Christ, what have I done?" said the man at the door squinting at the card. "A detective chief Inspector? It must be serious."

"There is no need for alarm, Mr Coulson. It is Mr Coulson, isn't it?"

"Yes," said the man. "You'd better come in. We're not open yet."

"Thanks," said Francesca. "I didn't want a drink." Gary had made his way to the front of the pub by this time and Francesca introduced him. "This is Detective Constable Clarke," she said.

Jed Coulson nodded in recognition. "What would you like?" he asked when all three of them were inside the pub. "I take it not alcohol since we're not open yet and it is a bit early in the morning but I could rustle up a tea or coffee."

"No, thank you, Mr Coulson. As I said, I don't want a drink. We'd like to get on with things. It's about something that happened in this pub on Sunday night. I don't know whether you're aware of it but one of your regulars was assaulted as he made his way home from here that night."

"Rob, you mean? I'm not surprised. He had a pretty eventful evening."

"Yes. We gather he was unmasked as having three lovers. We're trying to find them. To eliminate them from our enquiries. He seems to think it was a man who did it but we feel they could help us get to the bottom of this."

"Have you asked him who they are?"

"Yes, but he won't tell us. We know one of them was Miranda Headley – but that's as far as we've got. We thought you might be able to help us."

"I'm not sure I should be giving away information about my customers' private lives," Jed began.

"But if you don't we'll have to come back during opening time and quiz your regulars. I don't mean to be threatening, Mr Coulson, but we need to know and we will find out. It's just that you could make it so much easier for us,"

Jed nodded. "And it's not as if I'm giving away any trade secrets," he said. "Well, the first one was Sue Plummer. She's in charge of school meals at Bass Street primary school. The third one is a classy woman – Jackie Quesling. She runs a flower shop in the town centre. Jackie's."

"Do you know much about them?"

"No, they only drink here with him,"he said."I suppose I may have lost their custom after Sunday night. Miranda is married. I know that. She occasionally came in here with her husband – Aaron, I think his name is. As for the other one, Jackie Quesling, I think we would have been a bit downmarket for her – although she did come in with Rob a few times. I think he was the cause of her splitting up from her husband."

"Oh?"

"You do tend to pick up bits of conversation as you clear away the empty glasses."

"Can you think of anyone who would be likely to assault Rob Corcoran?"

"You mean, apart from those three women and Miranda's husband? Well, yes, funnily enough."

"Go on."

"I don't think he parted on good terms with his wife, Trish. She runs a charity shop in the town centre. I can't remember which one."

"What's her name?"

"Trish Corcoran. She still goes under her married name."

"Still carrying a torch for him?"intervened Gary.

Jed looked at the young detective. "No, sonny," he said. "Just lazy."

"Don't call me sonny,"snapped Gary.

"All right." Francesca motioned to cool things down. She noted that Jed did not apologise. "Will that be all, then?" he added – a trifle stiffly.

"Yes. thanks,"said Francesca. "You've been most helpful."

"Have I?" said Jed. "You wouldn't have thought so from listening to this young man."

"No,"said Francesca."Possibly not."Once outside, she turned on Gary. "Do you have to screw up every relationship we have? That guy was being exceedingly helpful."

"That's going a bit far. I don't like being called sonny, ma'am."

"No," said Francesca, "and I don't like being called ma'am."

• • ● • •

"Enter work mode," said Rivers as he and Jo arrived at the office that morning. "Right, what have we got on today?" he asked.

"I don't have anything," said Jo apologetically.

"Oh, dear, that's a bit grim," said Rivers. "How are we going to sustain two people working here if there's nothing to do?"

Jo shrugged his shoulders. "We can't really create work in our line of business," he said.

"No, but" – Rivers paused for thought. "I wouldn't mind betting that at some stage we get involved again with Rob Corcoran – but we can't do anything yet. He doesn't want us putting our noses in the trough and the police around here are too sensible to jump to the wrong conclusions and arrest the wrong person so that they then need help from us – unlike some forces I know."

"Too sensible?"

"Francesca Manners. I have great respect for the way she works."

"And fancy her?"

Rivers thought for a moment. He found it difficult to keep secrets from Jo. "And that, too," he mumbled under his breath. He then cleared his throat and spoke more positively. "... But I'm happily married now and I have to put thoughts like that on the backburner."

Jo smiled at him. "You've changed," he said.

"Well spotted," said Rivers. "You'll make a great detective one day." He rustled some papers on his desk – to no effect. "When you were in the office on your own yesterday morning," he said, "did nothing come in?"

"As a matter of fact it did," Jo said.

"Good," encouraged Rivers..

"Not good," said Jo firmly. "He was a racist. Some black people were making a noise in a house near him and he wanted you to investigate it and shut them up. He didn't want me to help him. In fact, he ended up by saying that he wouldn't use the services of a firm like yours because of the type of people they were employing, i.e me."

"Oh, dear," sighed Rivers. "Not a good baptism for working here."

"No," said Jo. He thought for a moment. "You know, Rivers," he said. "This place has changed."

"This place?"

"This country," said Jo correcting himself. "There was that policeman investigating the assault on Rob Corcoran saying 'us lot' were unreliable and there was an atmosphere in that pub, the Dog and Partridge, when I walked in. They were all cases of racism, man."

"Yes," said Rivers. "I think things have changed. Some people nowadays seem to think they can get away with saying what they were previously only thinking. I think there always were as many racists about. It just that they feel they can be more open now."

"Why?"

"The vote we had on whether we wanted to remain a part of Europe. Those who voted 'no' wanted to pull up the drawbridge. It was all about cutting down on immigration – joining together in a little England against the world."

"And Wales and Scotland and Northern Ireland?"

"Sadly Wales," remarked Rivers. "You can take two crumbs of comfort, though. One is that they're just as anti some of the white races in Eastern Europe – although I accept that's not a positive finding. And secondly, I believe there are still just as many good people around as there always were."

"I'll have to see that to believe that."

"Just keep talking to the likes of me and Nikki and Francesca and you'll find that. I can introduce to one or two others, too.

Can I ask you, though? Is it changing your opinion as to whether you want to remain in the UK at all?"

"It could do. Back in Calicos, you don't have that sort of problem. And we aren't racist towards the whites."

"In Nassau, though? I seem to remember from staying with Susan (Susan was Rivers' sister who was living in the Bahamas) that there were a few hard-line white racists there."

"You have a point."

"Just remember, Jo, I'm just as upset about the growth of open racism here as you are and I feel I've got to combat it."

"You're not just as upset, Rivers. You're not black. You can't be."

Rivers conceded the point. "But I am upset, though," he said. He thought for a moment. "I ought to start introducing you to one or two of my friends so you get a more balanced view of what UK people really feel. I'll get Nikki to organise a dinner party."

"Good idea, Rivers," said Jo.

• • ● • •

"We'll try the school first," said Francesca as she and Gary drove away from the pub. Francesca glanced at her watch. It was well before lunchtime – even for a primary school – so hopefully Sue Plummer would have time to talk to them. They drove into the car-park in front of the school's main entrance and made their way to the reception desk – where they showed their warrant cards.

"Detective Chief Inspector Manners and Detective Constable Clarke," said Francesca. "We've come to see Sue Plummer."

"Have you got an appointment?" asked the woman behind the desk.

"We don't make appointments," said Gary surlily.

The secretary looked at him – as if he was an infant who was misbehaving. "Then you can't be surprised when people aren't in," she said.

"She's the school meals supervisor for Christ's sake," he said. "It's lunchtime. She must be in."

Francesca shot him an irritated glance. "If you could just check for us," she said.

"Okay, Detective Constable," came the response.

"No, I'm the Detective Chief Inspector," said Francesca, smiling.

The secretary seemed a little bit happier to do the police's bidding at this news. She rang an internal number. After a brief chat, she turned to Francesca. "Miss Plummer will see you now. She'll come out and fetch you."

"Thank you," said Francesca. They only had to wait for about a minute – and Sue Plummer joined them in reception. "Miss Plummer?" asked Francesca.

"Yes," she said. "What's this about?"

"We're investigating an assault on Rob Corcoran. I believe you know him." After this brief introductory comment, the two detectives went through the rigmarole of showing their warrant cards.

"Rob?" she said. "Is he hurt?"

"Not badly. He suffered a blow on the head on Sunday evening."

"And you think I might have delivered it?"

"We're in the process of eliminating people from our enquiries," said Francesca diplomatically. "I gather you had an altercation with him outside the Dog and Partridge on Sunday night?"

"That's one way of putting it. I found out he was a lying, cheating rat."

"So you're not kindly disposed towards him," said Gary butting in.

"Would you be if your wife had cheated on you?" asked Sue.

"I don't have a wife," said Gary.

"All right, then, I wasn't kindly disposed towards him."

"Can you tell me where you went after you left the pub on Sunday night?"

"Flounced out of the pub would be a better description,"

reflected Sue. "I went straight home. Had a couple more stiff drinks and then went to bed."

"Can anybody corroborate this?"

Sue thought for a moment. She was reluctant to expose Debra to police scrutiny because of her vulnerability but then surely she could cope with just telling the police the time she arrived back from the pub. "Yes," she said. "As a matter of fact, they can. Debra," she said shouting towards the kitchen area. "Come here a minute."

"Yes, Sue," said the young girl. "What do you want?"

"These two people are police officers, Debra. They think I may have assaulted Rob and want to know where I was on Sunday night."

"I told you you should have done," said Debra. "He deserved it."

"But did I?" said Sue firmly – a note of irritation coming into her voice.

"No. You came back from the pub about 9.30pm, had a drink and went to bed."

"Thank you," said Francesca. "I think that's all we need from you."

"Wait a minute," said Gary. He turned to Debra. "You think he deserved a beating, do you?"

"He really upset Sue," said Debra.

"So did you do it – or organise a friend to carry it out?"

"Hold on a minute," said Sue. "Do you really think Debra could beat Rob up. She's barely five foot and not the most athletic of people."

"I wonder if she could answer my question," continued Gary.

"Are you treating her as a suspect?"

Francesca intervened. "No, we're not," she said. "Detective Constable Clarke is out of line with his questions."

"I'm glad to hear it."

"I didn't beat him up," intervened Debra – as if hurt by the suggestion. "I said he deserved it but I didn't do it. And I don't know anybody else who would do it."

"You seem to have your answer, Detective Constable," said Sue.

Gary said nothing but followed Francesca out of the school. Francesca turned to face him when they were out of earshot. "Do you ever get any results, Gary?" she asked.

"I beg your pardon, ma'am?"

She sighed. It was pointless, she thought, to remind him again that she did not like being called ma'am. "It's just that you seem to want to antagonise everybody – even when they're being friendly and co-operative," she said.

"I find it can jerk them into making admissions that they want to keep secret," he said. "It's not as if we've got very far from using your softly, softly approach."

"Policing sometimes takes time," said Francesca. "And you can't just go around accusing everybody. If that girl had confessed you couldn't have used it. You'd have had to arrest her and caution her before you started interviewing her. How the fuck did you get through training school?" Francesca seldom swore. It was a measure of her exasperation with the new colleague she had had forced upon her.

"I did very well, actually," he said.

"Well, bully for you. Can I insist on some ground rules? You leave the interviewing to me and only come in when I invite you to. Is that clear?"

"Crystal," he said.

Francesca glanced at her watch. "It's coming up to lunch time," she said. "Let's try the one that doesn't go out to work. Miranda Headley."

It took only about five minutes to drive from Sue Plummer's school to Miranda's home on a new private estate near the centre of Hertford. They were lucky – she was in and invited them to join her in a cup of coffee, an offer which they declined.

"Can I help you?" asked Miranda. Gary couldn't help himself thinking that here was an attractive woman – slimmer than Sue Plummer, more elegantly dressed despite the fact that she was at home while Sue had been at work. She seemed, thought Gary, to be taking a pride in her appearance – something that Sue did not. Why tie yourself down with a woman like Sue, he thought, when you could have this classy lady. He kept his thoughts to himself and remembered he had agreed to allow Francesca to do all the questioning.

"I'm here about an assault on Rob Corcoran," she began.

"Oh, yes, how is he?" she asked fervently.

"You knew about the assault?" she said.

"It's common gossip," she said.

"And you received this gossip from where?"

"I....er...." Miranda was at a loss for words.

"Only we've just been to see another woman who works in a school where – doubtless – quite a few people would know Rob Corcoran and could have found out what happened to him. But you – you work from home. There's not so much opportunity to tap into gossip."

"I must have heard it from one of the neighbours. I've had nothing to do with Rob since Sunday night."

"When you fell out with him, had a blazing row and found he was two-timing you – no, three-timing you with two other women."

"Two other women?" said Miranda. "I only saw him with one."

"What did you do when you left the pub on Sunday night?"

"I came straight home and went to bed."

"Just like that?"

"Well, I may have had a stiff drink first, but...."

"And your husband?"

"Aaron?"

"Yes, I assume you've only got one husband." It was a cheap jibe and, on reflection, Francesca thought, it was not worthy of her.

"Well."

"I mean, I can imagine the scenario. You come in from the

73

pub, obviously agitated, pour yourself a stiff drink and go to bed. He's not going to ask you: 'What's the matter?'"

"Oh, well, yes, he did. I said that I didn't want to talk about it."

"And he accepted that?"

"Yes."

"And went to bed, too, after possibly pouring himself a stiff drink, too."

"I assume so."

"You assume so? You don't sleep together then?" Miranda bit her tongue. It was her first mistake and she wondered how she was going to get out of it. The detective chief could read into her reply that there was something wrong with the relationship, she thought.

"I think he went to bed in the spare room. He was annoyed I wouldn't speak to him."

"You think he went to bed in the spare room? In other words, you don't know. He could have gone out."

Miranda tried to look Francesca straight in the eyes. "I'm pretty sure he did. Go to bed in the spare room, I mean."

"He couldn't have had an inkling about what happened – possibly from you – as you sought to explain your agitated state and then gone out to find Rob Corcoran and show him what he thought of him?"

"I would have heard something," Miranda mumbled.

"But you really can't give him a cast iron alibi for Sunday evening?"

"No, I suppose not."

"And he can't give you one?"

"I wouldn't hurt Rob," she said. "I really wouldn't."

"Despite the fact he hurt you?" Miranda didn't respond to this question. "Right," continued Francesca. "Where does your husband work?"

"He's a salesman," said Miranda. "He's out on the road today."

"What time do you expect him to be back?"

"I don't know. About 7pm?"

Francesca nodded. "We'll be back to question him then," she said. "Right, Detective Constable Clarke," she said. "We're done here. Thank you, Mrs Headley. You've been most helpful."

Miranda sighed – realising she hadn't meant to be. Should she warn Aaron about what he was facing, she wondered. She should, she reckoned, tell him the police might be about to call on him but she should not reveal all the details of the conversations she had had with them. Her actions on Sunday night had told her that honesty was not always the best policy.

Once back in the car, Francesca turned to Gary. "Thanks for not interrupting me there, Gary," she said. "You're learning."

Gary flinched at what he saw as a back-handed compliment. "I think we've got someone in the frame now," said Gary.

"Yes, Aaron Headley."

"Should we abandon the other women, then?" he asked.

"No," said Francesca. "We must be thorough." Their next port of call was Jackie Quesling's flower shop. She took them into an office at the back of the shop where – she told them – they could have more privacy.

"What can I do for you?"

"It's about an assault on Rob Corcoran."

"Oh, yes."

"You knew about it?"

"Yes, I met someone who had been to visit him in the planning department on Monday."

"If I'm right," said Francesca, "you were the last person to have a row with him at the Dog and Partridge on Sunday."

"The last person?"

"There were three altercations."

"I only witnessed one other."

"So after you'd given him a piece of your mind, you…."

"Went home and, no, no-one can confirm it. I live on my own. My friend, Pauline, did come round later but that won't nail it""

"That's a shame," said Francesca.

"I think he went back into the pub after we'd had our row," she said. "We didn't leave together. We wouldn't have, given what had passed between us."

Francesca made a snap decision. "I don't think we need detain you anymore," she said. "There is no evidence linking you to the assault. You may not have that good an alibi but that's the only thing that counts against you. We'll be on our way – although we may need to talk to you again as evidence emerges."

Jackie smiled at them. "You know where I am," she said.

• • ● • •

Rob Corcoran noticed a van parked opposite his home when he returned from work that afternoon. It said: McCarthy and Higgs: Scrap Metal Merchants. He thought nothing of it but – as he put his key in the lock – a voice called out to him.

"Excuse me, sir, could we have a word?" The man had a gruff East London accent. Rob looked at him. He was thickset, wore a diamond bracelet and had close cropped brown hair. He was sporting a leather jacket and wearing jeans. His companion was an altogether weedier individual, slim with a knitted waistcoat and ill-fitting suit which was too big for him.

The thickset man made his way up the stairs. "We'll come inside," he said. There seemed no question of waiting for an invitation.

Rob watched helplessly as the two men walked past him and entered the living room. "Bruiser's the name," the thickset man said. "I won't bother to tell you how I got it."

"Best not to ask," said the second man.

"McCarthy and Higgs?" said Rob. "You're scrap metal merchants?"

"Yes, but you've no need to worry about that. We haven't come for any scrap metal – unless, of course, it's holding your body together after an operation." Bruiser laughed at his own joke.

"Might have to – after we've been," said the second man shaking his head as he spoke.

"You're the people Jerry Vincent mentioned as being his friends in low places?" said Rob. "I don't think I've anything to say to you."

"We don't need you to say anything. Just listen." The thickset man paused for dramatic effect. "Oh, where are my manners?" he said. "This is my colleague Eel – as in slippery as an eel."

Eel offered his hand for a shake but Rob made no move to accept it. "Do as the gentleman suggests," said Bruiser. "It would be disrespectful – and we don't like disrespect." Reluctantly Rob shook Eel's hand. The latter's handshake was weak. "And now me," said Bruiser. Rob put his hand forward only to find it held in a vice-like grip by Bruiser who then yanked his little finger back, breaking it in the process. Rob gave a cry of pain. "I'm so sorry," said Bruiser. "Stupid of me. That was my attempt at a mason's handshake. I take it you're not a mason."

"No," said Rob, nursing his little finger.

"Never mind." Bruiser then acted as if he was thinking through his next step carefully. "It has come to our attention, Mr Corcoran, that you are giving grief to a certain acquaintance of ours," he eventually said.

"Jerry Vincent."

"Never a good idea to mention names," continued Bruiser. "We're very protective of our friendships – aren't we, Eel?"

"I should say so."

Bruiser approached Rob menacingly. "Very ... " He slapped him on the cheek. "Protective ...." Another slap. "Of ..." A third slap. "Our ...." A fourth one. "Friends ..." A full blooded punch to the nose which sent Rob reeling. As he lay on the floor Bruiser came towards him and put his foot on his chest. "Now, we understand our mutual friend asked you to stop making enquiries into certain planning matters," he said.

"He's no mutual friend."

Bruiser transferred all his weight on to the foot that was on Rob's chest. "Best not to speak when you're being spoken to," he said. "Now where was I?"

"You were saying about Mr Corcoran making enquiries into planning matters" prompted Eel.

"That are of no concern to him," said Bruiser taking over the conversation. "Yes," he continued, "what was your response to our mutual friend's – I warn you, don't say anything." He lifted his foot as if to crash it down on Rob again as he felt him squirming. The blow did not come, though. "About our mutual friend's friendly advice? You went straight to the boss of the planning department and talked to him about skullduggery and corruption. Not sensible. Perhaps you'll heed the well intentioned warning you're getting now?"

Rob nodded. It was useless to defy the two men, he reckoned. He could leave any decision as to his next move until after they had gone, he reasoned.

"There," said Bruiser. "That's better now." He lifted Rob to his feet. Rob winced with pain as he felt the damage done to his ribs and his finger – and, indeed, to his face. "Now, where are our manners?" he said. "Eel, we've not even offered the gentleman a cup of tea."

"A cup of tea coming up," said the other man.

"There's no need," said Rob as he winced with pain again. He wanted to be shot of his two companions as soon as possible – but they did not seem inclined to leave. Eel made his way into the kitchen and – without asking – found tea, milk and a cup and a drink for Rob.

"We'll not bother with tea, thank you," said Bruiser. "We don't want to outstay our welcome." He moved closer to Rob as he sipped the tea that Eel had prepared. "Just be quite clear, if we hear you've still been pursuing your enquiries, we'll be back. Rest assured of that. And we won't be so gentlemanly next time. Funny thing. No-one seems to relish a second visit from us, do they Mr Eel?"

"No," came the reply.

"And a third visit? Well, that never happens, does it Mr Eel?"

"No."

Bruiser was now only inches away from Rob's face. "Well," he said, "let's hope it's au revoir and not adieu. Yes, Mr Eel and I are cultured people." With that, he took the cup of tea from where it had been placed by Rob on a table next to him and threw it in his face. He and Eel then departed leaving Rob to ruminate on the events of the last few minutes.

• • ● • •

"Should we visit the wife?" Gary asked Francesca as they left Jackie Quesling's flower shop.

"I think so," said Francesca. "After all, the publican did tell us in no uncertain terms that she had it in for him. She works in a charity shop, we know that. There are about three in the town centre. We'll soon find her."

They did. "You want to question me about the attack on Rob?"

"You know about it?" said Francesca as part of her well-ordered routine.

"I saw him yesterday. Not a pretty sight. He was attacked on Sunday night, you say?"

"Yes."

"Well, at the time of the attack, I didn't know about the arguments at the Dog and Partridge. I was only told about them later – by one of the regulars. So I wouldn't have a reason to attack him."

"In your case, the arguments aren't the reason. We understand things were not entirely amicable between you and him."

"That's one way of putting it. He doesn't give me a penny."

"So you feel aggrieved about the way you split up?"

"Yes, but punching him won't help. Far better to do what I did yesterday and go and see a solicitor and demand a settlement from him."

"Certainly more sensible," acknowledged Francesca.

"Anyway, I have an alibi for Sunday night," she went on. "I had a phone call from Colin Standen from the Dog and Patridge at 10.30pm that evening telling me what had happened in the pub. He phoned my landline so I had to be at home to take it. He'll corroborate that if you ask him."

Francesca nodded. "We'll do that," she said. She looked at Trish. She couldn't help thinking she was somewhat on edge – as if there was something she was not telling her. Without anything more than just a gut feeling, though, there was nothing more that she could do about it. "Well," said Francesca, "we'll let you get on with your work. Come on, Gary." Trish saw the two of them out, reflecting as they went that she was glad that she had not told them about the other bit of news that the solicitor had imparted to her – that, as she was still married to Rob, she was still entitled to inherit from him if he died.

Francesca, meanwhile, confessed her gut instincts to Gary. She got no feedback, though. Gary appeared to be drooling over Jackie Quesling. "Why was it so difficult for Corcoran to make a decision over these three women?" he asked. "One's a frump, the second is married – although I grant you she's quite dishy and the third just oozes class – she's got her own business."

"Not part of our remit, Gary, to think about that. Ours is just to find out who is the most likely person to have carried out the assault."

"Aaron Headley?"

Francesca nodded. She glanced at her watch. "We'll go back to the station," she said. "We'll try and catch him around 7pm – before he settles down and has time to talk through things with his wife." He nodded. They were interrupted by a call on Francesca's mobile. "Detective Chief Inspector Manners," she said on answering it. "Oh, sir," she said. There was silence for a moment as she listened to the voice at the other end. "Will do, sir," she finally said before switching her mobile off.

"That's the chief super," she said. "He wants to see me about something at 6.30 this evening. I'm afraid you'll have to take charge of the visit to Aaron Headley."

"Fine, Francesca." She smiled at his reply. It was further evidence that he was trying to put things right between them. He had remembered she was Francesca when they were alone together. No more of that horrible epithet, ma'am, she thought.

"I'll arrange for one of the other detective constables to go with you for support," she said, "but you should be able to manage being the main inquisitor."

"Thank you, ma....Francesca." It was still a struggle, noted Francesca.

• • • • •

Rob fished the card out of his pocket. He glanced at his watch. It was probably too late to go and visit the private detective in his office. After all, he worked in Finchley and that was half an hour's drive away – at least. Instead, he tentatively telephoned Rivers' mobile. "Philip Rivers?" he asked on hearing a voice at the other end of the line.

"Yes," said the private detective. "Who is this?"

"Rob Corcoran. Remember me?"

"Of course."

"I need help," he replied. "Could you come and see me?" Rivers needed no second bidding. Apart from anything else, it was very quiet at the moment and he had nothing else on. Also, the tone of Rob Corcoran's voice made it sound urgent. He sounded worried. He was at Rob's home within half an hour. "That was quick," said Rob on ushering his visitor into the living room.

"It sounded urgent," said Rivers.

"I think it is," said Rob. Rivers noticed his little finger was bandaged and he seemed to be clutching his ribs as he talked.

"You've been attacked again?" said Rivers.

"Yes, and this time by professionals." He told Rivers about the visit of Jerry Vincent the previous evening and of the follow-up by Bruiser and Eel earlier that evening,

"Bruiser and Eel," said Rivers incredulously.

"That's what they call themselves. In reality, they're McCarthy and Higgs, scrap metal merchants. One's called Bruiser because he bruises people and other's called Eel because he's a slippery customer."

"Right."

"They as near as damn it threatened to kill me if I didn't stop my enquiries into corruption in the planning department. They said they'd come back and – to put it in their words –'wouldn't be so gentlemanly' if they heard I was still pursuing my allegations. No-one liked a second visit from them, they said, and no-one ever needed a third."

"They're trying to put the frighteners on you," said Rivers.

"They've succeeded," he said. He appeared to be shaking as he spoke.

"I'll get on to it as soon as possible. I doubt if they've killed before, though. They'll want to remain as under the radar as they can be. I'll check tomorrow if they're known to the police."

"Don't tell them it's because of me."

"Don't worry," said Rivers. He laid a reassuring hand on his shoulder but even this seemed to trigger pain in his ribs. "I think you'd better tell me about the corruption in the planning department." Rob looked as if he was about to protest. "No," said Rivers, "this wouldn't constitute a furtherance of your enquiries and trigger off a return visit by Bruiser and Eel. I just need to know as much as I can about the situation before I take your case on." Rob looked surprised. "And yes, it will cost you," said Rivers. "I'm not a charity."

"Of course not, I'm sorry." He told Rivers about Jerry Vincent's planning applications, how they always seemed to get approval from the authority even if they contravened planning policy and how Roger Broadbent, one of his colleagues, was awash with free tickets for Wimbledon and Lords' and seemed to have no trouble affording extra work on his house.

"You told your boss about all this?" asked Rivers when he had finished.

"Yes."

"And he did what?"

Rob paused for a moment. "Well, nothing, really," he said. "He said he wanted me to give him chapter and verse in a report before he acted."

"And have you?"

"I've been too busy getting beaten up and dealing with woman trouble to get round to it."

"Do you suspect anyone involved in the corruption of being involved in the attack on you?"

"No," said Rob. "I didn't make a complaint until the attack."

"But these people were the ones you were talking about when you said you feared you were involved with some people who were far more dangerous than the ones connected with your mistresses?"

"Yes," said Rob.

"Leave it to me," said Rivers.

"What will you do?"

"I might pay Messrs Bruiser and Eel a visit. They'll have to be more careful if they think somebody is monitoring what they're doing."

"Let's hope so."

● ● ● ● ●

Miranda had gathered the names of her two love rivals from one of the regulars at the Dog and Partridge. She was worried that Aaron would face charges over his attack on Rob Corcoran that Sunday evening. She wondered whether the three women acting together could bring pressure to bear on Rob to refuse to co-operate with the police enquiry into the assault. She didn't know that was exactly what he had been doing. She had had no contact with him since Sunday evening.

She began by ringing Jackie Quesling on her mobile number. "Hallo," she said nervously when the florist answered. "I'm the woman who saw you with Rob at the Dog and Partridge on Sunday night. I'm a bit worried about this assault investigation."

"Well, I'm not," Jackie cut in. "Why are you worried?"

"It seems to me a court case could result in all our names being dragged through the mire." She neglected to add " and my husband jailed for an assault on Rob". Her point seemed to strike a chord with Jackie. "We should perhaps meet together and maybe make a joint approach to Rob to do his best to have any suggestion of criminal charges over the assault being dropped."

"Did you carry out the assault?"

"No."

"You're married, aren't you?"

Miranda could not deny it and realised that Jackie could be putting two and two together at the other end of the telephone. "That's got nothing to do with it," she said unconvincingly.

"Of course not," said Jackie sarcastically. "I've no objection to us meeting," she said. "Perhaps we could think of ways of teaching Rob a lesson."

"How about eight o'clock tonight?" Miranda asked. It would give her time to forewarn Aaron about the impending police visit and perhaps stay with him at home while he was being questioned by them.

"Where should we meet?"

"Not at the Dog and Partridge. Too public," said Miranda.

"Your house?"

Miranda thought for a moment. "No," she said. She didn't

want to Aaron to be confronted by the three love rivals – thus stirring up memories of her infidelity with Rob.

"Okay, mine," said Jackie.

"We should invite Sue Plummer, too," said Miranda.

"Sue Plummer? Is that her name?" said Jackie coldly. Miranda could sense that Jackie would prefer to scratch her eyes out rather than meet her. "Very well, then. Would you invite her?"

"Yes," said Miranda. She put the telephone down and dialled Sue's home number. It was Debra who answered. "Hallo," said Miranda. "Could I speak to Sue Plummer?"

"She's not in yet," came the reply.

"I wonder if you could ask her to ring Miranda Headley." Miranda gave her the number.

"Are you one of the other women?" asked Debra.

"I don't know what that's got to do with you," retorted Miranda. The implication of her comment was so clear that Debra realised she was speaking to one of Sue's love rivals. "I just want to meet up with her." She gave Debra Jackie's address and said the two of them would be meeting there at 8pm.

"Are you planning to do something about Rob?" Debra asked. Miranda ignored the question. "If you are, then good luck to you," said Debra finally.

● ● ● ● ●

"I don't like what you're getting me into," said Roger Broadbent.

"What do you mean?" said the voice on the other end of the telephone line. It was Jerry Vincent.

"Rob Corcoran has come into work today. He's got a cracked rib and a broken finger."

"My goodness," said Jerry. "How alarming. Have you any idea how that could have happened?"

"Don't give me that," said Roger. "You know very well."

"Be careful, dear boy, we don't want to be making unfounded allegations. Is he there?"

"No, of course not. I wouldn't ring you if he was."

"Glad to see you've got some common sense. What exactly is it you're worried about, my old thing?"

"Well, being involved in violence."

"Are you?" said Jerry sounding surprised, "Why, what have you done?"

"I've done nothing," said Roger with a heavy emphasis on the "I've".

"Exactly. You haven't lifted a finger towards anybody. You haven't even threatened Rob Corcoran despite who knows how much provocation. For all I know, you might even have an alibi for last night – although, goodness knows, you don't need one."

"Last night?" queried Roger sounding alarmed.

"I gather that must have been when the new attack on Rob Corcoran happened," said Jerry. "After all, he went home from the office yesterday without a cracked rib and broken finger and he arrived at work this morning with them. It doesn't take a genius to work out when he suffered those injuries. You don't need to have had any connection with causing them to work that one out."

"No," said Roger slowly. "I suppose not."

"You suppose right, old boy. Anyhow, I doubt if you'll have any further need to be worried about him. I'm sure he'll have been persuaded by now to drop his enquiries."

"You think so?"

"Yes."

Roger laughed – a nervous laugh. "Well, I beg to differ. I heard him on the telephone this morning. He was speaking to a Philip Rivers."

"Should I know this man?"

"From the gist of the conversation I heard, he's a private detective he's hired to protect himself."

"A private detective? Now that's rather naughty of him."

Roger froze for a moment. He wondered whether it had been a good idea to pass this information on to Jerry Vincent. "Just thought I should tell you that," he mumbled unconvincingly.

"Now that's very disappointing," said Vincent. "We're getting close to the point where he may need a second visit to deter him from carry on with his enquiries."

"I'm sorry," said Roger. "I can't be a part of this." With that, he put the receiver down.

Vincent shook his head – ruminating on how little backbone Roger Broadbent had. He sighed heavily and immediately reached for the telephone again. "Bruiser?" he said when a voice answered at the other end.

"Yes?"

"It seems you weren't at your persuasive best last night. Corcoran's only gone and hired a private detective to protect his interests. A Philip Rivers. Ever heard of him?"

"No."

"I think it may be time for a second visit."

Another voice chipped in. "Is that wise?" said Eel. "I mean, with a detective milling about?"

"If you persuade him to stand the detective down and to drop his enquiries, yes. Is that beyond you?"

"Not beyond me," said Bruiser.

"Best not to go too far in this second visit," said Vincent. "Be at your persuasive best. No more. The accent should still be on persuasion as a result of this visit."

"We can manage that," said Bruiser confidently.

● ● ● ● ●

"What did you want me for, sir?" Francesca asked Chief Superintendent Gleeson as she entered his office.

"Come in and sit down," he said motioning her to a chair

opposite him. "I wanted to find out how you were gelling with our new recruit, Gary Clarke."

"Honest answer, sir?"

"Always."

"He's a bit bumptious. Has the knack of getting people's backs up – even when they're co-operating with us. He's learning but it's a slow process."

"The Chief Constable thinks quite highly of him. Thinks he should be on the fast track to promotion. He's got a degree."

"I'll bet it's not in communication skills," said Francesca wryly. "I have left him holding the fort while we have this conversation. We'll see how he copes."

"That doesn't sound like a ringing endorsement."

"No, sir. It's not."

"I'm sorry," said Gleeson. "Down to more important matters," he added – switching the subject. "It's the chief constable's summer ball tomorrow night. Would you like to accompany me to it?"

Francesca thought for a moment. Normally only the most senior officers gained an invite. Although she had been promoted to Detective Chief Inspector, she was still technically with another force. It was the sort of do she would normally try to avoid. "What about Mrs Gleeson, sir?"

"Very thoughtful of you to have thought of her," said Gleeson. "She can't stand these do's – and frankly nor can I. It is a chance to network, though. If you ever thought you'd like to stay with Hertfordshire, it would give you a good opportunity to impress the right people. You would also make an older man very happy."

"An older man?"

"Me."

"Oh." Francesca blushed.

"These events are, shall we say, not noted for the literary standard of conversations. I think I would enjoy myself more chatting to you than making polite conversation with the Chief Constable's minions."

"That's very kind of you to say so, Sir." So long as it remains at literary conversations, she thought. She didn't want to give Gleeson the impression that there could be anything more on offer. To be fair, though, there was no evidence that he expected anything.

"It would mean leaving Gary Clarke holding the fort again. But he's got to learn."

"Yes, sir."

· · · · ·

Gary Clarke had asked one of the detective constables to accompany him to the Headley's home that evening for him to conduct the interview with Aaron Headley about the assault on Rob Corcoran.

"I think we've got him by the short and curlies," Gary confided to his companion. "No alibi. His wife having it away with the victim."

They were a little late in getting round to the Headley's. It was well past eight o'clock by the time they got there and they found Aaron on his own. "I've been expecting you," said Aaron.

"I suppose your wife told you we'd be coming," said Gary. "I've got to admit it. Things are looking bad for you. Your wife couldn't give you an alibi. She'd just told you she was having an affair with this guy."

"How did you know that?" asked Aaron.

"I am right, though, aren't I?" said Gary.

"Just hold on a minute. Am I a suspect? Do I need a lawyer?"

"At the moment we just want you to answer a few questions but if you'd prefer us to do it at the station."

"No," said Aaron. It was at that moment that Gary's mobile went off. He took it from his pocket. He noticed it was from the duty sergeant at the station. "I'm sorry, Mr Headley, I've got to take this." He moved away from Aaron to the corner of the room in the vain hope that he could have some privacy for his call. The other detective constable stood silently by Aaron's side. "What?" he said when he had digested the information from the duty sergeant. "Fuck me. We'd better get over there as soon as possible. What? He paused for a moment. "No, no need to disturb her for the moment. She's in a meeting with the Chief Super. I can handle it." He ended the call and put the mobile back in his pocket. "Come on," he said to the other detective constable. "Urgent business. I'm sorry, Mr Headley, we'll have to leave things as they are. We'll come back tomorrow. Fix a time later."

The two detectives then left the room with the second detective constable panting to keep up with Gary. "What's happened?" he asked.

"Rob Corcoran. He's been attacked again," said Gary. "This time he's been killed. Run down in the street by his home."

"Don't you think you'd better call your boss?"

"What" asked Gary. "No, I've got to show I can cope. Impress her."

"If you're sure," said the other man doubtfully.

They sped round to Rob's house. It was in a normally quiet cul-de-sac off the main road. This time, though, there were two police cars with their blue lights flashing and an ambulance parked outside the house. A body lay straddling the pavement and the road. A quick glance from Gary determined that it was Rob.

"What happened?" asked Gary.

One of the police constables came over to him. "No-one actually saw the incident," he said. "It looks as though he was knocked down while he was crossing the road, then – according to the tyre tracks – the car must have reversed over him and then driven off, driving over his body again."

"So no accident?"

"I wouldn't have thought so, sir. We've arranged for forensics to come down. They'll be here in a minute."

"And nobody saw the car?"

"No-one. One guy came out of his house when he heard a noise but by the time he'd made it to the street the car had driven off."

"How long ago did this happen?"

"According to the neighbours, it must have been half an hour ago."

Gary looked at the body. "Can you get me some gloves?" he asked the police constable." We should be checking for clues. Ironically, we were interviewing a suspect over an assault on this guy on Sunday evening when the call came through. Pretty much got him bang to rights but I guess he's got one of the best alibis he could have for this attack." The police constable looked at him quizzically as if he had not followed his train of thought. "Me and Detective Constable Johnson."

Gary turned his attention to the body. "He had something in his hand when he was knocked down," said the police constable. "It was a card. It's in the evidence bag. Shall I fish it out for you?" Gary nodded. The police constable lent over to where the bag was and took a card out."Philip Rivers – private detective," he said.

"Maybe he should be our first port of call," said Gary. It had a mobile number for the private detective. Gary rang it. "Mr Rivers?" he asked when someone answered. "It's Detective Constable Clarke from Hertfordshire CID here. We need to speak to you urgently. Where are you?"

"At home," came the reply.

"Where's that?"Rivers gave him the address. Gary recognised it as being in Finchley – some thirty minutes' drive away. "We'll be round in 20 minutes," he said optimistically.

"Don't you think you ought to stay here and see what else they find?" Johnson asked when he had got his colleague's attention.

"No," said Gary. "We'll find out more from Rivers." A crowd appeared to be forming outside Rob Corcoran's house. It appeared to be growing by the minute. "Get these ghouls out of here," he said to the PCs – whereupon they started clearing people away. Gary took a look at the crowd as he got into the police car he had arrived in, Johnson was driving. He noticed a face he recognised on the fringes of the crowd but couldn't place it for the moment. He thought long and hard as Johnson drove off and then said: "That was Debra. Debra," he repeated. "She's the flatmate of one of the women we questioned about the earlier assault on Mr Corcoran. It's a long story but she threatened to do him harm." He made a mental note that he should go round and see her the next day or when he was through with Rivers. What he didn't see as he drove off was a car approaching the cul-de-sac. It was stopped by one of the constables. "I'm sorry, madam, but you can't go near there," he said to the driver. "It's a crime scene."

"What's happened?" said the driver.

"I'm afraid I can't tell you but you'll have to reverse." The occupants then saw a covered up body loaded into the ambulance van. "Whoever that is, they are dead. It could be Rob. Looks like somebody got to him before we did – to deadly effect," said Jackie Quesling to her two fellow occupants of the car – Sue Plummer and Miranda Headley.

· · ● · ·

"Detective Constable Clarke, what's happened?" said Rivers as he opened his front door to Gary. He had already rung Francesca Manners in an attempt to find out but her mobile phone had been on voicemail.

"Could you tell me about your relationship with Rob Corcoran?"

"Rob Corcoran? Has something happened to him?"

"If you could answer the question, sir."

"Look," said Rivers, "you might find that I'm in a better position to help you if you tell me what's going on."

"I'm sorry but I can't disclose evidence from an ongoing investigation." Johnson looked at him with a baffled expression on his face. It seemed to say "surely you can".

"OK," said Rivers. He thought for a moment. "Well, all I can say is that he hired me to protect him."

Gary laughed. "Well, if you'll pardon me, you don't seem to have done a good job of that."

"Why? What's happened?"

"I've told you I can't tell you."

"But you hint at it through smirks and what you consider to be jokes. Why not just tell me instead of letting me guess at what's happened? I would imagine he's been attacked again – possibly even killed. Your demeanour seems to suggest this is a serious situation."

"He hired you to protect him. From whom?"

"He thought he was getting involved with dangerous company because he had uncovered some corruption in the planning department where he worked. He was also in danger from attack as a result of his private life. You know he was exposed as a womaniser at the weekend."

"Yes. Tell me more about this corruption."

Rivers thought for a moment. He was unhappy with Gary Clarke's bull in a china shop attitude. He would have felt more comfortable imparting the information to Francesca Manners. "I'd rather speak to your boss," he said.

That was like red rag to a bull to Gary. "Are you obstructing the police in the course of their duty?" he asked.

"No, I'm telling you that I'll give you the information – but only when your boss is here."

"Maybe you'll change your mind after a few hours in a cell," said Gary.

"What?" said Rivers incredulously. "That's totally unnecessary."

"I need to get cracking on this investigation as soon as possible. We can't wait for my boss."

"Have you informed her of this evening's events – whatever they are?"

"I'm in charge of this investigation this evening," said Gary a trifle petulantly.

It was at that stage that Rivers' mobile rang. "Hallo," he said. "Oh, Francesca, thank you for ringing back. I wondered if you could tell me what happened to my client Rob Corcoran this evening? What? You don't know. Well, your DC won't tell me either. At the moment he's threatening to arrest me for withholding information. What? You'd like a word with him? Sure." Rivers handed the mobile over to Gary. "She'd like a word."

Gary took it from him. "Yes, ma'am," he said. "Well, Rob Corcoran's been killed. I didn't think you should be bothered. I can cope. Yes ma' "He remembered in time this time. "Francesca." He handed the telephone back to Rivers. "She suggests the three of us meet to discuss the situation." "You mean the murder of Rob Corcoran?" said Rivers.

"Yes."

"And I'm not under arrest?"

"No."

"Then I'm happy to help you and Detective Chief Inspector Manners."

"We could give you a lift to the police station," Gary volunteered in an attempt to smooth over their differences.

"No, thanks," said Rivers. "I'll drive over there. It'll give me a bit more confidence that I can leave of a time of my own choosing." He smiled as he passed Detective Constable Johnson on the way out of his flat.

CHAPTER FOUR

"So how the hell did we get into a situation where we nearly arrested Philip Rivers – who may have vital information to help us with our enquiries into Rob Corcoran's death?" asked Francesca, sounding exasperated.

"He was being obstructive."

"Oh, yes. How?"

"He only wanted to speak to you, ma'am."

"I'm not surprised considering the approach you took to him. Look, Gary, first rules of detective work. You have to develop antennae as to who could be helpful to us and who is being evasive – and treat them differently. Not everyone is seeking to hold out on us."

"Sorry ma'... Francesca." Again he remembered in the nick of time to call her by her first name.

"Anyhow, let's try and show a united front for the rest of the evening."

At this juncture Rivers returned from obeying a call of nature. He sat down opposite the desk in Francesca's office without waiting for an invitation. "Philip, what can you tell me about Rob Corcoran?" asked Francesca softly.

"He was a frightened man," he said. "Shortly before his death he rang me to ask if I would look after him." Gary snorted at this juncture but Francesca shot him a severe frosty glance. "I didn't – and I guess he didn't – realise how much imminent danger he was in. He had been adamant up until yesterday that he didn't want my help over anything. If you ask me, he was embarrassed over the contretemps with the three women at the Dog and Partridge. Wanted to put that behind him. I don't think he was worried about reprisals from them."

"But he was assaulted on the Sunday night because of that?"

"Yes."

"We have a fairly good idea of who was responsible for that. Miranda Headley's husband."

"Oh," said Rivers. "In the frame for the murder, then?" Rivers sounded surprised that this might be the case.

"He would be," said Francesca – a smile beginning to form on her face, "but he has a rather good alibi for the time of the killing."

"Yes?"

"He was with Detective Constable Clarke at the time."

Rivers laughed. "So your deputy does have his uses?" he said.

"It would appear so," said Francesca. Gary bristled at the exchange between the two of them. "So what made him change his mind about needing protection?"

"He had uncovered some information about a corruption racket at the planning department where he worked," said Rivers. "He told me he thought these people were far more sinister than the ex-mistresses and their partners – or, more correctly, partner. He'd been beaten up a second time before he was killed. A much more professional job." He recorded how Corcoran had had his finger broken and ribs cracked.

"Who was responsible?"

"Have you ever come across two individuals called Bruiser and Eel?" asked Rivers.

Francesca reflected for a moment. "Their names ring a bell." She was deep in thought. "Ah, yes," she finally said. "Larry Green mentioned them to me. You know, my predecessor as Detective Chief Inspector." Rivers nodded. "He said they were the kind of people you shouldn't visit on your own if you had something on them. I think they were debt collectors. Their real names are on the tip of my tongue – McCarthy and Higgs. That's it."

"Well, they paid Rob a visit to put the frighteners on him –

and succeeded, I'll be bound."

"Not quite," said Francesca.

"What do you mean?"

"Well, he did come to you for help. That's not the action of a frightened man. They could have construed your intervention as a sign that he was planning to continue with their enquiries."

"How would they have known about me? He wouldn't have told them."

Francesca shrugged her shoulders. "Somebody must have told them," she said. "The thing is, though, they're not likely to have carried this out all on their own. Somebody must have paid them to get involved."

"A property developer by the name of Jerry Vincent," said Rivers. "He was the one who was in receipt of favours from the planning committee. I doubt whether there would be any evidence to connect them though – especially now Rob Corcoran is dead."

"Precisely the reason that makes it likely they killed him," said Gary – sounding enthusiastic about where the enquiry was leading. "We should question him immediately."

"No," said Francesca, holding up a restraining hand. "Bruiser and Eel should be our first port of call."

"Let me question them first," said Rivers. "They're more likely to threaten me. They'll just stay silent if you start questioning them. I can bring any evidence to you."

Gary looked at Francesca as if he was questioning the wisdom of this move. "No, Gary," she said. "I think it's a good idea."

"I'll go and see them tomorrow morning," said Rivers.

"Remember what Larry Green said," Francesca urged. "He said he wouldn't want to go and see them on his own if he suspected them of anything."

"Don't worry," said Rivers. "I'll take Jo with me."

• • • • •

Jerry Vincent spluttered into his wine glass as he heard the lead item on the local news bulletin that evening. It said a 57-year-old Hertford man had been murdered earlier on in the evening. It mentioned no name but left a clear imprint in his mind that it was Rob Corcoran. It talked of the victim having worked for the local planning department. He decided to ring Bruiser and Eel immediately. He used Bruiser's mobile number to contact them.

"'Allo," a gruff voice responded. "Bit late to be ringing, isn't it? I need my beauty sleep."

"Have you gone beyond your brief this evening?"

"Who is this?"

"You know who this is, dear boy."

"I do now. What's up, Mr Vincent?"

"Have you heard the local news tonight?"

"Can't say as I have."

"Rob Corcoran's been murdered."

"Blimey."

"You were going round to see him tonight."

"Yes," said Bruiser. "We got there but there were loads of people outside. We decided to call it a day."

Vincent sighed. "So you've got nothing to do with what happened tonight?"

"What do you take me for?"

Vincent decided not to respond to that question. A small-time thug, he thought to himself.

"Were you in your van last night?" he eventually asked Bruiser. "With McCarthy and Higgs emblazoned over the vehicle?"

Bruiser thought for a moment. "Yes, I suppose we were," he said. "I don't think anybody saw us, though. We weren't there for long. We hightailed it out of there."

"Let's hope you're right." With that, he put the receiver down.

• • • • •

Rivers drove into the scrap metal yard early the next morning with Jo in tow. "Remember," he said to his friend. "This could turn nasty." He got out of the car and made his way over to the shed that Bruiser and Eel used an office. "Anyone at home?" he asked.

"Who wants to know?" It was the gruff voice of Bruiser.

"My name's Philip Rivers. I'm a private enquiry agent. I'm calling on behalf of a client," he said.

Bruiser emerged in the doorway. He was still wearing his leather jacket and jeans from two days ago. "No offence," said Bruiser, "but fuck off."

"None given but I'm not going to fuck off," said Rivers. "Do you know a Rob Corcoran?"

"You heard what I said." Bruiser moved menacingly towards Rivers at which point Jo emerged from the other side of the car. The Bahamian was taller than Bruiser and cut an imposing figure as he stood just a few inches away from him.

"Actually, I want to amend what I just said," said Rivers. "You do know a Rob Corcoran because you visited him a couple of days ago. You broke his finger and cracked his ribs – and threatened you'd be back to create more damage if he didn't drop some enquiries he was making into a planning application made by a property developer I believe you're acquainted with – Jerry Vincent."

"Dunno what you're talking about," said Bruiser. At this stage Eel emerged from the ramshackle office. "You're causing serious offence – so push off before I push you off."

"You might like to hear what I've got to say before you're hauled in for questioning on a murder charge," said Rivers. "My client was murdered last night. I'm trying to work out whether you were responsible."

"I've told you. I don't know this Corcoran bloke."

"Not true," said Rivers. "But tell me where you were last night."

"I don't have to tell you anything."

"No, you don't but – if you do have an alibi for last night – it might just affect the report I give to the police on the two of you."

Bruiser picked up a metal spike and moved a couple of inches towards Rivers. "You may not be in a position to give a report to the police,"he said menacingly.

Jo moved quick as a flash and wrestled the metal spike from Bruiser's clutches and threw it to the ground. "Oh yes, he will be,"he said.

"Boys, boys,"said Eel intervening for the first time. "Let's have no more of this macho nonsense. Just tell him where we were last night, Bruiser." Bruiser looked at Eel as if he had to take his cue from his lanky companion. "We were in the pub down the road,"he said. "Stayed there until it was nearly closing time."

"Oh, yeah,"said Bruiser.

"The Clarendon Arms. Take the first right on getting back on to the high street. You can't miss it."

"So you see we can't possibly have been in Hertford."

"Hertford?"said Rivers. "Who said anything about Hertford?"

"I thought you did."

"No," said Rivers,"but it is where my client lives – lived. But then you knew that, didn't you? Because you broke his finger and cracked his ribs at his home a couple of days ago – and then went back last night to run him over. You knocked him down, reversed over the body and then drove off over the body again. Callous, calculating, cold-blooded murder."

"Mr Rivers," said Eel, "I think you ought to check our alibi out before you go throwing out accusations like that. The Clarendon Arms?"

"I'll go," said Rivers,"but -– quite frankly, pal – I don't hold out much hope of you surviving this enquiry with the attitude you've got." The last few words were addressed to Bruiser.

"Remember, next time you're questioned, it'll probably be the police," he went on, "and they'll probably be a bit more persistent than me." At that, he got into the car and drove off. Bruiser picked up the spike and flung it at the departing car. It missed by yards.

"Right," said Rivers. "The Clarendon Arms."

It took them less than five minutes to find the pub. It wasn't yet open but persistent ringing of the doorbell brought a half-dressed manager to the door. "Yes?" he said in an irritated voice.

"Sorry to trouble you," said Rivers, "but we're private enquiry agents. We wondered whether you were in the bar last night."

"Yes, I was," the other man replied.

"We're investigating a crime and a couple of the prime suspects say they were drinking with you last night."

"Who are they?" the publican asked.

"You may know them as Bruiser and Eel – but their actual names are Mr McCarthy and Mr Higgs."

"Ah, Bruiser and Eel." The publican thought for a moment. Rivers thought he was weighing up whether he could afford to cross McCarthy and Higgs by telling the truth.

"Well, then?" asked Rivers.

"Well then, what?"

"Were they here last night?"

"Of course they were," replied the publican. "I remember being worried about them."

"Worried about them?"

"Well, Eel was supposed to be driving them home but he'd had a bit to drink. I suggested to him he leave the car and take a taxi but Bruiser was having none of it. Are they all right?"

"Why do you ask?"

"Well, you said you were investigating a crime that they were the prime suspects for. I wondered whether they'd had an accident on the way home."

"No, nothing like that," said Rivers. "Thank you for your help." Rivers could not help but sound bad tempered as he uttered these words – he wondered whether the publican was being entirely honest with him. "We'll be on our way, then," he said.

The publican nodded. "Glad to be of help."

"To Bruiser and Eel," said Rivers as he made his way back to his car.

The publican waited for them to go and then returned inside to ring the telephone number of the scrap metal yard. "What have you boys been up to?" he asked when Bruiser answered the telephone.

"I don't know what you're talking about," said Bruiser gruffly.

"Bruiser, this is me talking. Dan" said the publican. "I said you were both drinking here until closing time. I embellished it a little. I said I was worried about Eel driving you home because I thought he'd had too much to drink."

"Thanks," said Bruiser.

"No worries – but what were you doing last night?"

"That's for me to know and you not to ask questions about," said Bruiser.

• • ● • •

"Have you heard the news today?" Colin asked as he rang Trish that morning.

"Haven't had time to listen to the news," she said.

"Then what I'm going to say may shock you," he said.

"Go on."

"It's Rob," he said. "He's dead. Run over by a car. The police think it was deliberate."

"Bloody hell," said Trish. "I need to sit down." She was in her charity shop. She asked one of the volunteers if they could deal with all customers for a while and walked into the office at the back of the shop – still holding her mobile telephone. "God," she said. "I feel so bad."

"Why?"

"I was wishing him dead earlier this week," she said. "When

I found out I was still going to inherit from him. I didn't mean it."

"I know you didn't but you should be careful what you say," said Colin. "You'll probably be questioned by the police soon."

"I can't tell them anything," she said. "Rob? Dead? I can't take it in. I've been cursing and swearing at him so much over the last few months – well, longer than that, really. It just doesn't seem possible."

"It is," said Colin. "Just put the local news on. That'll tell you all about it."

"I don't know that I want to know the details."

"That's understandable," said Colin soothingly, "but do you think you should carry on working today? I could come round and look after you if you like."

"Thanks, Colin. That'd be sweet of you. I might very well give up work for the day and go home and put my feet up." She put her mobile back in her pocket and went up to one of the volunteers and explained what had happened. The volunteer expressed no surprise that she would rather be at home taking it all in – instead of working. She was joined in her cottage by Colin a few minutes later. "Thanks for coming, Colin," she said.

"I've got a bit of time on my hands now," he said, "after being made redundant. I could take you out to lunch – a cheap pub lunch. I haven't got that much in the bank these days."

"Don't worry about that," said Trish. "I suppose I'll be coming into some money soon so I can afford it. Let's go out of Hertford, though, I don't want to be accused of being the merry widow – living it up after her partner's popped his clogs."

"I don't think anyone would accuse you of that," he said. He moved as if to kiss her. She didn't withdraw but offered him her cheek so it ended up not being as passionate an embrace as he would have liked. Decorum, he thought to himself. You've got to take these things slowly.

• • ● • •

Ralph Corcoran shuffled across the mortuary floor to the exit door. Francesca could tell he was Rob's father – there was a family resemblance. Masses of curly hair – although white in Ralph's case. He walked uneasily across the floor clutching his wife Patricia's arm. She, for her part, looked quite sprightly for her age. Francesca put both of them in their late seventies.

"Hardest thing anyone ever has to do," muttered Ralph to no-one in particular. "Identify the dead body of their offspring. You wish –" here he squeezed Patricia's hand for further support –"you wish you could have gone first. That's the natural order of things," he added.

"We'll get the bastard who did this," said Gary Clarke intervened. His naturally brash exterior was all in pieces. Francesca could even tell that he was holding back tears as he spoke. It was, after all, the first case of murder that he had had to deal with. She put a comforting hand on his shoulder. "Thank you Francesca," he said.

Francesca smiled. He had still forgotten the golden rule: Francesca in private, Detective Chief Inspector Manners in public. This time it was excusable, though. "I share Detective Constable Clarke's sentiments," she said to Ralph."It's shocking what happened." She ushered the couple over to a table and picked up a bag to hand to Patricia Corcoran."Rob's belongings," she said.

Patricia looked inside the bag. There was not much there. A blue denim shirt, underpants. A wallet, watch and a pair of glasses. No socks, no shoes. "Not much for 57 years on this earth,"she said.

"No," agreed Francesca. "It seems to indicate he was lured out of his house by someone he knew and then run over. It seems to indicate there could have been two people involved in the murder – although we can't be sure."

"Thank you,"said Patricia.

"There is one thing more," said Gary stopping them as they

were about to leave. He put his hand in his pocket and drew out a business card. "This," he said, handing it to Ralph.

"Philip Rivers," said Ralph, reading it. "Who's he?"

"He's a private detective. Rob seems to have been frightened or at least worried that something might happen to him. He hired Rivers as a precaution."

Ralph gave off a nervous laugh. "It doesn't seem to have worked out," he said.

"To be fair to Mr Rivers, I think he was only hired a few hours before Rob was murdered. I don't think anyone realised how serious the situation was."

"No," said Ralph, "I don't suppose they did."

"We'll keep you in touch about any further developments," said Francesca. "In the meantime, you have our deepest sympathy."

"Thank you," said Ralph. He seemed to grip Patricia's arm a little tighter as they made their way from the mortuary.

"Your first time?" asked Francesca when they were out of earshot as if to confirm what she was sure was the case.

"Yes," said Gary. "I've never had to be present before when relatives identify a body."

"I'd like to say you get used to it," said Francesca, "but I think if you did it would make you less of a human being."

"Where to now, Francesca?" asked Gary. There seemed to be a new-found confidence in his voice – as if he was determined to deliver justice to the Corcoran's.

"Interviews with the usual round of suspects," said Francesca. "We'll wait until we hear from Rivers before we tackle Bruiser and Eel. I vote we start off with Sue Plummer again."

"Yes," said Gary. He thought for a moment. "Francesca?" he said hesitantly.

"Yes?"

"You said there might have been two people involved in the murder?"

"Yes. One to lure Rob Corcoran out of his house and one to run him over."

Gary paused for a moment to let the information sink in. "There's something I forgot to tell you last night," said. "That lodger of Sue Plummer's. She was hanging around outside Rob Corcoran's home last night."

"Any idea why?"

"No," he said. "I was just leaving to go and interview Rivers." Francesca shot him a sidelong glance. "I know, I know, wrong call," he said holding his hands up, "but perhaps we can find out what she was doing if we go and interview them this morning."

"To the school, then," said Francesca.

Meanwhile, Rob's father Ralph was still wrapped in thought as he and Patricia left the mortuary. He took Rivers' card out of his pocket again. "Perhaps we ought to go and see this guy," said Ralph. "He might know a bit more about what was going on. They were very nice – those detectives – but I don't think they have a clue."

"They don't like to give much away."

The couple got into their car and resolved to drive to Rivers' office address – given on the card. As luck would have it, they arrived at his office at exactly the same time as Rivers and Jo returned from their visit to Bruiser and Eel.

"Mr Corcoran?" said Rivers to the couple as they approached his door.

"Yes," said Ralph. "How did you know?"

"There's a strong family resemblance," said Rivers.

"Except that I'm twenty-five years older than Rob," he said. The words seemed to make him feel sad.

"Come in," said Rivers, "and sit down. This, by the way," he added pointing to Jo, "is my assistant Jo."

Jo smiled at the couple and shook each one by the hand. He was relieved the question of his race didn't seem to bother them – unlike the first potential client he had dealt with after joining Rivers' employment.

"We've just come from the mortuary," said Ralph. "The police said Rob had hired you."

"Yes, on the night he died. I'm sorry I didn't realise what an imminent danger he was in. I would have started work immediately."

Ralph waved his hand at Rivers as if to tell him not to worry about it. "Why did he hire you?" he asked.

"He was worried. He'd been attacked twice in two days."

Ralph glanced at Patricia who looked horrified. "We had no idea," he said.

Rivers looked thoughtful. "I don't know how much you knew about your son," he began.

"I'm beginning to feel not much."

"Well, the first attack was because of women trouble. It seems he was dating three women at the same time – one of whom was married. They found out about each other on Sunday."

"And one of them attacked him?"

"Can't be sure of that," said Rivers. "In fact I doubt it. More likely to have been the husband of one of them."

"And the second attack? Was that as a result of this, too?"

"No," said Rivers. "Your son had uncovered some corruption in the planning department. A couple of heavies were sent round to his house to warn him off making further enquiries. That was a much more professional job – and was what persuaded him to seek help from me. Help that to my eternal regret I was unable to give."

"You seem to know a lot more about Rob and what he was involved in than the police do," said Ralph.

"I think they're just being cagey with you."

"Nevertheless," said Ralph. He looked at Patricia. "I was thinking, Darling, we should ask Mr Rivers to continue to look after Rob's – our interests," he said. She nodded in agreement.

"Would you be prepared to do that, Mr Rivers?"

"I'd be delighted to," said Rivers. "It will cost you, though.

Unlike the police, I'm not a free service funded by the taxpayer."

"No, I realise that," said Ralph, It did not take them long to negotiate a contract at a figure which guaranteed Jo's wages as well as Rivers' for the duration of the case.

● ● ● ● ●

"I'm afraid she's not here," said the school receptionist after she had telephoned through to Sue's office to tell her the police had arrived and wanted to interview her. "Taken the morning off sick. The headteacher would like a word with you, though."

Francesca glanced at Gary as if to ask him if he could think why the head had made that request. Within minutes, they had their answer as the headteacher – a slim bespectacled woman with an austere look on her face appeared before them. "Would you accompany me to my study?"she said. It was a command not a question and Francesca and Gary dutifully traipsed behind her into her office."I can't think of the last time I was summoned to the head's study,"Francesca whispered to Gary as they followed her into the room.

"Now," said the head. "How many more times are we going to have visits like this?"

Francesca looked at her as if she didn't understand the reasoning behind the question. "I don't know," she said. "I'm conducting a murder enquiry – and I go where the evidence takes me."

"And it takes you to Miss Plummer?"

"She is one of many people we have to interview in connection with this murder. She was close to the victim."

"So she is a suspect?"

"I didn't say that."

"Only, as I expect you will appreciate, Inspector…"

"Detective Chief Inspector," intervened Francesca frostily. Teachers should get their facts right, she reasoned to herself.

The headteacher waved her hand as if the difference between the two was of no consequence. "As I expect you will appreciate, it does the reputation of the school no good to have the police constantly on the premises."

"And the reputation of the school is far more important than us catching the brutal killer of a man well liked in the community?" Gary butted in. For once, Francesca did not see any reason to restrain him.

"More important to me, yes," the head said stiffly. "Now, you've been told that Miss Plummer is at home so you can go. I might add that should you wish to interview her again in the future you will also find her at home. She is being suspended from duty as from today."

"That's a bit harsh," said Gary.

"That decision is nothing to do with you, young man," said the head stiffly.

"No," said Francesca, "but if everybody we interviewed in connection with this case was suspended from their job, it wouldn't be good for the economy of Hertford."

"Would you leave now?" said the head curtly. "I have told you Miss Plummer is not here,"

"We're not quite finished," said Francesca. "We'd like to interview her flatmate, too, who I believe also works in your school meals service."

"Is that really necessary?"

"Yes. Why do you ask? Do you need evidence so you can suspend her too?"

"Perhaps we should interview the entire school meals staff," said Gary. "Ask them if they have noticed anything different in Sue Plummer's behaviour of late. Of course, it could take some time."

"I'll get Debra for you," said the head gruffly. "You could do the interview here rather than shout it from the rooftops in reception."

"Thank you," said Francesca. They waited patiently while Debra was summoned from her work station and brought before them. "Debra," began Francesca, "I don't know whether you know but Rob Corcoran died last night. He was murdered."

"I saw the police cars. And the ambulance."

"Yes," said Francesca. "We understand you were there outside his house when it happened."

"I saw them."

"Why were you there?"

"He'd hurt Sue. I wanted to tell him how badly he had hurt her."

"Did you?"

"I didn't see him. Not to talk to."

"So you just went there and came away again?"

"Yes."

"Thank you, Debra," said Francesca. "That will be all." The two detectives then thanked the head for the use of her study. "We'd better get round to Sue Plummer's home, then," Francesca said to Gary.

"And apologise to her for being the cause of her losing her job?" said Gary. "Honestly, what a blinkered decision."

Francesca nodded in agreement. She also sympathised with Sue Plummer when she found herself imparting the news of the circumstances surrounding Rob's death to her. "I have to ask you," she went on "Where were you last night?"

"Here for the most part," said Sue.

"You didn't think about going round to Rob Corcoran's?"

"I did think about it," she said. "I couldn't help thinking that our relationship needn't be at an end. That if I gave him one more chance – but that's all water under the bridge now." She began sobbing and broke off to fetch a tissue from the kitchen. "I'm sorry, I can't believe he's dead. I've lost everything. My job, my boyfriend." Whatever it was she wanted to say disappeared in another round of sobbing.

"You haven't lost your job," said Francesca. "You're only suspended."

"And you think they're going to take me back again? Pigs might."

"Can I ask you?" said Francesca. "Who do you think has done this to Rob? Is it one of his former mistresses? One of their partners?"

"There's no-one else in my life," said Sue. "Only Rob over the last few months. I can't speak for anyone else, though."

Francesca nodded. "Okay, we'll leave it at that, then," said Francesca. She touched Sue's knee in sympathy as she got up to leave. Gary nodded politely as he made his way to the door.

● ● ● ● ●

"What are you doing here?" Douglas Roulay seemed alarmed by the presence of Jerry Vincent in reception.

"Don't worry, I haven't come to see you," said the property developer. "I just wanted to check on the progress of my planning application. With Roger."

"Roger's not in," said Roulay. "He's taken the day off sick."

"Oh, I am sad to hear it," said Vincent. "Perhaps I should take some flowers round to his home. I do hope he makes a quick recovery."

"I doubt if he'll want to see you," said Roulay. "In fact, I doubt if anyone will want to see you."

"Now that's not very friendly, dear boy," said Vincent. "You know, you really shouldn't panic. One would almost think you've got something to hide."

"You know you should keep a lower profile."

"Darling, low profiles and I just don't gel together. Like chalk and cheese." He looked at Roulay. "Well, I mustn't take up any more of your time. Toodle pip."

"Where are you going?"

"That, my dear boy, is none of your business."

"Don't go round to Roger's. He's nervous enough already."

"In that case, I might very well have something that will calm his nerves. Possibly permanently." He laughed at what he perceived to be Roulay's discomfort at this remark and left the planning department. As he was approaching his car, his mobile went off. "Bruiser, my old pal," he said on ascertaining who the caller was. "You're not panicking, are you?"

"Panicking?" asked Bruiser. It was as though he did not understand what the word meant. "I don't think so."

"Well, if you don't think you're panicking, then you're not. No-one's mentioned seeing your van last night so I think you could be in the clear."

"I should tell you that Rivers has been sniffing around here. Wanted to link us to the killing of that Corcoran fellow last night. Luckily Eel and I managed to whistle up an alibi. We were in the pub all night last night."

"Of course you were, my son. Is that what you wanted to tell me?"

"No," he said. "I think we're going to get a visit from the police."

"I shouldn't worry about that, old boy. If you've got a cast iron alibi for last night, you're all right."

"But I don't think Rivers is going to give up."

"Then, me old fruit, you're going to have to make him give up."

"How?"

"Come on, dear boy, you're the persuader."

"It won't be enough just to threaten him," said Bruiser. "He's a determined bugger."

"Then look for his weak spots. Has he got a wife? Children? Threaten them – not him. I shouldn't need to tell you your job. Tail him for a while. See how he lives. What threats present themselves. Do what's necessary to take him out of the equation. But don't keep coming back to me. The less chance they can trace any communication between the two us the better. Understand?"

"Yes, boss."

Vincent shook his head. "If you can keep your head while all around are losing theirs," he mumbled to himself. He drove on until he reached Roger Broadbent's home. He noticed the curtains twitching as he turned his Aston Martin into the newly gravelled driveway. Newly gravelled courtesy of him, he thought to himself. He jumped out of the car and strode over to the doorbell. "Come on, Roger, I know you're in there," he said "No point hiding."

A nervous looking Roger opened the door. Vincent walked past him and into the living room. "Come in and sit down," said Roger nervously after the property developer had done just that.

"I heard you were poorly," said Vincent, "so I came to pay my respects. No grapes, I'm afraid, though."

"Pay your respects?" Roger seemed alarmed at the choice of words.

"Well, wish you well then," said Vincent. "You know, you don't look ill. No sniffing nose. No sore throat or loss of voice. You just look anxious."

"Well, wouldn't you be?"

"Wouldn't I what?"

"Look anxious in the circumstances."

"No, I'm full of the joys of spring. So should you be. You've got tickets to the test match at Lord's next week. The sun's shining. It's going to be a great game. Your house looks wonderful. Especially the new driveway. Everything's tickety-boo." He got up from his chair. "Let's see what else we can do for you round the house." He made his way into the bedroom. Suddenly a reproachful voice called out. "Oh, Roger, what are you doing? You're packing?"

"I want to get away for a few days – until this whole thing has blown over."

"No, Roger. You're going to face it out." he looked at Roger's crestfallen face. "Oh, you haven't bought tickets, have you? And you've told the wife you're taking her away. Trying to get back together again." He shook his heads. "Sad," he said. "All that will have to wait. Give those tickets to Uncle Jerry and I'll get a refund for you – or re-arrange it for a month or two hence." He held his hand out and clicked his fingers. Roger moved over to the sideboard and got a folder out. He handed it to Vincent. "Thanks," said the property developer. "You see. There's nothing to fear. Corcoran isn't going to make any more enquiries."

"Rivers?" said Roger tentatively.

"Any threat from Rivers will be taken care of – just trust your Uncle Jerry. The planning application will go through next month's meeting. Don't backtrack on your report. That would be feeding the vultures. You'll watch the test match and England might even win."

"All right," said Roger reluctantly.

"So it's back to work tomorrow morning as if nothing ever happened." He gave Roger two friendly slaps on the cheek. "Eh?"

Roger nodded.

• • ● • •

"Look, if Bruiser and Eel say they were in here last night, they were in here last night," said the man – in his mid-thirties – as he gulped down some ale.

"Does that mean they were here last night?" asked Gary. "I don't understand."

"It's simple," said the man. "It doesn't matter whether they were here or not. If they say they were, they were."

"And if we find they were somewhere else, we could charge you with obstructing the police in the course of their duty. At the very least."

"Whatever. It's better than what they would do to me."

Gary sighed. At least this punter was being honest with him. The other drinkers in the Clarendon Arms had to a man ... there were no women in the pub ... sworn they had seen Bruiser and Eel in the pub the previous evening. Gary went to rejoin Francesca. "It seems to be the Bruiser and Eel fan club in here tonight," he said. "They're queueing up to give them an alibi."

Francesca nodded. "We're not going to be able to shake their alibi," she said.

The landlord came over to them at this juncture. "Have you got what you wanted?" he asked.

"No," said Francesca.

"That's one of the problems you have if you start an investigation with a pre-conceived notion," he said. "Bruiser and Eel were here last night. I saw them."

"And we're going to have to accept what you say until we can prove otherwise," said Francesca.

"As I told the other chap who was enquiring, I was a bit worried about whether Eel was fit to drive home," he said, "but you challenge Bruiser and Eel at your peril."

"What have they got on you?"

"The power of persuasion."

"Well, thank you for your courtesy – if not help," said Francesca. "I think the day would not be quite complete if we didn't now go and see Bruiser and Eel." With that, she and Gary departed from the pub and did the five minute drive to the offices of McCarthy and Higgs.

"What do you want?" asked Bruiser gruffly as he responded to their knock on his office door.

"We're police," said Francesca as the two of them flashed their warrant cards. "We just wanted to ask you about your relationship with Rob Corcoran."

"I don't have any relationship with Rob Corcoran," he said. "What do you think I am – a ruddy poofta?" It was an attempt at humour.

"We know you were at his house on Monday evening."

"Got a witness have you?"

"Rob Corcoran."

"Oh, and they're going to wheel him into court. Knock once if Mr McCarthy and Mr Higgs came round to your place. Knock twice if they didn't. Do me a favour."

"He told someone you were there. Someone who is very much alive."

"You're talking of Philip Rivers? I wouldn't rely too much on him."

"Oh? Why not?"

"I'm just saying. Listen, bint. Fuck off out of here. It's time for me to go down to the pub."

"To thank everybody for supplying you with an alibi?" said Gary.

"Whatever. Look, you've got nothing to hold me on, charge me with or whatever so I'm making my way to the pub. If I were you, I wouldn't come back until you've got some evidence to charge me and Eel with."

"We will be back," said Francesca as she and Gary made their way to their car. "Charming couple," she said as she sat in the passenger seat.

"The sort I'd love to put away."

"Yes," said Francesca. She glanced at her watch. "Damn," she said. "I'm going to be late for the Chief Constable's ball if I don't get a move on. Could you take me home, Gary, instead of to the office so I can get myself ready?"

"You've been invited to the ball?" said Gary. He sounded surprised.

"Yes, as guest of Rory Gleeson." Gary looked surprised. "Don't worry, there's nothing going on there," she said. "It's just that his wife hates balls."

"Lucky that Rory Gleeson hasn't got any, then," he said tartly.

"That's a bit harsh," said Francesca. "Where did you get that idea from?" Gary didn't reply.

· · ● · ·

"Aaron, tell me it wasn't you." said Miranda as her husband returned home from work that evening.

"What wasn't me?"

"You know," she said.

"Oh, that killed Rob Corcoran? What do you take me for?"

"Someone who assaulted him on Sunday night."

"All right, it wasn't me. You can talk to my alibi if you don't believe me."

Miranda looked at him quizzically. "Who would that be?" she asked.

"Detective Constable Gary Clarke. He was here interviewing me when the call came through saying Rob Corcoran had been killed. Can't get a better alibi than that." He poured himself a glass of whisky from the cabinet. "How about you?" he asked.

"You surely don't think?"

"You seemed to think that I could have killed him. I'm just turning the tables on you. Where were you last night? You weren't here with me, that's for sure."

"I didn't think you wanted me around."

"That's a good explanation as to why you weren't here but it doesn't explain where you really were."

"Out."

"You're impossible, Miranda. Is that answer supposed to satisfy my curiosity?"

"I'm afraid it will have to do."

"Oh? So you were with another lover, were you?"

"No, I wasn't," she said indignantly. "There is no-one else. Now."

"Now," repeated Aaron, "so I've got a lot to be thankful for to the killer of Rob Corcoran. He's brought my wife back to me."

"And will you have her back?"

Aaron took a sip from his whisky. "I've been thinking about it. I'd like us to make a fresh start. But – no lies in the future. And that's why it's important you tell me where you were last night."

"I was with a couple of friends," said Miranda.

"Yes – and who were they?"

She sighed. "Sue Plummer and Jackie Quesling if you must know."

"Wow'!" said. The news was sufficiently surprising for him to pour himself another whisky. "Why?"

"We were going to confront Rob about what he'd done."

"And did you?"

"No, we drove up outside his house to find the police cars and an ambulance outside. We just drove away again."

"The witches' coven," said Aaron. "That's what you were. I'm almost beginning to feel sorry for the guy. So many people seem to have had a grudge against him."

"Yes, that's true," said Miranda, "but we didn't kill him."

Aaron took another sip from his whisky. "I believe you," he said. He opened his arms to her and she snuggled up to him. "I didn't really believe you could have killed him," he added. She remained silent – snug in his arms. He would have liked her to have said: And I didn't really believe you could have done either. The words were not forthcoming, though. He was glad, he thought again, of the alibi that Gary Clarke could give him.

● ● ● ● ●

"That's a stunning dress," said Rory Gleeson as Francesca opened the door to her house. She was wearing a full-length crimson dress with an accompanying white jacket and high heeled shoes.

"Thank you, sir," she said.

"Rory," he corrected. "You're my date for tonight. I don't think you should call me sir."

"Possibly not," said Francesca. He ushered her to his car. "You're driving?" said Francesca surprised.

"I won't be drinking," he said. "I'm not a party pooper but I'd rather have a car to get me home tonight than not be sober and rely on a taxi."

Francesca breathed a sigh of relief. What little doubt she had as to his intentions seemed to evaporate. "It's not as if you can't enjoy yourself when you're not drinking," she said.

Gleeson nodded. He helped her into the passenger seat and then made his way over to the driver's side. "How are things going?" he asked.

"Things?"

"The murder enquiry."

"No real leads yet. We know Rob Corcoran was beaten up by a couple of professional thugs the night before he was murdered – but they have an unshakeable alibi for the night of the murder. That doesn't mean they didn't do it. Just that we can't prove it was them."

"Do you think it was them?"

"I'm keeping an open mind as they say," she said. "They had motive. They were trying to warn him off pursuing his enquiries into corruption in the planning department – but there was evidence he was still carrying on. But the more sensational aspect of the case is the three lovers he had – who found out about each other at the weekend. That, I think, is the one the media will be running with tomorrow morning."

"Right. And how are you getting on with Detective Constable Clarke?"

"It's an up and downer. He was really moved when the parents of the victim came to identify him this morning – so he has got a heart. We just have to work hard on reminding him

119

of that fact. Otherwise, he can be quite embarrassing during interviews."

"Right," said Gleeson. "One thing," he said.

"Yes?"

"Don't be quite so open with your comments about Clarke if the Chief Constable asks you the same question."

"All right, sir," said Francesca. "Any particular reason?"

"He values Clarke quite highly."

By this time they had arrived at the local club where the ball was being held. Rory Gleeson was the perfect host – opening the passenger door for Francesca and then chaperoning her into the club. As they entered the room where the ball was being held, a line of people had gathered to be introduced to all new arrivals. Most were senior members of the police force but it also included the Police and Crime Commissioner and members of the police committee.

Chief Constable Adrian Paul made a point of greeting Francesca. "Detective Chief Inspector Manners, I believe," he said.

"Yes, sir," she said.

"I'm pleased to meet you. I wanted to ask you: how's my nephew getting on."

Francesca started. "Your nephew, sir?"

"Yes. Gary Clarke."

Francesca shot a sideways glance at Gleeson. He remained poker-face, though, engaging in small talk with the Police and Crime Commissioner. "I didn't realise he was your nephew, sir," she said. "I'm sorry."

"I told them not to tell you. I thought it might influence the way you treated him but I don't think there's any need to hide it from you anymore. Not now that he's got his feet under the table, so to speak."

"No, sir."

"Well?"

"Oh, he's getting on well, sir. He's had a baptism of fire.

We've had a murder case thrust upon us."

"Yes, I heard about that. Pretty gruesome, I gather."

"Yes, the body was run over three times by a car to make sure the victim was dead. I think your nephew was quite moved when the parents came to identify the body."

"That's Gary for you," said the Chief Constable. "Always had a bit of a soft streak in him."

"Well, he hasn't let it show on many occasions."

"Good. Anyhow, I must get on and greet the other guests. Perhaps we can talk a bit later?"

"That would be delightful, Sir," said Francesca as she moved along the line. She hardly listened to what the other people she was introduced to were saying. Instead, she reflected on the fact that the Chief Constable's nephew had been placed under her wing without her knowledge,

Gleeson was behind her in the line-up and was introduced to the Chief Constable himself after she had moved on. "Very attractive filly, that Manners," said the Chief Constable. "You and she an item?"

"No, sir. Just work colleagues."

"Bad luck, old boy."

"I'm afraid my wife doesn't revel in these do's," he said.

"Nor mine," said the Chief Constable, "but unfortunately she's here tonight." He pointed to the top table where a couple of women not invited to take part in the line-up had gathered. "Usually, try and ignore her as much as possible." Gleeson smiled politely. That's possibly why she doesn't enjoy these do's, he thought to himself. He hurried through the rest of the line-up and rejoined Francesca.

"You might have warned me," said Francesca.

"I was under specific instructions not to," said Gleeson. "I am sorry, though. I didn't know he was going to come out – as it were – tonight as Gary's uncle."

"I like to think of the Chief Constable coming out," said

Francesca mischievously. "That would be an interesting thing for him to do."

"Anyhow," said Gleeson, "would it have made any difference to your treatment of Gary Clarke if you had been aware that he was the Chief Constable's nephew?"

Francesca reflected for a moment. "No, sir," she said, "I don't believe it would have."

"Well, then, there you are. And it's Rory, not sir. Remember?"

She smiled. It was ironic that she was being chided for the same mistake that Gary had been making over the few days that she had been working with him. It seemed both of them had a problem in dropping the deference towards their superiors. "All right, Rory."

He smiled. "And will it make a difference to your treatment of him in the future?"

"No."

"That's why I chose to embed him with you. I was pretty sure you would be straightforward in your treatment of him."

They sat down in their allocated places. Gleeson had not been awarded a place at the top table – a fact that didn't seem to bother him one iota. He was the perfect host – ensuring her glass was always replenished and making conversation which didn't depend on discussing the minutiae of police work. He danced with her when the ball got under way – only to be interrupted by the Chief Constable after his first foray on to the dance floor.

"Let me dance with Francesca for a moment," he said to Gleeson. She smiled and consented to a dance with the Chief Constable as her partner. The sequence was only broken by a call on her mobile. She excused herself to take the call.

"Hallo, it's Nikki Hofmeyr as was Rivers as is," said the voice on the other end of the telephone. "I hope I'm not interrupting anything."

"No, you've been a godsend. I was dancing with the Chief

Constable at his annual ball. He's got two left feet."

"I was wondering whether you'd come round to dinner tomorrow night. We thought we ought to throw a dinner party to help Jo get to know people. I'm going to invite Mark Elliott, the journalist, and his wife as well."

"I'd be delighted to come," said Francesca. It would be a bit more relaxing than the current evening's events, she thought.

"Good, we'll see you about eight," said Nikki

"Look forward to it." With that, she put her mobile telephone away and returned to the Chief Constable on the dance floor. Luckily for her, at the end of the dance, he was badgered by his wife to take more notice of her. He smiled pleasantly at Francesca. "If you would excuse me," he said.

"Certainly, sir," she said and went back to Gleeson's table.

"We can go if you like," said Gleeson. "Make out you're on an important case and need to get up early in the morning."

"I am on an important case."

"Which is more than can be said of any of these bigwigs here," said Gleeson. With that, he got up from the table and accompanied Francesca to his car. "No need to say our goodbyes to anyone," he said. "They won't remember." He drove her home and she got out of the car – motioning to him not to worry about getting out and opening the passenger door for her. "Thank you, Francesca," he said, "for helping make the evening more bearable than it otherwise might have been."

"Likewise," said Francesca.

"A word of warning, though."

"Yes, sir."

"The Chief Constable's a randy old sod and I think he took a shine to you."

"Thanks for leaving me with that thought, Rory." Damn, she thought as she made her way to her front door. She could do without having to fend off amorous advances from the Chief

Constable while she was training his nephew and investigating a murder. Perhaps Rory had been wrong, though.

• • ● • •

"I don't understand," said Jo. "Are we just paying our respects?"

"It's a little bit more than that," said Rivers as he drove his car in the direction of the crematorium in Stevenage where Rob Corcoran's funeral was taking place. It was a humanist funeral – Rob had never had much time for religion. Rivers wondered who would be saying a few words on his behalf. None of the women he had been involved with, he reasoned. "We're looking out for who turns up – and who doesn't turn up. I'd also like to see how the three mistresses relate to each other. I want to find if there's any sign that they know each other. That sort of thing." He drove into the spacious car park. It seemed he was not the first person to arrive. He stepped out of the car and went into the chapel.

"Sorry, sir, would you mind waiting?" said one of the staff at the crematorium, "if you're here for the Corcoran funeral, that is. There's another service going on at the moment." Rivers nodded and waited outside the door. He looked around him. Ralph and Patricia Corcoran were already there. He made a point of going over to have a word with them.

"Thank you for coming," said Ralph. "It's most appreciated. I think they'll let us in soon." Rivers nodded. He touched Ralph on the arm and went back to where Jo was standing. At this juncture Francesca Manners and Gary Clarke walked in. Francesca, too, went to pay her respects to Ralph and Patricia. After having done so, she moved over to where Rivers and Jo were standing. A woman dressed in a black suit was the next to appear – just as the earlier service was ending.

"Trish Corcoran," Francesca said to Rivers.

"I'm glad you came along," he replied. "I've never met these people. I'm on the case by the way. The Corcorans have hired me to find out what happened to Rob."

"Good," said Francesca. "The more the merrier. I don't have a feeling about this case yet."

"Except I'd like to pin it on Bruiser and Eel. Get them put down so they stop making people's lives a misery."

"Easier said than done. The words 'unshakeable' and 'alibi' come to mind. Oh, this is Sue Plummer coming in now – with Debra, her flatmate." She was dressed in trousers and a sweater and a black jacket. Debra was holding her hand. Sue acknowledged Trish as their eyes met.

So they know each other, thought Rivers. That was not surprising, though, he thought. They were not love rivals.

Douglas Roulay was the next to appear through the doorway. He looked around but did not see anybody he knew so just stood quietly by the door to where the funeral was to take place.

A crematorium official appeared through the doorway. "You may go in now," he said. He went over to Ralph and Patricia. "I think you should sit in the front row, sir," the official said to Ralph. "You'll be giving an address." Ralph nodded.

Roulay noted they must be Rob's parents and went over to them when they were seated. "I was Rob's boss," he said to them. "Douglas Roulay. I'm so sorry about what happened to him." He then turned around and made his way to an inconspicuous seat in the middle.

"That must be the head of planning," Francesca said to Gary. "I just caught a bit of what he said to Ralph and Patricia. We'll need to interview him sooner or later." Gary nodded.

"I'm going to sit nearer the back," Rivers said to Francesca. "If Jo could sit with you, so you could tell him who people are."

Francesca nodded. "Before you go," she said, "this next person just coming in now is Jackie Quesling – the flower shop owner."

Jackie walked past the pew that Sue Plummer was sitting in. To Rivers' mind, she seemed to be making too much of an effort not to have eye contact with Sue. She sat by herself – a couple of seats away from Roulay. She was followed by half a dozen men, chatting amongst themselves. "The regulars at the Dog and Partridge," said Francesca to Jo.

"Yes, we've met them," he said.

Colin was amongst them and gave a sidelong glance and smile to Trish. He thought it best not to go and sit next to her. After all, any relationship between them had hardly started yet. The pub regulars were then followed by Miranda Headley as the service got under way. Jo turned to Rivers and gave him a big wink after Francesca had explained who it was. There was an obvious seat left next to Jackie Quesling but Miranda decided to ignore that and sat on the other side in front of the pub regulars.

The service lasted about half an hour with a humanist celebrant giving details of Rob's life before Ralph made a short speech. The celebrant then asked if anyone from the congregation would like to say a few words. There was general silence but then Sue Plummer got up to speak. "Rob wasn't a bad bloke," she said. "Oh, I know he let people – especially women – down but deep down he cared for people. Whoever killed him should know that society has lost someone who was caring through their actions. The world is not a better place as a result of what happened to Rob." She began to sob and Debra placed a comforting hand on her shoulder. She sat down again.

The congregation filed out slowly once the service was over. Ralph and Patricia were the last to leave. Again, the three mistresses appeared to have no contact with each other. Once outside, Rivers was reunited with Jo, Gary and Francesca.

"Well?" said Francesca.

"Interesting," said Rivers. "I'm sure those three mistresses were pretending that they didn't know each other."

"It isn't just that they haven't ever met," said Gary.

"Sue and Jackie would have met at the Dog and Partridge. Miranda would have seen Jackie at the Dog and Partridge.

Maybe they were trying to ignore each other because they didn't like each other," said Francesca.

"Maybe," said Rivers sounding unconvinced. "One interesting thing."

"Yes?" said Francesca.

"Douglas Roulay from the planning department was here but the guy he shared an office with wasn't."

"Well, he was accusing him of corruption."

"All the more reason to turn up. You know. No hard feelings. You got it all wrong, I forgive you."

Ralph Corcoran approached the foursome. "We're going to have a drink at the Dog and Partridge," he said. "Rob's friends tell me it would be an appropriate way of celebrating his life. You're welcome to come if you'd like."

"I think we'd better get back," said Francesca. "We've got quite a few interviews to conduct."

"I'd like to come," said Rivers.

CHAPTER FIVE

"I wouldn't have thought you'd have wanted to come to the funeral," said Rivers to Jackie Quesling as he helped himself to a pork pie in the Dog and Partridge.

"Why? We had been close."

"Yes, but after what happened on the Sunday. Still, it seems all three of you decided to turn out today."

"Yes,"

"You know the other two?"

"I've worked out who they were."

Rivers nodded. "I'd like to ask you where you were on the night Rob died," he said.

"Surely, this is neither the time nor the place to go into such matters?"

"I have been hired by Rob's parents to find out what happened to their son. And that's what I intend to do."

"Very well," said Jackie. "I was at home for most of the evening."

"With anyone?"

"No."

"So no real alibi?"

"No."

Rivers decided to ask for another soft drink. The pub's real ale was tempting but he had to drive back to his office after the wake so – in his book – it was a non-starter. He already had a past conviction for drink driving. As he sipped his drink, he started to circulate and introduced himself to Sue Plummer.

"I must say," he said to her. "Of all the three ex mistresses, you are the one that looks the saddest here today."

"That's because I am sad, Mr Rivers."

"Do you know the other two?"

"Not really," she said. "I mean, I recognise that one." She pointed to Jackie Quesling. "She was the one that found us in the pub that night."

Rivers nodded. "Have you seen her since?" he asked.

"No, I haven't."

"Look," he said. "I've got to ask you this. I've been hired by Rob's parents to find out what happened to him. Where were you on the night Rob died?"

"Oh. When was it?"

"Last Tuesday."

She racked her brains. "I think I was at home for most of the evening." she said.

"And presumably your flatmate can corroborate this?"

"I'd rather you didn't ask her."

"Oh? Why?"

"Debra has learning difficulties. She can become quite confused about things. It wouldn't be a good idea to burden her with formal questions like that."

"Okay," said Rivers, "but she may face more formal questioning from the police at a later date."

"I'll cross that bridge when I come to it," said Sue.

"Okay." You don't mean that, thought Rivers. What you do mean is that Debra couldn't corroborate your claim that you were at home. Either that or she would have to lie and you're too decent a person to put her in that position. He took his leave of Sue and walked over to where Miranda was sipping a glass of wine. "Terrible tragedy this," he said in an effort to strike up a conversation with her. "Can I introduce myself? My name's Philip Rivers. I've been hired by Rob's parents to find out what happened to their son."

Miranda seemed to be nervously shifting from one foot to another. "Mr Rivers," she said.

"I wonder if you'd mind me asking you where you were on the night of Rob's murder."

"I don't wish to talk to you, Mr Rivers," she said firmly. "I don't have to."

"No, that's true but I would have thought you wanted me to be able to give Rob's parents some closure as to what happened on Tuesday night."

"I'm sorry but you're a private detective. You can't compel me to talk to you."

"No, you're right there."

"Then good-day, Mr Rivers." With that she moved to another part of the bar and started talking to one of the regulars at the Dog and Partridge.

Interesting, thought Rivers. Of course, you're the one of the three mistresses who can't say they were at home on the night of the murder because Detective Constable Clarke knows you weren't – seeing he was at your flat interrogating your husband when the murder happened. So none of the three mistresses had an alibi for the night of the murder. Was that just a coincidence? he wondered. Or were all three of them together?

He was becoming bored with the wake and thought he had done all the detective work he could do – and was just about to leave when he realised he should have spoken to Rob's wife, Trish. She was standing by the bar – deep in conversation with one of the regulars at the pub. He went over to them. "Philip Rivers." he said offering a hand to Trish to shake.

"I remember you," said the regular. "You were in this pub the night that Rob's world came crashing down all around him."

"Yes."

"Colin Standen," the man said offering his hand to shake. "I was a friend of Rob's." He looked at Trish. "And of his missus."

"I'm a private detective," said Rivers. "I've been hired by Rob's parents to find out what happened to their son."

"I wish you luck," said Colin.

"You think I'm going to need it?"

"Well, there were a lot of people who bore Rob a grudge."

"I'm beginning to realise that," said Rivers. "I wonder if you could help me eliminate at least one of them from my enquiries." He turned to Trish as he asked the question.

"I'll try."

"Where were you on the night Rob was killed?"

"Last Tuesday? I was at home all evening."

"With no-one to corroborate that?"

"I suppose not, Mr Rivers."

"And you?" he said turning to Colin.

"Me? Why do you want to know where I was?"

"Force of habit," said Rivers. "Sorry."

"Well, I think I was in here for a good part of the evening – but whether anybody else's memory would let them corroborate that, I don't know."

"Thanks," said Rivers. It seemed like there were a heck of a lot of people minding their own business and on their own on the night that Rob had died.

• • ● • •

"Have you got something you'd like to tell me, Gary," said Francesca as they made their way back from the funeral to the police station.

"I don't think so," he said – racking his brains as to what she might be alluding to.

"Well, you see I found out something about you when I went to your uncle's ball last night."

"Oh. Who told you?"

"He did."

"Well, I hope it won't make any difference to you, ma'am."

"No, I suppose I'll have to be a bit more lenient with you when you keep calling me ma'am but otherwise I don't think it should."

Gary fidgeted nervously. "I wouldn't like to be known as the

Chief Constable's nephew," he said. "I'd rather be judged on who I am and how I do."

"Don't worry. You will be as far as I'm concerned."

"Did you get to speak to my uncle last night?"

"I was introduced to him. He insisted on having a dance with me – something that my male colleagues would never be subjected to."

"Subjected to?"

"He has two left feet. But I wouldn't like that to get back to him."

"Don't worry," said Gary. "I'm not the sort that would go running to him with every bit of gossip I pick up. As I said, I'd rather he wasn't my uncle."

"In which case we should get along fine," said Francesca.

· · ● · ·

"Did you find out anything?" Jo asked Rivers as he returned from the wake that lunchtime.

"That the entire population of Hertford were on their own on Tuesday night when Rob Corcoran was killed. And nobody saw them. Oh, except for one guy that was in the pub but nobody can be sure which night that was either. In other words, we have no clues as to what happened to Rob."

"A waste of time, then?"

"I wouldn't say that. We know that at least one of the mistresses wasn't at home that night. Miranda Headley. We know that because the police were at her home that evening – questioning her husband. Trouble is, she's the only one that's refusing to speak to us. If you ask my advice, I think all three mistresses were together that night. But I can't prove that and I don't know what they were doing."

"There's only one thing that would have brought them all together," said Jo.

"Rob Corcoran?"

"Precisely."

"But what were they planning to do with him?"

"It wouldn't have been friendly," said Jo.

"But if they were all together in the same place, wouldn't it make sense to tell us? We could check it out." Rivers thought for a moment. "They were somewhere where there was no-one around to corroborate what they were doing. So they couldn't have been at Miranda's because the police were there. They probably weren't at Sue's because Debra would be around and – although she would be sympathetic to anything Sue was trying to do – I got a taste of how loyal Sue is to her today. She wouldn't want to involve her in anything like this."

"Like what?"

"I don't know," said Rivers. "So in all probability they were round at Jackie Quesling's house. Were they there all evening? What time did they leave? Could they have fitted in murdering Rob Corcoran into their timetable?"

"That's a bit extreme," said Jo. "They don't strike me as the murdering sort and ‑‑ whereas I can see maybe one of them carrying out a crime of passion – to picture all three in that position takes a leap of imagination."

"Time to use some subterfuge," said Rivers. "We go to them. Tell them we know where they were and what they were doing and shake the tree – and see what apples fall out."

"Okay," said Jo.

"This enquiry is going in two directions," said Rivers. "It's either one of the mistresses or one of those caught up in the fall-out from Rob's probing of corruption in the planning department. We'll divvy up the work between us. You take responsibility for the ex-mistresses. I'll work on the planning angle."

"Right," said Jo.

"Go down to the pub and pick up what you can," said Rivers. "Then work on Miranda. I know she wouldn't talk to me but if you tell her that we know what she was doing – that she was round at Jackie's plotting some fate that would befall Rob you never know – she may spill some of the beans. Then visit the other two."

"I seem to have my work cut out," said Jo.

"Yes," said Rivers. "In the meantime I'll go round to the planning department and interview the boss. Also try and find out why Rob's co-worker wasn't at the funeral today." Rivers smiled. At least he felt in a more positive frame of mind than he had done when he left the Dog and Partridge earlier that day.

• • ● • •

Douglas Roulay sat back in his chair after returning from Rob's funeral. He, too, had noted that Roger Broadbent was an absentee from the proceedings. He picked up the telephone receiver in his office and dialled Roger's number. A nervous voice on the other end of the line identified the number as Roger's.

"What are you playing at, Roger? Why aren't you in work?"

"I don't feel well."

"You'll draw attention to yourself if you continually feign illness. You should have been at Rob's funeral."

"I couldn't make it," said Roger. "I didn't feel right attending."

"People will think you killed him."

"They'd be wrong," insisted Roger. "Look, I'll make every effort to come in tomorrow but not today – I need some time to unwind."

"All right, Roger." Roulay thought for a moment. "On second thoughts, if you're still in a jittery frame of mind, stay at home. You'll be no use nor ornament here. I've got someone coming in to cover for Rob tomorrow. I could always put in for another replacement."

Roger thought for a moment. "No, I'll try my hardest," he

said. Roulay's suggestion that it would be thought he had killed Rob made him think he should try harder to get back to normal.

Roulay sat back in his chair when he replaced the receiver. He looked at his diary. It was the planning committee meeting that evening. Arranged several weeks beforehand. Rather unfortunate, he thought, that it coincided with Rob's murder. Perhaps they should postpone it as a matter of respect. After all, Jerry Vincent's homes development was on the agenda. It might look a little unfeeling to push through a planning application where Rob had raised suspicions of corruption. He was about to pick up the telephone again and discuss the matter with Vincent when his secretary entered the office.

"There's a Philip Rivers to see you," she said.

Without waiting for a welcome, Rivers shot past here and was soon facing Roulay across his desk. "You still here, then?" he said by way of an opening gambit.

"I resent your tone, Mr Rivers."

"Rob Corcoran had brought his suspicions about corruption in the planning department to your attention, I believe. They implicated one of his fellow officers, Roger Broadbent, I believe. Can I ask you what you've done about it?"

"I asked Rob to outline his suspicions and evidence in a report. I guess I'll never get that now."

"That would be a safe assumption. So what do you do now?"

"There is no evidence. There can be no confirmation that any corruption took place."

"So the murderer did the right thing – from his or her point of view?"

"I'm sorry?"

"Well, kill the complainant and the complaint gets dropped. Surely you could launch an investigation on what Rob had told you – allied to his murder?"

"It's all a bit vague, Mr Rivers."

"It didn't sound so to me. Roger Broadbent writes a favourable report on a planning development put forward by Jerry Vincent. In return, he received Wimbledon and Test match tickets plus free repairs to his home. Rob, for his part, is visited by a couple of heavies who break his finger and crack his ribs. Yes, I'm sure you could conclude from that that everything is hunky-dory in the planning department. Especially if you were on the take as well."

"I resent that implication, Mr Rivers."

"It's not an implication, Mr Roulay."

"If you have any proof of that allegation or can substantiate what Rob was saying, you should tell me."

"I'd rather tell the police – who are investigating Rob's murder."

Roulay squirmed. "Let's not be hasty, Mr Rivers," he said.

"I don't see any evidence of anyone being that," said Rivers.

"You said Rob was attacked by a couple of heavies? That's the first I've heard of that."

"It's true," said Rivers. "That's why – just a few hours before his death – he hired me to protect his interests. Sadly, I wasn't able to."

"Do you know who these heavies were?"

"They were a couple of scrap metal dealers. Rob was convinced they were hired by Jerry Vincent."

"Did they actually say they had been?"

"They didn't have to. Who had the most interest in closing down the investigation? The answer has to be Jerry Vincent." He mused for a moment. "Or it could be Roger Broadbent."

"If you knew Roger Broadbent, you'd know he wouldn't move in those kind of circles."

"Or you."

Roulay gave him an exasperated expression. "I won't dignify that allegation with a comment," he said. "Leave it with me, Mr Rivers. In view of what you've said, I will open an inquiry. If I find any evidence of corruption, I will take appropriate action."

"You'll pardon me if I don't hold my breath?"

"What does that mean?"

"I'm investigating Rob's murder and I think his concerns about the planning department are an integral part of that investigation. I shall continue my investigations."

"You're free to do so," said Roulay. Rivers nodded and made his way from the room. Roulay immediately picked his telephone up and dialled Vincent's number. "Jerry," he said when the other man answered. "I think we have a problem."

"One that I'm sure you can solve," said Vincent icily.

"I'm going to propose that we delay a decision on your housing development – and postpone the whole meeting as a mark of respect for Rob." There was silence on the other end of the line. Roulay was unaccustomed to Vincent remaining silent on any issue. "I'm going to have to launch an inquiry into Rob's corruption allegations," he added. "I've just found out he told this private detective Rivers that two heavies – whom he believed were hired by you – assaulted him on the night before he died. It's not looking good."

"Not for you, either," said Vincent.

"I can use this enquiry as a stalling device until the heat dies down."

"Or Rivers ceases to make any further investigations," said Vincent. "It seems to me if he is out of the equation, then we're back to square one. No evidence from Rob. None from Rivers. No need to pursue the matter any further."

"I'm not sure I like the drift of what you're saying. Rivers goes the way of Rob?"

"I don't care what you like or don't like. You look after your interests. I'll look after mine."

• • • • •

Jo made his way to the Dog and Partridge early that evening. As luck would have it, the regular group of drinkers were gathered by the bar. They seemed in sombre mood. Jo sought out Jed Coulson to seek his permission to ask his customers some questions. "Go ahead, lad," he said. "I remember seeing you in here with Philip Rivers the night Rob Corcoran's private life unfolded before him."

One of the regulars overheard the conversation. He approached Jo. "We're all pretty raw about Rob's death still," he said. "We could do without you blackening his name so if I were you, I'd keep it buttoned."

"It's not my intention to blacken his name. On the contrary, I'm trying to find out what happened to him – something which, as friends of his, I would have thought you supported."

"Do you live round here?" asked another of the drinkers.

"I don't see that's relevant."

"Only we wouldn't want you becoming a regular in this pub."

"I see," said Jo. He noticed that Jed Coulson had moved out of earshot. "Might I ask you why you wouldn't want me to be a regular? My money's as good as anybody else's."

"No offence, mate, but you're not exactly English, are you?" said the second drinker.

"Next you'll be asking me to go back to where I came from," said Jo.

"Good idea," said the drinker.

"My address is Flat 8, Maidenhead Hall, Finchley, London N3. I'll go back there, shall I?"

He received no reply and decided to carry on with his original mission. "I wondered if any of you could tell me about the relationship Rob Corcoran had with any of his mistresses. Also whether you knew anything about them? How they were likely to react on finding out he was two-timing them?"

"Strictly speaking, he was three-timing them," said one of the regulars – not one of the two who had just made comments to Jo. His remark brought forth tremendous guffaws from his drinking mates.

"I take your point," said Jo in an effort to be friendly to them and encourage conversation.

"Look mate," said one of the two original drinkers to comment. "As far as we're concerned, the police are investigating Rob's murder and any evidence we have we will give to them. We don't need some Johnnie-come-lately coming round here trying to make fast buck out of Rob's tragic death."

"Do you know who hired me?" There was silence from the group. "Rob's mother and father," he said. "They believe the police enquiry is progressing too slowly and they want some answers. Don't they deserve your respect?" The group still remained quiet. "Would you be reacting the same way if my boss, Mr Rivers, was asking you the questions?"

"Send him round and you'll find out."

"Yes, and we might have some words to say to him about the kind of company he hires."

At this stage Jed Coulson re-appeared at their side of the bar." He poured a pint out for Jo. "Have this one on the house," he said. "I'm sorry for the reaction you've got tonight. But it might be worth bearing in mind people are still grieving for Rob and the last thing they want to do is talk about him to a stranger."

"You can keep your drink." Jed looked offended. "No, it's because I'm not drinking. I'm driving," Jo explained. He turned to the two drinkers who had behaved most aggressively to him. "You know, when I was last in this pub – drinking with Rob Corcoran and Mr Rivers, Rob was unfailingly polite towards me. I felt no sense of antagonism. You would do well to reflect that was the kind of man he was and behave accordingly." With that, he turned on his heels and was gone.

One of the two drinkers stretched his hand across the bar. "I'll take that," he said putting his hand round the pint Jed Coulson had poured for Jo.

"You'll bloody well pay for it," said Jed.

• • ● • •

"Well," said Nikki, "it looks as if the person we've thrown this dinner party for is a no show," she said. The assembled guests – Rivers, his journalist friend Mark Elliott who lived down the corridor and his wife, Prunella, and Francesca Manners – were all gathered in the living room.

Jo, however, was nowhere to be seen.

"He'll be here," said Rivers. "He's quite assiduous in his work, though."

"I wonder who he takes after," said Mark.

"Not you, Darling," said Prunella. With that, there was the sound of a key turning in the lock and Jo entered.

"Jo," said Nikki. "I want you to meet our friends, Mark and Prunella." He shook them both by the hand. "I think you know Francesca Manners."

"Yes, yes, I do," he said smiling at the detective.

"You seem a bit subdued," said Rivers.

"Oh, it's nothing," said Jo – aware that he should not spoil the party mood. "Nothing that a good drink won't cure," he said.

"What would you like?" asked Rivers.

"A beer. A pint of bitter."

Rivers poured him a bottled ale. "That's the best I can do," he said.

"Thanks," said Jo. He swallowed from the glass. "No, I've had a rather disappointing session at the Dog and Partridge."

"Oh?"

"Racism showing its ugly face again. They made it clear they didn't want me to become a regular at their pub – and they wouldn't answer any of my questions about Rob Corcoran."

"I'm sorry" began Rivers.

"It's not your fault," said Jo quickly. "You know, this country of yours seems to be divided between racists and non-racists. I know whose company I'm in tonight."

"I'll go and give them a piece of my mind," Rivers said.

"I can fight my own battles," said Jo.

"Yes, I know, but it does no harm to remind them they are not in the majority in this country."

"That's the point," said Jo. "I'm not sure they're not."

"I think Jo's right to a certain extent," said Francesca. "Ever since the Brexit vote people have felt they can utter thoughts which previously they kept private."

Nikki, who had disappeared into the kitchen soon after Jo's arrival, then returned. "Time to eat," she announced. "Come into the dining room," she added. She had split the two couples up so that Prunella sat next to Rivers and she was seated by Mark. Francesca and Jo were together at the table, too.

"Tell me a little bit more about yourself," Francesca said to Jo.

"There's not much to tell," said Jo. "I was happily operating a ferry service in the Bahamas when this man – he pointed at Rivers – came into my life. I helped him out with a murder enquiry over there. I was even imprisoned for a while for my sins. When I came out, he offered me a job over here and I was happy to snap it up. In those days, Britain seemed a more welcoming place to people like me."

"Imprisoned?" said Francesca latching on to this tit-bit of information.

"I killed someone who was bent on killing Rivers," he said. "The court decided I had used too much force. I think they weren't convinced he was going to kill Rivers. But that's water under the bridge now."

"It explains why I felt honour-bound to offer him a job when he came out of prison," said Rivers.

"Even though I knew nothing about detective work," said Jo.

"Do you enjoy your work?" asked Francesca.

"Ask me on another night when I've been dealing with the non-racists in the UK," he said. "I might say 'yes' then."

"Fair point."

"Do you have any family?" persisted Francesca.

"Not here. I've just had to bury my mother back in Calicos

Island in the Bahamas. I have a brother who's a fisherman over there, too."

"And you're living with Philip and Nikki?"

"Staying with them would be more accurate,"he said. "I hope to get a place on my own at some time in the not too distant future. Tell me about yourself."

"She's had a meteoric rise to Detective Chief Inspector," Rivers butted in. "Very much merited. She's not afraid to take the establishment on in the police force if she feels it necessary. So far that doesn't seem to have made her too many enemies in the force,"

"So far," said Francesca crossing her fingers and showing her hand to the assembled company.

"Are you single like me?" said Jo.

Francesca frowned. "At the moment, yes."

"Oh," said Jo. "Is that likely to change in the near future?"

"I didn't mean that," said Francesca. She sighed. "I was let down by someone a few years ago. I just haven't found anyone to replace him – not that I'm looking, though."

Jo nodded. "Relationships and me are always a disaster area," he said.

"I can't remember any you've had," said Rivers.

"Precisely," said Jo.

"I guess we're the boring couple here," said Mark. "Married 20 years."

The conversation carried on until the early hours of the morning. The wine flowed. It was only broken when Francesca decide she would have to go home to prepare herself for work the next day. She called a cab and made her exit. "It's been really nice meeting you, Jo," she said as she was leaving. "Just remember we're not all racists."

"I know," said Jo, smiling.

Mark and Prunella took their cue from Francesca to leave. "If you ever wanted to see how a newspaper works, I'd be proud to show you round my place," said Mark.

"I'd like that very much."

"And if you're ever in need of pampering I could show you round my place," said Prunella. "I work as a beautician."

"I think I need that less," said Jo.

"Oh? Beautiful enough?" asked Rivers. They all laughed.

When they had all gone, Jo sat down again. "One more?" asked Rivers. Jo nodded. "Make it a whisky this time," he said. "I notice you don't have any rum." Rivers did as he had been bidden.

"Do you two need to talk some shop before you retire?" asked Nikki. "If so, I'll make my way to bed."

"Thanks," said Rivers. He turned to Jo when the two of them were alone. "Well, where do we go from here?" he asked.

"Francesca," said Jo. "I like her. Would you have any objections if I asked her out? I mean, it wouldn't breach any protocol between police and private detectives?"

"I guess not," said Rivers.

"Fine. I'll ask her out, then."

"Don't expect too much," said Rivers.

"What do you mean?"

"Last time I broached the subject, she said she was still too cut up about what had gone wrong to contemplate a new relationship. She was the victim of a two-timer."

"Whoa," said Jo. "I said I'd take her out. Not marry her. I just think I should start organising some kind of a social life for myself – instead of relying on you and Nikki to set one up for me."

"Fine," said Rivers. "Sorry. I didn't want to put a dampener on things."

"You haven't," said Jo.

Rivers looked at his friend. Jo and Francesca – possibly the two people in life that he was closest to outside of his marriage to Nikki. He had already come to terms with the fact there would be no relationship between him and Francesca – despite the fact that he had wanted one at one stage. He was dedicated to making his marriage work and he had to admit that – since Nikki had stopped working as his assistant in the detective agency – it had been much easier to keep things on an even keel. He was sure he would not be jealous of any relationship between Jo and Francesca – however much it was only in its formative stage.

• • ● • •

Francesca made it into work the next morning a little late as a result of her dinner chez Nikki and Rivers. As a result, Gary Clarke was already sitting over the other side of the room.

"Good morning, Francesca," he said.

"Good morning," she replied. "Right," she added as if she felt the need to do something decisive as quickly as possible. "I think we should go down to the Dog and Partridge today and give them a hard time."

"For any reason?" asked Gary. "As you know, I'm all for giving people a hard time but I just wondered what had prompted this."

"You know Jo, the black detective who works with Philip Rivers?"

"Yes."

"Well, he met a certain amount of racism when he went to get some background from the pub regulars yesterday. I think we should make it clear we're not going to tolerate a racist pub in our midst in Hertford."

"Fine," said Gary.

"No time like the present," said Francesca.

"You'll only find the landlord there now," said Gary. "Best wait a bit until it gets busy. Also, I think there's something you should attend to before we go." He nodded in the direction of her desk. "I took a message for you earlier on this morning."

Francesca saw there was a scrawled note on the pad on the desk. "Ring the Chief Constable's office", it said. The number was written underneath. "Do you know what this is about?" she asked Gary.

"No, I only know that my uncle is anxious to see you." He noted from the lack of enthusiasm on her face that she wasn't so anxious to see him.

"Do you know what it's about?"

"No," said Gary.

Francesca picked up the telephone and dialled the number on the pad. "Is that the Chief Constable's office?" she asked when a voice answered.

"Yes," came the reply.

"It's Detective Chief Inspector Francesca Manners here," she said. "I gather the Chief Constable was trying to get in touch with me."

"Oh, yes," she said. "He was wondering whether you could meet him for an early dinner tonight."

"Do you know what it's about?" asked Francesca.

"No," came the reply as if the secretary were surprised this question has been raised. "Normally, people are only too pleased to receive an invitation from the Chief Constable," she said a little haughtily.

Until they get along there and find themselves being groped, thought Francesca – recalling Rory Gleeson's words of warning to her on the night of the Chief Constable's ball. "Of course," said Francesca diplomatically. "I would be delighted to attend." Only Gary could detect the insincerity in her voice.

"He suggests the Red Lion in Hertingfordbury at 6pm." It was a little village outside Hertford – somewhere where there would be unlikely to be any other police officers present. Or was she being just a little bit paranoid following Gleeson's warning?

"I'll be there," said Francesca. She replaced the receiver but thought the better of making any comments in case he had a hotline back to his uncle. In reality she felt like saying that it was one invitation she could do without.

"Can I detect a certain lack of enthusiasm for the encounter?" said Gary.

"You might detect it – I couldn't possibly comment," she said diplomatically.

"He's all right," said Gary. "Bit of a crusty old cove. I expect he'll want to know how I'm getting along."

Francesca fervently hoped that was the extent of his interest in her. "Come on," she said. "Let's get down to the Dog and Partridge," she said.

Gary followed her to her car and within minutes they were in the bar of the pub. Gary had been right. Jed Coulson was the only person there. It was 10.30am and the pub had just opened for morning coffee. "What can I do for you?" asked Jed.

"I gather there was a bit of an incident in here last night," said Francesca.

"An incident? I don't think so."

"You were less than helpful and at times blatantly rude to a colleague of mine who is investigating Rob Corcoran's murder."

"Not me. A couple of regulars were a bit insulting to him."

"On the grounds that he was black?"

"Racism may have played a part in it."

"What did you do about it?"

"Offered him a pint."

"You know what you should have done?"

"Tell me."

"Barred them from the pub. You don't want to get the reputation for being a racist pub – a reputation that could easily be spread through the police force. It won't do your business any good."

"I appreciate that," said Jed. "I did offer the bloke an apology."

"Well, if he comes back and has some questions he wants answered, just answer them – politely."

"I will. Was there anything else, Chief Inspector?"

"No," said Francesca, "except I wonder if you've kept your

ears open for any gossip following Rob Corcoran's death."

"I may have kept my ears open – but I've heard nothing."

"The three mistresses – have they been in here since that Sunday evening?"

"Only to attend the wake – which you didn't attend."

"No," said Francesca.

"I overheard Philip Rivers talking to them. I think he unearthed the fact that none of them had an alibi for the night of Rob Corcoran's murder. I don't know if that's of any use to you. His wife didn't have an alibi, either, except she was on the telephone from her home later on in the evening in conversation with another of my regulars, Colin Standen. Rivers seemed to think there was something significant in this."

"Thanks for the tip off," said Francesca. "Come on, Gary, we must be on our way."

Once outside, Gary turned to Francesca. "What was all that about? Your questioning of him seemed to me very much like an afterthought."

"I suppose it was. I just wanted to put the suggestion in his mind that he should bar the racists. Jo is a friend of mine and I don't like him being treated the way he was. If I can do something about that, I will. We benefit if people are open and helpful to Philip Rivers and Jo. They're not in competition with us and would share any information they get."

And, as you said, Jo is a friend of yours, thought Gary.

• • • • •

"Good of you to make it in today, Roger," said Douglas Roulay as he ventured across the corridor to greet his employee.

"Well, you said I should if I could," said Roger. He had black rings under his eyes as if he had not been sleeping much. "What happened last night?"

"Last night?"

"To the planning application from Jerry Vincent."

Roulay frowned. "You'd better come and discuss that in my office." He jerked his head in the direction of the new temp – who was filling in for Rob and sitting opposite Broadbent. "It is a bit of a delicate matter." The two of them filed into Roulay's office "Sit down," he said. "First, last night's meeting. It was postponed as a mark of respect for Rob," he said. "All business will be carried over to next month's meeting."

"What does Jerry Vincent think about that?"

"I don't care what he thinks," said Roulay. "It was the right thing to do."

"You've changed your tune," said Roger.

"I beg your pardon?"

"Well, you've always wanted to grease Jerry Vincent's palm."

"You're a fine one to talk," said Roulay, Then he bit his tongue. He shouldn't be engaging in this kind of banter with his employee. He had a duty to perform. "Roger," he said. "You know that Rob Corcoran made certain allegations against you?"

Roger stared at his boss intently. He instinctively felt he did not like the direction in which this conversation was going. "Yes," he said tentatively.

"Well, these have been embellished by a private detective – Philip Rivers. He alleges that Jerry Vincent hired a couple of people to dissuade Rob Corcoran from continuing with his investigations."

"And you're surprised at that?"

"I have to investigate this. If I don't Rivers is going to take the whole matter to the police. I see it as a stalling operation but first I have to tell you that I am suspending you from duty pending investigations being completed."

"And what about you?"

"What do you mean?"

"Well, you're just as much involved in all this as I am."

"I don't think so, Roger," he said. "There's no evidence connecting me to the enquiry."

"I could supply them with the information if you suspend me."

"I don't think you understand, Roger. There is no 'them'. It's just me. I'm hopeful that the enquiries will discover there is insufficient evidence to lay charges against anyone – in which case you can be reinstated and a couple of months down the line the planning application can go through. But we have to play it by the book."

"And Rivers?"

"What about Rivers?"

"Is he going to accept this state of affairs?"

"I don't think he'll be a player in the game by then."

Roger winced. "I don't think I like the sound of that," he said.

"He'll be all right. He'll just have been dissuaded from pursuing his enquiries."

"I wish I could share your confidence in that."

"It doesn't matter whether you do or don't Roger. Now pack your things and go home. I'll let you know when you have to give evidence to the inquiry and when you can resume your work."

"I will be able to resume my work?"

"I would imagine so."

• • ● • •

Rivers' suggestion that he should concentrate on Miranda as the weakest link of the mistresses' chain was preying on Jo's mind. He wasn't sure it was going to be the most productive thing to do. If left to his own devices, he would have gone after Jackie Quesling. After all, it was at her house that the meeting between the three mistresses was likely to have taken place. Rivers was the boss, though. That was why he found himself ringing Miranda's doorbell early that evening.

"Yes?" a male voice answered.

"Could I speak to Miranda Headley?"

"Who is it?"

"I'm a private detective investigating the death of Rob Corcoran."

Miranda was listening in on the exchange. She shook her head. "I've told him I don't want to talk to him," she said. "Tell him to go away."

"Go away," said Aaron to Jo. "She's already told you she doesn't want to talk to you."

"No, she hasn't," said Jo. "She may have talked to my boss but I have some information which means I would like to eliminate her from my enquiries." Jo smiled. He had often heard those words used in crime thrillers – never dreaming that he would be uttering them himself.

Aaron turned to his wife. "Might be an idea to hear what he's got to say," he said. "He's not the police. He won't arrest you and it might be best to be fore-armed for when the police do call – if they call."

Miranda digested what Aaron was saying. She nodded and Aaron pressed the buzzer to let Jo in. Jo showed them his business card after entering their living room. "We know where you were on the night of the murder," Jo said confidently. "You were with Jackie Quesling and Sue Plummer at a meeting at Jackie's house. The three of you can only have been plotting to do something about Rob Corcoran." Miranda remained silent. "What time did that meeting break up?"

"You tell me. You seem to know so much," said Miranda.

"She was back here at about 10 o'clock," volunteered Aaron. Miranda shot him a sidelong glance as if to tell him not to intervene.

"Rob Corcoran was killed at around nine o'clock or just before. That puts you right in the frame for his murder."

"No, no," said Miranda. "I was with the girls."

"Where?"

"I'm sorry?"

"It's a simple question. Where were the three of you? At Jackie's house. At Rob's house? Or were you on your own?"

"We were at Jackie's house."

Jo felt she sounded less than confident about her answer. He questioned to himself whether she was telling the truth. "I will continue my investigations," he said. "If you're lying, I will find out. Best to tell the truth now than be found out in a lie." Miranda said nothing.

"I resent you calling my wife a liar," said Aaron.

"Why?" said Jo. "Has she never lied to you? About her affair with Rob Corcoran, for instance." That left the two of them at a loss for words. Jo smiled and took his leave of them.

"Were you telling him the truth?" asked Aaron when Jo had gone. Miranda remained silent. "Come on now – no more lies between us. You owe me that."

"I'm sure the girls will back me up on my alibi."

"It's not a convincing one. Three wronged women each citing each other. Why were you together? What were you planning to do?"

"We planned to confront Rob. Find out what he wanted. We didn't want to kill him."

"And did you confront him?"

"We were too late. When we drove up outside, the police and ambulance were already there. Rob was already dead."

Meanwhile, Jo was already half way to Jackie's home. There was a car in the driveway when he arrived but he decided against going and confronting Jackie with his new information first off. Try the neighbours, he thought. Had they seen or heard anything on the night Rob died?

He knocked on the door of the house on her right. A woman – possibly in her late fifties and smartly dressed for someone who was spending an evening at home – appeared at the door.

"I'm sorry," she said. "I don't want anything."

"And I'm not going to give you anything," said Jo. "I'm a private investigator looking into a murder." He showed her his business card. "I just need to ask you a few questions."

"A murder you said? Surely if it's a murder the police will be investigating it?"

"They are," said Jo, "but we – that is my employer and I have been employed by the victims' parents to find out what happened to their son. I would be grateful."

"No,"she said, making a movement to close the door. "I don't hold with private investigators."

You've probably never met one before, thought Jo."I'm sorry to hear that,"said Jo. "Why is that?"

"We have a perfectly adequate public service to deal with criminal matters."

Jo looked at her intently. If he were a betting man, he would lay odds that she would be amongst the first to decry the public services for wasting taxpayers' money and applaud attempts to make savings by turning them over to the private sector in other circumstances.

Her dress and what he could see of the inside of the house – not ostentacious but smart and well looked after – told him the inhabitants were conservative. With a small 'c' possibly. "The questions won't take up much of your time,"he ventured.

"Alfred," she called. A man slightly stooped wearing a suit came to stand by her at the door.

"This man says he's a private detective."

"I'm sorry,"said Alfred. "We don't answer questions from the likes of you late in the evening. Now do as my wife says and clear off."

"What do you mean by 'the likes of you'?"

"Well, you're obviously not from around here,"said Alfred.

"No, I'm from Finchley,"said Jo. "You know, the constituency Margaret Thatcher used to represent."

"I'm not going to get into an argument with you,"said Alfred. "Now clear off."

Jo reckoned he had tried his best and there was nothing to be gained from further conversation. "Thank you," said Jo.

"I'm in touch with the police. I'll tell them you're obstructing the investigation into Rob Corcoran's death. I'm sure you'll be hearing from them."

"You do that," said Alfred. "I doubt if they'll listen to you."

Jo waved his hand at them as he turned away. They stayed standing in the doorway until he had left their property. He decided to take his chances with the neighbours on the other side of Jackie's house. He thought he might have better luck when a younger woman wearing a kaftan and stroking a cat answered the door.

"Hello," he said, bringing out his business card. "I'm a private detective investigating a murder and I believe you could have information which could help me with my enquiries."

"I doubt it," said the woman. "It's very quiet around here. I don't think we've ever had a murder."

"No," said Jo, "the murder wasn't actually round here but I wonder – were you in last Tuesday evening?"

"Yes, with my husband."

"Did you hear any comings and goings from the house next door?"

"Funny you should mention it, but yes. She – that's the lady who lives next door – had a couple of visitors round. They must have arrived at about eight o'clock. I remember the theme tune from Holby City playing as they arrived."

"Did you hear them go?"

"I think it was about half an hour later. Holby City was still on."

"How many of them left?"

"The two visitors, I think."

"Leaving Jackie behind?"

"I can't swear to it but that would be the logical conclusion."

"Did she leave the house herself?"

"Yes, I remember walking the dog soon after nine o'clock and there being no cars outside the house then."

"You have a cat and a dog?" asked Jo.

"Yes, they get on very well with each other."

Jo nodded. "Did you hear the third car go?"

The woman thought for a moment and then shook her head. "No," she said, "but we got quite engrossed in Holby City. It's a very good programme. Do you watch it?"

Jo had to confess he had never heard of it. "So just to recap – there were three cars outside the house next door at eight o'clock, two of them left half an hour later and the third a little later on but you don't know when."

"That's about the size of it," she said.

"Great," said Jo. "You've been very helpful." He took his leave of her and marched up to Jackie Quesling's front door. "Good evening," he said as she answered. He showed her his card. "I'm investigating the death of Rob Corcoran. I wonder if I could come in."

Jackie looked reluctant to admit him but in the end invited him into the living room. "What can I do for you?"

"Where were you on the night Rob was murdered?" asked Jo.

"I was here for most of the evening," she said.

"Yes," he said. "You had a meeting at about eight o'clock with Miranda Headley and Sue Plummer – but it didn't last long. No need to ask what you were discussing. You only had one thing in common."

Jackie ignored his last comment. "Miranda and Sue left about 8.30pm," she said. "I stayed here."

"Not for long, though."

"I'm sorry?"

"Your neighbour reports your car had gone by just after nine o'clock. Where did you go?"

"What business is that of yours?"

"You need an alibi for Rob's murder and – as yet – you haven't supplied me with one."

"All right," said Jackie. "I went into town to meet up with Miranda and Sue again. We planned to go and visit Rob."

"That sounds very chummy. I bet it was not."

"The meeting didn't happen. By the time we got there the police and ambulance had arrived. Rob was already dead."

"Was that your intention, too?"

"What?"

"To kill him?"

"No," she said. "We wanted him to explain himself. I think one of us – Sue – thought there was still a chance she could revive her relationship with him. Miranda and I just wanted to give him a chance to explain where we stood with him."

"So you left here to go to Rob Corcoran's place?"

"After picking up Miranda and Sue."

"From where?"

"In the centre of town."

"And when did you get to Rob's?"

"Around 9.30pm, I suppose. I wasn't really clock-watching."

"What did you do on seeing the police and ambulance outside his house?"

"We just left."

Jo nodded. "You didn't think it would look good if three ex-lovers were found outside his home just a few minutes after he was murdered," he said. It was a statement not a question.

Jackie blushed. "Exactly," she said.

"You're right," said Jo. "It doesn't."

• • ● • •

"Would you like an aperitif?" the Chief Constable asked Francesca as she sat down opposite him in the pub restaurant.

"That would be nice. A bloody Mary, please."

Adrian Paul raised an eyebrow at her choice of drink. "Not a gin and tonic merchant then?"

"No," Francesca said.

"Beer's my tipple," he said. "I like a nice cold lager on a

summer's evening."

I bet that's not all you like, she found herself thinking but she dismissed the thought from her mind. Give him the benefit of the doubt, she thought. He might really have something he wanted to put to her. Instead, she smiled.

"There were a couple of things I wanted to put to you", he said. "First off, I'd like to ask you whether you're happy here."

"Yes, sir. Rory Gleeson's a good man to work for." Better than "Pratt-by-name, Pratt-by-nature" – the man she had left in Barnet, she thought to herself.

"Is there anything going on between you?"

"Sir?"

"Sorry, perhaps I shouldn't ask."

"As a matter of fact, there isn't," she said. "He's happily married."

"And you?" His voice tailed off, hoping that she would pick up the slack.

"I believe my private life is my private life," she said. It sounded pompous, she thought, especially when there was no private life to speak of.

Adrian Paul nodded. "You seem to have fitted in very well following your transfer," he said.

"I'm glad to be able to help out," she said.

"You know you're standing in for an illness?"

"Yes, sir."

"Well, I have it on good authority that Detective Chief Inspector Brett is unlikely to return to work so it could be a full-time vacancy. I'd be happy to put in a good word for you – if you were interested."

"I would be, sir." Perhaps this dinner was not going to be too much of an ordeal. The waiter approached their table and this juncture and took their order. Francesca decided to have the calamari followed by what looked like a fairly exotic sea bass dish.

"Vegetarian?" asked Paul.

"No, sir, sea bass fanatic."

"Good choice," he said. He ordered a prawn cocktail followed by a well done sirloin steak and chips.

"We'll return to the possibility of a permanent job here later," he said. "I also wanted to ask you how Gary was getting on. I know I did at the ball but that was hardly the atmosphere for anyone to say anything significant."

"Well, sir."

"Adrian, please," he said waving her words aside.

"Adrian." She could hardly resent him asking her to call him Adrian. After all, it was the same request that she had made to his nephew. "He has one or two rough edges that need to be ironed out," she said. "He has a tendency to go in like a bull in a china shop."

"You'd make a good couple, then."

"Sir?"

"Well, I gather you're fairly methodical in your approach."

"Sometimes if he cuts in too abruptly, he ruins what I've been trying to set up through a methodical approach," she said, "but he's learning."

"I venture to think he couldn't have a better teacher," he said tucking into his prawn cocktail. By now they had ordered wine – they had compromised on white even though Paul would have preferred red to go with his steak.

"Thank you, Adrian."

The meal continued with small talk but – by the time they had got round to deserts – a crème brulee for Francesca and sticky toffee pudding for Paul – he had returned the conversation to the possibility of a vacancy in Hertfordshire. "I should know for definite in the next couple of weeks," he said. "I'll let you know when I do."

"Thank you," said Francesca.

"Now," he said. "That's something I can do for you. I wondered if there was something you could do for me?"

"What might that be?"

"I wanted to get to know you better."

She felt a hand being placed on her knee. Oh dear, she thought here it comes. She decided to ignore it for the moment. She remembered the case of a politician who had claimed it was only the flapping of a tablecloth that had touched his dinner companion's knee in order to escape a charge that he had acted inappropriately towards a subordinate. She wanted more proof of his intentions before she acted. Encouraged by the fact she did not appear to object, he carried on – the hand moving further up her leg. "I have a safe house nearby – which is not being used at the moment," he said. "We could go there after we finish the meal."

"Excuse me, sir," she said, "but would you get your hand off my knee."

"Francesca," he said. "I could make things so easy for you. A good word from me."

"And my future position here is dependent on your hand wandering further up my leg, is it?" she said frostily. "I told you to get your hand off my knee."

"Don't be like that, Francesca. We could get on so well together. On the other hand, if you're obstructive."

"Yes?"

"I could make life very difficult for you."

"Difficult?"

"Yes, you'd have to watch your back. The slightest complaint. You know the sort of thing. On the other hand, we could have a very pleasant relationship."

"We are not going to have a relationship, sir."

"That's sad, Francesca. There really are quite a few other people interested in the full-time job here."

"Don't threaten me."

"Threaten you? I will, of course, deny it. Only you and I are privy to these conversations. I'll deny any threat."

"You'll find it difficult," said Francesca.

"What do you mean?"

She opened her jacket to reveal a small tape recorder in the inside pocket. She rewound it for a bit and then started playing it. "Excuse me, sir, but would you get my hand off my knee." She wound it on a little and then started playing it again. "And my future position here is dependent on your hand wandering further up my leg, is it?" the tape recording said.

"Francesca," he said. "Why have you done this?"

"Because I don't relish the idea of being groped by a senior officer. I was warned about you. It seems that nobody has had the courage to confront you beforehand about your activities. Nobody has had the proof, I suppose. I wonder what will happen when we play this tape recording to a disciplinary committee."

"You don't intend to do that, do you?" he said.

"At least you're not bothering to threaten me anymore," she said. "I think I should go now." She took some money from her purse. "This should cover the cost of my meal, I think," she said. With that, she put the tape recorder back in her inside pocket and left him stunned at the table on his own.

• • **•** • •

"What?" said Gary Clarke as he received the message from the station. "There's a body inside?"

"Yes, sir. The constables called to the scene have radioed in. She's hanging in the living room. Looks like a suicide but I thought CID ought to be informed."

"Thank you," he said. "I'll get down there."

"Neighbours were alerted to what happened by screaming. Turned out to be a flatmate of the dead woman. She'd found the body."

Gary nodded and got into his car. He looked at the address he had been given. It was familiar. It was Sue Plummer's house. He decided – after his last faux pas – that he had better alert

Francesca. "Hallo," he said when she answered her mobile. "I'm sorry if I'm spoiling your dinner with my uncle – but I thought I ought to tell you. There's been a body found at Sue Plummer's flat. I think it's her."

"No need to worry, Gary. The dinner's over. I'll join you there as soon as possible." They both arrived at the scene within minutes of each other. Sue Plummer was hanging from a light bulb fitting in her bedroom. Debra, her flatmate, was sitting in the kitchen drinking a strong cup of tea and gently sobbing. "Hallo, Debra," said Francesca, "Remember me? I'm Detective Chief Inspector Manners. What happened?"

Debra was full of grief, though. She rocked backwards and forwards in her chair, saying to herself: "Why did she do it? Why did she do it?"

"That's what we've come to find out. When did you discover her?"

"No, no," screamed Debra. "She shouldn't have done it. He wasn't worth it."

"Who wasn't worth it? Rob?"

One of the neighbours who had alerted the police then came over to speak to Francesca. "She's not right in the head, you know, Inspector," she said. "She should have someone with her if you're going to question her."

Francesca nodded. "Yes, I take your point." She walked over to Debra again. "Debra, is there anyone you'd like us to call to be with you?"

"I want Sue," said Debra. "There's only Sue."

Francesca turned to the neighbour. "Do you know anything about her circumstances?" she asked.

"No."

"Could you be with her?"

"I'll try," the woman said. She walked over to where Debra was sitting. "Debra, it's Muriel from next door. I've come to look after you."

"No," screamed Debra. "I want Sue."

"Well, you can't have Sue. She's dead and we want to find out what happened to her," said Gary intervening.

"That was just a touch too bullish, Gary," said Francesca reproachfully.

"Well, how do you propose to get some sense put into these proceedings?"

Muriel took Debra by the hand and sat her down at the kitchen table. "Darling," she said. "These people just want to know what happened. Now I heard you screaming and that was why I came over. I've got a key for emergencies so I came in and found you staring at Sue's body and screaming."

"She was the only one who ever befriended me. She gave me a job. Took me in. What's going to happen now?"

"Nothing that you don't want to happen," said Muriel soothingly. She kept holding Debra's hand. "Did you come in and find the body?"

"Find the body," repeated Debra. It set off another round of wailing.

Muriel turned to Francesca. "I don't think you're going to get much sense out of her tonight," she said. "You know she's retarded?"

"We'd be best getting her to hospital and sedated," said Gary to Francesca. "She's in a state."

"Wouldn't you be if you found the only person who had cared for you dead in your home amidst obvious signs that she had killed herself?"

"Don't take her to hospital," said Muriel. "Me and Stan – that's my husband – can look after her for tonight. I don't think she can help you very much. She must have come in and just found Sue hanging there. It's awful."

"You say 'must have'," said Francesca. "You don't know that. She's not the type to go out much. She could have been in the flat – in which case she could have evidence that would be useful."

"It should be me that's dead," said Debra. "It should be me."

"Why do you say that?"

"I'm the one." She stopped in her tracks. "No," she said, "I can't tell you." Gary made a note of what she was saying.

"She's afraid of something," said Francesca to Gary. "Look – she's all tensed up."

"Of landing herself in it, most likely."

Muriel overheard his comments. "You can't think she's got anything to do with this," she said. Neither Francesca nor Gary responded. "I'll take her back to my place," she added. "The sooner we get her out of here the better."

"Yes, all right," said Francesca. She turned to the two police constables who had arrived first on the scene. "Did you find a note?" she asked.

"No," said one. "We looked but found nothing."

Francesca nodded. She wandered into Sue's bedroom. By now her body had been taken down. Ambulance staff had arrived to take it to the mortuary. She looked round the room. "Something's not right," she said to Gary. "If she killed herself in a fit of remorse over Rob..."

"What? You mean, because she had killed him?"

"Possibly? Or maybe just over a relationship that had ended. If she had done that wouldn't she have wanted to make a clean breast of it and told someone why she was doing it? Especially if she was Rob's killer?"

Gary remained silent. He had another theory. He couldn't forget that Debra had wanted to punish Rob – even kill him – for what he had done to Sue. Had she? Had Sue found out and then blamed herself for Rob's death because she had not done enough to stop her.

"Well, I guess we're not going to find the answers tonight," said Francesca. "Best sleep on it."

CHAPTER SIX

"I didn't expect to see you in here again," said Jed Coulson as Rivers walked up to the bar in the Dog and Partridge.

"This is not a social call," said Rivers tersely. "I came here to protest at the treatment my assistant Jo received here yesterday."

"Quite right," said the landlord.

Rivers eyed him suspiciously. "So what are you going to do about it?" he asked.

"What have I done about it, you mean?"

"Yes," said Rivers sneeringly. "Offered Jo a free pint of bitter."

"More than that," said Jed. "I've barred the two people who insulted Jo from the pub. Last night. I thought about what had happened. I should have acted sooner and done it at the time."

"I was going to read you the riot act this morning. Tell the local people how my friend suffered racist insults in this pub."

"You wouldn't have been the first." admitted Jed.

"Oh?"

"Detective Chief Inspector Manners came in yesterday and told me in no uncertain terms what she thought of the way Jo had been treated."

Rivers smiled. "Ah," he said. Perhaps a bond was being created between the detective and his assistant. "I'm glad you acted," he said.

"Yes," he said. "I told them they had to treat all the pub's customers with respect in future. I think you'll find they'll be willing to co-operate in future if either you or – Jo, is it?" Rivers nodded. "If either of you have any more questions."

"Good," said Rivers. "I must confess to having an ulterior motive for wanting to sort this out. I'm buying a house in

Hertford and would like to make this pub my regular. Your ale's really good."

"Would you like some?"

"Best not," said Rivers. "I'm driving, on duty and all sorts of things."

"Come back one evening when somebody else is driving," said Jed."In fact, one of our regulars said he might have some information for you. I'll introduce him to you. Colin Standen's his name."

"Okay but this time I think I'll let you introduce him to Jo. It'll do his confidence no end of a good if he ends up getting somewhere as a result of visiting this pub." Rivers ordered a coke. "He's had a rough time since he came back to be my assistant."

"Racism?"said Jed as he passed the drink over.

"Yes," said Rivers taking a sip of coke."You know, he worked for me for three or four years before but he had to take a break when his mother died. Now he's back, things seem to be different. More people are prepared to take a pop at him because of his race. I'm not sure he'll stay."

"That would be sad,"said Jed. "If he went as a result."

"It's not that there aren't plenty of friendly people. There are. It's just that whenever he goes out to interview people he's not sure of the reception he's going to get."

"Send him here to chat to Colin Standen. Colin's in here most evenings. And that free pint's still on offer. That is, if he doesn't think I'm demeaning what happened to him by offering one."

"I'll suggest he comes along this evening."

• • ● • •

"Only one thing to do today," said Francesca as Gary Clarke entered her office that morning.

"What's that?"

"Go back and see if we can get some sense out of that Debra woman about what happened that night."

"Yes," said Gary. "Have we got the post mortem on Sue Plummer yet?"

"No. Later on today. We'll get the interview with Debra out of the way first." With that, they took off in Gary's car and called round at Sue's neighbour's home to see if Debra was still there.

"Yes," said Muriel as she greeted the detectives. "She's not up yet. Well, she's not come out of the bedroom. I'll go and tell her you're here. Do sit down and make yourselves comfortable."

"Thanks," said Francesca taking advantage of Muriel's offer. "Come on, Gary," she said. "You'll make her feel nervous. You're even making me nervous shifting about from one foot to the other."

"Isn't that the point?" said Gary. "Might it not be good to make her feel nervous?"

"Kid gloves today, Gary. She's been through a lot. Let's not worry her any more until and unless we find we have some cause to do so." Gary shrugged his shoulders but eventually did her bidding and sat down.

Muriel appeared from the bedroom Debra had been sleeping in. "She'll be in in a minute," she said.

"How's she been?" asked Francesca.

"I don't really know. She just shut herself in the bedroom soon after coming here last night. That's the last I heard from her. Except some sobbing during the night."

"She didn't get a good night's sleep? asked Francesca.

"I don't think so," said Muriel, "but then nor did I. It's not every day you find a dead body next door. Especially if it's someone you've been friendly with."

Francesca nodded sympathetically. "Had you seen her since Rob Corcoran's murder?"

"Once or twice. Not to speak to. Just putting out the rubbish, actually."

"How did she seem?"

Muriel thought for a moment. "Well, she was upset at Rob's

death," she said. "Obviously. I saw her a couple of days earlier and she told me they'd split up. She was sad about that, too. But I never would have guessed she would go and do this."

"No," said Francesca sympathetically. At this juncture Debra walked into the room. Her tear-stained cheeks and the black rings under her eyes told a story. "Hello, Debra," said Francesca. "How do you feel?"

Debra wiped a hand across her eyes and just looked at Francesca. "Sue's dead," was all she said.

"Yes, I know, love," she said. She didn't usually use such language when interviewing witnesses but she actually felt sorry for Debra. She didn't know whether Debra could manage on her own. Sue had been a tremendous support for her – offering her a home and securing a job for her. On top of the grief she must be feeling for losing a close friend in such a dramatic way, there must be a feeling of angst about what was going to happen to her now. "Just take your time," said Francesca. "We need to know what happened last night."

"It wasn't meant to happen," Debra blurted out,

"What do you mean?" asked Francesca.

"Sue dying."

"No," said Francesca tentatively. "Why do you think it did?"

"Rob."

"What about Rob?"

"His death." She buried her face in her hands at this juncture and said no more.

"Debra," said Francesca leaning forward towards her in an attempt to seem to be soothing. "We really need you to help us. What happened to Sue? Were you in all evening or did you come home and discover her?"

"It was Rob's death," she said. "She was really upset about that."

"And that's why she killed herself?"

Debra covered her face with her hands again. "It's my fault," she said emphatically.

"Why?" said Francesca.

Debra shook her head. "I can't tell you," she said.

"Did she kill Rob? Is that what happened? Did she confide in you?"

"It's my fault," she said again. Gary started fidgeting on his chair. He took a notebook out of his pocket and scribbled a note to Francesca. Tell her we'll have to continue this conversation down at the station, it said. She shook her head on receipt of it. "I should never have told her," Debra continued. A look of worry came over her face. "I shouldn't have said that," she said.

Francesca ignored her last remark. "Shouldn't have told her what?"

"No," she screamed. "No, don't ask me."

"Let's go back to the beginning," said Francesca. "Where were you last night before you discovered Sue's body?"

"Out."

Francesca heaved a sigh of relief. At last they seemed to be getting somewhere. "Out where?" she asked hoping the answer to this question would not be too upsetting for Debra as it didn't involve bringing back the memories of the death scene.

"My classes."

"Your classes?"

"I go to exercise classes – yoga – twice a week. They help calm me down," said Debra. It was the most forthcoming she had been since the incident. Shame we can't send you back there again today, thought Gary.

"I see," said Francesca. "And when you came back you found Sue?"

"I tried to get her down," said Debra fidgeting as the memory came back to her. "I tried to get her down but I couldn't."

Francesca stretched forward and put a hand upon her knee. A look of disgust came over Gary's face. "She was probably already dead by the time you came home," said Francesca. "There was nothing you could have done." She thought for a moment.

"Did you touch anything else in her room?" she asked.

Debra shook her head violently. She began sobbing again. "I want to go to my room," she said looking at Muriel who – in turn – looked at Francesca who nodded. "Thank you," said Debra quietly.

Muriel escorted her to her bedroom and then came back. "I'm a bit worried about looking after her," she said. "I can't keep an eye on her night and day."

Francesca nodded. "Do you think she's suicidal?" she asked.

"I don't know but I wouldn't rule it out. I'm not a doctor."

"We should call one. Or social services."

"She wouldn't be a priority," said Gary. "She's 22, lives independently and has her own job."

Francesca nodded. "A doctor then," she said. "I'll ring and get one to make a house call. Perhaps you could continue to look after her until then?"

"Yes," said Muriel, "but what then? I don't like the idea of returning her to her own home."

"We'll cross that bridge when we come to it."

"I'm sure the doctor will only prescribe sedatives," said Gary.

Francesca turned to face him. "So what's your solution?" she snapped at him.

"I don't think we've got the half of what she knows out of her," he said, "but I don't have a solution." Muriel and Francesca looked at him – each trying to weigh up in their own minds whether he was right or not.

• • ● • •

"I'm pleased," said Jo. "It's a nice pub. Shame about the people."

"Not all of them," said Rivers.

"Not all of them," repeated Jo. "I will go back there and talk to Colin Standen. And I'll accept that free pint – with good grace."

"Hold on a minute," said Rivers. "Who's driving?"

"Haven't you heard of trains?" said Jo.

Rivers smiled. "You know Francesca went down there to read them the riot act over what happened?"

Jo smiled. "Then I shall thank her tonight," he said. "I'm meeting her for a drink," he said by way of explanation.

"Good," said Rivers. "Now," he said, "let's recap on where we are on this little matter of Rob Corcoran's murder." Jo gave him a stare. "I don't want to belittle what happened to you, Jo, but we do appear to have sorted it and we don't appear to have sorted what happened to Rob."

"No," agreed Jo.

"As far as the planning department goes, there is now an inquiry into Rob's allegations and I am giving evidence of the treatment that he received from our two friends, Bruiser and Eel. Roger Broadbent has been suspended but Roulay's conducting the inquiry. I'm not so sure about that. I think he may be involved, too."

"Think?" queried Jo.

"Only think," agreed Rivers. "Rob had no evidence and neither do I."

"But there is someone who would," said Jo.

"Who?"

"Roger Broadbent," said Jo, "and now he's been suspended by Roulay he just might be feeling a little bit aggrieved. Worth going to see him?"

Rivers nodded. "You're right," he said. "Now," he said. "The mistresses."

"Which reminds me," said Jo. "I should have told you earlier."

"What?"

"My third port of call last night was Sue Plummer."

"Yes."

"I didn't get to see her."

"Oh?"

"When I rolled up there were police cars and an ambulance

outside her home. They wheeled a body out."

"Sue Plummer?"

"It must have been. I could see someone else sobbing in the corridor who looked as though she lived there."

"Murder or suicide?"

"I don't know."

"Find out from Francesca tonight." A wry smile came over his face. Normally, he would be getting the information he needed from Francesca. It was one of the best relationships he had ever had with a police officer. He was quite happy to let Jo do the running in that department now, though. "If she killed herself," he said, " it could be because she killed Rob and felt remorse. In fact that's the most likely explanation. On the other hand, if she was murdered?"

Jo thought for a moment. "It was probably because she found out who the real killer was," he said eventually.

Rivers nodded. "Who's likely to be able to help us over that?" he asked.

"The flatmate."

"We'll have a word with her," said Rivers. "Anything else, Jo?"

"Yes," he said. "Miranda Headley is lying about where she was on the night of the murder," he added emphatically. "She says she went round to a meeting at Jackie Quesling's house about 8pm and returned home a couple of hours later."

"And she's lying because?"

"Jackie says the meeting was over by 8.30pm and the other two drove off to meet again in the town centre about an hour later and drive out to Rob's place to have it out with him."

"Have it out with him?"

"Find out what he was planning to do about his relationship with the three of them. Jackie's version of events is confirmed by a neighbour who says she heard two cars arriving for the meeting at 8pm and two cars leaving at 8.30pm. That would be Sue and Miranda."

"And she's sure of the timing?"

"Because she was watching Holby City."

"And what happened to Jackie's car?"

"The neighbour didn't know because Holby City became quite gripping during the second half."

"That's a first," said Rivers,

"You watch it?"

"Not anymore."

"Anyhow, getting back to the evening in question. Jackie's car had left by just after 9pm because the neighbour noticed it had gone when she went to walk her dog after Holby City was over."

"So none of the three have an alibi for the time Rob was actually killed?"

"I suppose not," said Jo, "although Jackie would have had to have acted quite sharpishly if she didn't leave her home until later and picked the other two up at 9.30pm."

"Unless the excitement created by Holby City happened soon after 8.30pm," said Rivers wryly.

Jo laughed. "Are you suggesting we watch a re-run of the programme?"

Rivers smiled. "No," he said. "I suspect our definition of what amounts to excitement might differ from the neighbour's."

"So what's to do?" asked Jo.

"Interview Miranda again. Tell her you have proof that she lied to you the first time you spoke to her. Rattle her cage and see what falls out."

"Should we wait until we find out what happened to Sue Plummer?"

"Why?"

"On the grounds that if she killed herself that's an end to the matter?"

"I don't think it would hurt to rattle Miranda's cage," said Rivers.

• • • • •

"Is that you, Bruiser?" In reality, Jerry Vincent did not need to ask. The gruff tones of the person who had answered the telephone call told him all he needed to know – but the reply came back in the affirmative. "I need your services again," he said.

"Friendly persuasion?" asked Bruiser almost guffawing as the words came out of his mouth.

"Something a little bit more, dear boy," said Jerry. Bruiser winced down the other end of the line. He did not like another man calling him "dear boy". "Someone is paying some unwelcome attention to my business interests."

"Who?"

"Philip Rivers."

"Hearing that name is like music to my ears," said Bruiser in an unusually elegant response for him.

"I want you to be a bit fly this time, though."

"What?"

"Clever."

"Oh." It was as if Bruiser didn't understand the word. "I'll get Eel," he said.

Eel took over from him on the other end of the line. "What did you have in mind?"

"I don't think you'll be able to warn Philip Rivers off by making threatening noises and breaking a few bones." Bruiser snorted as if his favourite cake had just been pinched from under his nose.

"So what do you suggest?"

"Hit him where it would most worry him."

"And that is?"

"Over his family."

"Yes. Who are we talking about?"

"I don't know. Follow him home. Do a little detective work. I suspect he's got a wife. She's the one you must threaten. If he has, make it clear that she's a target for your specialist talents. That should be enough to set the cat amongst the pigeons.

Don't do anything just yet but leave him in no doubt that you're threatening her."

"How?" asked Bruiser.

"Do I have to spell everything out for you?"

"No, you don't," said Eel interrupting. "We follow him to his home. Make it clear that we can get access to it by getting inside – obviously when neither him nor her are there. Send him proof that we've done it and…."

"Bob's your uncle," said Vincent. "I knew you'd catch on, Eel. That's why the two of you are so effective a partnership,"

"So what's the state of play with this Rivers?" Bruiser mimicked his colleague's middle class tones as he asked the question.

"He's investigating my planning application. He's already persuaded the head of the department to hold an inquiry into it. He's suspended my mole in the town hall and he's minded to put my application on ice for the time being. Meanwhile, Rivers is digging even deeper. He's taken over from Rob Corcoran in heading up an investigation."

"How soon do you want us to put this plan into effect?" asked Eel.

"As soon as you can. Rivers isn't resting. Nor should we be."

• • • • •

Jo gave Francesca Manners a friendly peck on the cheek when they met for a drink that evening. He decided to put visiting the Dog and Partridge on the back burner for the evening. After all, Rivers had been assured that Colin Standen would be in the pub every night. Also, the murder enquiry was stalled until they had more information about Sue Plummer's death – and Francesca was the person who could supply them with that. All in all, he reasoned to himself, it made sense to keep to his original arrangement with Francesca than go off on what could be a wild goose chase. "How's things?" he asked her.

"Hectic," she said. "I've got something I want to ask you about," she said.

"And I you," said Jo.

"You go first," Francesca insisted.

"All right," said Jo. "I saw you last night – at Sue Plummer's house. I was just going round there to question her about Rob Corcoran's murder. My journey, it seems, was superfluous."

"Yes," said Francesca.

"Did she kill herself?" Jo asked.

"It looks like that. Her flatmate, Debra, had been out for the evening at a yoga class and came back to find her body hanging from a light bulb fitting in her bedroom."

"Does that mean what I think it means?"

"I don't know. I can't read your mind." She smiled. "Yet," she added.

"That she was driven by remorse after having killed Rob Corcoran?"

"That's the most logical explanation."

"But you have your doubts?"

"Not based on anything really; we've found no signs of foul play. But something doesn't add up. She didn't leave a note. Most people in that distressed state of mind would have done. Also, her neighbour says that – while she was clearly upset about breaking up with Rob and his death – she didn't detect any signs that she was contemplating suicide or was even depressed, in the clinical sense of the word. Then there's the behaviour of the flatmate. She keeps on saying it was her fault. Well, if Sue killed Rob and then killed herself, it's hardly her fault."

"Have you questioned her about that?"

"Of course," said Francesca. "She's a bit – well, not quite all there. She has learning and communication difficulties. She relied on Sue who gave her a home and got her a job. I'm not sure you can trust anything she says – not because she's lying but she's not in control of her faculties. She's also very worried about what might happen to her. Will she be able to keep on the home? Will the job still be there without Sue's patronage?"

"I see."

"Have you got anything to add to the murder investigation?" she asked, turning the tables on Jo.

"Other than the fact that all three of the mistresses could be in the frame for the murder, no," he said. "Miranda Headley is definitely lying about where she was and the three mistresses were planning some joint action against Rob." He went into the details of what he had gleaned from his interviews the previous evening. "Have you had a post-mortem carried out on Sue Plummer?" he asked after he had finished.

"We're in the process of having one done. There have been some delays. I don't quite know why."

Jo nodded. "Anyhow, what was it that you wanted to ask me about?"

Francesca sighed. "A little local difficulty within the police force," she said. "I was invited out to dinner by the Chief Constable last night."

"Very nice," said Jo.

"No, not very," came the reply. "He propositioned me."

"Oh."

"Put his hand on my leg and – whilst he was moving it upwards – asked me if I'd like to go to a safe house with him for the night. When I asked him to stop, he threatened me – warning me a rejection of his advances might have implications for my career."

"My God. The bastard."

"Precisely my sentiments."

"So what did you do?"

"Well, I'd been forewarned that he was a randy old goat so I had a tape-recorder running through our dinner. I played it back to him – and he backed off."

"I'll bet he did," said Jo.

"Now I'm not sure what to do," she confessed. "The very fact that I have the tape recording makes it certain that he won't take any action to threaten my career. It's insurance if you like so I could do nothing in the knowledge that nothing nasty is going to happen to me."

"Yes." Jo sounded tentative in giving any approval to this kind of action.

"On the other hand, if he has this reputation in the force, he's going to try it on with another woman at some time and she might not be as forewarned as I was."

"He's also obviously tried it on in the past," said Jo.

"Yes," said Francesca, "so part of me feels that I'm duty-bound to lay a complaint against him to stop him behaving this way in future."

"Yes," said Jo thoughtfully. "You know – there are no half measures when it comes to racism and sexism. Take racism. I suffered racist insults in the Dog and Partridge last night – the publican tried to smooth it over and get me to forget about it by offering me a free pint of bitter but it wasn't enough. Rivers was seething about it this morning and went down to sort it out. When he got there, he found the landlord had barred the two men who made the comments to me. Result. It sends a message out to anyone else who is thinking of insulting someone because of the colour of their skin. Don't. There are consequences. I would have just left it and boycotted the pub."

Francesca smiled. "You know," she said. "I might just have had something to do with the landlord's decision to bar the two racists last night. When I heard about it, I went to the pub fully intent on launching both barrels at the landlord. That might have prompted his change of heart."

"Very possibly," said Jo. He touched her hand in an effort to show gratitude for what she had done.

"So I was very clear what should happen in the case of a racist insult. You should not leave it be. I should be just as clear in the case of the unwanted sexual advances made to me. I should lay a complaint against the Chief Constable. God, why do I always end up in these situations?"

"What do you mean?"

Francesca smiled. "Earlier in my career, I came across a case of my superior trying to fit someone up for a murder. I laid a complaint which was initially ignored – but I persevered and was proved right."

"Nobody will be able to ignore you this time," said Jo. "You've got the tape recording."

"Yes, if he's got any sense, the Chief Constable will resign." She looked at her watch. "Look, Jo," she said. "It's ten o'clock. We've both got busy jobs. Would you mind if I went home now? We can get to know each other better next time we go out."

Jo smiled. He raised his glass. "To the next time," he said. Francesca clinked her glass with his.

• • ● • •

It could do with a lick of paint, thought Rivers as he saw the outside of Roger Broadbent's cottage. Nice view, though, a smart new gravel drive at the front of the house and a sizeable garden.

Difficult to sustain on the salary of an official in the planning department, he surmised. He knocked on the door. Roger Broadbent answered. He looked apprehensive. His hair was unkempt. There was the slight trace of a beard beginning to grow. His trousers looked as if they hadn't seen the inside of a washing machine for quite a while.

"Mr Broadbent?" said Rivers.

"Yes?"

"Philip Rivers, private detective." He showed the other man his business card. "Do you mind if I come in?"

"Er – it's not convenient."

Rivers was not taking no for an answer. He pushed past

177

Broadbent and went into the living room where he promptly sat down on the settee. There were the remains of a meal which had not yet been cleared away on the adjacent table. "Live here on your own, do you?" asked Rivers.

"What business is that of yours?"

"Sorry, Mr Broadbent. I was just putting my skills as a private detective to good use. You don't have to answer."

"If you must know, my wife left me last year."

And you still haven't got round to hiring a cleaner, thought Rivers. "Oh, at about the time you got into bed with Jerry Vincent," he said.

"I resent that implication."

"Resent it all you like but it is true, isn't it, that you have been suspended from work as a result of your links with Jerry Vincent?"

"Alleged links," he said quietly.

"You're contesting the case?"

"I will be."

"How do you feel about your suspension?"

"I beg your pardon."

"Well, you were suspended by your boss who – some say – might have similar links to you as far as Jerry Vincent goes."

"Oh, I see what you mean."

"So how do you feel?"

Broadbent thought for a moment. "Aggrieved," he said eventually. "Aggrieved."

"Would you care to elaborate on that?"

"I don't think I did anything wrong. Mr Vincent's planning application would bring with it – if approved – more than 100 new homes in the neighbourhood. Homes that the government says are desperately needed. They want us to build on green belt and conservation areas to provide homes. Approving such a scheme is a legitimate decision to take."

"And the test match and Wimbledon tickets and the new

gravel pathway are immaterial?"

"You have no proof that they were paid for by anybody else than myself."

"I'm sure we can get it. Lords and Wimbledon would have records on who paid for their tickets. But I'm here on a much more serious matter than corruption in the planning department. I'm investigating a murder."

"You surely don't think I did it?"

Rivers looked at him intently and then looked round the room. "No," he said, "you don't look as if you have the wherewithal to arrange your own supper let along carry out a murder. But, as far as suspects go, you are the only one in the planning department. The victim, Rob Corcoran, was alleging corrupt practices – specifically against you. Unless, of course, you think he might have uncovered something else if he had been allowed to carry on with his enquiries?"

"I don't know. I'm not saying anything."

"Are you content with being the fall guy? Just think about it. Unless you widen the net, you are in very real danger of becoming the police's main suspect in this murder enquiry."

"So why haven't they come to talk to me?" said Broadbent – a gleam suddenly coming to his eye as if he had discovered a flaw in Rivers' argument.

"They will do, Mr Broadbent," said the private detective. "They will do. In fact, I should scrub up the family home for when they come. You look like a man who's not coping as a result of the guilt he has." He took a business card and pressed it into Roger Broadbent's hands. "Look, I appreciate that what I've told you might have come as a little bit of a shock," he said, "but – if you think about it and you think there's something you want to tell me, then don't hesitate to call." With that, he took his leave of Broadbent – who stared after him as if a little bemused by the visit.

• • • • •

"Trish," said Colin as he stood on the doorstep of Rob Corcoran's former wife's home. "I just thought I'd come and see how you were."

"You've been doing that quite a lot lately," she said.

"Well, it's difficult times. You want to know who your friends are."

"Thank you, Colin," she said. "Rob and I were separated."

"Yes, but you must still feel something for him."

"Must I?" she asked "Look, Colin, I appreciate what you've been doing for me but…."

"But what?"

"I don't want a relationship with you."

"I wasn't aware that was what I was offering you."

"Well, if you weren't, then all well and good. I'm just about to come into some money."

"Yes." Trish looked at him. He wondered if he had been a bit too quick off the mark in acknowledging her future wealth. "I'm sorry," he said. "Go on."

"I'm just about to come into some money and it will give me a new lease of life. I want to use it to my own advantage. See a little bit of the world. Act as if I'm footloose and fancy free. I don't want to be tied down in another relationship. It's too soon."

"Oh."

She looked at him. "I know I've upset you, Colin." He opened his mouth as if to protest.

"No, no, I know that I've upset you." There was an accent on the word "know". "I'm sorry about that but it would be wrong to string you along." The truth is, she thought to herself, you're boring. You've lost your job, there doesn't seem any sign of anything else coming your way, you're in the pub every night, you don't seem to want to do anything else but eat and drink – and drink some more. I could do so much better for myself than you.

"How could you?" he said. "I've done so much for you."

"Pardon me, Colin, but you've held my hand at a time which has been very difficult for me. You've made sure I've had company when I could have felt very morose at being on my own. But you've not done – to use your words –'so much' for me."

"I can see now that you don't appreciate what I've done." He came to a halt. "I...." He was at a loss for words.

"I think you'd better go, Colin." she said. "I'm sorry but I thought I should get things straight between us."

"If you say I've got to go, then I must go, but mark my words – you'll regret this – you'll regret this." He sounded angry rather than sad now.

Trish looked after him as he made his way back to his car wondering if his last words were supposed to convey some sort of threat – or whether Colin was just meaning to indicate that she would regret losing his friendship in the times to come. She didn't wait to see him drive away, shutting the door before he had got the car started. Once inside the house, she lay back against the door and breathed a sigh of relief.

Colin, for his part, got into the car and ignited the ignition. Then, before he drove off, a wave of anger came over him and he crashed his fist down on the dashboard. It had little impact other than to bruise his fist. "Fuck," he shouted as he nursed his fist with his other hand. "Fuck."

• • ● • •

"You wanted to see me?" Francesca said as she entered Rory Gleeson's office.

"Yes, sit down," he replied. He shuffled some papers on his desk – in a manner which almost made her think he was nervous. "You've laid a complaint against the Chief Constable?" he asked

"Yes," she confirmed.

"I hope you know what you're doing."

"I do," she said. "I wouldn't do it if I wasn't sure of myself."

"You accuse him of inappropriate behaviour towards a junior officer – i.e. bullying, sexism... and unwanted sexual advances.

"Putting his hand on my knee and working it up my leg. Disgusting behaviour."

"If true."

"I have it on tape."

Gleeson relaxed. "Thank God," he said. "I was going to warn you it would only be your word against his and there would be no proof of his behaviour and that – in the circumstances – you had better watch your back."

"Unnecessary," she said.

"What persuaded you to tape record the encounter?" he asked.

"If you mean who, it was you."

Gleeson stared back at her in astonishment. "Me?" he said puzzled.

"You said he was a randy old goat – or words to that effect – and that you thought he had taken a shine to me at his ball."

"I seem to remember saying something similar," he said slowly. "Wow." He sat back in his chair. "Of course a disciplinary panel will be summoned and normally he would have the right to be questioned by an officer senior to himself. In this case they will call in a Chief Constable from another constabulary to conduct the disciplinary hearing," he added.

"What do you think will happen?"

"In view of the overwhelming evidence, he would be best advised to resign," Gleeson said. "I don't know whether he will. Of course, your complaint may flush out others from women officers who have been too frightened to come forward." He cleared his throat. "Of course, the complaint wasn't the only reason I called you in today," he added.

"No?" she said.

"No," he added. "One of your old cases has come back to haunt you. A guy in Brighton who was sent down for a string of burglary offences is appealing against his sentence. Prosecution seems to think he hasn't got good grounds for appeal but they want you to stand by in the court-room to give evidence. Means a couple of days by the seaside."

"And takes me out of harm's way in the run-up to the disciplinary proceedings?"

"You've got such a suspicious mind," said Gleeson. "Actually, I don't think that will be necessary. Adrian Paul has been suspended from duty pending the hearing in view of the serious nature of the allegation against him. It's not just the harassment of a female officer but the fact that he was prepared to use police property as a knocking shop – if you'll excuse the phrase."

"I see," said Francesca. "That would never do," she added wryly. "I mean, it would be all right if he had a caravan."

Gleeson smiled. "I can't see Adrian Paul functioning well in a caravan," he said. He then adopted a serious tone again. "There are senior officers within the Hertfordshire force who are friendly towards the Chief Constable. I suppose they might be tempted to give you a hard time. Better keep that tape recorder running."

"I hope you're not serious, Rory?"

"Not really. Better to be safe than sorry, though, if you do find yourself called in a for a chat by any other senior officers" He thought for a moment. "What about Gary Clarke?"

"He doesn't like to play on the fact he's the Chief Constable's nephew," she said. "I don't think there'll be any issue there."

"You'll be leaving him in charge of the enquiry into Rob Corcoran's death for a couple of days – and this new case, the hanging of Sue Plummer. Is that suicide or murder?"

"I'm still awaiting the results of the post-mortem."

"Still awaiting the results? She's been dead for 36 hours."

"I think they're snowed under."

"They always say they are. I'll get in touch with them and chivvy them along."

"Thank you."

"To go back, though, you have no qualms about leaving Gary in charge? I can get him another detective constable to help him out but senior officers are a bit thin on the ground."

"I think it'll be okay," said Francesca, determining to have a word with him before she went.

• • • • •

Rivers returned to his office later that afternoon to find Jo sitting at his desk. "Any further developments?" he said.

"No," replied Jo. "I went round to Miranda Headley's but I didn't find her in. I was going to leave it until about 5pm and then go back again."

"Good." He walked over to the coffee point which was next to a street facing window. He stared at the street scene as he poured himself a cup of coffee. "Would you like one?" he asked Jo. His eye alighted on a thickset man in a leather jacket and jeans standing by a white van. He was handing a cup of tea or coffee to someone inside the van in the passenger's seat. "Come over here a minute," he said to Jo.

Jo obliged. "What is it?"

"Look at that guy over there," he said – pointing out the thickset man. "Recognise him?"

Jo squinted in the direction to which Rivers was pointing. "Yes," he said. "It's our old friend Bruiser."

"In a white van – not the McCarthy and Higgs van of his scrap metal firm. Presumably he wants to remain incognito?"

"He ought to change his clothes then," said Jo.

"Right," said Rivers. "It's no coincidence that he's parked opposite our office, I would presume." He looked again at the van. "I can't see very well but it looks as though that could be Eel in the passenger seat," he said. "Look," he added. "I've nearly finished for the day. Why don't I go home and see what happens? You keep your eye on Bruiser and Eel and see what they do."

"Okay."

So saying Rivers got up to leave his office. His car was parked in the car park at the rear of the offices but he made a point of coming out of the front entrance and going past Bruiser and Eel – if it was them – parked in the street outside the front of the office block. Jo was just behind him but waited until he saw the white van draw out before he turned into the street himself and followed it. It was just a short drive to the block of flats where Rivers lived. He went into his parking spot to see the white van drawing up in the street next to it and coming to a halt. Jo was still following it but took up his allotted place in the car park on reaching Rivers' home. He was fairly confident Bruiser and Eel had not spotted him and decided not to get out of his car until they had disappeared to avoid recognition. Rivers was soon inside the block of flats and – as he disappeared inside – Eel walked over to the entrance. He looked at the intercom and buzzer and saw Rivers' name by flat number eight. He walked back to Bruiser.

"He lives at number eight," he said.

"Right," said Bruiser.

"We'd better hang around," said Eel. "See if anyone else like a wife or partner comes home to that address. I'll hang out by the door. I look less suspicious than you."

"Okay," said Bruiser wondering to himself why he looked suspicious. To Eel, though, he had the look of a man who should have a knuckle-duster in his hand. It was 4.30pm and Eel wondered how long he would have to wait to see if Rivers had a partner. A couple walked up to the front door and he smiled at them. "Are you waiting to get in?" said the man.

"No," said Eel. "A friend's coming down and we're going for a drink."

The man nodded and put his key in the lock and disappeared inside.

The next arrival at the door was Nikki laden with baskets

of shopping. "Can I help you?" asked Eel.

"No, it's all right," she said. "I'll just buzz upstairs and see if my husband's home." She did so and Eel could see she was buzzing number eight. "Oh, hallo, Philip, darling," said Nikki. "I'm glad you're home early. Could you let me in?" She smiled at Eel as she disappeared inside.

Eel walked over to Bruiser. "Philip Rivers lives at flat number eight," he said, "and he has a wife or partner – that rather lovely looking woman who just went indoors."

"There's no justice in this world," said Bruiser – philosophically for him.

Eel gave him a strange glance. "She also said that she was glad he'd come home early so – if this is her regular home time – the flat is unoccupied until 4.30pm/4.45pm," he said. "The residents seem friendly; one even offered to let me in. I don't see that we will have any problems getting into the flat tomorrow."

"What are we going to do?" asked Bruiser.

"Steal something that will make it clear to Rivers that we can get access to his flat at any time. In fact, it might be a good idea if I did it by myself. No sense in drawing attention to ourselves." He decided to be polite in suggesting to Bruiser that he could be a liability if he was seen hanging around the flats with him. In no way did Bruiser look like the sort of person who would live in a block of flats like these.

"Okay," said Bruiser.

With that, Eel got back into the van and the two of them drove off. Jo watched them go before entering the block of flats himself.

"What happened?" asked Rivers as Jo opened the door to number eight.

"They waited until Nikki came home," he said. He turned to Nikki. "In fact, the man who offered to help you was one of them."

"Gosh," said Nikki.

"Then they just went."

"They got what they wanted," said Rivers. "They know where I live and who I live with. Now we've got to figure out just what the hell are they going to do?"

· · ● · ·

"I've got to go away for a couple of days," Francesca told Gary on returning to her office. "That leaves you in charge of the investigations. Just keep an eye out for the post-mortem results from Sue Plummer," she said. "Tell them to get a move on. Ring them first thing tomorrow morning if you haven't got them by then. Gleeson is going to get you help – I think it will only be Detective Constable Johnson, though."

"Don't worry, Francesca, everything will be fine," said Gary – quite relishing the prospect of taking charge.

"I know it will be," said Francesca. She thought she ought to broach the subject of his uncle, Adrian Paul, "I suppose you've heard about the Chief Constable," she said tentatively.

"That he's been suspended? Yes."

"After a complaint I made against him."

"Yes," said Gary. "Look," he added, "I don't hold a torch for the guy. If anything I'm embarrassed by the fact that he's my uncle. It means it takes people a long time before they can relax with me and trust me. If he's done what he's said to have done, then that's a serious misdemeanour. End of. I just hope nobody believes I would behave in that way."

"I never thought that for a moment," said Francesca.

"Do you think he'll have to leave the force?" asked Gary.

"I really don't think I should speculate about things like that," said Francesca. "Best let the disciplinary hearing take its course."

"Can I just say, ma'am?"

"Francesca," she corrected.

Gary smiled. "Francesca. I'll get it right someday."

"You do get it right some of the time," said Francesca encouragingly.

Gary blushed. "Thank you," he said. "Can I just say," he repeated, "that if he did the things he's alleged to have done to you, then I admire your courage in coming forward and making a complaint? I hear you've got a tape recording of the incident so I guess it must be true."

"Thank you, Gary. I mean that sincerely." With that, she picked up her belongings from her desk and made her way out of the door.

"Have a good time in Brighton," he called after her. When she had gone, he sat back in his chair and thought for a moment. He had two days ahead of him. Two days in which to make some headway with the Rob Corcoran case and impress his superiors. He knew where he would first try to make his mark. He was convinced that Sue Plummer's flatmate, Debra, knew more than she was letting on about the murder of Rob Corcoran.

● ● ● ● ●

"So," said Trish as she sat herself down on a chair in Amit Raina's office, "can you tell me when I can expect to get hold of my inheritance?"

"Not just yet," said Raina. "There are complications."

"Complications?"

"Your husband was murdered,"

"Yes?"

"Until the police clear up what happened to him, you will not be able to obtain access to your inheritance. I don't know how to put this to you." He hesitated for a moment. "You are a person of interest to them," he eventually added.

"A person of interest?" she said – a smile forming on her lips. "That sounds rather exotic."

"Believe me, you don't want to be," said Raina.

"Why?"

He heaved a sigh. "Well, it's as good as saying that you are a suspect in the murder investigation."

"What? I didn't do it. I shouldn't be penalised."

"Believe me, I believe you when you say you didn't do it. But that's not the same as convincing the police you didn't do it."

"God," said Trish. She began to sound worried. "But I've given evidence to them," she said.

"And what did you say?"

"Well, there wasn't much I could say. I told them I was at home on the night Rob was killed."

"Alone?"

"Yes."

"There you are, then," said Raina. "You haven't eliminated yourself from their enquiries. Don't get me wrong – the fact that you were alone at home doesn't mean that you killed him – it just means you can't prove you didn't."

"I thought the law worked the other way round," said Trish. "That you were innocent until proven guilty."

"It does," said Raina patiently, "if you are finally charged." Trish raised an eyebrow here. "Which you won't be, I'm sure," he added. "In the meantime, you just have to wait until they come up with some evidence proving somebody else did the murder."

"How long is that likely to be?"

"How long is a piece of string?" replied Raina. "Just one thing," he added cautiously. "If you are questioned by the police again, it may not be a good idea to give the impression that you are anxious to claim your inheritance as soon as possible. Speaks to motive."

"What does that mean?"

"In simple layman's terms, it will make them believe you were anxious for him to die so you could get your hands on your inheritance."

Trish nodded sullenly. "Pity," she said. "I was looking forward to treating myself."

"Also, not a good idea to spend lavishly in anticipation of the inheritance. Speaks to your mindset."

"That I want to enjoy myself in spite of my husband's death. What's wrong with that? We had separated. I don't have to don sackcloth and ashes over his killing."

"It might be an idea to show a little remorse," encouraged Raina, "even if you don't feel it."

"Couldn't it work the other way round? If I spend in advance of getting the inheritance, it will show I'm confident I will get it and that I'm not worried that I'll be charged with his murder and therefore forfeit it?"

"You could argue that," said Rania, "but somehow I don't think so." He thought for a moment. "But really I'm overstepping my brief," he said. "I shouldn't be telling you how to behave. All I should be doing is telling you that you won't be able to access your inheritance for a while."

Trish nodded and got up to go. "Thanks a bunch," she said.

• • ● • •

Jo rang the intercom as she approached Aaron and Miranda's flat. "It's me again," he said when Miranda answered. "The detective from Rivers' agency. Can I have a further word with you?"

"I've told you I've said all I'm going to say. I'm waiting for the police to interview me."

"Only we have conclusive proof that you were lying to us when you spoke about your movements on the night of Rob Corcoran's murder. I thought you might like to clear things up."

"Not with you," she said firmly. "I don't have to."

"You're not being very clever, Mrs Headley," said Jo.

"What do you mean?"

"Well, if I were in your shoes, I would want to know where I'd been caught out lying – even if just to avoid making the same mistake when the police come calling." There was silence on the other end of the intercom. It sounded as if she had moved away from it and was about to discuss what Jo had said with her husband. "Well, Mrs Headley?" said Jo. "What is it to be?"

She was back by the intercom now. "You'd better come up," she said.

Jo entered the sitting room and was motioned to a seat by Miranda. She sat down on the edge of a chair opposite him. She looked nervous. Aaron stood by the fireplace as if he was only half paying attention and clasping what looked like a glass of whisky in his hand. "Mrs Headley," said Jo, "I have to say you are the only person that I'm aware of who is lying to us about your whereabouts on the night of Rob's murder."

"Why do you say that?"

"Well, you told us you were at Jackie Quesling's house until about 9.30pm on the night of the murder and then went over to Rob Corcoran's after he had been killed. Well, Jackie Quesling says that you and Sue Plummer left her house at 8.30pm – and then met up again about an hour later to go to Rob Corcoran's flat."

"Maybe she's lying?" suggested Miranda.

"No, her evidence is independently corroborated."

"Who by? Not by Sue Plummer, I would suggest. I've heard that she also is dead."

"You heard correctly," said Jo. "No, a neighbour of Jackie Quesling's heard two cars departing from the house at 8.30pm. Obviously, it would make sense if those two cars were yours and Sue Plummer's. It was, after all, Jackie's house."

"So – that's the big lie?"

"That you weren't at Jackie Quesling's at the time of Rob Corcoran's murder. Yes, that's it. You gave a false alibi."

"But surely, the death of Sue Plummer means that it's likely she was the killer and that she took her own life because of what she had done."

"Maybe that's what you want me to think, Mrs Headley. Anyhow, who said it was suicide?"

"She was found hanging from a light fitting in her bedroom according to the local radio news," said Miranda. "Surely that means suicide?"

"I must admit it does look like it," confessed Jo, "but I'm sure the police are keeping all options open at the moment. And so are we." He fixed her with a stare. "So in the light of all this would you like to tell me where you were at the time of Rob Corcoran's death?" he asked.

"I came home for a while and then went to the bottom of Port Vale – the main road from Hertford through Bengeo – for my rendezvous with Sue and Jackie," she said.

"No," said Jo.

"What do you mean 'no'?" she asked.

"Your husband was here being interviewed by Detective Constable Clarke. Detective Constable Clarke would have mentioned it had you been here, I feel sure. Besides, you husband told me you didn't get back here until 10pm that night the last time I questioned you. So where were you?"

"I....er.... I just went for a drive," she said. "I wanted to think about things. Work out whether I thought what we were going to do to Rob was right or not."

"What were you planning to do?"

"There's no point in telling you. We didn't do it." She paused for a moment. "We weren't going to kill him, though."

"Thank you, Mrs Headley. I take it no-one saw you on this drive of yours?" he asked.

"Not that I can recall," she said.

"Thank you then." He got up to go and Aaron showed him to the door. "I think you will soon have a visit from the police," Jo said as a parting shot in Miranda's direction before he departed.

Aaron shut the door and approached Miranda. He looked at her accusingly, "Did you kill him?"

"Aaron," she said shocked. "I'm surprised you have to ask me that."

"Well, did you?"

She sighed. "Well, if I can't convince you of my innocence, what chance am I going to have with the police?" she said.

• • ● • •

"Come on, Johnson, let's go round and see Debra again," said Gary. "Put the wind up her."

"If you're sure," said his fellow detective tentatively. Ryan Johnson was another fairly newish recruit to the investigation team. He had worked his way up, though, from being an officer on the beat rather than the fast-track scheme that had seen Gary propelled into office. Francesca had left Gary in charge, though, as he knew more about the background to the case. Johnson went along with what he was suggesting.

"I expect she'll still be round at that next door neighbour's," said Gary. "I doubt whether she'll have wanted to go home yet."

The two of them soon arrived at Muriel's home. Gary banged loudly on the door.

"What is it?" came a voice from inside. "If you're a reporter go away."

"Police," shouted Gary sternly. "We need to speak to Debra again."

"Oh, sorry," said Muriel as she opened the door, "Only we've had one or two reporters round. Bit of a nuisance."

"Is she in?" said Gary gruffly as he pushed past her and into the living room. Debra was sitting on the sofa. Johnson was altogether more polite as he walked past Muriel into the room.

"Debra Paget?"

"Yes," she said.

"I should like you to accompany me down to the station to answer a few more queries we have about the murder of Rob Corcoran."

Muriel, puffing, had made her way back to the sitting room. "Is that really necessary?" she asked. "Couldn't she answer the questions here?"

"I should like you to come down to the station with me but – if you refuse – I shall have no option but to arrest you on suspicion of murder."

Debra went as white as a sheet. Muriel stared at Gary – as if she could not believe what he had just said. Ryan Johnson shuffled his feet and tried not to look anybody in the eye. "Darling, I'll come with you," said Muriel.

"That won't be necessary," said Gary.

"Perhaps not for you," said Muriel firmly, "but for me and Debra it will be."

"Come with us," said Gary to Debra beckoning at the same time to Johnson to escort her to their car.

"There won't be room for you in the car," he said to Muriel. "You'll have to make your own way there."

"Don't worry, I will," said Muriel. "Don't worry," she added turning to Debra. "We'll make sure you get a good solicitor."

"That's not your call," said Gary tersely. "She's an adult. She can make up her own mind."

"Oh, really?" said Muriel. "That's what you think, is it?" She turned to Debra. "Make sure you get a solicitor, love," she stressed.

With that, the two detectives departed with Debra in tow. Muriel, short of breath, raced to get her car and follow them to the station. She arrived about five minutes later than them and there was no sign of them as she approached the front desk at the station. "Where are they?" she asked the sergeant at the front desk as she arrived out of breath. She was a plump woman in her mid-sixties and was finding all this a bit of a strain.

"Where are who?"

"Don't tell me you've had that many visitors tonight. A young girl brought in by two detectives just a few minutes ago."

"They've taken her straight to the interview room."

"Where's that?"

"Nowhere you're going," said the sergeant bluntly.

"She needs help," said Muriel. "She can't look after herself."

"Are you her mother?"

"No," said Muriel. "She's lodging with me at the moment. She's been traumatised. The woman she was living with has been killed."

"You'll just have to wait until they've finished with her."

Muriel sat down and gave a big sigh. "She's had the doctor round earlier today," she said to the sergeant. "He prescribed some tranquillisers. She's not in a fit state to be interviewed."

"The detectives know what they're doing," said the sergeant, "but – if you like – I'll go and tell them you're here."

"Thank you," said Muriel. "Thank you."

The sergeant got up and disappeared inside the station. He knocked on the door of the interview room. "Come in," said Gary's voice. When he got inside the room, he saw that Gary and Ryan Johnson were sitting opposite the young girl who looked terrified. "Well?" asked Gary.

"Just wanted to tell you that the girl's landlady is outside."

"Thank you," said Gary. He then waited until the sergeant had left. "Now, Debra, you understand why you're here?" he continued.

"To answer questions?" she said in a hushed voice.

"Yes," said Gary. "You can have a solicitor present if you feel you need one. We will get one for you. It's your right but, if you're innocent, you've got nothing to fear."

"It's my fault," said Debra.

"You keep saying that," said Gary, "but what's your fault and why?"

"Sue's death. It's my fault. I should have done something."

"Done what?" Debra said nothing. She started fidgeting with her fingers and looked down at the desk top. "Why did she kill herself? Was it out of remorse after the death of Rob Corcoran?"

195

Debra nodded. "Did she kill Rob Corcoran?" Debra shook her head fiercely.

"So why did she feel responsible for his death?" Gary left the question in the air for the moment. He then pretended a sudden thought had struck him. "I've got it," he said. "She felt responsible for his death because you had killed him. Is that right? Did she say she wanted him killed?" Debra nodded. "And you killed him?"

"I should have done something, I could have stopped it."

"What?"

"Sue's death."

Gary leaned forward against the table as if to speak confidentially to Debra. "Look, Debra, if you did kill Rob, it's best to get it off your chest. You'll feel much better. Also, if you're going to be charged with Rob's murder, the court will think much better of you if you've confessed to it and made a clean breast of it. They're bound to be more lenient with you when they know the circumstances."

"I saw them," she said. "On the night of the murder I saw them."

"Saw who?" asked Gary in an irritated voice. "Oh, yes," he said. "I remember you telling me. You saw the police and ambulance staff come round to his house on the night of the murder. That means you were there, doesn't it?"

Debra nodded. "I told Sue."

"You told Sue that you were there on the night of the murder?" Debra nodded. "That you killed him?" Debra remained silent. No matter how hard Gary tried he could not wring a confession to the murder out of her. After a while, though, he tried another tack. "You've been here a while, Debra, and we're going round in circles," he said. "I have to tell you I think you're wasting police time – but we're going to stay here until we've got the truth out of you. Once we've done that, we'll bring this interview to a close and you can rest. I shall get angry if we waste much more police time." Johnson shot a sidelong glance at him. "But if you confess, it'll all be over and we can all three take a break and go to our beds to sleep. You understand me? Now, one more time, Debra, did you kill Rob Corcoran?"

"I....er.... yes." With that, she put her head in her hands and started sobbing.

"You killed Rob Corcoran?"

"Yes," she said still sobbing.

"In that case, Debra Paget, I am arresting you on suspicion of the murder of Rob Corcoran." He cautioned her then added: "I shall take a formal statement from you tomorrow morning in the presence of a solicitor." He looked at Ryan – a smile having formed on his face. "Get a constable to take her to a cell for the night," he said. "We're finished here for the time being."

"Can I go home now?" asked Debra.

"No," said Gary, "you'll be sleeping in a cell tonight."

"But you said we could go home to our beds if I confessed."

"No," said Gary, "I think you'll find I said we could go to bed. Your bed tonight is in the police cell. You've just confessed to murder. You have to stay here." At that stage a constable entered the room and took Debra by the arm to escort her to a cell. She started crying again. "Well," he said – turning to Johnson, "a good night's work, I feel."

"You think so?" said Johnson.

"We've found our killer," he said. "We'll make sure she has legal representation tomorrow, signs her statement, fills in one or two of the details. We'll have her in court before you know it."

"She only confessed because she was tired and wanted a break."

"Where's the evidence for that?"

"Well, you more or less told her everything would be all right if she confessed."

"Did I?", said Gary. "Where's the evidence for that?"

CHAPTER SEVEN

"Colin Standen," said the man propping up the bar offering his hand to Jo to shake.

"Jo from the Philip Rivers detective agency," said Jo accepting the handshake. Jed Coulson smiled in the background – glad that Jo had at last received a friendly welcome on a visit to his pub. "I gather you might have some information for me."

"Yes," said Colin. "I just happened to go out walking my dog at the time Rob Corcoran was killed. I saw a car pull into the cul-de-sac where he lived. The driver just sat behind the wheel as if waiting for something. It was only a few minutes before he was murdered."

"And?"

"Well, I thought she was acting suspiciously."

"She?"

"Yes, it was Rob's wife, Trish. I didn't see her do anything but I know her reasonably well. I know she stands to benefit from his will. They were not divorced. I thought I should tell somebody about it." That should cook her goose and cause her a few unpleasant moments, he thought to himself.

"Thank you," said Jo. "How well do you know her?"

"Oh, we're just acquaintances. Drinking buddies if you like."

"I wondered if you'd ever had a chat with her about Rob?"

"Oh, nothing substantial. I think she was pretty sore about him gallivanting with all those women."

"Gallivanting?"

"Going out with. Flirting with. Shagging, I suppose."

"Did she have hopes of getting back together with him, do you think?"

"Oh, no, not at all. She was fed up with the way he behaved when they were married." Colin smiled a little and gave a nervous laugh. "She was quite keen to get her hands on his money in the event of his death but, of course, he'd have to have died before he settled down with somebody else for that to happen."

"Keen enough to have wanted him to die before he married someone else? Keen enough to speed that process along?"

"Come, now, Mr....?" He realised he did not know Jo's surname.

"Jo. The name's Jo."

"Mr Jo. I wouldn't rat on a friend like that and suggest she might have had murder on her mind."

Thank you, thought Jo. I think you are trying to give me that idea. "Of course not," said Jo smiling. "Another pint?"

"Thank you," said Colin handing Jo his glass.

Jo summoned Jed over. "Another pint for my friend here," he said, "and I'll have another coke. Still driving."

"You know, if anybody offers Colin a drink these days, he always says 'yes'," said Jed.

"Bit of a lush?" said Jo now he was out of earshot.

"Not really," said Jed. "Just sad. He lost his job a couple of months ago and hasn't managed to find anything else to do. Great pity really. I thought he might settle down with Trish. They seemed very friendly at one stage."

"They can't be now," said Jo.

"Oh, why?"

"I think he's trying to plant the seed in my mind that she killed Rob."

"No," said Jed – finishing pouring the pint for Colin. "She wouldn't have. She's not the type."

"I bet you say that about all the girls."

"I'd have said that about Sue, too."

Jo raised an eyebrow. "So you don't think she'd have killed herself in a fit of remorse for killing him?"

"I wouldn't have said so – no," he replied.

Jo nodded and walked back to where Colin was standing, handing him his drink. "Thanks for confiding in me," he said.

"No problem. Does the information help you at all?"

"It does in some ways – but then in others it just means another person with a motive for murdering Rob is floating about near his home on her own in the night in question."

Colin supped his ale. It wasn't the original story that he'd planned to tell Jo but then he had developed a motive for dropping Trish in it over the past couple of days and, following his rejection by her the previous day, it was the one he now wanted to tell. As for the other story, well, he thought he might go and see the person concerned and see if he could attract some mileage out of them now that he had lost his way into sharing Trish's fortune. He took his mobile phone out of his pocket and dialled a number. "Planning department?" he asked when somebody answered on the other end of the line. "Could I speak to Roger Broadbent?" he asked.

"I'm sorry, sir, but he's not working with us at the moment," came the reply from the other end of the line.

"Oh." Colin turned his mobile off and determined to go and visit Roger at his home.

Meanwhile, Jo returned to the bar to have a friendly word with Jed before he left. "You know, there's one thing Colin forgot to say when he was dumping on Trish," he said.

"Yes?"

"It puts him in the picture, too. Near Paul's home at the time of the murder. With his dog, mind you. Very difficult to commit a murder if you've got a dog in tow."

"To the best of my knowledge Colin hasn't got a dog," said Jed. "He's never brought a dog in here – and we are a dog friendly pub."

Jo rushed to the door to see if he could catch up the departing Colin to put this point to him but he seemed long gone. It was a stupid claim to make, thought Jo – that he was walking his dog if he didn't have one. So easy to check on.

• • ● • •

"Right," said Gary, "are we ready to bring Debra back to the interview room?"

"Are you sure we're doing the right thing, Gary?" said Ryan Johnson.

"She's confessed to the murder."

"Under duress. A clever lawyer will unearth that."

"We get her to sign a statement today in the presence of her solicitor and we're there," said Gary.

"She's not all there, Gary," insisted Ryan. "Her landlady said she'd been given tranquillisers and she's two bits short of a picnic even before you take that into account."

"She's of an age where she can look after herself, she lives an independent life, she holds down a job. What more do you want?"

"So you think she's got the nous to steal a car and then deliberately run Rob Corcoran over and reverse and go forward over the body – and then dump the car. It's beyond her – always assuming she can drive. And have we checked that out yet?" He could see from the look on Gary's face that the answer was "no". He grimaced but then added: "Then you've got the evidence that Rob wasn't wearing his socks and shoes. He'd been lured out of the house by somebody he knew and trusted and who – more than likely – had to have an accomplice to kill him. She's unlikely to be able to lure him out of the house, anyway. He wouldn't fancy her."

"It doesn't have to be someone Rob fancied who lured him out of the house. She could have pretended to have a message or some information from Sue. You heard her say that Sue wanted to kill Rob – and she would have been fired up by that."

"We say we want to kill people but we don't always mean it."

"Thanks a bunch," said Gary, "So I'm supposed to ignore evidence of murder threats now as well, am I? Come on, Ryan, if we get a collar by the time Detective Chief Inspector Manners comes back from Brighton, it'll be a feather in our caps."

"All right," said Johnson, "but I'm not at all happy about the way things are progressing. Do you really think in your heart of hearts that she did it?"

"Yes," said Gary, "and your unhappiness is noted." But ignored, he said to himself.

• • ● • •

Jo got into the car after his chat with Colin Standen. What next, he thought to himself. The only avenue he hadn't explored was the death of Sue Plummer. He had rung the police station and found out that Francesca wasn't there. Chances were that Gary Clarke wouldn't pass information on to a private investigator so for the moment he would have to wait and see if the police released any information to the media about how Sue Plummer had met her death. The only other source of information would be Sue's flatmate, Debra, who – he saw in the local paper – had been the one to find the body. He drove up to her home and rang the doorbell. There was no reply. However, he was soon accosted by a call from her next door neighbour.

"Can I help you?" asked Muriel.

"Yes, I wanted to speak to – is it Debra Paget? I'm from the Philip Rivers detective agency. Investigating Rob Corcoran's death."

"She's not there." said Muriel. "The police took her away for questioning. They kept her in a cell overnight. I'm very worried about her. I was going to try and get her a solicitor this morning but I really don't know what I'm doing." Muriel sounded flustered.

"All right," said Jo. "Tell me what happened."

"They were very gruff. She was very worried. God knows what she'll say to them." Muriel, a staunch Catholic, crossed herself for taking the Lord's name in vain. "They said they just wanted to question her but that – if she didn't go with them voluntarily – they would arrest her on suspicion of murder. I went down to the station with her. They didn't tell me very much. Just said they were keeping her in overnight because of developments – and there was nothing I could do so I might as well go home." She puffed a bit at her exertions. "Honestly," she said. "I'm too old for all this at my age."

"Never mind," said Jo, touching her on the arm. "I'll take over from here. I just want to alert my boss as to what's happened." He dialled Rivers' number on his mobile phone. "Rivers?" he said when a voice answered at the other end. "Where are you?"

"I'm in the office."

"We've got a development," said Jo. "We think Debra Paget – Sue Plummer's lodger – has been arrested on suspicion of Rob Corcoran's murder. She's down at the police station helping them with their enquiries and has been since early yesterday evening." Jo shot a sidelong glance at Muriel who nodded. "Her landlady thinks she may be in trouble."

Muriel motioned to Jo to give her the telephone. "Mr Rivers?" she said. "Oh, thank God. She needs help. The doctor's put her on tranquillisers and she's not able to cope with heavy questioning. She's also – well, a bit slow – she won't understand the implications of what she's saying."

"All right," he said. "I'll get down to the police station. Has she got a solicitor?"

"I don't know," said Muriel. "I told her to ask for one but I didn't see one arriving at the police station when I was there last night."

"All right," repeated Rivers. "Would you hand me back to Jo?" Muriel did as he asked. "Is this Francesca's decision?"

"No," said Jo. "She's been called away and left Gary Clarke in charge."

"The man who decided the most appropriate action in the immediate aftermath of Rob Corcoran's murder was to threaten me with arrest."

"You're lucky he hasn't taken you in for questioning again."

"I'll get her a solicitor," said Rivers. "Someone who will stand up to Mr Gary Clarke. I'll also ring Francesca. Have you spoken to her?"

"No, I tried but she was on voice mail."

"Did you leave a message?"

"Not at that stage. It wasn't urgent."

"Could I have another word with Mr Rivers?" said Muriel when there was a break in conversation. "Mr Rivers, I didn't know Debra until this shocking death next door. I'm not very well. I've got a heart condition. I don't think I can continue to look after her if she's released from the police station."

If she's released, thought Rivers. That's a very big proviso. "I hear what you say," he said. "Don't worry. I'll sort some accommodation out for her if it comes to that."

"Thank you, Mr Rivers. I didn't want to burden you with all this, though."

"You've done your bit for her," he said. "Now, I must get on." He said goodbye to Jo and then immediately rang Francesca's mobile number. It was still on voice mail and Rivers surmised she might still be in court. "Francesca," he said, "it's Philip Rivers here. Can you get back to me? Your lackey – Gary Clarke – has just arrested Debra Paget. We've got some worries about her fitness to be able to deal with questioning." He then rang a solicitor friend of his in the Finchley area, Richard Wrexham, and asked him to give him the name of someone locally who could handle a client about to be charged with murder.

"Not me," said Wrexham, another acquaintance of Rivers from his days in the Bahamas when he had also met Jo, but he managed to give Rivers a couple of names to work with – the first of which, James Russell, happened to be free that morning after a long night at Barnet police station the night before. Rivers arranged to meet him at the police station in Hertford in half an hour.

• • ● • •

"Right," said Gary as he, Detective Constable Johnson, Debra and a duty solicitor, Charles Rutherford, gathered together in the interview room at the police station. "We are here to conduct a formal interview with Debra Paget about the murder of Rob Corcoran. Before we switch the tape on, I'd just like to recap on what happened last night. Debra, you confessed to the murder of Rob Corcoran?" Debra nodded. "Thank you," he added," but when we put the tape recorder on you will have to speak up for it." He nodded to Johnson who switched on the machine. "Debra, you have pleaded guilty to the murder of Rob Corcoran," he began. Debra nodded. "For the tape, could you speak?" he asked.

"I have," she said nervously. She then hid her face in her hands.

Rutherford leant over to speak to his client. "Debra, are you comfortable with this?" She nodded. "Do you know what's going on?"

"Yes, I'm being questioned about the murder of Rob Corcoran," she said.

"And?"

"I have pleaded guilty to the murder."

"You haven't actually pleaded guilty," said Rutherford. "This is no court of law – but you have confessed to it, as I understand it?"

"Yes," said Debra.

"Right," said Gary, trying to move things on. Gary then went through a formal caution again before adding: "The purpose of this interview is to agree a statement that you can sign about the murder of Rob Corcoran. Before that, though, there are one or two questions I need to ask you. How did you kill him?"

"I'm sorry?" said Debra looking confused.

"How did you kill him? How did he die?"

A look of recognition seemed to dawn on Debra's face. "He was run over by a car."

"Your car?"

"No, I don't have a car."

Gary swallowed. His next question was crucial. "Do you drive?"

"Yes." Gary shot a sidelong glance at Johnson with a broad smile on his face as if to say "thank goodness".

"What kind of car do you have?"

"I drive Sue's car sometimes. I've passed my driving test."

"What kind of a car is it?"

"It's a red one."

"No," said Gary, "the make?"

"What?"

"He wants to know what make of car it was," intervened Rutherford. "What type of car it was – not the colour."

"Oh. It was a Fiat. I don't know more than that."

"And did you use that car to kill Rob Corcoran?"

"No."

"Oh," said Gary. "You stole a car, then?"

Debra just stared at Gary. "Answer his question," said Rutherford, " or – if you don't want to – just say 'no comment'."

"No comment," said Debra.

Gary sighed. If she was confessing to murder, why would she be so reluctant to admit to stealing the car? "You said Rob Corcoran was killed as a result of being run over by a car?" he asked.

"Yes."

"What kind of car was it?"

"It was a Skoda Octavia."

"And what happened?"

"He came out into the road and the car ran him over."

"The car you were driving."

"No comment."

"You have already said you killed him and that he was run over by this car – the Skoda – so surely it's a logical assumption to make that you were driving the car."

Debra was listening to him intently and replied. She thought for a moment and then repeated his words. "Yes. It is a logical assumption."

"So you ran him over – and then what happened?"

"The car reversed over the body and then drove over him again before driving off."

"Before you drove off in it?" Debra nodded. "For the tape, please," said Gary. Debra started crying. "It must have been you driving the car if you killed him," said Gary exasperated. She could feel the exasperation in his voice. She did not want to go through the same aggressive – as she saw it – questioning as she had faced the previous evening. "You're right," she said. "It must have been."

"Good," he said. It all fitted in. The tyre marks on the body and around it had been shown to be compatible with a Skoda Octavia. In fact, it was one of the first cars that the pathologist had named as being responsible for Rob's death. In addition, the car did knock him down, reverse over the body and then drive away. None of these facts could have been known to Debra unless she had been a party to the accident. "Now," he said, "where is the car now?"

"I dunno," she said.

"Did you dump it?"

"I ....er...."

"Well, it's not in Rob's street. It must be somewhere else."

"Yes."

"Where? Did you dump it somewhere? Have you forgotten where you dumped it?"

"I don't know where it is," she said firmly before crying again and resting her head in her hands.

"I think my client is finding this very stressful," said Rutherford.

"Maybe it's time to take a break?"

"We could have a break and get together a statement from what Debra has just said," said Gary, "but there are a few more questions I wanted to ask." Rutherford acquiesced to his request. "Why did you kill him?"

"Sue wanted to kill him."

"And you thought you would be pleasing her if you killed him?"

"I thought he deserved to die because of what he did to Sue."

"I see."

At this stage Johnson intervened. "I've got one question, Debra," he said. "How did you lure Rob Corcoran out into the street that night in order to run him over?" She looked at him as if she did not understand the question. He repeated it but she still remained silent.

"Debra?" prompted Rutherford.

A look of understanding came over her face. "Oh, yes," she said. "No comment."

"Debra," said Gary earnestly sitting forward in his seat until his face was only a few inches from her. "You've confessed to the murder. There's no point in you saying 'no comment' to events that are put to you surrounding the night of the murder. The court will be much more pleased with you if you answer the questions – and you want that, don't you?"

Debra did not respond. She buried her face in her hands again. "I really think the time has come for a break," said Rutherford.

"All right," said Gary. "We'll draft a statement for you to sign from what you have said. We'll show it to you and you can suggest amendments to anything you disagree with but – for the present – interviewed terminated at – he glanced at his watch – 11.48am." Johnson switched the tape recorder off and he and Gary then left the room with the tape recording.

Rutherford turned to Debra. "Can I get you something to drink – or eat?" he asked. A constable entered the room -– presumably to chaperone Debra during the break in proceedings. "I could organise for you to be taken back to your cell if you wanted a break – to sleep," said Rutherford.

"I don't want to go back there again," she said firmly. "I want to go home. I want to go home to Sue's house."

"I don't think that's going to be possible," said Rutherford. "You have confessed to a murder. You did do it, didn't you?"

She sighed. "It wouldn't be safe to go back there, anyway, I suppose," she said. "Best to stay here. Make the best of a bad job. That's what my mother always used to say."

"I asked you a question," repeated Rutherford. "You did do it, didn't you?"

"I confessed, didn't I?" she said a touch of anger entering her voice.

"I'll go and get us some food and drink," he said. He smiled at the police constable as he made his way from the room – returning a few minutes later with some tea and some sandwiches. He passed one packet of sandwiches to Debra plus a cup of tea. She just nibbled at the sandwiches but drank the tea quickly. It was not long before Clarke and Johnson re-entered the room.

"We've drafted a statement," said Gary. He gave copies to Debra and Rutherford who read it carefully. "I don't think you'll find there's anything there you would disagree with. It just gives details of who you are and your confession that you killed Rob Corcoran. It describes how he was killed and what your motive was for killing him. If you could sign it, we'll get it entered into the records." Johnson switched the tape recorder back on again and Clarke described the process they were going through and the details of the statement. He paused for a few moments until Debra looked up from reading the statement. "If you'd sign it." He reached across the table. "just here," he said pointing to the line where she should sign.

Debra was looking white as a sheet. She leant forward to take a pen from Gary's hand but suddenly slipped from her chair and ended up motionless on the floor. Rutherford looked concerned. "She's fainted," he said. "Get medical help." He got off his seat and leant down beside her. As he did so, she struggled to rise from the floor. "Are you all right?" he asked.

"I felt faint," she said. Clarke and Johnson were just staring at her. "Get some help," said Rutherford angrily. "In fact, we should get an ambulance to take her to hospital. We need to get her checked over."

"We could take her in a police car," said Johnson. "It would be quicker," Rutherford nodded and Johnson left the room to make arrangements for Debra to be taken to hospital.

• • ● • •

Rivers arrived at the police station with solicitor James Russell in tow just in time to see Debra being carried off in a police car to the local hospital. Rutherford, the duty solicitor, had helped her into it and turned round to go back inside the station.

"Excuse me," said Rivers. "Who are you?"

"He's the duty solicitor," said Russell. "Charles Rutherford."

"What's happened?"

"I'm sorry," said Rutherford, "and you are?"

"My name's Rivers," he said. "I'm a private detective." He showed his card to Rutherford. "At the moment I'm looking after Debra Paget's interests."

"And who's authorised you to do that?"

"I have," Rivers said. "It doesn't look as if anybody else is so I've taken it upon myself."

"Very noble, but you have no jurisdiction here."

"Precisely what I was going to say," said Gary Clarke who came out into the forecourt at this juncture. "I just wondered how she was," he asked Rutherford.

At this stage James Russell intervened. "Actually, Charles, it's you who've got no jurisdiction from this point onwards," he said. "I've been hired to represent her."

"Who hired you?"

"That's irrelevant. The point is I am now her legal representative."

"Has she consented to this?"

"I was just going to ask her but she appears to have fainted as a result of the oppressive treatment she's received at this police station," he said.

"Steady on," said Gary. "Oppressive?"

"Yes, oppressive. She is an adult who is a slow learner and has difficulty understanding complex issues. Can I ask you, Detective....?"

"Detective Constable Gary Clarke," said Gary.

"Detective Constable Gary Clarke, has she been accompanied and represented throughout the interview process here?"

"Mr Rutherford has been representing her."

"I gather she was brought into the station for questioning last night. Was he representing her then?"

"She waived her right to representation."

"Oh, she waived her right to representation and then no doubt – after you had kindly found her accommodation for the night – sat down and completed an A-level chemistry paper before you woke her for breakfast."

Gary stared at him uncomprehending. "I'm sorry," he said. "An A-level in chemistry? What's that about?"

"I'm being sarcastic. What is the state of play with my client?"

"She's confessed to murdering Rob Corcoran," said Gary trying to summon up a triumphant edge to his voice."

"I see – and this confession was made when?"

"Last night."

"When she was alone and unrepresented."

"She confirmed her confession this morning and we have drafted a statement for her to sign before submitting the papers to the Crown Prosecution Service asking it to give us the go ahead to charge her."

"A state of affairs which so alarmed her that she fainted and has had to be carted off to hospital." He turned to Rutherford. "Are you still here?" he asked irritatedly. Rutherford shuffled off without saying his goodbyes. "Now, Detective Constable Gary Clarke, I'd like you to do a few things for me. One, could you furnish me with a copy of the statement." Gary handed him one. "Which I see is unsigned."

"She was going to sign it when she fainted."

"Oh, of course. She didn't faint, you don't think, when she realised the enormity of what she had done?"

"She was not pressurised into anything," he said.

"No, of course not. I expect she faints all the time."

It was Rivers turn to intervene. "Do you seriously think that she has the wherewithal to arrange to steal a car and then run Rob Corcoran over three times?"

"She described the car she stole and the method of death accurately," said Clarke.

"I'd like to have a copy of the tape recording you made of the interview you did with her this morning. I think if you pursue this matter to a charge or a trial – we shall be taking legal steps to declare that confession null and void."

"I'll get you a copy of the tape," volunteered Johnson. He left the gathering outside the police station.

"I think – when we've got that – we should repair to the hospital to consult with Debra about all this."

Rivers nodded. "But don't think you've heard the last of this," he said to Clarke. "I shall be in touch with your superiors about the way you've handled this – frightening a vulnerable young woman not to say worrying an elderly woman with heart trouble, too."

"I still think she's guilty of murder," said Clarke.

"If I were you, I'd hold on to that thought," said Rivers. "I don't think that anybody else will be doing so."

• • • • •

Clarke and Johnson had few words to say to each other as they made their way back to the office. It was only when they inside that the ice between them broke. "Well," said Clarke, "say something."

"I said all I had to say earlier this morning," Johnson replied. "I think we were wrong."

"Very charitable of you to say 'we'," noted Gary. He sat down at his desk and the telephone rang. He picked it up. "Yes," he growled irritatedly into the receiver. He listened intently to the caller for a moment. "Thank you," he said indicating the call had finished. Oh, and well done." He turned to his fellow detective constable. "That was traffic. They've found the car that ran over Rob Corcoran. It's a Skoda Octavia. Been found in a field outside Hertford. There's some blood on the front bumper which is consistent with it being involved in an accident and knocking someone down. We're having it checked out to see if it's a match with Rob. The pathologist is doing it now."

"Great," said Clarke.

"By the way, talking about the pathologist. Have you got back to him?"

"About what?"

"The post mortem into Sue Plummer's death. He rang yesterday and three times this morning."

"I was interviewing a suspect."

"Seems he thinks he's got some important news for you."

"What's that?"

"Well, he wouldn't tell me. You'd better ring him. He did drop a copy of his report by, though, this morning. I left it on your desk."

Clarke rummaged around and soon found it. "What's that?" asked Johnson.

"The post mortem into Sue Plummer's death." He began reading it. After a while, he let rip an expletive. "Christ," she said. "She was murdered."

"Murdered?"

"Apparently, she was drugged up to the eyeballs. There are also bruise marks to the upper part of her body – and blood from a scratch mark on her leg which was probably caused when it came into contact with a nail. The pathologist has surveyed the bedroom where she was found and says there is such a nail in the bedroom which itself has a splattering of blood on it. The bruise marks, he says, could have been caused by trying to lift the body and hang it from the light fitting. In other words, she was drugged and then hung from the light fitting by somebody else – someone who murdered her."

"Wow," said Johnson, "and we could have had this information yesterday afternoon."

Gary sighed. "It would appear so."

"Before we brought in Debra Paget for questioning?"

"I still think there's a strong case against her."

"Do me a favour," said Johnson. "Our case against Debra rested partially on the fact that Sue Plummer had so much remorse about encouraging Debra to kill Rob Corcoran that she went and hanged herself. If she didn't, where does that leave us? Are we saying she killed Sue Plummer as well?"

"Maybe," said Gary slowly. "Maybe she was so shocked at what she had done that she decided to confide in Sue – but Sue wasn't as sympathetic as she thought she would be. She realised that – in order to escape prosecution – she now had to get rid of Sue as well."

"Do me a favour," said Johnson. "She worshipped Sue Plummer. She would never have killed her. No, if it's murder, it must have surely been committed by the same person who killed Rob Corcoran. It would have had to be committed by someone with a fair amount of strength to have dragged her drugged body around the bedroom and hung it from the light fitting. Not someone undernourished like Debra."

"So what do we do now?" said Gary.

"We grovel as unobtrusively as we can and apologise to Debra for her arrest."

"I suppose so," said Gary reluctantly. "Would you go down to the hospital and explain the situation to her?"

"No," said Johnson, "I think this is one for you."

"I am in charge of this investigation."

"Precisely," said Johnson. He was tempted to add but for how long.

"Come on, let's go," he said, making his way out of the office. "Give me some moral support at least," he said. When they arrived at the hospital, they found Debra lying on a bed in the accident and emergency department. Rivers was still with her – as was a police constable. "You can go now," Gary said to the constable. "I have some news," began Gary gravely. "There have been some fresh developments."

"Oh," said Rivers."

"The post mortem on Sue Plummer. It indicates she was murdered." Debra gave a little gasp. "I should probably convey this information to your solicitor, Miss Paget."

"You can tell her," said Rivers. "And me."

"Well, we have no evidence linking you with the murder of Sue Plummer and there is good reason to think that the murders of both Miss Plummer and Mr Corcoran are linked, so that means we shall be dropping criminal proceedings against you."

"And admitting that you held her under duress – extracting a confession from her?"

Gary ignored the remark. "So, when you're discharged from here, you're free to go – back to your home." A smile came over Debra's face. "I'm sorry," Gary added to Rivers. "I really did think I was doing the right thing."

"That's what's really worrying," said Rivers. "Your initial reaction to Rob Corcoran's death was to try and arrest me on some charge or other, your next reaction was to go for the most vulnerable person and try and break her."

They were interrupted by the return of the consultant who had been dealing with Debra to say that they could find nothing wrong with her and that the fainting must have been caused by stress and brought on by under-nourishment. She told her to take it easy but that she was being discharged. "Is there somebody to look after you at home?" she asked.

"No, but I'm staying with a neighbour."

"I don't think that option is open to you anymore," said Rivers. "Muriel is reporting suffering from stress as a result of what's happened,"

"I'm not letting you go back to live by yourself – without help. You need at least a week's rest to recover," said the consultant.

"All right," said Rivers. "She can stay with me. I'll just have to square it with my wife, Nikki."

Gary got up to leave. "So we can find you at Mr Rivers' address if we need to talk to you again," he said.

"You won't need to," said Rivers. "Or at least if you do, you won't be welcome."

• • ● • •

The hedgerow in Roger Broadbent's front garden looked overgrown, thought Colin Standen as he approached the house. That morning's papers were still stuck in the letter box even thought it was two o'clock in the afternoon. Everything about the house spoke of neglect, he thought. Ah, well, I've come to add one more bit of misery to his life, he thought. He rang the doorbell. After what seemed an age, Roger opened the door. He was wearing a dressing gown over underpants and a shirt stained with tomato ketchup and bacon grease.

"Yes?" he said sharply.

"Roger," he said. "It's Colin. Colin Standen from the Dog and Partridge. I don't know if you remember me."

"It's a long time since I've been in there," he said. "What

brings you out this way?" he asked suspiciously.

"It's Rob Corcoran's murder," he said. "I have a bit of information I wanted to talk over with you before I decided whether to pass it on to the police."

"Oh." Roger sounded less than enthusiastic at receiving this news.

"Could I come in?" he asked.

"I'd rather you didn't. It's a bit inconvenient."

"I won't stand on ceremony. It's just that I don't like discussing private business on the doorstep."

"Why not? Nobody can hear." Roger's home was a way away from his nearest neighbour's. However, in the end, he relented and allowed Colin inside. The interior of the house was as badly looked after as the outside, Colin realised. Several plates with food stains on them had been left in various parts of the living room. "Now, say your piece," said Roger, a touch aggressively.

"It's just that – on Tuesday evening – I saw you coming out of Rob Corcoran's home."

"Yes," said Roger. "You would have done. So what?"

"That was the night that he was murdered."

"But he wasn't murdered in his house – and I wasn't coming out of it at the time he was murdered. It was a good hour and a half beforehand."

"Why were you visiting him?"

"That's none of your business," said Roger tersely.

"But it will be the police's business and – once I tell them what I know – they'll be round here as quick as a flash to ask you questions. You need to work out what you're going to tell them." Roger decided not to react to Colin's comments. "There is another way round this," suggested Colin tentatively.

"Oh, yes?"

"Give me some money and I'll forget all about it."

"So that's it. You've come to bribe me. How much do you want?"

"I was thinking of about £1,000," said Colin.

"Bollocks."

"Ok, you tell me how much you think my silence is worth. Aren't you forgetting one thing?"

"What's that?"

"Well, let's think for a moment about what the reason for your visit could be. It's well known Rob was making enquiries into what he thought was evidence of corruption in the planning department. The only reason you would have gone round to his place is to have asked him to drop his investigations. Now, if he said no, you might have felt it was necessary to take more extreme action to stop him uncovering more evidence. I'm sure that's what the police will think."

"And if I took that more extreme action and killed him aren't you in rather a worrying situation? I assume you haven't told anybody you're here – so it would be easy for me to engineer you disappearing without trace. On the other hand, if you don't believe I killed him, why should the police? And why should I pay you £1,000?"

"To avoid the embarrassment over being questioned about being involved in a murder at a time when you're at your lowest ebb. I can see you're not coping. You've presumably been suspended from work?"

"I don't think I want to continue this conversation with you," said Roger. He walked to the front door and opened it. "Kindly go," he said. "You know, I always thought the Dog and Partridge catered for an altogether more discerning class of person than a filthy blackmailer."

Colin got up to go. "I hope you won't be sorry about your decision," he said.

"I'm sorry about a lot of things," he said. "I'm sorry about getting involved with the wrong kind of people through my work at the planning department, I'm sorry about being suspended from work which could lead to me forfeiting my income if things go badly for me – but I'm not sorry about making the decision to have no truck with you."

He watched as Colin disappeared down the driveway. He felt a bit more self-confident about himself after having turned him away. It would have been easy to pay him off – and not risk a police investigation into his dealings with Rob Corcoran. After all, he still had the wherewithal to do so as his wages were still being paid while he was suspended. In the long run, though, could he have guaranteed that Colin would not have come back for more money? He thought not.

Colin, meanwhile, trudged away wearily – his attempt to earn himself an extra crust having been thwarted. He decided to go and spent what little money he had on a pint in the Dog and Partridge. As luck would have it, the recipient of his earlier attempt to try and spread information about Rob Corcoran's murder was also there. Jo came over to him. "I've got something to ask you," he said.

"What?" asked Colin.

"It may seem a trivial matter – but you said you saw Rob's wife's car outside his home while you were walking your dog. According to Jed Coulson, who probably knows you as well as anybody, you don't have a dog."

"Slip of the tongue," he said. "I walk the dog of a friend of mine who's not so mobile as I am."

"I see," said Jo.

"Can I interest you in some more information?"

"What?"

"I also saw Roger Broadbent from the planning department visiting Rob Corcoran at his home on the night of the murder."

"At what time?"

"About seven o'clock."

"Well before the murder?"

"Yes, but he could have come back."

"In which case you would have seen him because you were

walking somebody else's dog and saw Rob's wife hanging around the area. Frankly, Mr Standen, I don't know whether to believe anything you say – although I can't quite work out what benefit you get from passing on duff information. Perhaps you just want to make mischief for people."

"No," protested Colin. "I just want to help."

"I don't believe you, I'm afraid."

• • ● • •

Miranda stretched out in the double bed and yawned. Aaron was no longer with her – he had had to get up to go out to work. It was no slight. She smiled to herself. It was the first night they had spent together since that awful Sunday night when she had found out that Rob Corcoran had been cheating on her. Perhaps things could go back to where they were – especially as Rob was no longer around to offer a distraction. Her thoughts were interrupted as Aaron returned from the bathroom.

"I won't be too late tonight," he said. "Perhaps we could go out for a bite this evening?"

She sat up on the bed and smiled at her. "A sort of celebration meal?" she said.

"That might be pushing it too far," said Aaron. "Just a recognition that we're back together again." He walked half-dressed towards the bed. "I do realise that my neglect of you played a part in all this," he said taking her hand in his. "For that part, I'm sorry."

"And I'm sorry for what I did." She did not feel it was necessary to elaborate on what that was. She kissed his hand and seemed deep in thought. "What would you say to us going away for a few days?" she asked.

"I'd love to," he said. "What do you have in mind?"

"I don't know. Just a cottage in the country or something. I need to get away from all this talk of murder. Honestly, I feel like I'm the prime suspect in the eyes of that detective."

"I think you are," said Aaron.

"I suppose, though, we don't need to worry about him," she said. "It would be a different matter if he was the police."

"Ah, the police," said Aaron. "You know, I think the most sensible thing I have done over the last fortnight was to go and punch Rob Corcoran's lights out."

"How do you come to that conclusion?"

"Well, if I hadn't assaulted him, I'd never have been interviewed by the police on the night of Rob Corcoran's murder and never had had the most watertight of alibis."

"I suppose there is that," said Miranda.

"You know," he continued, "I think they're also going to drop any suggestion of an assault charge against me. After all, it becomes small beer now he's been murdered. That's something to celebrate tonight, too."

"For you, not me," said Miranda.

Aaron looked at her thoughtfully. "Are you ever going to tell me where you were between leaving Jackie's flat that night and returning home at 10 o'clock."

"If you must know I decided to go for a drink with Sue before meeting up with Jackie again."

"Where did you go? Not the Dog and Partridge, I hope."

"No, it was a pub on the road back into the centre of town from Jackie's place. I can't remember the name of it. We just agreed to meet in the first pub we came across. It was choc a bloc with people, though, so I don't suppose anyone would remember me."

"So you've just put forward another alibi that cannot be corroborated?" said Aaron.

"That's why I didn't mention it to that detective."

• • ● • •

Bruiser pulled into the car park at Rivers' block of flats. "Right then," he said turning to Eel. "Are we ready?"

"I am," said Eel. "You just sit in the car and wait." He glanced at his watch. "It's three o'clock in the afternoon. We've got a couple of hours before Mrs Rivers comes back from work."

"You don't need help?"

"No, and the last thing we want is you frightening the neighbours." Eel had a respectable suit on that day – the sort that would help him blend in with the business people and office staff who lived in Rivers' block of flats. He wore a trilby, too. Bruiser was still sporting jeans and a leather jacket.

"Okay," said Bruiser reluctantly.

"Shame we didn't bring a paper so that you could do the crossword," said Eel.

"I ain't doing no fucking crossword," said Bruiser.

"No," said Eel. "I'm sure you're right there." With that, he got out of the car and walked over to the entrance to Rivers' block of flats. As luck would have it, a woman with a baby in a buggy arrived at the doorway a few minutes later. Eel, who had been standing in a nearby alley way, emerged as she struggled with opening the door and held it for her until she had got the buggy inside. He then followed her in.

"Thank you," she said as she made her way to one of the ground floor flats. Eel doffed his trilby and then set off in search of flat number eight – the number that the intercom said was inhabited by Rivers and Hofmeyr. Hofmeyr, he reasoned, must have been Nikki's maiden name. He soon found it and – assuring himself that no-one was looking – managed to pick the lock and get inside Rivers' flat.

Once inside, he had a quick look round. There was a photograph on the mantelpiece – a foursome. Rivers and his wife were smartly dressed – as were another couple. Eel reasoned it must have been a wedding photograph. Not quite the sort of thing he'd had in mind, he thought. He went into the main bedroom – and there on the table by the side of the bed was a picture of just Rivers and his wife. Just the ticket, he thought. He took it out of the frame and brought a sharp knife out of his pocket. He sliced the photograph down the middle – thus separating Rivers from his wife. He donned gloves now and carefully put the photograph of Rivers back in the frame and placed the one of the private detective's wife in an envelope he brought out from his pocket. He looked at his watch. He still had a little time left. He wondered whether to trash the flat in an obvious statement to its occupants that he had gained access to it. No, he thought. That might just tip them over the edge and make them call the police. Just the subtle doctoring of the photograph would be enough to make them wonder what on earth the intruder was up to. He took one last look at the photograph as he left the bedroom. That would be enough to put Rivers on edge. He made his way back to Bruiser's van. "Got what I wanted," he said – brandishing the photograph in front of Bruiser's eyes.

"What do we do now then?""

"We send it to Rivers," he said.

"Oh, great. Like that's going to scare him off."

"It'll make him realise we can get access to the flat and that we plan to target his wife if he doesn't drop this investigation he's doing."

"I don't see it," said Bruiser.

"You will do," said Eel. "You will do." So saying he brought the sharp knife out of his pocket again and carefully carved one of Nikki's fingers off from the photograph. "That," said Eel, "we will tell him, is what will happen to his wife if he doesn't drop the investigation he's pursuing."

"Great. So we kidnap her?"

"You're catching on, Bruiser. That's exactly what we'll do."

Bruiser smiled – giving himself a mental pat on the back for his foresight in understanding what the plan was. "When do we do it?" he asked.

"Tomorrow – or the day after," said Eel. "We need to have concrete signs that he's going on with the investigation before we do."

"And if he drops it?"

"We drop the kidnap plot." Bruiser seemed a little disappointed at this. "I don't think he will," Eel added.

• • ● • •

Rivers took his mobile phone out of his pocket as he left the hospital that afternoon. He saw it was Francesca on the other end of the line.

"I'm sorry not to have got back to you earlier," she said. "What's happening?"

"Have you been in touch with your deputy, Gary Clarke?"

"No," she said. "I've tried but he doesn't seem to be answering his mobile."

"I'm not surprised," said Rivers. "With any luck he's ashamed of what he's done."

"What has he done?"

"Arrested Debra Paget, grilled her for hours on end and broken her until she confessed to murdering Rob Corcoran. He then tried to get the facts to bolster up the story. He's failed, though, but not before Debra ended up in hospital as a result of a fainting fit."

"Oh."

"Is that all you can say?"

"Philip, I've been in court the last couple of days. There was nothing I could have done to restrain him."

"Sorry," said Rivers. "It's just that I'm a bit mad about what's happened. She's a vulnerable girl. She needs help not bullying. The woman who was looking after her, her next door neighbour, was also suffering from stress and she's had to stop looking after her, too."

"We need to get social services involved."

"She'll hardly be a priority," said Rivers. "Anyhow, the bleeding hearts have come to the rescue."

"Oh, good. Who? I take it from the phrase you used it's not some official agency."

"No, I'm definitely not that."

"You?"

"Yes, Nikki and I have taken her in for our sins."

"I'm pleased." said Francesca.

"I'll give you my verdict on my feelings in a couple of days' time," said Rivers. "Anyhow, are you coming back?"

"Yes, the court case is over. I should be back in harness tomorrow morning."

"Well, after you've bollocked Mr Clarke, perhaps we should have a catch up."

"Bollocking Mr Clarke, as you so neatly put it, is not as easy as it sounds. He's the Chief Constable's nephew."

"I'm sure you can find a way round that," said Rivers.

"What do you mean?" asked Francesca with a heavy emphasis on the word "do".

"Well, the Francesca Manners I know wouldn't let a senior officer let alone a subordinate get away with doing something that she knew was wrong."

"I'll take that as a compliment," she replied. "Until tomorrow then?"

"Until tomorrow."

● ● ● ● ●

Adrian Paul looked out of the window at his home after he heard the knock at the door. He could see a colleague of his – the Chief Constable from Lincolnshire, Ray Ellis, who was supposed to be conducting the hearing into Francesca's allegation that he had made unwanted advances to her – standing in the driveway.

"This is a surprise, Ray," he said as he opened the door. "A nice surprise – even though I would have thought a little bit unethical. Come on in."

"I'm sorry you see it that way," said the other man. "This is not an official visit, Adrian. I just thought that – as colleagues over the last few years – you might appreciate an honest appraisal of where you stand."

"Where I stand?" he said. "Do you not mean where you stand?"

"You're in trouble, Adrian. I'll not mince my words."

"Tell me about it."

"What are you planning to do?"

"Well, there's no point in denying that I made an advance to Detective Chief Inspector Manners. She's got it on tape."

"Exactly."

"I wanted to pass it off as a moment of madness. She's a very attractive woman and I feel I fell below the moral standards that we as a force set ourselves. I thought I would apologise."

"Stop clutching at straws, Adrian."

"What?"

"You know you don't mean that."

"Well," he said. "I'm not so sure."

"I am, Adrian." The Lincolnshire man sat down in a chair opposite Paul's desk. "Are you aware of what's happened since she made her complaint?"

"Well, I've been suspended. I'm facing a disciplinary hearing. Some colleagues have offered me their support and others have shunned me."

"And what support can those who have offered to help you realistically give you?"

"Well, they can give me character references. You know the sort of thing. Entirely out of character for the Chief Constable who's been a fine and outstanding police officer. That sort of thing."

"In other words, diddly squat. That sort of help is going to be of no use to you." Ellis started toying with a paperweight on the desk in Paul's living room. "The thing is," he said leaning forward in his chair,"it's not entirely out of character, is it?"

"What?"

"Adrian, since Detective Chief Inspector Manners' allegations became known and people realised you had been suspended, there have been four other allegations made against you."

"What?"

"Four other allegations made against you."

"Who?" said Paul sounding exasperated.

Ray Ellis reached into his brief case and brought out a sheaf of papers. "Two of the women you took to the safe house and had sex with," he said. "You offered them advancement. In one case you managed to deliver on your promise. In the other, the woman left the Hertfordshire force and was transferred elsewhere to avoid her becoming – I think the word you used was 'troublesome'. Do I need to remind you of their names? Are there so many others that have not come forward?"

Paul buried his face in his hands. "No, you don't need to."

"The other two – like Detective Chief Inspector Manners – declined your advancement. You were as good as your word to them, too. They got no advancement. They claimed they were almost shunned by your senior management team. As a result, one of them left the force altogether – the other one struggled on in her post until she got a transfer to another force."

"They didn't come forward at the time, though."

"Which is irrelevant, Adrian. The point is they have now – and this is all going to come out at your disciplinary hearing."

Paul nodded. He clasped his hands together and looked at his fellow officer in the eyes. "So what do you want me to do?"

"It's not a question of what I want you to do. You have to make the decision yourself. My advice to you is the best course of action you could take is to resign."

"Resign? But I've got five years of service before I become eligible for my pension. And what about my marriage?"

"You don't seem to have been considering the effects on that while you were pursuing these female officers, Adrian. As to having five years until you become eligible for your pension, do you honestly think you're going to make it through to then in the force?"

Paul looked crestfallen. "Serving in the police force has been my life," he said.

"It's not the end of the world," said Ray Ellis. He dived into his briefcase again and brought out another brochure. "See this," he said waving it at Paul. "A shopping development on my patch. Opening later this year. They need a head of security."

Paul reached out across the table. "It's in Lincolnshire," he said tentatively.

"Well spotted Adrian," said the other man, "but it's the only area I have influence in. Now, I've spoken to the managing director of the company running this, and he agrees with me – you have all the credentials necessary to do a fine job for them."

"Have you told them about – about my dilemma?"

"Yes, and they're willing to overlook that for your expertise," said the Lincolnshire man. "Of course, if you were to start propositioning the women who work for them, I think it would be curtains for you."

"There's no danger of that, Ray," he said.

"We'll see," came the reply. "You know, Adrian, I would never have thought in a million years that you would have been guilty of something like this – making inappropriate sexual advances to female officers – so I take your promise with a pinch of salt. Fortunately for you, the head of this development takes a different view and the fact that he does neatly wraps things up for us. It gets you out of the way without ruining your family's financial stability." He started to put the allegations from the four other police officers back in his brief case but left the brochure about the shopping development on the table. "You know, Adrian, I hold no brief for making your family suffer," he said when he had completed the task. "Only you – and I know you will suffer if you have to resign from the force in ignominy."

"Yes," said Paul slowly.

"So what's it to be, then, Adrian?"

"My resignation letter will be with the powers that be tomorrow morning," he said reluctantly.

"Good," said Ray Ellis. "That way we can avoid unfortunate publicity for the force dragging on for months to come. We can make a clean breast of this and find a suitable replacement for you whose not going to place his grubby paws up the skirts of female officers in the force. Good-day, Adrian."

Adrian Paul got up from his desk. He offered his hand to Ray Ellis for a handshake. "Good-day, Ray," he said.

Ray Ellis refused the offer of the handshake. "For the record, Adrian, I think you're a disgrace to the force," he said. With that he made his way to the front door. "You'll be hearing from the managing director of the shopping development by the weekend," he said. "With any luck, I shall never set eyes on you again."

CHAPTER EIGHT

"The man's a waste of space," said Jo to Rivers. "You can't believe a word he says."

"I know you think that," Rivers replied, "but you should still check them out. He may just have uncovered something. Leave no stone unturned."

"Anyhow, what does it mean if Roger Broadbent did visit Rob Corcoran on the night of the murder? No-one saw him go back later."

"Shows he was concerned about the hornet's nest Rob Corcoran was stirring up. If he felt he was getting nowhere, you never know. It could have driven him to murder. There's certainly a motive there."

"Well, if you think I should I will, of course. What about Standen himself? I said to him if you saw Trish Corcoran there on the Tuesday night at the time of the murder doesn't that you mean you were there as well."

"With his dog. Clear that bit up. Find out whether he did walk a neighbour's dog. If he didn't, I'll grant you it makes his evidence less compelling."

"I'll get on to it," said Jo.

Rivers nodded. The two of them were in the office alone which, Rivers believed, made it easier for him to broach his next subject. "Jo," he said tentatively.

"Yes?"

"We've got a new lodger."

"Oh, who?"

"Debra Paget."

"Debra Paget? Can we take on responsibility for her?"

"She's been through a lot. She has no-one else to turn to. It'll only be temporary."

"What makes you think she has us to turn to? We're private detectives investigating a murder? We're not a branch of social services."

"Jo, I would have thought that you of all people would have wanted to show her compassion."

"Why me of all people?"

"You're against discrimination. Race, sex, disability. You would, I think, believe that anyone in these categories struggling to cope deserves support."

"Oh, so you'd lump us all together – the ethnics, the women and the disabled. We all need you to be bountiful towards us."

"I'm not being bountiful towards you. I'm not being bountiful towards her. I just believe she needs a helping hand at this stage. You don't. You're more than capable of standing on your own two feet."

"Thanks for that vote of confidence," said Jo. "I'm sorry, Rivers. I shouldn't have jumped down your throat but it does bring me to something I wanted to say to you. I'm looking for my own accommodation."

"Fine," said Rivers.

"If I'm to have a social life outside of the office, then I need to have my own place. Your flat is a nice pied a terre for a married couple – or any kind of a couple, I guess. Three's a crowd. Four certainly is."

"Three's a crowd," ruminated Rivers. "I guess that thought could have occurred to Rob Corcoran, too. Miranda, Jackie and Sue." He changed the subject. "So how are you getting on with Francesca?"

"Well. I haven't seen her for two or three days. As you know, she's been away."

"She's back now. Reading the riot act to Detective Constable Clarke if I'm not mistaken – probably as we speak."

Jo nodded. "So how are we going to cope with this new-found foursome?"

"I'm not asking you to give up your room, you'll be glad to know," said Rivers. "Debra will have to bed down on the settee in the living room. It converts to a bed."

Jo nodded thoughtfully again. "Was there any reason for Detective Constable Clarke to take her in for questioning?" he asked. "Or was it just that he thought he could get a quick collar?"

"She knows more about Sue Plummer than anybody else around here – but it wasn't over Sue's death that he was questioning her." He thought for a moment over Jo's question. "No, there was no reason to question her but she may have some evidence – maybe even evidence that she doesn't know she has – that could help us with Sue's or Rob's deaths. One thing's certain, though, after her treatment from Gary Clarke, she'd certainly be wary of being questioned by anybody again."

• • ● • •

"Good morning, ma'am," said the desk sergeant in an authoritative voice as Francesca entered the police station. Francesca looked at him and smiled. Normally he did not look up from his papers when anybody arrived for work in the morning. As she went through the reception area and headed off towards her office, a senior colleague coming the other way made an elaborate detour to get out of her way. "Don't want to run the risk of brushing up against you," he said. "Could be the ruin of my career."

She smiled a forced smile. If it was meant to be funny and a reference to her complaint about the Chief Constable, she did not share her fellow officer's sense of humour. The funny thing was, though, that she had passed exactly the same officers in the corridor three days previously – after she had submitted the complaint - and he had not given any reaction. She wondered what had happened.

"Good morning, Ryan," she said to Detective Constable Johnson as she entered her office. Johnson was alone in the office – Clarke did not seem to have arrived yet.

"You're back, ma'am," said Johnson as a way of greeting her.

"I can see how you became a detective, Ryan," she said. Her attention returned to the reception she had received. "What's going on out there?"

"What do you mean?"

"Well, people are either avoiding me or being incredibly deferential," she said.

"You haven't heard, then?"

"Haven't heard what?"

"The Chief Constable's resigned. Handed in his notice this morning. The gossip mill suggests there have been four more complaints laid against him following yours. Seems he just couldn't fight it anymore."

Francesca sat down and heaved a sigh of relief. "I'm glad," she said. "I wasn't looking forward to giving evidence to a disciplinary committee."

Before she could get down to any work, Rory Gleeson popped his head round the door. "Could I have a word, Francesca?" She nodded and followed him to his office. "It seems you've brought down the old bugger," he said.

"And you," said Francesca.

Gleeson looked at her in surprise. "What do you mean?"

"Well, I wouldn't have brought him down if you hadn't warned me he was a randy old goat. I don't think those were the exact words you used – but they were the sentiments. I'd never have taken a tape recording along to our supper if you hadn't done that. It would then just have been his word against mine – and the other complainants may never have come forward."

Gleeson blushed. "Probably best not to mention that to anyone else," he said.

"Oh, really?"

He blushed again. "I'm a candidate for his job," he said. "It wouldn't look good if it came out that I had played a part in his downfall – and then stood to gain from it."

Francesca looked at him intently. She wondered if he had had today's outcome in mind when he warned her of Paul's character. She decided it didn't matter. Paul deserved to lose his job over the way he behaved and – if Gleeson had helped bring that about – so much the better. She looked at him again. He would make a fine chief constable. During the evening they had spent at the chief constable's ball, he had never once made a pass at her. Not that that was the only criterion that should be considered in selecting for such a key post. "Don't worry, Rory, I don't intend to say anything to anyone about my part in his downfall – let alone yours."

His blush was replaced by a smile. "Well, I suppose we ought to return to more mundane matters," he said. "You've got two murders on your plate, I understand?"

"Yes."

"Any closer to solving them?"

"I'd like to have a word with Detective Constable Clarke before I answer that," she said, "but I think it's fair to say we've made no progress. Detective Constable Clarke followed his own instinct and arrested a suspect yesterday. It turned out she had nothing to do with it."

"Yes," he said. "I gather she fainted as a result of the interview process and had to be taken to hospital."

"I will have words with Detective Constable Clarke about that," said Francesca.

"Tell him he's no longer the Chief Constable's nephew," said Rory.

"Yes, sir."

"Right," said Rory, "keep me posted on any developments."

Francesca went back to her office. By this time Gary Clarke had emerged and was sitting at his desk. "Ryan." she said.

"Thanks for your help over the last couple of days but we no longer need you now I'm back." She looked at the door and Johnson took the hint to depart. "You don't seem to have made tremendous progress since I left, Gary," she said. "Would you mind telling me why you were so fixated with the idea that Debra Paget did the murder?"

"She seemed to be hiding something," he said. "I wanted to find out what that was."

"So you dragged her down here, convinced her she didn't need a solicitor and wheedled a confession out of her when she could no longer stand up to the questioning you were subjecting her to?"

"She was a functioning adult."

"I'm glad you use the word 'was'," said Francesca. "I'm not so sure she is now after having to go to hospital."

"She was holding down a job and living independently. I don't buy this garbage that she's vulnerable and needs protecting."

"You don't?" queried Francesca. "Do you remember the evidence we collected immediately after Rob Corcoran's murder? That he was lured out of his home by someone who knew him – and then run over by a car – making it quite likely that there were two people involved in the murder. Tell me, was it Debra the Mata Hari that did the luring or was she driving the car that killed him?"

"She accurately described how he was run over – giving more details than we have divulged to the media."

"So you think she drove the car?"

"Yes," he said.

"Right," said Francesca – a note of sarcasm becoming apparent in her voice. "So she drove the car and persuaded someone else to lure Rob Corcoran out of his house? She couldn't have been the lurer. I don't think Rob Corcoran cared much for her."

"Could have been Sue Plummer," said Gary.

"And Debra bossed the operation getting Sue to lure Rob

Corcoran? This also all assumes that she had the nous to steal the car in the first place. Get a grip, Gary. Yes, she lives independently and holds down a job. But she's a slow learner and would never have been able to plan all those things in advance. She was also besotted by Sue Plummer – and a frail young woman. Would she have had the strength to drag Sue Plummer's unconscious body into the bedroom and hang it from the light fitting if you're saying she killed her as well?"

"Sue Plummer could have killed herself out of remorse" began Gary.

"But we have the pathologist's report which says it was murder."

"I wasn't aware of that at the time."

"Only because you were so obsessed with trying to find Debra guilty that you neglected the fact that it was ready and complete."

"I'm sorry, Francesca."

"That's better," she said. "I'd rather have you apologising for the fact that you got things wrong than continuing to bluff it out." She paused for a moment to let her words sink in. "Remember," she added, "you're no longer the chief constable's nephew so you don't have to impress him anymore." Gary looked crestfallen. Francesca felt she had done her job in making him realise the error of his ways. "The awful thing is that I agree with you on one point – that Debra Paget may very well be holding something back. She's in the best position to know the details of Sue Plummer's last few hours. We're not going to find out what that is – if there is anything because she's now frightened of the police. We'll just have to hope Philip Rivers can coax whatever she knows out of her." Francesca paused again. "So don't go trying to arrest him again," she said emphatically.

• • ● • •

Jo approached the charity shop where Trish worked. He showed her his card and they retired to the back office.

"What do you want to know?" she asked sullenly as if she did not relish her encounter with him.

"We've been asked by Rob's parents to investigate his murder," said Jo, "and we've come up with a witness who says he saw you outside Rob's house in your car at the time of the murder."

"Really? Whoever it was that told you that is wrong. I was at home all evening."

"But nobody can verify that."

"My daughter came home at about 11pm. You might ask her if I was in a murderous frame of mind then or was acting oddly. I was in fact watching the telly. They were re-running an old episode of Foyle's War."

"You would have had the perfect motive for murdering him. I gather you were still married to him and stood to inherit?"

"Yes, but I didn't hate him. I know you'll be able to find people who will say that I was dead chuffed to find out I was still going to benefit from his will – Colin Standen for one." She paused for a moment. A flicker of recognition came over Jo's face. "Ah," said Trish, "so it was Colin Standen who told you I had been seen outside Rob's house that night. Well, well, well, hell hath no fury like a man scorned."

"I'm sorry," said Jo. "You've lost me."

"Was it Colin Standen who gave you this information?"

"I can't really divulge the source of my information," said Jo haltingly.

"Your face just has," said Trish. "Let me tell you about Colin Standen. Ever since I found out I was the benefactor in Rob's will, he's been sniffing about me like a dog on heat. Oh, I know he's been a friend and I'm really grateful for the company he has given me since I split up with Rob but there's nothing between us. In fact yesterday, I had to make the position plain to him –that I really didn't want to enter into a relationship with him. He kind of went off with his tail between his legs. This allegation, I fear, is his way of getting back at me. It should be given no more credence than that."

"I see," said Jo.

"I suppose, though, it's a question of whether you believe him or me?"

"Hmm," said Jo. "All this talk of dogs being on heat and tails between legs reminds me; does Colin own a dog?"

"No," said Trish. "I've been round to his place a couple of times and there's never been a dog there. He never takes one to the pub, either. Why?"

"Well, he said he spotted you while taking his dog for a walk."

"There you are then. He's lying."

Jo was still not quite convinced. "He didn't have a friend who had a dog? Someone who was too frail to walk it?"

"Not that I know of." She racked her brains. "He did rather go on about one of his neighbour's dogs. I think he liked dogs. He would like to have owned one. He might have been walking it, I suppose, but why tell you it was his dog? I bet he wasn't even there at the time he says I was."

"Thank you, you've been most helpful." Jo turned to go but then a thought struck him. "Mrs Corcoran?"

"Trish," she said obviously by now happy with the private detective's presence.

"I just thought I'd ask you – do you know which of his three women Rob was fondest of?"

"That's easy – Sue Plummer. The other two are mutton dressed as lamb."

Jo look baffled. "I've never come across that expression before," he said. "What does it mean?"

"It means they've got airs and graces – and are pretending to be something they're not. Not Rob's type. No, my bet would have been that once this fuss over the three mistresses settled down, Rob would have gone back to Sue. They were well suited." She smiled. "Two scruffy individuals with a shared outlook on life. Rob just couldn't see it."

● ● ● ● ●

238

"How are you feeling?" Nikki asked her new lodger when she finally awoke that morning. "You look a lot calmer."

"That's the pills," said Debra. "I must have slept for ten hours – and at least I don't have that policeman breathing down my neck firing all those questions at me."

"Take your time to recover," said Nikki. "I thought I'd take the morning off so we could have a little chat." Debra started. She looked apprehensive and defensive again. "No," said Nikki, "I'm not going to ask you about the murders or anything like that – just talk about you." Debra looked as if she was reassured. "I'm sorry I can't offer you more than a converted settee to sleep on," she said. "Have you thought about what you want to do?"

"I suppose I ought to try and get back to work soon," she said. "They won't wait for me forever at the school – and I suppose they're already down on staff because of what happened to Sue."

"I don't think you need to worry about that," said Nikki. "I'm sure they'll give you until the start of next week at the earliest."

Debra nodded. "You know, I don't really want to go back," she said. "Sue and I – we were happy working together. It'll bring everything back."

"Time is a good healer," said Nikki.

Debra ignored her. "Sue's home, too," she said. "I really can't get that picture of her hanging from the light fitting out of my mind." She started to cry and Nikki held her hand.

"You know, you can stay here as long as you like," said Nikki, "but at some stage you have to think about the future."

"I'm scared," said Debra. "Supposing whoever did that to Sue went on to do it to me as well?"

Nikki's memories of her time working for her husband's agency were still fresh enough in her mind to know how to question a vulnerable suspect. "Is there any reason to suppose that whoever it was might have it in for you, too?" she asked.

Debra nodded feverishly. "It was my fault that Sue died," she said.

"Why?" said Nikki perplexed.

"I can't tell you," she said. She started biting her fingernails furiously.

"All right," said Nikki seeing that she was becoming upset. "Maybe you'll be able to tell me later."

Debra fervently shook her head. "It was my fault that Sue was killed," she said again.

• • ● • •

"Hallo, Francesca, nice to see you," said Rivers as he realised who his visitor was. "Jo's out," he added.

"I can still pop round and see you if I want you," she said. She got straight to the point. "I'm sorry about Gary Clarke's behaviour," she said.

"You don't need to apologise," said Rivers. "He does. He's left behind him one very frightened girl. I won't say woman because I don't think Debra has developed to the stage where she's a fully functioning adult." He paused for a moment. "What was he thinking about – questioning her for hours on end without a solicitor or any adult present?"

"I sometimes wonder whether he's a fully functioning adult," she said.

"Yes," said Rivers. "I was tempted to punch him when I saw him at the station yesterday. I really wanted to but – in the end – I thought he wasn't worth putting my private detective's licence in jeopardy. That bit of card that tells you I have approved membership of the Association of Private Detectives. The organisation doesn't take kindly to people who punch police officer's lights out."

"Good. Someone still respects us," said Francesca. "Anyway, he's no longer going to get away with things because he's the chief constable's nephew."

"I'm sorry. I don't get your drift," said Rivers.

"The chief constable has resigned today. He tried to seduce me over a meal a few nights ago but I had a tape recorder running and laid a complaint against him. Turns out four other women have come forward with complaints since I laid mine – so he had no option but to resign."

"Blimey, Francesca," said Rivers, "do you always have a tape recorder running when you go out for a meal with someone? If so, I'll tell Jo to watch out."

"No, of course not," she said. "I was just warned about what he might get up to." She suddenly looked thoughtful. "Philip," she began, "I don't want you to read too much into the fact that Jo and I went out with each other. I like him. I like his friendship but...."

"Best tell him that," said Rivers cutting in quickly..

"I will," she said. "Why? Has he said something to you?"

"Private detective's instinct," he said tapping his nose. "More reliable than the nephew of an ex chief constable's."

"There are two reasons why I would be cautious – one, the break-up I told you about is still less than four years ago. I'm not wallowing in sadness but it was a great relationship – and it hurt to find out he was cheating on me. I'm not sure I could believe it if another relationship looked as good as that one once had and I value Jo's friendship too much to want us to end on a sour note. Secondly, it is almost like dating someone at the office – something I never think is good idea. It might also cause a bit of awkwardness between you, me and him."

"No," said Rivers emphatically. "Look, you two are probably the two people I most respect in life. I want to see the two of you happy – but it's up to you to decide how to reach that state."

"Thank you, Philip," she said, placing a hand on his arm. "Now," she said, "down to business. Debra, how is she?"

"In the sort of state where I wouldn't recommend an interview with the police in the near future," said Rivers.

"I wasn't going to suggest that," she said, "but I wondered if you could act as a proxy for us? I still think she might well have information that could well be of use to us."

"It'll take time to gain her trust but I'm fully aware of your feelings."

"Thanks," she said and turned on her heels to go. Rivers watched as she walked down the stairs. Plucky woman. Bloody attractive woman, too. Never afraid to stand up to any bad apples in the force. She'd seen off the chief constable and a corrupt police officer in an earlier case the two had worked on in tandem. If she did ever decide that it was right for her to start up a relationship and settle down with someone, that person was going to be incredibly lucky, he thought as she finally disappeared from vision.

• • ● • •

Jo drove up to Roger Broadbent's house after visiting Trish Corcoran. In his mind he was laying to rest the second piece of so-called evidence that Colin Standen had handed on to him. Broadbent answered his knock on the door. The suspended planning official was wearing a suit for the first time since he had had to leave the council buildings. He had shaved and altogether looked a more respectable sight than the one that had confronted Colin Standen the previous day.

"Roger Broadbent?" asked Jo.

"Yes," came the reply.

Jo showed his car again and was admitted to the house. "Some new information has come to light linking you with Rob Corcoran's death," he said. "You were seen leaving his house on the night of the murder."

"At about seven o'clock, yes," said Broadbent. "And you came upon this information when?"

"Yesterday evening. I wanted to ask you why you were visiting Rob Corcoran."

"To get him to drop his investigation into the town hall planning department. I thought it would play badly for me."

"And did he?"

"No."

"So how did that make you feel?"

"Worried, but not worried enough to go back to his house later on that night and kill him. It's not in my nature – although I accept I can't insist that you believe that." He finished making a cup of tea for the two of them and handed one cup to Jo. "Look," he said. "I've been a weak man and I've made some wrong decisions. I have been in the pay of a property developer, Jerry Vincent, and I acknowledge I shouldn't have been. He's the type of man, though, that once you get into his clutches, it's difficult to leave. I'm going to make a clean breast of all this."

"Oh, yes?"

"I've booked an appointment with the chief executive tomorrow morning," he said. "I shall be naming names."

"Doesn't that make you nervous in view of what happened to Rob Corcoran?"

"I thought you'd come here to put me in the frame for Rob's murder – not to warn me I might be the killer's next victim. I doubt if anybody but you and the chief executive knows I'm going in to see him tomorrow morning so I don't really see why I should be afraid."

"Okay." Jo sounded far from convinced.

"By the way, shall I tell you who gave you the information about me going to visit Rob Corcoran?"

"I know who it was," said Jo wryly.

"I know, but I can also tell you why he did it."

"Go on. Astound me."

"It was Colin Standen." He paused for a moment to soak up Jo's reaction to his news. "Impressed?" he said when he detected none.

"Go on. I'm interested in the why bit."

"He was here yesterday afternoon. He told me he'd seen me and he promised he wouldn't mention it to a soul if I just coughed up £1,000. In a way, I think I've got to be thankful to him. He made me realise what sleazy company I was getting into which convinced me I should make a clean breast of things. Funny that. I turned him down, of course."

"The names you're going to name. Could you tell me who they are?"

"I think it's best if I leave it until after I've met the chief executive. You might go and interview them. That could turn out badly for me."

Jo nodded. He accepted the argument. "Do you think any of them could be responsible for killing Rob Corcoran?" he asked.

"Goodness," said Broadbent, "that's a leading question. Just look what they did to Rob – the assault on the night before he died. Breaking his finger, cracking his ribs. It shows you what they're capable of."

"Bruiser and Eel."

"That's as maybe. I don't know them. But forget about them. They're only the hired hands. You want the man who hired them."

"Jerry Vincent. We know that."

"Well, you – and whoever else is investigating this case – have done sweet f.a. about it. The council will have to act after my testimony tomorrow. They'll have to call in the police. I realise it might mean a jail sentence for me. I haven't got my head in the clouds. It will be worth it. As it is, I'm thoroughly ashamed of myself. Now, if you don't have anything else to ask me, please let me get some rest."

"Will do," said Jo and he left the house.

• • • • •

"I shouldn't be seen talking to you," said Douglas Roulay through gritted teeth as he arrived for the planning meeting that evening and was confronted by Jerry Vincent.

"Keep your hair on, dear boy," replied the property developer. "Nobody seems to have cottoned on to your scurrilous role in planning affairs. After all, Roger Broadbent is the only person suspended as a result of your inquiry." There was heavy emphasis on the word 'your' as if to stress to Roulay that he was in control of events. "Anyhow, I'm only exercising my right as a member of the public to attend tonight's meeting," he continued.

"It might not be to your satisfaction."

"Dear boy, do you want to go to Wimbledon or not?"

"Wimbledon's over for this year," interposed Roulay.

"You know what I mean."

"Of course, what you don't know – and I've heard through the grapevine – is that Broadbent is going to see the chief executive tomorrow morning. It could be the nail in your coffin – and mine for that matter. Now, if you don't mind, the meeting starts in a couple of minutes and I need to distance myself from you."

"Charming," said Vincent. "Don't worry about Broadbent, by the way. I've a feeling he can be dissuaded from attending that meeting tomorrow morning. Leave it to me."

Roulay did not respond to Vincent's last remarks. If he was going to use heavy handed tactics to deter Broadbent from going to the meeting, he did not want to know. He made his way into the committee room – where around six councillors sat round a table. A couple of members of the public sat in seats set out along the wall. One of them was Jackie Quesling.

Vincent made a bee-line for her. "I've a feeling it could be your night," he said.

"Oh."

"Roulay's taken my name off your planning application so there's no mention of the developer who designed the house to be built on your site. You're not tainted with being associated with yours truly," he said.

The chairman of the planning committee called the meeting

to order. "I have to inform the committee that allegations of corruption have been made over a specific development before us tonight," he said. "You will see a housing development has been submitted by a Mr Jeremy Vincent – item three on the agenda. There is a favourable report on the development from one of our planning officers despite the fact it runs contrary to our current policy. Douglas, perhaps you could tell us what has happened?"

"Yes," he said. "Allegations have been made that one of our planning officers received inducements to support this application. He has now been suspended from duty and an inquiry launched into the allegations. In view of this, it was thought prudent that the application should be withdrawn from tonight's meeting – and held in obeyance until the inquiry is completed."

"So move," said one of the councillors. The suggestion was seconded and the committee unanimously voted in favour of it.

"Thank you," said Roulay. "I will, of course, keep you abreast of any further developments."

"If we might move on to the next item on the agendas," said the chairman. "An application by Miss Jacqueline Quesling to build a house on land she owns at Barton Terrace. You will see there is already one dwelling there. It is in a conservation area but the department is recommending acceptance on the grounds it will have minimal impact on the surrounding properties and will help keep us abreast of government policy to encourage the building of more domestic property."

"Mr Chairman," said one of the councillors. "The report on this development is written by the same suspended officer, I see."

"Yes – but there is no suggestion that this small-scale plan was the subject of corruption allegations."

"Move support," said the councillor who had moved the motion blocking Vincent's housing development. Again it was seconded and then passed with five votes in favour and one abstention – the councillor who had raised his concern that the approval was being recommended by Roger Broadbent. In the public seats, Jackie Quesling beamed and got up to leave the meeting after the vote had been taken. Vincent followed her out.

"Happy?" he said when the two of them were out of earshot of the committee.

"Yes," she said rather abruptly. "I don't think I should be seen talking to you."

"Oh come on, you've got what you wanted courtesy of Uncle Jerry. The least you could do is be courteous to him in return."

"I can do courtesy," she said, "when we've left the building."

"No need to invite me out for a drink," he said as they returned to the car park. "I've still got a bit of work that I need to do. Nice to see one satisfied customer. You're potentially £750,000 richer as a result of tonight's meeting."

Jackie did not respond but opened the door of her car, got in and drove off. Vincent took his mobile out of his pocket and dialled a number. "Hello," he said. "Got a job tomorrow morning. Could you stop Roger Broadbent attending the town hall tomorrow morning?" He listened to the response from the other end. "Play it by ear," he said. "If you think you've managed to use your powers of dissuasion to stop him from testifying, all well and good. If not, then it might have to be a case of plan B."

• • ● • •

Roger Broadbent looked out of his window as he prepared to leave for the council offices and his meeting with the chief executive. There was a car parked opposite. He sighed. He was no match physically for the two individuals he could see but – as he busied himself with his preparations – they made no effort to approach the door. They're going to take me when I go outside, he thought. He took his wallet from his pocket and took out a business card which had Jo's number on it and rang it.

"Jo," said the voice on the other end of the line.

"It's Roger Broadbent," he said. "I need help. There are a couple of heavies sitting in a car outside my home. I don't they've just come here as part of a drive out into the country."

Jo looked at his watch. "Realistically," he said, "I can be with you in twenty minutes. Can you hold them off until then?"

"They don't seem to be making any attempt to come into the house."

"Right," said Jo. "I'll be as quick as I can."

Broadbent put the receiver down and went over to the window again. The two men – who were in fact Bruiser and Eel – appeared not to have moved. Eel noticed the twitching of the curtain, though. He waved at Broadbent. "What are you doing that for?" asked Bruiser. "We don't need to draw attention to ourselves."

"On the contrary," said Eel. "I think we do. If we frighten him into staying in his house, he doesn't go to the meeting with the chief executive. Mission accomplished without any resort to violence."

Bruiser appeared disappointed at this. "It's not how I saw the morning going."

"No," said Eel. "You'd have been in there – all guns blazing – and kidnapped him from his home leaving signs of a struggle for all to see. This way, we either maroon him in his house or pick him up outside. Either way, there's no evidence at all that we were ever here."

"It's bloody boring," said Bruiser. He reluctantly agreed to go along with Eel's suggestion and settled down for the wait. It was not for long. Jo had made good progress from his Finchley home and drew up outside Broadbent's house precisely twenty minutes after he had been telephoned. He pipped his horn as he sat in the driveway – looking over to Bruiser and Eel's van as he did so.

"It's that black git from the detective agency. What do we do now?" asked Bruiser. "Surely we don't just sit and do nothing?"

By now, Broadbent was coming out of his house and had made his way over to Jo's car and climbed into the passenger seat.

"Not much we can do," said Eel. "Drive after them. If we get a chance, we could run them off the road." It was an unequal struggle, though. Bruiser and Eel's sturdy old white van could not match Jo's four-seater for pace and Roger Broadbent was soon being delivered to the council offices for his morning meeting.

● ● ● ● ●

"Stick with him," Rivers said to Jo as he received a progress report on Broadbent's journey to the council offices that morning. "You've got him to the point where he's giving evidence but Bruiser and Eel could have a nasty surprise for him when he leaves the building. It's all very well for him to give evidence to the chief executive this morning – but he'll need to follow it up by giving a statement to the police, give evidence in any ensuing court case. We've got to keep him out of their clutches."

"Easier said than done," said Jo.

"Persuade him to go away somewhere. Abroad or somewhere in the north. He should leave a forwarding address – given to as few people as possible. The chief executive and us, say. Just keep him away from Bruiser and Eel."

"Okay."

Rivers sat back in his office chair after he had finished the call. There was a couple of days mail for him to open as he made himself a cup of coffee. One letter with his address in handwriting caught his eye. He opened it carefully. A picture of Nikki fell out from it. It was accompanied by a piece of paper with an almost illegible scrawl written on it. He picked up the photograph of Nikki from the floor. It was then that he noticed that she had a finger missing – carefully cut out from the photograph. He shook his head and went on to pick up the scrap of paper.

He screwed his eyes up and managed to read it. "If you don't drop your investigation, this is what'll happen to your wife," it said. Bastards, he thought to himself. He pondered the letter for a moment. Perhaps he ought to go to the police, he thought. Trouble is, though, they wouldn't have the resources to mount a twenty-four-hour watch on her. Also, although he knew from what he had already seen, that the letter and the photograph were Bruiser and Eel's work, he had no proof of that. No, if he wanted Nikki to be protected, he would have to take care of the matter himself. One thing was certain, what with this letter and that morning's show outside Broadbent's house they were beginning to get desperate. He rang Jo back again. "Jo," he said when the other man answered his call, "get back here as soon as possible after you've seen Broadbent safely off the premises. There's one or two things we need to discuss."

• • ● • •

"Come in, Roger," said Dan Macfarlane, the council's chief executive. Broadbent noticed he was accompanied by a senior member of the council's legal team. Macfarlane had a kindly face – but he knew from experience his outward demeanour masked a razor-sharp mind. A slightly portly man, possibly from all the lunches he had imbibed in his role of chief executive, he was wearing a sports jacket and open-necked shirt accompanied by a cravat -– the kind of dress that would make him blend in well with a gathering of farmers. By contrast, his colleague from the legal department was dressed in a very sober dark suit. He was sitting to Macfarlane's right, pen poised to take notes of the meeting. "I gather," said Macfarlane, "that this is not intended to be a formal meeting but that you wish to place on record your reaction to the allegations of corrupt practices levied against you."

"Yes," said Broadbent. He began by listing the "freebies" he had received from Jerry Vincent – the test match tickets,

Wimbledon tickets, the new gravel pathway outside his home. "Nothing straightforward like money exchanged hands," he said. "Mr Vincent was very clear about that so he could escape detection."

"Over how long a period were these offers made to you?"

"A year or so. They covered at least five planning applications. Substantial housing developments in a couple of cases. I also know that Mr Vincent was not averse to threatening people who got in his way. Rob Corcoran, for instance."

"You can implicate him in Rob Corcoran's murder?" interjected Macfarlane.

"No, sir," he said, "just in an attempt to frighten him when he realised Rob was investigating him. He was not averse to frightening anybody who got in his way. He employed two 'heavies' to do his dirty work for him. I can give you their names."

"Were you worried about what he might do if you refused to go along with him?" asked Macfarlane.

"I wasn't, sir," he said, "but these same two heavies were outside my house this morning as I prepared to come here."

"It sounds as if you might need police protection."

"Thank you, sir. I have my own protection for the time being."

"Good." Macfarlane studied his witness for a moment. "Did this corruption stretch beyond you?"

Broadbent remained silent for a moment as if weighing up his response. "How do you mean sir?" he asked.

"Were any other officers involved in this corruption?"

He should have been anticipating this question. He had to decide once and for all whether to reveal Douglas Roulay's relationship with Jerry Vincent. For the first time since entering Macfarlane's office that morning, he hesitated. "I have no proof anyone else was involved," he said, swallowing hard. Roulay had been a work colleague of his for years. At the very last, he could not bring himself to implicate his colleague.

"But you think they might be?"

"I can only repeat what I said before – I have no proof anyone else was involved."

Macfarlane chose to ignore him. "And if somebody else was involved, it could only have been Douglas Roulay. Rob Corcoran couldn't have been. The reaction to his allegations tells us that. I think by the phrasing of your words in answer to my question, you are telling me that Douglas Roulay was involved."

"I can't say that, sir."

"You don't have to." Macfarlane shuffled some papers on his desk. "Right," he said. "We'll get what you have told us written up in a statement for you to sign. I have to tell you that – as a result of what has transpired between us this morning – it is almost certain you will face criminal proceedings but I guess you knew that already." Broadbent nodded. "I shall be suspending Douglas Roulay from his job pending further enquiries. We will probably need to be in touch with you in a couple of days to sign your statement – but, until then, that will be all."

Broadbent got up as if to go. "Just one thing," added Macfarlane added as he made his way out of the office. "Don't leave the area in the meantime."

"That may be difficult advice for me to follow," said Broadbent. "I don't want to be a sitting duck for Vincent's heavies."

"You should get yourself down to the police station immediately and report them to them," said Macfarlane.

"Yes, sir," he said. Realistically, though, he knew the amount of protection he would be afforded was unlikely to be enough. As he walked out of the offices, he found himself surrounded by Bruiser and Eel on the pavement outside.

"I think you need to come with us," said Bruiser gruffly, grabbing him by the arm. At that moment Jo's car screeched to a halt just by them and the passenger door was flung open.

"Get in," shouted Jo. Broadbent tried to but Bruiser was exercising a strong grip on his arm. Jo jumped from the driver's side of the car, pushed Eel out of the way and then confronted

Bruiser. "Let him go," he shouted bringing his hand down in a karate chop on Bruiser's arm. This forced the man to relinquish his hold on Broadbent's arm. Bruiser made as if to grab at Broadbent again but Eel shook his head. By this time a number of people had gathered to watch the spectacle. "Too many witnesses," said Eel, shrugging his shoulders as Broadbent clambered into the passenger seat and heaved a sigh of relief. Jo made his way into the driver's seat and the two of them sped off, leaving Bruiser and Eel exasperated on the pavement.

"That was a bit too close a call," said Broadbent.

"Yes," said Jo. "Now we need to make sure you hole up somewhere where you can be safe for the rest of this investigation."

"I have a cousin in Scotland I can visit," said Broadbent.

"Good," said Jo, "just leave me a forwarding address and I'll make sure the chief executive can contact me to get hold of you in the future."

"Thank you," said Broadbent.

• • • • •

"I just wanted a copy of the police tape," said Rivers as he entered James Russell's office. "I guess you have no more interest in it."

"Only if we want to pursue a case for damages for wrongful arrest," said Russell.

"You think we would have a strong case."

"Listen to it," he said and began to play it to Rivers. "It's very interesting. She agrees with Detective Constable Clarke that she had confessed to killing Rob Corcoran but in this tape she never admits it again. She describes the murder exceptionally well – and accurately, according to the police themselves, and says she is responsible for Sue Plummer's death, which we now know to have been murder. What does that mean to you?"

"I never thought she did it." He shrugged his shoulders.

"You've had more chance to study the tape than me. What do you think?"

"She comes across as frightened, too," said Russell, "especially when she's asked why she thinks she was responsible for Sue Plummer's death. I'll tell you what I think. I think she gives such an accurate description of the murder of Rob Corcoran that she must have witnessed it herself. She knows who killed him."

Rivers nodded. "And?" he added.

"Well, if she saw that, it must have been troubling her and – if she was troubled by something like that – what would she do?"

"Tell Sue," said Rivers thoughtfully.

"Yes and – after she tells Sue – Sue gets murdered herself. Why would that happen?"

"Maybe Sue attempted to follow up what Debra had told her – and the killer realised Sue knew what they had done and killed her, too."

"And that's why Debra's so afraid. She thinks if she says anything to anybody she'll be killed, too."

"Sue probably wouldn't have told whoever it is that it was Debra who told her – so the killer may not know that Debra could bring about their downfall."

"But Debra doesn't realise that – and that's why she's so scared," Rivers thought for a moment. "Of course, it wouldn't take a genius to deduce that Sue had got her information from Debra so she may be quite right to be scared. Now all we've got to do is try to coax the information that Debra has out of her."

"Rather you than me," said Russell. "She wouldn't take kindly to more questioning as a result of the grilling she received at the police station."

"Bloody Clarke," said Rivers. "He's got a lot to answer for. Still, I think we're beginning to gain Debra's trust now we're putting her up. We might be able to get somewhere with her."

"If I were you," said Russell tentatively, "I wouldn't mention what you suspect to the police – not even Detective Chief

Inspector Manners. They wouldn't be able to restrain themselves from coming in and doing the questioning themselves."

"No," said Rivers, "I think Francesca understands where we're at over Debra."

"Francesca?"

"I know her well," said Rivers. "I've worked with her on a couple of cases beforehand. I trust her."

"Good," said Russell.

"Well, if that's all, could I have the tape now?"

"By all means. You know there are so many flaws in that so-called confession I think they could be shitting themselves over whether they're going to face a case for wrongful arrest. I'd love to take it on if Debra agrees."

"I don't think she would," said Rivers. "We've got to use kid gloves with her to find out what she knows. I don't think she'd be very co-operative if she thought there was going to be another brush with the police at the end of the day."

"All right," he said. He handed Rivers the tape. "So I get nothing for my pains in intervening to help your client?"

"The best I can do is clear some expenses for you with Rob Corcoran's parents. After all, they have briefed me to find out what happened to their son. By stopping the police from going through with Debra's arrest, you could argue that I was making it more likely that they would devote their energies in capturing the real killer."

Russell smiled. "I'll accept that," he said.

•   •   **•**   •   •

"Morning, Gary," said Francesca as she made her way into the office.

"Boss," he said in a tentative voice as if he was about to frame a question. Boss, she thought. One stage better than ma'am but still not what she wanted to hear from him. "Boss?" he continued.

"Francesca," she said correcting him. "What do you want, Gary?"

"I want to make an unreserved apology for the way I've been behaving on this enquiry so far. I ballsed it up over Debra Paget."

"I couldn't have put it more eloquently myself," said Francesca. "What's brought on this realisation?"

"Well," he said. "I think as the Chief Constable's nephew I was conscious of the fact that I needed to make an impression."

"You have, Gary," she said. "At times it's been a very bad impression."

Gary was undeterred. She felt that he must have decided to make this speech and that nothing was going to deter him. "I felt I needed to make some initiative, gain some glory if you like – so that you, or anybody who worked with me, thought at least he's got some skills and I've not just been saddled with the Chief Constable's nephew. I realise that now. I was wrong. It is, as you said once, a long ball game." Francesca frowned. She did not recognise the language he ascribed to her. "And I don't have to make a spectacular collar to gain people's attention."

"I think you have gained people's attention all right," said Francesca. "Rory Gleeson is worried that we may face some sort of action as a result of your harrying."

"Harrying?" queried Gary.

"Yes, harrying," said Francesca firmly, "of Debra Paget. I'm glad, though, that you now see the virtue of playing what you called, I think, the long-ball game."

"Thank you, Francesca," he said. "Where do we go from her then?"

"That's a big question," said Francesca. "Do you mean you and I – or are you talking about the case?"

"Oh, the case," he said firmly.

"Let's talk about you and me first," she said. "I'm willing to put the past behind us and hope that we can work more fruitfully together in the future. As to the case, what do you think?"

He fidgeted. "I have to say I still think Debra Paget still knows a lot more than she's letting on."

"Congratulations, Gary, I think you, me and Philip Rivers have all come to the same conclusion there. It's just that we have different ways of handling that thought. You see, I wouldn't use the phrase 'knows a lot more than she's letting on'. I don't think she's withholding information from us for any malevolent reason – which the use of that phrase suggests. Still, it's good to see that we're all on the same wavelength. Just, for goodness' sake, Gary, don't you do anything about it."

Gary squirmed in his seat but reluctantly nodded his head.

• • • • •

Rivers dropped by his flat in the afternoon – just to check that Debra was feeling all right. On ascertaining there was nothing wrong with her, he suggested she accompany him to the office. "Be interesting for you to see where we work," he said. "You'll realise that if anything does worry you we're only a few minutes away." He unlocked the door on arriving at the office and invited her to come inside.

"So it's empty for some of the time?" she asked.

"Yes," he said. "Nikki used to work with me and she'd spend time making sure the office was manned but Jo is more involved in investigations so spends more time out of the office. I suppose we ought to hire a secretary to take calls etcetera but we're not made of money." He saw he had left the message from Bruiser and Eel on his desk and quickly moved it out of the way so Debra did not notice it. It might worry her, he thought. There were a couple of letters on the mat by the door and Rivers picked them up and began to open them. "Somebody wants us to run a check on their partner," he said to Debra after reading the first one. "She suspects him of cheating on her. That's the sort of bread and butter case that we get."

"What will you do about it?"

"I'll go round and see her when I've got a moment?"

"What happens if he answers the door?"

Rivers smiled. "Good question," he said. "I would invent some entirely plausible excuse for calling round and then depart. I won't claim I've come to read the meter. I wouldn't know how to. Thing is we're quite stretched at the moment dealing with the Rob Corcoran murder so we wouldn't be able to devote as much time as we should to following her case up."

Debra nodded. "You don't think I did it?" she asked.

Rivers smiled. "Good Lord, no," he said. "No, I don't really know who did do it. Who do you think it was?"

Debra froze. Rivers could tell she was feeling uncomfortable. Instead of saying she didn't know, though, she said she couldn't say which reinforced Rivers' suspicion that she knew who it was. He decided, though, to pretend that he thought she was in the same boat as him and didn't know who it was. "Thing is," he said, "it would be good if we did know who it was. They've already killed twice – Rob and Sue Plummer. We could stop them from doing it again if we knew." He looked at Debra and could see she was still feeling uncomfortable. He thought she might be debating with her conscience as to whether she should tell him what she knew. That would be a good sign but he decided that, instead of continuing to talk about the subject, he would give her a rest in the hope that maybe in the not too distant future she felt able to be honest with him about what she knew. It was at that juncture that the telephone rang. "Would you answer that?" he asked her as he pretended to be reading something on his desk.

"Rivers detective agency," she said very clearly on answering the phone. There was a pause before she answered: "Yes, we do deal with divorce cases. I'll put you on to Mr Rivers." She handed the telephone to him and he made an appointment for them to come in and see him in the office the following Friday morning. Having arranged that, he replaced the receiver.

"Well done," he said. "You handled that really well."

She blushed. "Thank you," she said. It had been the first sign of her taking control of a situation since she had been taken down to the police station three days ago.

Rivers stroked his chin. "What are you thinking of doing in the future?" he asked. "Do you want to go back to the school meals service? I'm sure they're holding the job open for you."

A perplexed look came over Debra's face. "No," she said. "Sue and I were happy working there together. I don't think it would be the same without her."

Rivers nodded. "Well," he said, "would you like to come and work for me? As a receptionist? I'm sure you could cope with the work. But how about we do it on a trial basis for a month? See if you like it."

Debra smiled. "Yes, please," she said.

Good, thought Rivers. He really was gaining her confidence and he felt she could make a contribution to the agency. After all, they were highly likely to have missed the divorce call if she had not been visiting the office. He never really liked being in the office. He would have found an excuse to have been elsewhere.

• • ● • •

"We've got to face up to it," said Eel as he dialled Vincent's number. "We messed it up."

"If we'd gone into the house in the first place, it would never have happened," mumbled Bruiser. He stopped moaning, though, as Vincent answered the call.

"I'm afraid he got away," said Eel.

"How?" demanded Vincent.

"A private detective was guarding him. The black guy who works with Rivers."

"So Rivers is still bugging us?" said Vincent.

"Yes."

"Then it's time to put the frighteners on him. Kidnap his wife. Do what you have to but make sure he gives up the case. In fact, you might be able to persuade him to tell you where Broadbent is. I take it he's no longer at home?"

"No," said Eel. "We'll do it tomorrow. We know her movements."

"Good. You've never let me down before, lads. Don't make it twice in a row or I'll have to think about getting someone else in."

Bruiser roused himself on hearing this. "I wouldn't do that if I were you," he said.

"Are you threatening me?" Vincent sounded incredulous.

"It's all right," said Eel. "He threatens everybody. It's one of his strengths."

• • ● • •

Jo arrived back at the office in mid-afternoon. Rivers and Debra were still there. "You wanted to see me?" he said.

"Wait a minute." Rivers did not want Debra to hear what he was going to say in case it unduly alarmed her. "Would you mind going across the road and getting us a couple of teas, Debra?" he asked. "There's just one or two things I have to talk to Jo about." He escorted Debra to the window and pointed out the tea shop to her.

"What is it?" asked Jo.

Rivers went back to his desk and picked up the letter and picture Bruiser and Eel had sent him. "Take a look at that," he said.

Jo scrutinised it for a moment. "My God," he said. "They don't mess about, do they?"

"No. I did wonder about calling in the police – but we've got no proof it was sent by Bruiser and Eel. Far better to catch them in the act of kidnap when they strike."

"Isn't that a bit risky? We don't know when they're going to strike."

"But we know where. They wouldn't have cased our flats if they hadn't meant to pull off the kidnapping there. Nikki's only ever there after four o'clock. We can make a good educated guess as to when they'll strike. They'll want to do it before we get home – or when they think we'll get home. That's six o'clock in their book."

"Okay."

"Jo," said Rivers suddenly adopting a more serious tone. "I want you to drop everything on the women and concentrate on protecting Nikki. Don't hang around her, though. I want them to be caught in the act thinking it was okay to strike. When you think they're going to strike, ring me. I'll be there as soon as possible – but go in without me in case I'm delayed."

"I can do that," said Jo. "It's only Bruiser who's a threat. Eel is quite a coward when it comes to potential physical violence, I think."

At that juncture Debra reappeared with the teas. "Oh dear," Rivers whispered to Jo. "That means we've got to stay and drink them now." He smiled and took a plastic cup from Debra. "By the way," he said to Jo. "Debra's coming to work for us for a while – as a receptionist."

CHAPTER NINE

"I'm feeling lucky today, Eel," said Bruiser. He clasped his hands together and made his fingers give off a cracking sound. "Very lucky."

"Good, Bruiser, glad to hear it," responded his companion. Eel smirked. It was only because he had a carte blanche to use any methods necessary to kidnap Mrs Rivers that he was feeling confident. None of this namby-pamby stuff of sitting outside waiting for their victim to emerge.

Their white van was parked in the car park outside the Rivers' flats. It was four o'clock in the afternoon. Soon Nikki (Mrs Rivers) would be coming back from work. If Bruiser and Eel had been a bit sharper they might have noticed a car they would recognise at the other end of the car park. Jo had just arrived to start surveillance of Nikki's home and was sitting in the driver's seat drumming – perhaps a trifle nervously – with his fingers. He was calculating the odds. It would be two against one effectively. He would go for Eel first, he thought. He would be easier to succumb, having no history of violence. Bruiser might try to come to his rescue. That would be the time to do his best to overcome him. Besides, it wouldn't take Rivers long to get there once he was alerted to the situation and that would even the score up.

The three of them didn't have to wait long. Nikki soon came round the corner and walked towards the front door of her flats. She seemed not to have a care in the world. She was even humming a tune quietly to herself. Rivers hadn't told her of the threat she was facing. He thought it would alarm her unduly and that he and Jo could deal with any situation that developed.

If he was honest with himself, he might have admitted that he wanted to catch Bruiser and Eel in the act and – if she had been forewarned – she might just have given a clue out to Bruiser and Eel (all right, then, to Eel, he thought) that she was expecting something to happen.

Bruiser and Eel got out of the white van and followed her to the door. Bruiser was all for following her into the flats before the door closed. Eel restrained him. "We've never found it difficult to gain entrance," he said. "Someone will let us in." He was right. The time was just ripe for stragglers from school to arrive home and, sure enough, a teenage boy let them in. They made their way up to number eight and then banged on the door to be let in. Meanwhile, Jo followed them into the block.

"Who is it?" cried a voice from inside.

"We have a delivery for you," said Eel.

"Oh," said Nikki. She sounded surprised – perhaps that a delivery could have coincided so equably with her return home from work. She opened the door, though. Bruiser was first through it and grabbed her by the arm. She screamed. While she did so, she noticed the other man – Eel – was putting the safety lock on the door.

"You're coming with us," said Bruiser gruffly. "Come quietly or it will be the worse for you."

It was at that moment that Debra appeared like a whirling dervish from the kitchen. She had a frying pan in her hand and jumped up in the air so that she could bring it down with maximum force on Bruiser's head. Bacon and mushrooms flew out of the pan – Debra had obviously been cooking herself a meal. Bruiser gave out a cry of pain – it was not only the force of the frying pan that was causing him pain. A red mark suddenly emerged on the side of his head as he suffered burns. The frying pan had just been used to fry the bacon and mushrooms and was still piping hot. Debra, quite excited by what she had done, moved towards Eel menacingly changing the frying pan from one hand to another. A devilish look came over her face as she contemplated dishing out the same treatment to Eel. He raised his hands – either in surrender or to protect himself from the force of the blow – it mattered little which it was.

"It's all right, Debra," said Nikki. "I think he gets the message." At that stage a groggy Bruiser came round on the floor where he was lying and tried to struggle to his feet. Quick as a flash, Debra hit him on his cheek with the frying pan with – again – as much force as she could muster. He gave a strangled cry and slumped to the floor.

As silence descended inside the flat, they could hear a banging on the door. Nikki rallied herself to take the catch off the lock whereupon Jo flew into the room – having decided his best option was to take a run at the door and break it open. He knocked the frying pan out of Debra's hand and trod on Bruiser on the floor before coming to rest. He surveyed the scene before him. "Good," he said, "you guys seem to have got everything under control." At this stage, Eel tried to slip through the open door – only for Debra to pick the frying pan up and chase after him. "Come back here now," she shouted with some authority. He obliged. Jo then noticed he had on him some masking tape – presumably with which to tie up his victim. He grabbed his arm and took him into the kitchen where he tied Eel to a chair. Bruiser was still out cold on the floor in the hallway. Debra was sitting on a chair next to him a devilish grin on her face and the frying pan still in her hand.

"I don't think you have to hit him again," said Jo. "He's out for the count." He prised the frying pan from her hand. She reluctantly let him take it away from her "Right, now," he said. "Police and an ambulance." He rang Francesca Manners on her mobile and explained what had happened. She promised to get to the flat with some support as quickly as possible. At that stage, Rivers suddenly emerged at the door. He noted Bruiser still lying on the floor – although he was squirming a little now much to the relief of Nikki and Jo who feared Debra might have killed him. Debra showed no relief whatsoever, though. Jo then telephoned for an ambulance as Rivers assessed the situation.

"You all seem to be enjoying yourself," he said. He went over to Debra. "Congratulations," he said. "It looks as though you've just foiled a kidnapping."

"I heard Nikki scream and then I saw this big man – she held her arms as widely apart as she could at this juncture – grabbing hold of her. There was only one thing to do. I had this frying pan on the go so I used it to try and knock him out."

"It looks as though you succeeded," said Rivers as he surveyed what surrounded him.

"She used it twice," said Nikki.

"Yes, I can see," he said pointing out the red marks on the top of Bruiser's almost bald head and on his left cheek. A thought struck Rivers. He and the solicitor James Russell had concocted this theory that Debra had been a witness to the killing of Rob Corcoran and that was what was scaring her. He wondered if that had played any part in the savage attack she had perpetrated on Bruiser. Had she seen him that night? "Debra," said Rivers softly," can I ask you? Have you ever seen this man before?"

"No," she said without hesitation. Rivers scrutinised her face for any reaction. It seemed a genuine enough response which meant that – if he and Russell were right – Bruiser was not responsible for the killing of Rob Corcoran, he thought.

Bruiser slowly managed to haul himself up and adopt a sitting position on the floor. "I'm fucking hurting," he said. "I need help." He rubbed the top of his head but it only seemed to hurt him more.

"Now you know what it's like to be on the receiving end," said Rivers. "Unlike your victims, though, we have arranged for an ambulance to take you to hospital."

"Could I have something to put on my head?" he asked.

"No," said Rivers. "Wait."

He did not have to wait long. The ambulance crew arrived before the police and took one look at Bruiser before telling Rivers: "Those are nasty injuries to his head and cheek. We'd best get him seen to in hospital. We'll take him to Barnet General. How did he get them, by the way?"

"His head came into contact with a frying pan," said Rivers non-commitally. "We've contacted the police. We'll let them know what happened."

The ambulanceman nodded. "Tell them where we've taken him," he said. Rivers agreed to do so and – just as they were leaving with Bruiser – Francesca appeared in the doorway.

"Anyone need any help?" she asked as she surveyed the scene before her.

"Yes," said Rivers. "This is the guy you should be concentrating on." He walked over to where Eel was tied to a chair. "Eel."

"Yes, I know."

"Caught in the act of trying to kidnap my wife," Rivers added.

"What have you got to say for yourself?" Francesca asked him.

"I want a solicitor."

"You'll need one," said Francesca. She turned to Rivers again. "I take it he was not acting alone?"

"Funny you should mention that," said Rivers. "No, he had an accomplice who came off slightly the worse for wear – courtesy of Debra here."

"I hit him with a frying pan," she said firmly.

It was at this stage that Gary Clarke entered the hallway. "Oh, no," said Rivers – recalling the detective constable's past history with Debra. "She was acting in self-defence," he said. "Well, in defence of my wife, actually."

Nikki moved over to where Debra was standing. "She's a hero," she said linking arms with the young girl.

"It's all right," said Francesca. "He's programmed not to arrest her now. We'll need to take statements from all of you. A couple of constables will be arriving soon. You can give them to them.

Who was this accomplice then?"

"Bruiser," said Rivers.

"As if I needed to ask."

"The ambulance has taken him to Barnet general."

"No rush, then," said Clarke, His remark was greeted with total silence. "I mean it's under pressure. It'll take ages for him to be seen by A and E."

"Better to be safe than sorry," said Francesca. She telephoned the police station and requested an officer be despatched to the hospital to guard Bruiser as soon as possible and that whoever it was should let her know when he was able to answer questions. "Right," she said approaching Eel. "Charles Ernest Higgs, I am arresting you on suspicion of attempted kidnapping." She went on to caution him before she and Gary untied him and took him off to the police station.

"You've got a remarkable memory for names," said Jo to Francesca.

"I looked up a file we had on him before I left the police station," she replied.

Now the four were on their own, Rivers went over to Nikki and put his arm around her. "Are you all right?" he asked.

"Did you know this was going to happen?"

"I had a pretty shrewd idea."

"I thought it was a bit odd – you and Jo arriving just after it happened. Why didn't you tell me?"

"I thought it might alarm you."

"That's all very well – but, if it hadn't been for Debra, it could have all ended in disaster. Jo couldn't get in because the one they called Eel had put the catch on the door."

"I'm sorry. Jo would have got to you eventually."

"Eventually is a long time," said Nikki. "Anyhow, where's the hero of the hour?"

Rivers shrugged his shoulders. "She's in the kitchen," said Jo. Rivers and Nikki walked over to where Debra was standing to congratulate her. She still had the frying pan in her hand. "I'm just making some bacon and mushrooms,"she said. "It was what I was doing before I was interrupted by those guys."

"Make some for us,"said Jo. The doorbell rang. It was the police again wanting to take statements. "We'll have them when they've gone,"Jo added, "and, don't worry, we'll help you with your police statement. You won't be incriminating yourself at all."

Debra smiled. At last, she thought, she was in the company of people she felt she could trust.

· · ● · ·

"I might as well make it plain from the outset I'm not going to tell you anything," said Eel as he faced Francesca and Gary across the table in the interviewing room at the police station. His solicitor – summoned on the recommendation of Jerry Vincent – sat there stony-faced beside him.

"That's your right, Mr Higgs."

Eel smiled at Francesca. "You can call me Eel,"he said.

"Look, Mr Higgs," said Francesca, leaning across the table menacingly. She had been granted leave by the local police to carry out the interview at their station on the grounds that – whilst the attempted kidnapping had taken place in their jurisdiction it stemmed from a case that she was already investigating. "This is no vicarage tea-party. You have been arrested on suspicion of a serious crime. We're not all going to be calling each other by cosy names and pouring each other cups of tea." Eel remained silent. "Right, let's go back to the beginning," she continued. "What we do know is that you broke into Nikki Rivers' flat."

"We didn't. She let us in."

"Under false pretences. You said you had a delivery for her." He shrugged his shoulders at this point. "You then grabbed hold of Mrs Rivers."

"I didn't."He stressed the word 'I'.

"All right, your companion did. What did you do when he did that?"

"No comment."

"Nothing – because you were going to tie her up and bundle her out of the flat and into your white van."

"No comment."

Francesca pushed two bits of paper across the table for Eel to look at. It was the note sent to Rivers' office with the picture of Nikki with a finger missing and a warning to him to drop investigating the charges of corruption in the planning department. "What do you know about these?" she asked him.

"Never seen them before in my life," he said.

"You could at least look at them. That way your words might just have a scintilla of credibility."

He looked down at the table and then picked them up. He pretended to look at them carefully and then put them back on the table, pushing them towards Francesca. "No, never seen them before."

"You're not being sensible, Mr Higgs. We will be scouring your offices tomorrow. We may find a notebook of the same size as this piece of paper with one page torn out. We may even find the imprint of those words on the next page. Your lies will not curry favour with a judge and jury. Telling us the truth might help you."

"You'd put in a good word, would you?" sneered Eel.

"Much as it pains me to say so – yes." She squared up to him. "You're small fry, whatever you might think, Mr Eel. I want your employer – not you. I want Jerry Vincent." She looked at him to see if he reacted. There was no reaction. "All right," she said," so we examine the other scenario. There was no-one else involved in this attempted kidnapping. It was all your idea – yours and Mr McCarthy's." She laughed derisively. "Well, I think if it's something concocted between the two of you, we know who the mastermind is. Mr McCarthy couldn't organise the proverbial piss-up in the brewery. It had to be down to you."

"You'd need to prove motive."

"Ah," said Francesca, "so you are saying it wasn't down to you and there was someone else who ordered you to do it. We've looked at yours and Mr McCarthy's phone records since you got here – and there appears to have been a telephone call to a property developer, Jerry Vincent, last night. Friend of yours is he?"

"No comment."

"Where were you going to keep her?" said Francesca, suddenly changing tack.

"Eh?"

"Nikki Rivers. Where were you going to keep her? Lock up garage, perhaps? Done this kind of thing before, have you?"

"You're fishing."

"I'll bet you have a lock up garage not far away from your business. Wonder what we'll find if we go round there? Incriminating evidence, I'll bet."

"No comment."

"All right," said Francesca. "That's enough for now. We'll be holding you overnight. We'll come back to you tomorrow morning when we may have some more evidence."

"Can't wait."

"We'll get a PC to take you to a cell," said Francesca, gathering her papers up.

"Wait a minute," said the solicitor. "Could I have a word with my client before he goes?"

"Certainly, sir. No problem."

Francesca and Gary withdrew from the room – leaving Eel alone with his solicitor. "Look, smart arse," said the solicitor, "when we agree a 'no comment' strategy, it's 'no comment' all the way down the line. No so called clever answers. You let things slip by them. For instance, they now know you were hired by somebody else because of what you said. Remember, I may be representing you but I'm being paid by someone else – and he

270

won't like what I've got to tell him about how things have gone. You'll be lucky if he keeps on funding your legal representation. And remember I charge more than you can afford."

Eel nodded sullenly. The solicitor got up to go and opened the door to the interview room. "Ready for you to take my client away," he said.

• • ● • •

"Ain't you going to ask me how I got this sore head?" said Bruiser to the police constable sitting by his bedside in the hospital. "I'm a victim here."

"Yes, sir, of course," said the constable sarcastically.

"I've been hurt."

"It's no use trying to get me to give you some sympathy. All I'm doing in staying with you until the doctors say you're fit to be interviewed. Then I hand you over to the detectives."

Bruiser scowled. "Nurse, nurse," he shouted. A nurse came to his bedside. "Am I fit to be discharged?" he asked.

"The doctor felt it would be best if you stayed in overnight so we can observe you. You've got a nasty head wound."

"I know. That's what I've been telling this police officer. You tell him. Then maybe he'll do something about it."

"You just stay there, sir," said the nurse. "We'll review your situation in the morning."

"Well, I'm going to discharge myself," he said. He sat up and tried to get out of bed but a sudden pain in his head forced him to cry out.

"Best to stay where you are, sir," said the nurse sympathetically.

At that stage Francesca and Gary came on to the ward and approached Bruiser's bed. "Oh, you again," said Bruiser. "I've been told I've got to stay here."

"We know," said Francesca. "We thought we'd just like to see how you were."

"Touching," said Bruiser sarcastically.

The two detectives ignored his remark. "We've been interviewing your colleague, Mr Higgs," began Francesca. "Most illuminating. We now know it wasn't your idea to mount this kidnapping – and that somebody else was going to pay for it. We have a pretty good idea who it was."

"Eel wouldn't have squealed."

"Do you know a Jerry Vincent?" persisted Francesca. Bruiser screwed up his face as if he was contemplating an answer to the question. The effort hurt him, though, and he just exclaimed "Ow!" and lay back on the bed again.

"I'll take that as a yes."

"You can take it how you like. I'm not telling you anything – unless you want to investigate this assault on me. I've been told it's an offence to use greater forced than necessary in defending yourself."

The police constable looked up, "He's been going on about that all the time," he said to Francesca and Gary,

"Are you going to charge that little girl with – oh, fuck –" he said as his head began to hurt again.

"We're going to charge that little girl - as you call her - with fuck all," said Gary. "She was going to the rescue of her landlady whom you were attempting to kidnap."

"There's no justice in this world," mumbled Bruiser as he drifted off to sleep.

"I don't think we'll get anything out of him this evening," said Francesca. "Let's go." She turned to the uniformed constable. "We'll get some relief for you but I think we'd better get going now."

"What do you think, Francesca?" said Gary as they left the hospital.

"I think he'll be all right tomorrow and then we'll be able to take him down to the station."

• • • • •

Rivers left his flat soon after the police had taken their statements. He left Jo, Debra and Nikki tucking in to bacon and mushrooms. He wanted to get to Vincent before the police did. He felt angry about what the property developer had been prepared to allow Bruiser and Eel to do to Nikki. He knew where to find him. Vincent obviously didn't worry too much about his own security. His home address was the same as his business address which was advertised on the internet. It was a mansion in the countryside just about five miles out of Hertford. It was a gated residence and he felt that he was unlikely to be granted admittance if he just pressed the buzzer and told the occupants who he was. He parked on the roadside opposite the house to think about his strategy. As he was contemplating what to do, what looked like a chauffeur driven car made its way down the driveway and exited along the road in front of him. As it passed him, he could make out two figures in the back of the limousine. One he couldn't really see on the far side of the car. It was a man, he knew that, because whoever it was looked as if he was wearing a rather flamboyant gaily coloured suit. The other was a woman, also dressed in smart clothing. He was sure it was Jackie Quesling. Surprised, he determined to follow them. They drove for about five miles along winding country lanes before they came to a stop outside a pub which advertised the fact that it had won awards for its meals. The two passengers in the limousine got out of their car and made their way to the restaurant area of the pub. Rivers thought it would be a risk that he would be recognised if he went into the pub. He hadn't actually met Vincent but, seeing that the property developer had ordered the kidnapping of his wife, he might very well have been told what he looked like. He had met Jackie Quesling at the funeral wake of Rob Corcoran in the Dog and Partridge. She would be bound to remember him. He was just contemplating leaving when another taxi drew up outside the pub. Out of it stepped Douglas Roulay. This, he thought,

273

was just too intriguing for words. Roulay went into the pub's restaurant area and as Rivers looked through the window he could see him getting a warm greeting from both Vincent and Jackie. Reluctantly, Rivers decided to leave – but scratched his head thinking about the best way to follow up the evidence of this link between the three people meeting in this fairly exclusive diner. It was far enough out of Hertford for them to believe they could avoid detection. Whatever bound them together must have something to do with planning. He resolved to try and find out the following morning.

Meanwhile, inside the restaurant, all three were sitting down at the table. "So glad you could come, Douglas," said Vincent beaming as he shook Roulay by the hand. "I felt I owed you this dinner."

"I won't argue with that," said Roulay. "You know now I've also been suspended from the council?"

Jackie looked surprised but Vincent was more philosophical. "I had heard," he said. "I'm sorry."

"I can only think Roger Broadbent landed me in it."

"Yes," said Vincent, "and he's gone to ground now." The waiter brought them a bottle of white wine and Vincent indicated that Jackie should taste it for them. "There are some things to celebrate, though," said Vincent. "Jackie is £750,000 richer as a result of last night's planning committee meeting. She's got you to thank for that, Douglas, and I've at least got the privilege of securing the contract to build the new house on her land. Sadly, though, I won't be around to carry it out."

"What?" Both Jackie and Roulay sounded shocked.

"I'm having to do a moonlight flit tonight. Two employees of mine have been arrested on an attempted kidnapping charge. There's no obvious link between us over the kidnapping but I prefer to be safe than sorry."

"Who were you having kidnapped?" asked Roulay.

"I'd prefer it if you re-phrased that question. It assumes guilt."

"Who do they say these people kidnapped?"

"They tried to kidnap Nikki Rivers – the wife of a private detective."

"Who is investigating the murder of Rob Corcoran," said Jackie.

"I had nothing to do with that," said Vincent. "Anyhow, while I say I won't be around to carry out the contract, there is a subsidiary company."

"There always is," said Roulay.

"It's run by a distant – very distant – cousin of mine and it will carry out the work." He turned to Jackie. "He'll be contacting you to sign the contract tomorrow morning. In the meantime, I've taken all the assets out of my company and I'll be flying to Spain tomorrow morning where I've arranged to access them through a newly established account."

"When were these two guys arrested?" asked Roulay.

"About five o'clock this evening?"

"Gosh, you don't hang about," said Jackie sounding impressed.

"I find it best not to."

"You do realise people will think you're responsible for Rob Corcoran's murder if you run?" said Roulay.

"Well, that'll be helpful for somebody."

"They'll put out an arrest warrant for you."

"I won't exist. Jerry Vincent will be no longer after tonight. Actually, I'll let you into a secret. He never did exist."

Jackie looked puzzled. "So who are you then?"

He took her hand in his. "Some people just ask the wrong questions," he said. "Douglas," he said.

At that moment, the waiter returned to the table. "There's a taxi outside for Mr Vincent," he said.

"Yes," he said to his two companions. "I won't be staying to eat with you. I've put £100 behind the bar for your meal. Enjoy!" With that, he was gone – arranging for the taxi to take him home where he picked up some essential items for his sojourn in Spain. A few hours later a Roger Bunting, complete with passport, boarded a flight from Stansted airport to Barcelona.

· · ● · ·

"I'm saying nothing," said Bruiser as he was confronted by Francesca and Gary across the interviewing room table the following morning. He had been discharged from hospital but arrested on suspicion of attempted kidnapping before he could leave it. A couple of police constables had then taken him back to the police station to await questioning.

"We'll see," said Francesca. "First of all, I have to tell you, Bertram Percival McCarthy, that you have been arrested on suspicion of attempted kidnapping." She had to pause at this juncture because of an uncontrollable outbreak of laughter from Gary.

"What's so funny?" snarled Bruiser.

"Bertram Percival," said Gary. "Who the hell gave you those names?"

"No comment."

Gary seemed to think Bruiser's response to this question was comical, too. "You poor sod," he said. "It's more embarrassing than Inspector Morse's first name in the TV series."

Francesca managed to establish a semblance of decorum and cautioned him again. "Now," she said, "we know you didn't plan the kidnapping yourself. It would considerably help your case if you were to tell us who did."

"So Eel didn't snitch, then," said Bruiser. "I thought not."

"So you're confirming, too, that the two of you weren't acting alone?"

"No comment."

"Come on, Bertram Percival, you might as well tell us who did hire you?" Gary couldn't control a snigger.

"Don't call me that," said Bruiser.

"Or you'll do what? Your days of threatening are over, Bertram Percival. Unless, of course, you want to take on a prisoner."

"I'll fucking kill you."

"I don't think you will, Bertie. Too many witnesses." Bruiser reached out across the table and tried to drag Gary off his chair. His solicitor put out a restraining arm and managed to calm him down.

"Let's get back to this case, shall we, Mr McCarthy?" said Francesca.

"It's not me that's taking the mickey," protested Bruiser.

"Were the two of you acting alone when you attempted to kidnap Mrs Rivers?"

"No comment."

"What did the two of you say to Jerry Vincent on the evening before the attempted kidnapping?"

"No comment."

"Come on, Bertie, you can tell us," coaxed Gary. Bruiser swung a wild punch at Gary and caught him on the jaw. "Right," said Gary, nursing his injured jaw, "that's you done for assaulting a police officer at the very least."

Bruiser's solicitor looked at him in exasperation. "You're not helping yourself, Mr McCarthy," he said.

"I see you're not on first name terms with your solicitor," said Gary laughing.

"If you're not careful you'll get my fist down your throat."

"Mr McCarthy," said Francesca, sounding irritated. "Will you stop threatening my fellow officer."

"I suggest you stop him from goading my client," said the solicitor.

"All that I can say is that he seems easily goaded. Brawn rather than the intellect that was needed to plan this operation successfully."

"That was Eel," protested Bruiser.

"Thank you, Mr McCarthy," said Francesca smiling. "That's exactly what I wanted to hear. So Mr Higgs planned this attempted kidnapping. What was his motive?"

At this moment, Bruiser's solicitor's mobile – on silent – started vibrating in his pocket. "Excuse me, I have to take this," he said. "Can we adjourn for a minute?"

Francesca nodded and turned the tape recorder off. The solicitor left the room only to come back a few moments later and ask if he could have a word with his client in private. "I've just received a message," he said to Bruiser once they were alone. "It tells me my client can now land Jerry Vincent in it if it helps their case. I suggest you do. After all, it will take some of the heat that you've placed on Eel off him."

Bruiser nodded. "I'd like to set the record straight," he said.

"We'll call the police back in."

"I'd like to make a statement," said Bruiser when Francesca and Gary returned. "We were hired by Jerry Vincent to do the kidnapping."

"Why?" asked Francesca.

"You don't need to know that."

"Why?" repeated Francesca.

"Tell her," said the solicitor. "It's all right."

"He was worried about Mrs Rivers' husband pursuing allegations of corruption in the planning department. He thought if we kidnapped her that he would stop his investigations."

"Thank you, Mr McCarthy, you've been most helpful."

Francesca switched the tape off. "Come on, Detective Constable Clarke," she said. "We have to pay a visit to Jerry Vincent. Call in one of the police constable's to take Mr McCarthy to a cell." She turned to the solicitor. "We will be seeking permission from the Crown Prosecution Service to charge your client with attempted kidnapping and then we'll be back to you." She noticed that Gary was having some difficulty unplugging the tape. "Leave that to one of the PC's," she said. "We've got to move quickly."

• • • • •

Rivers went back to Vincent's mansion in the morning. As he drove up to the gates, he could see a car had already gone through to the house. A sharp-suited man was placing a key in the door. He decided to press the buzzer to get the gates open.

"Who is it?" came a voice from inside the house. In all likelihood, it was the sharp-suited man he had seen entering.

"I have a parcel for Mr Vincent," he said.

"You're too late. He's gone."

"Gone?" repeated Rivers. "Gone where?"

"I don't know. I'm from the local estate agents. He's charged us with selling the property."

"He must have left you with a forwarding address."

"He's gone to Spain. He said he'd contact us when he had sorted out somewhere to stay. He's given us the name of a friend to deal with in the meantime."

"Could you give me that?"

"I don't know that I can. I've no proof of who you are. Anyhow, a delivery man wouldn't need to know that."

"Oh, come on," said Rivers. "I've no proof about you either."

"Sorry mate." By this time the man had come out of the house. He looked down the driveway at the closed wrought iron gates. He could see Rivers standing by his car. "You don't even look like a tradesman," he said.

"Sorry. Could you tell me what I should wear next time?"

The other man laughed. "Have a good day," he said, going inside the house and shutting the door behind him.

Rivers cut his losses. He decided he would drive over to Jackie Quesling's shop in an attempt to find out more about the previous night's dinner with Vincent and Roulay. "Hallo, Mr Rivers," she said as she greeted him.

"Just by chance," he said. "I happened to be drinking in a village pub last night. I saw you at a table with Douglas Roulay and Jerry Vincent."

"Is that any business of yours?" she said coldly.

"Yes, I'm still investigating the murder of Rob Corcoran. It strikes me the only reason the three of you would be dining together is because of a planning connection. Am I right?"

"It was a private dinner," said Jackie coldly.

"Did Jerry Vincent stay for the meal?"

Jackie was taken by surprise by this question. "I beg your pardon?"

"I think you heard. I wondered if Jerry Vincent stayed for the meal. Only I went round to his home this morning and it's empty. He's gone – put it on the market and left a friend to deal with the sale. That friend wouldn't be you, would it?"

"No," she said, sounding indignant. "Look, if you want to pursue Jerry Vincent, pursue Jerry Vincent. He's just a friend."

"As, I assume, is Douglas Roulay. Would he be the friend left in charge of selling the mansion?"

"You'd have to ask him that."

"The topic didn't come up for discussion last night?"

"Oh. As a matter of fact, it did take us by surprise when Jerry pulled out of the meal last night. He had arranged it."

"After a tête à tête with you beforehand."

"I'm sorry."

"I followed you and him from the mansion to the pub last night."

"You shouldn't read anything into that, Mr Rivers. Jerry and I are just friends."

"Who happen to have a joint interest in planning?" Jackie started. "Ah, I've touched a raw nerve there," he said. "Did you realise that – if Jerry hadn't done a midnight bunk last night – he would probably have been arrested by the police today?"

"No" she said.

"Two people he hired have been charged with attempting to kidnap my wife. They threatened to cut her finger off. Charming – the company you keep."

"That's nothing to do with me, Mr Rivers."

"I'm sure you'd never do anything so vulgar as chop people's fingers off," With that, he turned on his heels to go. "But remember, your friend would," he said as a parting shot.

"Mr Rivers?" she said, calling him back. "I've been thinking about what you've been saying," she said. "If Jerry Vincent is as you say – so vicious he thinks nothing of hiring people to cut somebody's finger off – doesn't it occur to you –." She paused for a moment. "Well, would he have stopped at murder if he knew that Rob Corcoran was investigating him for attempting to corrupt planning officials?"

"Nicely put, Miss Quesling. I'll think about that." It was his turn to think for a moment. "Perhaps the same could have been said about people who connived with him over planning corruption," he said. With that, he swiftly exited the shop before he could hear her riposte.

• • • • •

"Did you follow up those leads I gave you?" said Colin Standen as he noticed Jo at the other end of the bar in the Dog and Partridge.

"Yes," said Jo, "and you got one thing wrong."

"Oh?" said Colin.

"The dog."

"What about the dog?"

"You don't have one."

"I told you – I walk one for a friend."

"You told me that after I challenged you. Your friends don't seem to think you take enough notice of any neighbour's dog to make a mistake and tell somebody else it's yours."

"What about Trish, then?"

"You had a row with her earlier in the day and she dumped you. She was nowhere near Rob Corcoran's house when you were walking your non-existent dog. As for Roger Broadbent, yes – he did visit Rob Corcoran's house earlier that evening but there's no proof that he ever went back. You've wasted my time, Mr Standen and you're a waste of space."

Jo suddenly realised he had been speaking louder than he had meant to as a woman came over from the other side of the bar and started to remonstrate with him. "You shouldn't speak to my brother like that,"she said. "He's only trying to help."

"I tell you what your information does tell me," said Jo. "If there's a smidgeon of truth in it – and I think you are right about Roger Broadbent – all it shows me is that you were hanging around outside Rob Corcoran's home. I wonder why, Mr Standen. I wonder why."

"You're not accusing me of being involved with the murder?"

"I'd like to, Mr Standen. Believe me, I'd like to."

"Come on, Colin, we're not going to listen to this," said his sister. With that, she shepherded Standen out of the bar – leaving Jo to ponder the events of the last few minutes.

"What are you doing?"said Jed Coulson, the publican, sidling over to Jo. "Frightening my customers off?"

"I'm sorry,"said Jo.

"No, that's all right. That's one customer I wouldn't mind losing. He just hangs around. Never buys a drink. Or hardly ever. I suppose you have to feel sorry for him. He was made redundant a couple of months ago and – by all accounts – didn't get a decent pay-off. He's just on the cadge most of the time."

"Was he always like that?"

"No," said Jed,"he was quite a happy-go-luck punter at one stage. Always used to drink a bit too much, you know. You can't help but feel sorry for him. It must have been a shock to him when Trish dumped him. There he was – pretending to be her closest friend and father confessor. A role that he only took on when he heard that she was due to inherit Rob's money as she was still legally his wife. He must have thought he was in there. I blame her a bit – she didn't discourage him. Then she goes and dumps him immediately after Rob dies. No wonder he's crestfallen. He'll never get that close to money again – at least I doubt it."

Jo nodded. "Does his sister live with him?" he asked.

"We don't often see her in the pub. She's a bit – you know – rough and ready. I think her name's Felicity. No, I don't think we'll miss them if you've scared them away."

Jo was still looking at the door where they had just exited thoughtfully. Then he snapped out of his thoughts. "You might be gaining me as a regular," he said to Jed. "I've just rented a flat near the town centre."

"Oh, I thought you and Rivers worked in Finchley."

"We do," he said, "but it's not that far away. Anyhow, this is a nicer place." Jo still sounded half distracted, thought Jed. Obviously what he had said about Colin Standen had given him some food for thought.

• • ● • •

Rivers went straight from his meeting with Jackie Quesling to the council office planning department. He was not sure who to ask for upon arrival. Roger Broadbent was no longer there and Douglas Roulay would not help if he was. Instead, he just asked if he could see someone about a planning application. The receptionist rang to what had been Roger and Rob's office and a lanky young man with a smile on his face appeared.

"Sorry to disturb you," said Rivers. He showed the man his business card.

"Oh, are you investigating this planning corruption thing?" said the young man.

"You could say that. I've been hired by the parents of Rob Corcoran – one of your predecessors – to find out why he was killed."

"Yes, this is not a happy department," said the man. "One member of staff murdered and two suspended for corruption.

That's in a department of three."

"Two suspended?" queried Rivers.

"Yes, Roger Broadbent and the boss – Douglas Roulay."

"Do you know what was alleged against him?"

"I'm not sure I should be talking about it because it's sub judice but I think the allegations are much the same as those that were levied against Roger Broadbent."

"I'd like to look through the applications approved at the last meeting – and then compare them to the original applications."

"Okay," said the planning official. "Here's a copy of the agenda for the latest meeting. Nobody's typed up the minutes yet. But if you're particularly interested in any particular one I could probably find out what happened."

"Thank you," said Rivers. He took the planning agenda and began to read thoroughly through. He noticed the application to build homes submitted by Jerry Vincent and then his eyes alighted on one by a Ms Jacqueline Quesling to build an extra home on property she owned at the site of her present home. It had a scaled drawing of the proposed house and there was a report by Roger Broadbent recommending approval of the application. Broadbent's seal of approval had also been given to the housing development proposed by Jerry Vincent. He walked over to the planning office with the two applications in his hand. "What happened to these two?" he asked the official.

"Let me see," he said. "I can probably find out online." He played with his computer for a while. "Yes," he said, "the Vincent development was deferred. Not surprising, really. The Quesling one was approved. A bit controversial, that. It was against council policy being in a conservation area but then I suppose it is only a small scale development."

"She'd have stood to gain a lot of money from it."

"Oh, yes, a property like the one proposed would probably fetch around £750,000 to one million pounds on the open market."

"Thank you," said Rivers. "Do you have the original application?"

"Is that not it with the agenda?"

"I don't know," said Rivers, "but I'd like to check that out – see whether it's been altered in any way."

"Right," said the official. "All we need to do is key in a key word from the application once I've got the submissions list up and it should show us details of the application when it was submitted." He did as he had said and printed out the resulting application for Rivers who then scrutinised it carefully. "Anything in it?" asked the official.

"Yes, interesting," said Rivers. "The original application says that the specifications for the new development have been designed by Jerry Vincent and associates – but that's missing from the application that went before the committee. Somebody was attempting to cover up Jerry Vincent's involvement in the application. Who could that have been?"

"Well, the applicant wouldn't have access to our process to do that – nor would Jerry Vincent. The only people who could have done that would be staff in the planning department."

"So Roger Broadbent, Douglas Roulay and Rob Corcoran?"

"Yes."

"Well, I think we can rule Rob Corcoran out. He's the knight in shining armour. With Roger Broadbent, it depends when the substitution was made. Douglas Roulay was only suspended yesterday so he was the only one surviving until the meeting. I know who my money's on. Could I take a photo copy of these?"

"By all means," said the planning official. Rivers did so and bade his leave. "Good luck," the official said, "and thanks for brightening up my afternoon."

• • • • •

"Nikki," said Jo tentatively. "I've found somewhere to live. A two-bedroomed flat in Hertford. Really nice. It'll give you two some space."

Nikki beamed at him. "Might help you, too, Jo," she said. "You'll be freer to relax, kick off your shoes, invite Francesca round for a meal."

"There is that," acknowledged Jo, "although…."

"Although what?"

"When she came to the flat yesterday to arrest Bruiser and Eel, she never said a word to me."

"She was on duty. I was the attempted kidnapping victim, Philip was the senior partner in the detective agency. You shouldn't read too much into that."

Jo nodded. "I'm not all that good starting relationships," he said. He smiled. "Very good at finishing them, though."

"Philip and I have a lot of practice at both," said Nikki. "I was a bit upset yesterday that Philip hadn't told me I was in danger of being kidnapped. He said he didn't want to worry me and thought he had it covered. I'm not so sure that it wasn't really because he wanted to catch those two in the act of kidnapping."

"It worked," said Jo. "No-one was hurt." He smiled. "Except Bruiser by the frying pan. That is a lethal weapon in the hands of Debra. Where is she, by the way?"

"She's gone to collect more of her things from Sue Plummer's place."

"Oh. She should have waited. I could have given her a lift."

"I think she had some demons she wanted to confront. She wanted some time on her own."

Jo nodded. "I was going to ask her if she would like to move in with me."

"Be careful how you put that to her, Jo," said Nikki. "She might think you're after her body."

Jo smiled. "She's familiar with that area." He blushed at his double entendre. "I mean Hertford." he said. "I could give her a lift into work most days," he added.

They were interrupted by the arrival of Rivers. He almost burst into the room – so enthusiastic was his entrance.

"We're getting somewhere," he said. "Jackie Quesling stands to gain substantially from permission from the council to build a new home on her property. Guess what? The design was drawn up by Jerry Vincent and they got it through the planning committee by airbrushing any mention of him out of the application. That can only have been done by a planning department official and she had dinner with Douglas Roulay last night."

Jo nodded. "Good work," he said, "but I haven't exactly been slack either. Colin Standen was desperate for cash after having been made redundant from his job. He was wooing Trish Corcoran heavily when he found out she was due to inherit Rob Corcoran's money."

"Could he really be a killer?"

"He's a nasty bit of work."

Rivers thought for a moment. "Remember it could have taken two people to kill Rob Corcoran – one to lure him out of the house and the other to drive the car into him. It certainly could have taken two people to kill Sue Plummer. Difficult to hang someone from the ceiling by yourself."

"He's got a sister. I was going to try to find out more about her. Jed Coulson described her as rough and ready."

"Ready for what?" asked Rivers.

Jo gave him a knowing glance. "So I've told you who I think carried out the murders? Could Jackie Quesling have done them by herself?"

"Same answer as for Colin Standen. No," said Rivers. "But both Jerry Vincent and Douglas Roulay were in on the planning corruption. We can virtually be sure of that. It could have been either of them." He paused for a moment. "So have we narrowed our list of suspects down to two out of these five?"

"The new evidence does seem to point in their direction," admitted Jo. "Remember, though, Miranda Headley couldn't account for her movements between leaving Jackie Quesling's home and arriving at Rob Corcoran's after he had been killed. Trish Corcoran, too, stood to gain financially from her husband's death. And Roger Broadbent?"

"I believe Roger when he says he's making a clean breast of things," said Jo.

"Neither of the other two have an obvious partner to help them carry out the killing," said Rivers. "At least Miranda Headley does – her husband, Aaron – but he's got the best alibi in the world. He was being questioned by the police. Also, if you were investigating the case at the very moment Rob Corcoran died, you'd have to say there was a strong case for suggesting Trish could be in cahoots with Colin Standen. But she dumped him immediately afterwards. Dangerous thing to do if he'd committed murder for you. By the way, experience tells me not to go along with your theory that it's the nastiest bit of work that carried out the murder."

Jo smiled. "Okay," he said.

"And there are several contenders for nastiest bit of work. You'd have to put Jerry Vincent and Bruiser and Eel into that category." He reflected for a moment. "It's not Bruiser and Eel, by the way."

"Oh. Why?"

"If you believe the theory that Debra's tape recording at the police station shows she didn't kill Rob Corcoran but gives a strong indication that she saw who did, it isn't them. She said she'd never seen them before when they were here last night."

"Time, then, to get her to tell us who it was she did see."

"Yes," said Rivers. At that moment, the key turned in the lock and Debra arrived home with her bags of belongings. Rivers lent over to Jo, touching his arm. "We do this very gently," he said. "One on one. By me. We don't want to alarm her."

• • • • •

288

Francesca Manners pressed the buzzer on Jerry Vincent's entry phone. "Police," she said as a voice answered. The gates were opened and Francesca and Detective Constable Johnson accompanied by two police cars entered the driveway. By the time they got to the front door a young man – the man Rivers had met when visiting the property earlier in the day – was standing there ready to greet them. Behind him were a middle-aged couple, very smartly dressed. There was a four-wheel drive car in the driveway next to a more modest vehicle, which Francesca surmised belonged to the younger man. "We're looking for Jerry Vincent," she said.

"I'm afraid he's not here," said the young man.

"And you are?"

"Ed Franklin. I work for the estate agent's," he said, pointing to the board which had been put up at the entrance to the property. "I was just showing these people round," he said – turning to point to the middle aged couple who indicated they would like to leave. Francesca did not stand in their way. "Thank you, Inspector, you've just lost me a potential sale."

Francesca ignored the remark. "Where is Mr Vincent?"

"He's not here."

"That much is obvious," she said sharply. "Are you expecting him back?"

"I think he's gone away on holiday."

"So – if that couple had wanted to make an offer for the property – how would you have contacted him?"

"He's left a friend in charge of overseeing the sale."

Francesca was just about to ask him the name of the friend when a police sergeant approached her. "What do you want my men to do?" he asked.

"Search the property from top to bottom. You're looking for any papers that link to planning matters, anything that suggests contact between the owner – Jerry Vincent – and a couple of men named Bruiser and Eel or McCarthy and Higgs,"

"Right, ma'am," said the sergeant.

Francesca smiled. She might manage to coach Gary into stopping the use of the word "ma'am" but it was a completely different matter with the uniformed sector. Thinking of Gary reminded her. He was masterminding the search of Bruiser and Eel's yard. She rang him on her mobile. "Anything to report?" she asked.

"Not much," he said. "There is an address book. It has Jerry Vincent's address and telephone number in it but nobody else's you'd recognise. There are scraps of crunched up paper in the bin. One has Rob Corcoran's address on it – but we were pretty sure they visited him the night before he died so I'm not sure it proves anything."

"Bag them all and have them brought back to the station." She switched off the mobile and put it back in her pocket.

"I don't suppose there's anything else I can help you with?" said the estate agent.

"No," said Francesca, distracted for a minute as she contemplated whether Gary's findings had any significance. "Wait a minute," she said. "Who was this friend who has been put in charge of overseeing the sale of the property?"

"Let me get my brief case," he said. He walked over to his car and extracted it from the front seat. He pulled an envelope from it and started to read it. "His name's Douglas Roulay," he said. "We got a letter witnessed by two solicitors and signed by Mr Vincent himself this morning authorising Mr Roulay to take charge of the sale and – as Mr Vincent's agent – to receive any proceeds from the sale."

"Thank you, Mr Franklin," said Francesca. "You've been most helpful." She turned to Detective Constable Johnson. "Find me Douglas Roulay's address – quickly," she said. "People involved in this case seem to have a penchant for taking sudden foreign holidays." Within minutes she was speeding away from Vincent's mansion to an altogether more modest detached home on the outskirts of Hertford – where Douglas Roulay lived. She knocked on the door. "Police," she snapped again as it was opened. "Douglas Roulay?"

"Yes."

"I'm surprised to find you in," she confessed.

"You must have heard," he said. "I've been suspended from work because of allegations of corruption in my department." No suggestion there, she thought, that he was in any way culpable for what had happened. "Is that what I can help you with?"

"It's linked to that," said Francesca. Events had moved so quickly during the last twenty-four hours that she was not exactly sure what she was hoping to prove by questioning him – except confirming the link between him and Jerry Vincent. "I understand you know a man called Jerry Vincent," she said.

"Yes," he said. "He's a very difficult man to ignore. Look, if this is in any way linked to the corruption inquiry, I think you had better speak to my solicitor."

"Actually, it's not really you that we want," she said. "We're trying to find Jerry Vincent."

"Ah, Jerry. I understand he's gone abroad for a holiday. In fact, I know he's gone abroad for a holiday. I met him for dinner last night and he took off for the airport from the pub where we ate."

"Right. Do you know where he went?"

"I'm afraid not, Detective Chief Inspector. I think it was Spain but I couldn't be sure."

"Or which airport he went from?"

"Again, I'm sorry. I don't know."

"I believe he's left you in charge of the sale of his mansion."

"Yes," he said. "I received a letter to that effect this morning. I have to sign an agreement, get it witnessed but – in the end – I will be in charge of the sale."

"And when it's completed how will you communicate with him?"

"I understand that he will contact me at some stage with

a forwarding address," said Roulay. "Actually, that's rather the wrong word. I suppose he'll be in touch with me about a forwarding address. It was a complete surprise when I received this information this morning."

"Bit strange, isn't it? I mean the property must be worth £1.5 to £2million – money that will go into your bank account. You must be very good friends – otherwise, how's he sure you won't do a runner?"

"I assure you, Detective Chief Inspector, I have no intention of doing that."

"You're at the centre of a planning corruption scandal, you're potentially facing a criminal sentence. Quite nice to have the odd £1.5million to £2million to fall back on to escape justice. Maybe it's a payment from Mr Vincent as a sort of apology for landing you in it through persuading you to accept corrupt money?"

"I think you're getting ahead of yourself, Inspector," said Roulay, smiling politely. "As I said, if you wish to discuss the allegations of corruption, you had better speak to my solicitor. I'll get you his contact details." With that Roulay began to turn around and go back into the house.

"That won't be necessary," said Francesca. She felt she could do better things with her time than spend an hour or so sitting opposite a solicitor trying to stonewall on all her suggestions. "So, to sum it up," she said. "You are effectively now the beneficiary of the sale of Mr Vincent's property until you hear from him giving you a forwarding address. As he's on the run, I would have thought that was highly unlikely. Congratulations, Mr Roulay. You seem to have gotten your hands on a cool £2 million this morning without having to put any effort in." She made as if to leave but then turned round. "By the way, what were you doing on the evening of Tuesday, May 22?"

"May 22? What's this about?"

"Between the hours of 8.30pm and 10pm?" He thought for a moment. "That's the night of Rob Corcoran's murder, isn't it?"

"That date indelibly imprinted on your mind, is it? I wonder why."

"I was probably at home with my wife," he said. "Would you like me to go and check?"

"Don't bother," she said. "I'm sure we'll return to it again." She detected that he looked worried for the first time during the course of their interview. "Good-day, Mr Roulay." She got back into the car with Detective Constable Johnson. "I do hate the polite smile of the guilty middle classes," she said as she fastened her seat built. They drove away from the house. A glance back from Francesca revealed that Roulay was no longer smiling.

CHAPTER TEN

"Debra, you do trust me, don't you?" said Rivers after he had invited her to sit down on the settee opposite him.

"Yes," she said awkwardly. It was as if she was embarrassed about the potential intimacy of their conversation.

"You know also that I am trying to solve these murders to bring some settlement to Rob's parents and to avoid anybody else getting killed in the way Sue was?"

"Yes." She did not seem relaxed, he thought.

"I think you can help me," he said. "I've been reading through the transcript of your interview with the police." He could sense her tensing up. "Don't worry, Debra, that's not going to happen again – that sort of interview. Consigned to the dustbin." He thought he detected a smile almost breaking through the surface. "It seems to me that – although you confessed to Detective Constable Clarke – you only did it to get him off your back." She looked puzzled – perhaps, he thought, she was unfamiliar with the phrase. "I don't mean he was on your back," he said apologetically. "I just mean that you wanted him to go away – to stop." She nodded.

"Reading through the interview, it becomes obvious you didn't kill anybody. It's entirely foreign to your nature. You never mention killing Rob again but you do describe – very accurately, according to Francesca – my detective friend – how the murder happened." She nodded again – a little more warily this time. "It seems to me that you must have witnessed the murder," he said. "Did you?" His question was followed by silence. "Did you, Debra?" he said. "Did you see the murder?" She still failed to respond. "Are you frightened, Debra? Is that it? Are you frightened of what will happen if you tell me?" She nodded again – furiously this time. "Well, you said you trusted me," he said slowly, "and I won't tell anybody else you told me. In fact, I won't mention it to anybody – except Jo, and you trust him, too, don't you?"

"Yes," she said. "I like Jo. He's asked me to live with him."

Rivers took a sharp intake of breath. "I don't think he's quite done that," he said. "He's asked if you'd like to share his flat." Again the nodding was on the brisk side. It was obvious she did not realise the connotations that the idea of living together conjured up. In her book, she had lived with Sue Plummer. Now she was living with Rivers and Nikki. In the future, she would be living with Jo. No difference. "So I won't tell anybody what you tell me," said Rivers. "Debra, did you see the murder?"

"Yes," she said. "I was angry at the way Rob had treated Sue. I decided to stalk him so he couldn't forget what he had done. I was outside his house that night."

"And what happened?"

"I saw this woman knock on the door. She started waving her hands about and pointed to her car. He came out of the door. She called him over to the driver's side which was out in the roadway and pointed to something in the car. He looked at her and then bent over – as if to take something out of the car. He took something from the car and then backed out into the street and shut the door. It was then that a car came down the road – gathering speed – and knocked him over."

"Where was the woman?"

"She'd moved out of the way. She was back on the pavement."

"What happened then?"

"The car reversed and drove over Rob's body again. It came to a stop and then went forwards again – again hitting Rob as he lay in the road. The woman then left the pavement and picked up whatever it was Rob had taken from the car. I noticed she was wearing gloves. She then ran away down the road as quickly as she could."

"And what did you do?"

"I didn't know what to do. I was scared. I didn't know whether they had seen me or not. I thought I'd better get away."

"So did you see who it was?"

"I saw her. I was only on the other side of street."

"Who was it?"

"I don't know," she said hesitantly. Rivers sighed. "It's not much help, is it?" she asked.

Rivers momentarily chastised himself for sighing. "You've done really well, Debra. Really well. We now know there were two people involved in the crime." She smiled and nodded. "Tell me, Debra, would you recognise her if you saw her again?"

"Oh, yes," said Debra definitely.

"Good. And the driver of the car?"

"It looked like a man. He was thickset but I couldn't really see his face. I was concentrating on trying to hide when the car came down the road."

"I don't blame you," said Rivers. "I think I would have done, too." He paused for thought – trying to work out where this conversation was going to. "I tell you something," he said. "I think there are four women it could have been. Would you like to help me identify who it was?"

"Yes," said Debra.

"Because the woman who killed Rob could have had a part in killing Sue, too, and you'd like me to catch who killed Sue, wouldn't you?"

"Yes," she said in an unwavering voice.

"So what we're going to do tomorrow is visit all these four women," he said, "and you can tell me which one of them it was that killed Rob. Don't worry – I won't leave you alone in their company. We can just look at them from across the road if you like. There's no reason to be scared." Debra smiled. She reached her hand out towards Rivers and he grasped it. "Well done," he said. "That's what we'll do then." He held her hand firmly for a moment and then let go. "There's still one or two questions I'd like to ask you, if that's okay," he continued.

Debra nodded again. "Yes, that's all right," she said.

"What did you do when you got home that night? Did you tell Sue what you'd seen?"

"No, I was scared and she was so upset about what had happened to Rob. I didn't think it was the right time. I wasn't sure what she would do."

"I see – but did you tell her?"

"The following evening," said Debra. "I described the woman to her and she said she thought she knew who it was. In fact, she was more definite than that. She said she was certain she knew who it was."

"Did she tell you?"

"No but then it wouldn't have meant much to me," she said. "I don't think I should have told her."

"Why?"

"I think that caused her death. She said the following evening that she was going to sort it out."

"What do you think she meant by that?"

"I think she was going to have it out with the woman."

"Very dangerous in view of what she had done, surely?"

"She knew the woman," said Debra. "I think she thought she'd be all right."

"But the way you've described the murder, it was very meticulously planned."

"I think she was wrong to go and see the woman. After Sue was killed, I thought the same thing would happen to me if I told anybody. That's why I kept quiet."

"Yes, I can understand that – but now you've got the protection of Jo and me I think we can go and make sure this woman is brought to justice." He smiled as he finished speaking. "Don't you think so?" he added.

"Yes," said Debra, nodding again.

"How do you think she killed Sue?"

"I don't know. I was out on the night she died. I came back to find her body." She looked miserable for a moment. "I did the wrong thing, didn't I?" she said. "If I'd told the police instead of Sue, she would be alive today." Then she added firmly: "And I didn't have any reason to mistrust the police then."

"No," said Rivers. "Well, relax now," he added. "I know it's been a big ordeal for you getting all this off your chest but I want you to think of it as my worry now – not yours. How old are you?"

"Twenty-two," she said.

Rivers nodded this time. "Then would you like a drink? A glass of wine, perhaps?"

"No, thanks, it makes me tiddly."

"Yes," said Rivers, " but I think I'll have one all the same."

• • ● • •

"Actually, I was hoping you'd do me a favour," said Jo as he poured Francesca a glass of wine.

"And there was I thinking this would be an entirely social occasion," said Francesca. "A chance for us to get to know each other better. A chance to look round your new flat."

Jo smiled. "It's all of those," he said, "but there is just one thing."

"You sound like Columbo," said Francesca. Jo did not understand the reference. "He's a TV detective," she added. "He – oh, it doesn't matter. What is this one thing?"

"Could you do a check on someone for me? She's Felicity Standen. What we find out could help you as well as me."

"Any address for her?"

"She's staying with her brother, Colin Standen, at present. I don't have any other address."

Francesca nodded. "I'll get someone to make a check for me." She took her mobile phone out of her pocket and contacted Johnson in the office, whom she knew was on evening duty. He said he would ring her back as soon as possible. "Why do you want to check her out?"

"Colin Standen has a financial motive for wanting Rob Corcoran dead. He had high hopes of a relationship with Trish Corcoran at the time of Rob's death – but, as you have pointed out, he had to have an accomplice to lure Rob out of his house."

"It could have been Trish."

"No, she dumped him – or told him there was no chance of a relationship – as soon as Rob died. She wouldn't have done that if they had been plotting his murder together."

They were interrupted by the sound of Francesca's mobile. It was Johnson. "There is a Felicity Standen on our records. Lives in Dalston in East London. At least that's the last known address for her. She's thickset. Late twenties, early thirties, I'd say." Francesca repeated the description for Jo's benefit. He nodded. "Go on," she said. "It could be her."

"She's been inside for causing grievous bodily harm. Five years. Out about a year ago. Nothing else except a couple of shoplifting charges in her younger days."

"It must have been a serious crime," said Francesca.

"In a pub, apparently. In the East End. There's never much information on these files."

"Thanks, Ryan," she said. "That's very useful." She turned to Jo. "Well?" she said.

"In the frame, I'd think. Who's your money on?"

"I've still not ruled out Bruiser and Eel – through Vincent – although there's a part of me that says that – although they're nasty guys – Vincent would rather have them frighten people but stop short of killing them. He's clever. In a funny way, I think it's somebody who's not used to killing or getting involved in violence."

"It's not Bruiser and Eel," said Jo emphatically. "Debra didn't recognise them when they tried to kidnap Nikki yesterday. More wine?"

"Yes," said Francesca. She offered her glass to him and he filled it up. "I notice you've got three places set for dinner," she added.

"Yes, Debra's sharing the flat with me. This is her first night here. I didn't think I could tell her to stay away."

Francesca smiled. "No need to," she said.

"I'll just see to the jerk chicken," said Jo. As he got up, the landline rang. "That can only be one person," said Jo. "Rivers. He's the only one who knows I've moved in."

"And Debra," Francesca pointed out. Jo picked up the receiver. It was Debra. She told him she planned to stay the night with Rivers and Nikki as they had 'a big day tomorrow'.

"Looks as if we are on our own," said Jo. "She's staying in Finchley. She talked of having 'a big day' tomorrow. I think Rivers must be getting somewhere with her."

"Doubtless we shall find out in the fullness of time."

"Do I detect a note of sarcasm there?" asked Jo.

"No," she said firmly. "I have complete faith in Philip to keep me abreast of important developments – but he'll only tell me when they are important developments. I also understand he has to be careful about making any links between Debra and the police – thanks to my esteemed detective constable."

"How are you getting on with him?" Jo asked.

"I'm not sure that's not privileged information," she replied.

"This isn't," said Jo. "How are you getting on with me?"

Francesca smiled. "You don't waste words," she said and then added: "I like you." She leant forward to take hold of his hand. "I like you very much."

"But…."

"I'm not sure," she said. "And when I'm not sure I don't start anything. Let's take it steady. We can go to see a film, have nights

300

out and see what happens – but don't let's complicate things."

Jo smiled. "I told Nikki yesterday – when she was asking about you – that I was better at ending relationships than starting them," he said. "I think maybe you are too."

"Maybe," said Francesca,

"That jerk chicken will be ready by now," said Jo.

• • ● • •

"Ready?" said Rivers as they got into the car that morning.

"Yes, I think so," said Debra.

"You'll never be on your own," said Rivers to reassure her, "and I haven't even told Jo what you told me yesterday."

Debra looked surprised. "Why not?" she said. "I'm going to be sharing a flat with him."

"I guess I just haven't had the time yet – but you're relaxed about me telling him. That's a good sign."

"I can trust him."

"Yes, he's probably more trustworthy and honest than I am."

"Stop the car," said Debra suddenly. Rivers obliged. "What did you mean by that?" she asked. "Are you telling me I can't trust you?"

Rivers sighed. Debra took things at face value, he remembered all too late. If you said somebody was more trustworthy than you it meant you were less trustworthy than them. "It was a figure of speech," he said. "I was trying to make you feel good about him but I'm just as trustworthy as I was before I made that silly remark. You can tell that by the fact that I didn't even tell Jo what you had said." She still looked apprehensive. "Come on, Debra," he said patting her knee. "It's all right. I won't let you down." She relaxed again. "Can I start the car?" Rivers asked.

"Yes," she said quietly.

"Now the first person we're going to see is Trish Corcoran. Rob's wife. They were separated. She's one of the four women suspects. She works in a charity shop in Hertford. I'm going to pretend I've just bought a house in Hertford and we need some furniture and knick-knacks for it. You come in with me. Don't say anything but let me know when we get back into the car whether you've ever seen her before."

"All right," said Debra. They drove up to Trish's shop and parked outside it. They entered it together.

"Mr Rivers," said Trish in acknowledgement of the private detective's presence. "What do you want this time?" she asked suspiciously.

"Don't worry," he said. "I haven't come here to question you. I'm just stocking up for a new house I've bought in Hertford. I remembered you ran a charity shop."

She nodded. "Well, have a look round and tell me if you find anything," she said.

Rivers did precisely that. He took a toaster from off the shelves and went to Trish to pay for it. "I'll have this," he said. "I might bring my wife round to have a look, too." Trish nodded. "Oh, this is my niece," he said by way of explanation for Debra's presence. Debra looked at him quizzically but Trish nodded again. She stared after him as he started up the car and drove off. Funny to make a special journey just for a toaster but…. Ah well, she said to herself as she shrugged her shoulders and resumed her position sitting by the reception desk.

Meanwhile, outside Rivers turned to Debra. "Well?" he asked.

"Never seen her before," said Debra.

"That's as I thought," he said, "but we did well to eliminate her as a suspect. "Right," he said. "Next we have to go to Miranda Headley. She was one of Rob's three girlfriends."

Debra obviously had something on her mind. Her brow was furrowed. She suddenly turned to Rivers. "You do lie," she said. "I'm not your niece."

"No," said Rivers, "but it was the best explanation I could come up with to explain why you were there."

Debra had not listening to his explanation. "I wish I was," she said. "Your niece."

Rivers smiled and started up the car. A few minutes later they drew up outside the block of flats where Miranda and Aaron lived and pressed the entry buzzer. "Philip Rivers for Miranda Headley," he said when a male voice answered.

"She's not here."

"Oh," said Rivers. "Could we come up for a moment? There's just one or two questions I have for you."

"For me?" Aaron sounded surprised. "I would have thought I'd be off your list of suspects by now." However, he opened the door. "Come in."

They traipsed into Aaron's living room. "This is my niece," said Rivers to explain Debra's presence again. "I've been put in charge of looking after her for the day." He looked at Debra who smiled weakly. He was glad she was so slight of build that she could pass for much younger than her actual age of 22.

"You're lucky to catch anyone in," said Aaron. "We've just been on holiday. Only got back last night. I thought I'd delay going back to work until tomorrow."

"Very sensible," said Rivers.

"Now, what do you want?" Aaron asked.

"I just wanted to see Miranda." In actual fact, that was all that he wanted – to give Debra a chance to see Miranda and determine whether she had seen her on the night of the murder.

"She went straight off this morning – to visit some relatives in Scotland," said Aaron. "She still feels shaken up by what happened to Rob and doesn't like staying around here."

"Sounds as if she wants to avoid questioning by people like me and the police," said Rivers. "She still hasn't given a satisfactory account of where she was at the time Rob Corcoran was killed. I'd like to give her another chance to clear that up."

"I'll pass on your message to her."

"Thanks." He looked at Aaron squarely in the eyes. "Can I ask you?" he asked. "Are you satisfied that your wife didn't kill Rob Corcoran?"

"I wouldn't be sticking with her if I wasn't," he said.

"So you are?"

"I repeat – I wouldn't be sticking with her if I wasn't."

"Do you have a photograph of her?" he suddenly asked.

"Why would you want one? You know what she looks like."

"Yes," said Rivers, "but you never know when it might become handy."

"Well, I haven't," said Aaron. Rivers looked surprised. "I tore up all the ones I had the day after she confessed she'd had an affair with Rob Corcoran."

Rivers sighed then he added: "You know, you're really lucky you've got such a good alibi. The kind of temper you've got – I could see you being in the frame for Rob's murder if you hadn't."

"You were leaving?" said Aaron through clenched teeth..

Rivers nodded. "Come on, Debra," he said. "We're finished here." Once outside, he added: "Shame – we can't yet eliminate her from the list of suspects."

• • ● • •

Francesca and Gary thought they would attend the hearing at the magistrate's court where Bruiser and Eel would be charged with attempted kidnapping. It was all very straightforward. The two of them were remanded in custody until an appearance at the Crown Court at a later date.

Francesca watched them being taken down to the cellars to await transport to prison. "You know," she said, "we've done a service taking those two off the streets. My predecessor, Larry Green, warned me about them. Said to be sure I had a watertight case against them before I charged them with anything – otherwise they'd come after me for vengeance."

"You have, though, haven't you?" asked Gary.

"Oh yes, they won't be seeing the outside of a prison for a good few years. Shame we've only got them on attempted kidnapping. There's so much more that we could bring against them."

"Like what?"

"An assault charge on Rob Corcoran. Our main witness is no longer with us, though, on that one."

"You don't think they're linked to his murder?"

"It would be so nice and neat if they were but no, I don't think so. Vincent and Bruiser and Eel are all nasty bits of work but I think Vincent appreciates it's best to avoid getting involved in a murder rap. He'll have made sure Eel, for one, understood that."

"Bruiser might not."

"Agreed," Francesca said.

"So," said Gary, "where do we go from here?"

"We await developments," his boss replied. "I think Philip Rivers is getting somewhere with Debra – so fingers crossed. We could go and put a bit more pressure on Douglas Roulay. It would very much have been in his interests to have stopped Rob Corcoran from making further enquiries. Besides, I like goading him. Would you like to come with me?"

"Of course, Francesca," he said.

· · **·** · ·

"And now we're going to the pub for lunch," said Rivers.

"I don't really want a drink," protested Debra. "I don't think it would do me any good. I need to stay sober."

"Our prime purpose is not to drink," he said. "We should be meeting another one of the suspects. You can have an orange juice." She seemed uninterested in this thought. "Or a diet coke?" She smiled and nodded her head enthusiastically. "Two diet cokes," he said as he approached the bar at the Dog and Partridge," and do you have anything to eat?"

305

"We've got sausage rolls or sandwiches," said Jed Coulson.

"Sausage roll, then." He looked at Debra who nodded. "Make that two."

"I'll just heat them up for you."

"Thank you."

"I hope you'll start to make more social visits to the pub. You need to sample some of our finest ales," said Jed.

"I will do when I move out to Hertford." Jed nodded approvingly. "By the way," said Rivers, "is Colin Standen still drinking here regularly?"

"Regular as clockwork. He'll be in within ten minutes. You mark my words."

"With his sister?"

"I think so," said Jed. "He was with her last night."

"Thanks," said Rivers.

"You know, you're the only customer I've ever had who's been waiting anxiously for the arrival of Colin Standen. Most people try to ignore him. He's becoming a bit of a drunk."

"Oh, since when?"

"Since he was given the heave-ho by Trish Corcoran." Jed came back with the two diet cokes. He placed one in front of Debra. "By the way, who's this?" he asked. "I take it it's not your wife?"

"No," said Rivers. "I thought you'd recognise her. Debra Paget. Sue Plummer's lodger. I'm helping her move back to Hertford."

"Oh yes," said Jed. "You have been in here once or twice before, haven't you?"

"Yes, I came in a couple of times with Sue," said Debra, "but pubs aren't really my thing. I don't like drinking."

At that moment Colin Standen came into the bar. He was followed by a rather thickset woman whom Rivers assumed was his sister. He ended up standing at the bar next to Rivers. "You two know each other?" asked Jed.

"Philip Rivers," said Rivers extending his hand.

"I've seen you in here a couple of times but I'm not talking to you. I gave your man a couple of tips which I thought might help him but he just slagged me off for wasting his time."

"Maybe you were," suggested Rivers.

"Your usual?" Jed asked Colin Standen.

"Yes, please, and a pint for my sister, Felicity," he said. He noticed Debra for the first time. "I've seen you in all in here before," he added. "You're the woman that was sharing a flat with Sue Plummer."

Rivers watched Debra closely as Colin Standen spoke to her. She had said that she hadn't really seen the driver of the car – but it could be, he thought, if it had have been Colin Standen some of his mannerisms might just trigger her memory. She seemed quite unconcerned to be in his company, though. He introduced her to his sister. Debra shook her hand without – again – showing any signs of nervousness. "Well," said Rivers to Debra, "we've got a pretty busy afternoon. We should be getting a move on. We should get some flowers for Jo's new flat – and your new flat as well, of course."

Debra nodded. She seemed a little quiet now but quite disposed towards moving on from the pub. Once they were outside, Rivers turned to her again. "Well?" he said.

"Nothing," she said. "Never seen her before in my life."

"And him?"

"Him?" said Debra sounding as if she was surprised to be asked about Colin.

"Yes, Could he have been the driver of the car?"

"Oh, I see what you mean," she said. "I told you I never saw the driver of the car – leastways not so that I'd recognise him again."

"But there was nothing in Colin Standen's mannerisms or build that triggered any memories of the driver of the car that night?"

"No," she said definitely. "But I didn't think you were driving me round today to find the driver of the car as well as the woman."

"No, I'm not really," said Rivers, "but I thought it was worth a try as he was one of the people who had a motive to kill Rob Corcoran. I thought meeting the driver might trigger a memory."

"Well, he doesn't mean anything to me," said Debra, "although I don't think that tells you very much."

"Okay," said Rivers starting up the engine to his car. "Only one more visit to be made. Jackie Quesling. Another one of Rob Corcoran's mistresses. She runs a flower shop so we can get some new flowers for your flat." He debated with himself. Would it be best for Debra to stay in the car – or accompany him into the shop? There were usually flowers on display outside at a florist's so Debra could take the option of studying Jackie from across the road. On the other hand, he doubted whether Jackie would clock on to the real motive behind his visit – and he would be with Debra, too, in the case of anything untoward happening. Best put the dilemma to Debra when they arrived at the shop, he thought.

• • ● • •

"I'm supposed to be putting pressure on you to solve the Rob Corcoran and Sue Plummer murders," said Chief Superintendent Rory Gleeson after he had summoned Francesca to see him that morning. "Two unsolved murders on our patch. Not good for the image. Mind you, I can't say the Chief Constable is leaning on me to get a result."

"No," said Francesca. "I suppose you can't."

"And not necessarily for the reason you think," he added.

"I'm sorry?" said Francesca.

"Because I am the new Chief Constable. I've been appointed this morning. I can't really lean on myself."

"Congratulations, sir – er Rory," she said.

"Rory will do fine when we're alone," he said. "Sir had better be used when we're in public." Francesca nodded. "Smartest move I ever made was taking you as my guest to that ball," he said. He slapped his thigh. Sensing she didn't quite share his enthusiasm for what he had just said, he added: "Don't worry, Francesca. I jest."

"When do you start in your new role?" she asked.

"I start on Monday. No sense in hanging around. Adrian Paul has gone. There's a vacuum at the moment. There's no point in me hanging around here when I could be getting to grips with the new job, though." He paused for a moment. "I did ask you here, though, for a briefing on how the murder enquiry – or enquiries – are going," he added.

"I think well," she said. "There's no doubt in my mind that they were both committed by the same person or persons. In fact, definitely, persons. You must have read the briefing notes. Rob Corcoran was enticed out of his house by someone – hence ending up in the street without any socks or shoes. Also, it would probably have taken two people to stage the mock hanging of Sue Plummer. We think we have a witness to the first murder – but they're a bit afraid to come forward. I'm confident we can overcome that."

"Good," said Rory. "And relations with Detective Constable Clarke – the erstwhile nephew of the former Chief Constable?" "Are improving. He has made one or two spectacular mistakes since being assigned to me – but I think he realises what he did wrong. I've no doubt he will make a fine detective in time. He seems relieved that he's no longer the nephew of the Chief Constable."

"Good."

"You have no nephews, sons or daughters that I should be wary of?"

"No," he said. "None." He inched forward in his chair. "Francesca," he said in a more urgent tone. "I trust you.

You're a good detective and I'll fight to get you a permanent posting here. I'll also leave you alone as much as I can to conduct your own investigations. Obviously, there will be times when I'm under pressure to get results but I hope when that happens that I will realise that you're feeling the same pressures, too. I don't want any more of this 'them and us' regime where the bosses feel they have to be cracking the whip and laying down the law to their subordinates. I shall be on the interviewing panel for the new Chief Superintendent and I hope to be able to appoint someone who shares my own values – and, I know, yours. No more Adrian Pauls in here."

"Are you referring to his authoritarianism or his sexual predelictions?"

"I like to think both," Gleeson said. "Tell me – have you come across any sexism or unwanted advances from anyone else in the hierarchy?"

"No, I haven't," she said, "but I think I may have scared them off by – as they perceive it – getting rid of the Chief Constable. I did have one or two cases of senior officers making an exaggerated point of remaining as far away from me as possible so as to minimise the chance of any contact with me. That's died down now, though, and I'm just being left alone to get on with my job. I'm sure there are one or two officers who resent me for my role in the Chief Constable's demise but I can't help that. Whatever you do, you will always find you have one or two enemies."

Gleeson nodded. "I'm sure that's the case." he said. "Well, if there's nothing else, I bid you good-day and good luck in finding the culprits for the two murders."

"I should have something to report to you tomorrow or the next day."

"I'll look forward to it," he said.

Francesca walked down the corridor leading from his office with a much lighter step than the one she had employed reporting for the meeting just a few minutes earlier. If he meant what he said, things were going to improve in the local constabulary. She returned to the office. "We really must get down to Douglas Roulay's house," she said to Gary Clarke.

"No worries," said Gary.

"I've just been talking to the new Chief Constable," she said. "Rory Gleeson." She could see the name did not mean that much to him. Oh, he knew who Gleeson was but had not had any dealings with him himself. "The good thing is he hasn't got any relatives who are in the force," she said.

Gary smiled – but then composed himself to make a comment. "So you won't get anyone else appointed to you to take the pressure off me," he said.

"Afraid not, Gary," she said. "Afraid not."

• • • • •

"You again?" said Douglas Roulay – unable to hide the irritation in his voice as she answered the door to Francesca and Gary.

"Yes, me again," said Francesca, "and this is Detective Constable Gary Clarke."

"Pleased to meet you, I'm sure." He offered his hand for a handshake but there was no reciprocal move from Gary. "I gather this is not a social call, then," said Roulay.

"We don't tend to make them," said Francesca. "No, I was wondering if you could remember now where you were on the night of Rob Corcoran's murder."

"Yes," he said. "I was right here. I was at home. My wife confirms it. We watched Holby City on TV."

"Which is over by 9pm and would have given you time to have driven over to Rob Corcoran's and killed him by 9.30pm."

"Having stolen a car on the way, I suppose?"

"I'm sorry, sir?"

"Well, I read in the papers he was run over by a stolen car

so I would have had to have had one conveniently parked in my driveway or stolen it on the way. I don't think so, Inspector."

"Of course, it would help if you had an independent alibi."

"Unfortunately, I didn't know that I needed one."

"What about two days later when Sue Plummer was killed?"

"The same," said Roulay. "At home with my wife. Death in Paradise was on the TV. That runs between 9pm and 10pm. Is that better?"

"Again no independent alibi."

"I have a busy job."

"Had," said Gary, intervening.

"I have been suspended from work, yes, that's true," he said, "but I still have high hopes I'll be exonerated and be able to return to my job."

"I'm glad you've got high hopes, sir," said Francesca. "Your connections with Jerry Vincent won't hold you in good stead, though."

"Planning officers meet developers. It's one of those everyday occurrences."

"Even corrupt developers?"

"I had no idea Jerry Vincent was involved in corruption."

"Yet he rates you so highly he is willing to risk you having the estimated £2million he will get from the sale of his mansion."

Roulay gave a false smile. "Well, there's no accounting for taste, is there, Inspector?"

Francesca smiled at Roulay. This was normally the moment that high ranking officials mentioned they were friendly with the Chief Constable through the golf club or some such organisation. Roulay did not have that to fall back on. She wondered in the back of her mind whether anyone would use the name of Rory Gleeson in similar circumstances in the future. On the whole, she thought not. They might try – but it was unlikely to spread terror in the hearts of those who knew him. With a minimum of effort, she brought herself back to

312

the present. "Well, Inspector, if there's nothing else?" said Roulay.

"No."

"So you haven't got any evidence linking me to either of the murders? I said when you questioned me yesterday that – if you had any questions relating to planning matters you should refer them to my solicitor. I now think that goes for questions about either of the murders, too. I will not be talking to you in future without the presence of a solicitor."

"Do you not think that makes you seem more guilty – as if you've got something to hide?"

"I don't care, Inspector. I can see you've already made your mind up about me so I have nothing more to say to you. Good day."

"Good day, sir," said Francesca. "We'll be in touch."

"If you will insist on wasting police time."

Francesca indicated to Gary that they should depart the scene. "Do you think he did it. ... er, them?" Gary asked as they made their way back to the car.

"Surprising at it would seem to him, I do actually have an open mind."

• • ● • •

The young man from the planning department was nervous as he approached chief executive Dan Macfarlane's office. He had asked for the interview on the basis of what Rivers had found out leafing through the planning files the previous evening. He thought his boss should be aware of their content. At the same time Macfarlane had been unhappy about allowing so much time to a junior official. It concerned the planning department, though, and that was the bête noire of the council at the moment. "Do come in," he said as enthusiastically as he could.

"Thank you, sir," said the young man.

"What is it?" asked Macfarlane. "Are you still on your own in the department?"

"No, sir, another clerk has been appointed today."

"Good. Good." He adopted a sympathetic tone to the youth. "It can't be easy," he said, "working in a department where the previous incumbent has been murdered and two other officers suspended from duty because of allegations of corruption. But it could be a chance for you to make your name if you can get things running smoothly." He looked at the note his secretary had given him about the interview –"Ben."

"Thank you, sir. I wasn't sure whether to come to you or approach the independent panel you've set up to investigate this."

"We're still putting the independent panel together," said Macfarlane. "The wheels of authority."

"Turn very slowly," said the young man.

"Precisely. Now what is it that you wanted to tell me."

"We had a private detective in the office yesterday," said the other man. "I allowed him the same access as I would have granted a member of the public to the files."

"Quite right. Quite right," said Macfarlane.

"He uncovered another application that appeared to be supported by Jerry Vincent."

"Appeared to be?"

"Yes, when the application was first submitted, it said that the design work had been done by Jerry Vincent's firm. By the time it came to the planning committee all mention of Jerry Vincent's name had been removed from the application."

"I see. Do you know who by?"

"Well, it could only have been someone from the planning department. I eliminated Rob Corcoran. Sorry, sir, that's rather an unfortunate turn of phrase." Macfarlane nodded. "I mean, he wouldn't have been in league with Vincent as he was the one who was laying allegations of corruption against him. That meant it could only be Roger Broadbent or Douglas Roulay –

both of whom are now suspended. It depends when Vincent's name was airbrushed out of the application. I believe it happened after Roger Broadbent had been suspended."

"Believe?"

"Yes, Sir. Vincent's name wouldn't have been such hot property until Rob Corcoran had made his allegations."

"But you're not sure?"

"No, sir."

"Fine. I'll put this evidence before the independent panel when it is set up but – in the meantime – any more evidence that you can give us would be most welcome. You might have a bit more time to investigate this now that you have a colleague working with you."

Ben looked at Macfarlane. He would have thought the chief executive would have shown a little more enthusiasm for investigating the information himself – rather than leave it to a junior planning official to fill him in with what was happening. Be that as it may it would be good fun carrying out further investigations, though. Better than just sitting in the office showing planning applications to the public. "I'll do my best, sir," he said.

"Good." Macfarlane smiled as if Ben should take his cue to leave. The young lad did and made his way out of the office.

• • ● • •

"Do you want to come in with me or observe from across the road?" Rivers asked Debra as they made their way to Jackie Quesling's florist's.

Debra thought for a moment. "I'll come in with you," she said. "I did in the first shop."

"Okay," said Rivers. "We're nearly there. If you do recognise her, don't say or do anything. Just let me buy some flowers as if it's no out of the ordinary visit. Leave anything you've got to say until we get outside. Would she recognise you?"

"We've never met," said Debra, "so I don't see why she should."

Rivers nodded. They arrived at the florist's shop and Rivers parked the car. They crossed the road and entered the shop. An assistant was on duty. "Is Ms Quesling in?" Rivers asked.

"She's just popped out for a moment. Can I help you?"

Rivers wondered whether he could spin the visit out until Jackie got back. "It's just that I know her slightly," he said. He turned to Debra. "What kind of flowers do you think Nikki would like?" he asked.

"You should know better than me."

"I suppose so. Well," he said, perusing the stock in the shop. "I'd like that bouquet," he said pointing to one on display in window, " with just a dash of red. A red rose, perhaps." He turned to Debra. "I thought I should get her some flowers for having to put up with that attempted kidnap ordeal." In truth, he was feeling guilty about not telling Nikki about the risks she was facing. The visit to Jackie's shop provided him with an ideal opportunity to kill two birds with one stone – present Nikki with what would hopefully turn out to be a damage limiting gift plus sort out whether or not Jackie had been responsible for Rob Corcoran's death. The assistant was still putting together the bouquet for him when Jackie Quesling returned to the shop.

"Mr Rivers," she said, "what brings you here?"

"Oh, I was just buying some flowers for my wife," he said. "Nothing for you to worry about." Jackie nodded. Rivers could see her eyes turning to Debra. "Oh, Nikki's niece," he said. "I'm looking after her for the day because Nikki, my wife is working." Jackie Quesling gave a non-committal nod. Debra, for her part, was staring at her intently. Suddenly Rivers found her squeezing his hand hard. The assistant, meanwhile, finished parcelling up the bouquet and Rivers paid her. "I'll be on my way," said Rivers.

"You do that," replied Jackie. As Rivers and Debra made their way from the shop, Jackie watched them go. That's not Nikki's niece, she thought to herself. That's the little half-wit who shared Sue Plummer's flat. What, she wondered, were the two of them really doing at her shop?

Rivers, meanwhile, shepherded Debra across the road as quickly as her could. "I think I can tell what you're going to say," he said.

"That's her," said Debra. "That's her. She killed my Sue."

"You're sure? asked Rivers.

"Yes." She was still gripping his hand as they crossed the road – only relinquishing it when he had opened the passenger door for her and invited her to sit in the car. "What do we do now?" she asked.

"I telephone my friend Francesca Manners in the police force," said Rivers, "and we get her arrested."

"Can I come, too?" asked Debra.

"No, I don't think that's wise," said Rivers. "She might put two and two together and realise you were the witness that got her arrested."

"I want to see her arrested," said Debra.

"No," said Rivers, "safer to get her arrested and then you can go to the trial and see her being sent to prison for killing Sue and Rob Corcoran." He sensed the fear in Debra had gone and that it was now being replaced by anger. "You could give evidence at the trial. You could be the one that gets her put away."

"I want to be there when she's arrested."

"We'll see," said Rivers.

• • ● • •

Ben Hurst, the young planning official at the council offices, had no sooner sat down at his desk in the planning department than he began to think about what chief executive Dan Macfarlane had said to him. He had been charged with getting more information for the planning inquiry investigating corruption.

He could think of only one way of doing that. Douglas Roulay wasn't going to confess that he had altered the application. Roger Broadbent, he knew, had left the district since talking to Macfarlane. A couple of people had rung for him since Ben had started his new job. He had rung him at his home to try and pass messages on and had also tried his mobile – but it was to no avail. No, if anybody could give him chapter and verse as to when the planning application had been altered it would be the woman who had submitted it – Jackie Quesling. She could be an innocent bystander in all this, he reasoned to himself, just paying Vincent a retainer to help her with the application. There was no reason to be certain that she knew of any corruption involved in getting it through the planning committee. He looked at the address on the application. He would slip away early and see if he could challenge her about it and find out who had altered the application.

He bade his farewell to his fellow worker for the day and told the receptionist he would not be back until the following morning and drove to Jackie Quesling's house on the outskirts of Hertford. There was no reply to his knock on the door, though. He glanced at his watch. It was only a quarter to five in the afternoon. It was quite probable she was still at work but would be back soon. He resolved to sit and wait in his car until her return.

• • ● • •

"Hallo, Nikki," said Rivers on returning from Jackie Quesling's shop with Debra. "For you," he said thrusting the flowers into her hand. She looked at him. "I know," he said, "they're usually a sign that a bloke is guilty of something – done something wrong. This time is no different. I'm sorry for the way I treated you over the kidnapping threat. I should have told you what was happening."

She took the flowers from him and went into the kitchen to get a vase. "Yes, you should have done," she said.

"It won't happen again."

"I should hope not," she said. "I hope no-one will want to kidnap me again in the future."

"You know what I mean," he said.

"Yes," she said. "But you're not forgiven and it's not forgotten. I've been having nightmares about it. If Debra hadn't been there, it could have turned out very nasty for me."

"I know," he said.

"But the flowers are welcome," she said returning from the kitchen with them in a vase. "There is more joy in heaven over one sinner that repenteth." She smiled. "Anyhow, what are you looking so pleased with yourself about?"

Rivers looked at Debra, conscious of the fact he had promised her that he would not tell anyone other than Jo about her involvement in pointing the finger at Rob Corcoran's killer. "That's all right," said Debra. "I trust Nikki."

"Yes," said Rivers. "Well, we've – or that is Debra – has identified Rob Corcoran's killer."

"Great. So I take it it's not those two thugs who turned up here?"

"No, it's one of Rob Corcoran's three mistresses. She's a florist." He blushed. "Jackie Quesling."

"So you didn't make a trip to the florist for the sole purpose of buying me flowers?" she said. "I know you too well, Philip. I was an excuse so you could give a plausible reason for visiting her."

"The flowers are heartfelt," he protested.

"I'll believe you. So what do you do now?"

"Tell the police. We shouldn't waste any time." He rang Francesca's number on his mobile. "Francesca?" he said when she replied. "It's Philip Rivers. I think we've made some progress today. We've identified Rob Corcoran's killer."

"Great."

"It's Jackie Quesling."

"Was she identified by Debra?"

"Yes," he said taking the mobile into his bedroom so he could talk more confidentially to her.

"Do you think she'll testify?"

"I had to promise her I wouldn't tell the police about her role in putting the finger on Jackie Quesling. She seems keen, though, to see Jackie Quesling being sent down for the crime. She killed her closest friend, Sue Plummer, after all but I don't think I can ask her to give evidence or make a statement until after Jackie Quesling has been arrested."

"I can understand that," said Francesca. "So what do we now? I go out to Jackie Quesling's and tell her we've got a witness who saw her murder Rob Corcoran?"

"Yes. Jackie was the one who lured Rob Corcoran out of his house. We still don't know who did the actual murder. Debra is adamant she wouldn't recognise him. She only saw a thickset person behind the wheel of a car."

"Him?"

"Almost certainly, according to Debra."

"Right," said Francesca. "We'll play it by ear. You never know – Jackie may come up with the name of her accomplice after she's been arrested."

"We can but hope," said Rivers. "Are you going out there now?"

"I'll try and rustle up Gary Clarke and then go up there."

"I'll meet you outside. Will you wait for me?"

"Whoever gets there first can wait for the other," said Francesca.

"Thanks," said Rivers. He returned to the living room where Nikki and Debra were waiting expectantly. "The police are going to arrest her," he said. "I've just been talking to detective Chief Inspector Manners. I'm going out there, too."

"And me," said Debra.

"No," said Rivers. "It could be dangerous."

"You weren't at all worried about Nikki being around when it was dangerous for her from those two kidnappers," protested Debra.

"That was different," said Rivers. "Besides," he said taking a sidelong glance at Nikki. "I was wrong."

"You know how much Sue meant to me – and she killed her as well."

"I don't know," said Rivers. "What do you think, Nikki?" he said turning to his wife.

"I think Debra would be all right providing she took a frying pan with her," said Nikki. The three of them laughed.

"I'm going to be firm on this," said Rivers. "Besides, we don't want Jackie Quesling to know that you were the only person who identified her, Debra. She still may have an accomplice at large, remember."

Debra looked crestfallen but she could see that she had been beaten. "Okay," she said.

Rivers smiled. "It's for the best," he said. "I'd better be off." With that he was gone.

"Don't worry," said Nikki as she and Debra were left on their own. "I'm sure it'll all go well now. She'll be arrested and Philip will find out who the accomplice was," she said. "Look, I'm going to run a bath and then I'll make us some tea. How's that?"

Debra smiled. It had been a long day. She wandered into the kitchen to make herself a cup of tea. While she was waiting for the kettle to boil, her eyes alighted on a card which had fallen out of the bouquet Rivers had presented to Nikki. It had the address of Jackie Quesling's shop and her mobile telephone number on it. She took it and put it in her pocket. She still hadn't given up hope of being there for the moment her best friend's killer was arrested – but she realised she would have to find out the home address first. She would make her way to the florist's shop and see where she went from there. Having made up her mind, she slipped out of the flat while Nikki was in the bath.

• • ● • •

It didn't take Jackie Quesling long to work out the possible reasons for the visit by Rivers and Debra to her shop that afternoon. Debra, or that half-wit as she thought of her, must have evidence that linked her to the murders. Ironically, though, she came to the conclusion that what evidence Debra had probably linked her to the murder of Sue Plummer rather than Rob Corcoran. After all, she was Sue's flatmate. Perhaps she had come back in time to witness Jackie and her accomplice leaving the flat on the night of the murder. She wondered whether her accomplice had been identified, too. Best not to make contact, she thought, If Rivers had involved the police, it would not be long before the police would be monitoring her calls, she reasoned. She didn't want to incriminate either of them. What to do, though? Best to get away as soon as possible. "I'm going to go home now," she said to her assistant. "You can lock up, can't you?" she asked. Her assistant nodded. She got in the car and drove home – resolving to throw some things in a suitcase, grab her passport and make her way to an airport. She would use her mobile to try and book tickets for a flight abroad while she was in the car driving home. From Stansted. It wouldn't take her long to get there, she reasoned. As luck would have it, there was a seat available on a flight to Barcelona later that evening. She booked it. She would worry about accommodation when she got there. As she reached the driveway at her home, she saw there was another car parked there. Could it be the police? she wondered. As she got out of her car and made her way to the house, a young man got out of the driver's seat.

"Ms Quesling?" he asked. "Ms Jackie Quesling?"

"Yes," she said snappily, "Who wants to know?"

"My name's Ben Hurst. I'm from the planning department."

Jackie pushed past him and onwards towards her front door. "Not now," she said. "I haven't got time for this."

"I'm sorry, Ms Quesling. I've just got one or two questions for you."

"No," she shouted. "Go away."

This, thought Ben, was not the reaction of an innocent woman. Perhaps he had miscalculated and she was involved in the corruption, too. He felt he should continue to press his case, though. "Ms Quesling," he said, "I would appreciate just a couple of minutes of your time. In fact, there's only one thing I really want to ask you."

"Can't you see I'm in a hurry?" she said irritatedly.

"Just one question. Can you tell me when your planning application was altered so that the name of Jerry Vincent was removed from it?"

She had reached the front door by now and placed her key in the lock. Ben, for his part, was like a dog with a bone. He repeated his question. "Can you tell me when your application was altered so that the name of Jerry Vincent was removed from it?"

"I don't know what you're talking about." By this time she had opened the door and gone inside. She attempted to shut it but found his foot was stuck in it. "Mr Hurst, would you please go? I have nothing to say to you and I have a busy schedule. I am about to go on holiday and I have to pack."

In truth, Ben Hurst was enjoying his role as the inquisitor. To a young man who had only just left student life behind him, it was exciting to be in a situation where he appeared to be cornering someone who – by now – he believed to be a crook. "I would have thought you would have wanted to stay here and answer some questions – clear things up – rather than run away, Ms Quesling," he said.

"I am not running away," she said. "I have booked a holiday in Barcelona and I intend to catch my plane. Please leave."

"I notice you're not threatening to call the police," said Ben. "Is that because you don't want them involved with your affairs at present?"

Jackie was trying to think things out. She was already involved in two murders – so would another one be so damaging? On the other hand, she had not actually delivered the fatal blows that had killed her first two victims so she felt a bit squeamish about attacking Ben Hurst all by herself. Then again, if she let him go, he would probably call the police and alert them to the fact she was flying out of the country. She decided to calm down and invite him in. "All right, Mr Hurst," she said. "I'll give you a few minutes. But only a few, mind you. I only realised the name had been taken off the application when I saw the minutes of the planning committee meeting last week."

"When was the last time you saw the application with his name on?"

"Oh, I can't remember," she said. "Probably a couple of weeks beforehand."

"Think carefully, Ms Quesling. It could be vital in determining who removed the name."

"Well, it wasn't me, if that's what you think," she said.

"I don't think that, Ms Quesling. I don't think you could have had access to do that."

"No," she said firmly. "Is that all, Mr Hurst, only I am in a tearing hurry?"

"Were you aware that Mr Vincent was involved in allegations of corruption relating to another planning matter?"

"No, as far as I was concerned, he was only responsible for drawing up the plan of the building."

"Did you have any inkling that he could have been involved in corrupt activities to get your plan through the authority?"

"No, of course not. I wouldn't have been involved in anything like that. What sort of person do you think I am?" She began to congratulate herself at her forceful rebuttal at this stage.

She had regained her self-control. To think that she had only been a step away from deciding to kill this boy. "Now, Mr Hurst, if you have no more questions, I would like you to leave."

"Yes," he said. "I shall, of course, be giving a full report on our conversation to the authorities."

"I'm sure you will, Mr Hurst, and I'm sure it will be most thorough." Now get out, she thought to herself. Instead, she smiled and opened the door to him. "I'm sorry I was so rude to you at first – but you caught me unawares and I am in a hurry," she said. She shut the door as he got into his car and lay back against it, taking a deep breath before she moved on to her next task – packing for her sudden and enforced exit.

CHAPTER ELEVEN

Rivers honked his horn at the departing car. He had just parked across the road from Jackie Quesling's house and was about to ring Francesca to find out how long she and Gary Clarke would be when he saw a car with a familiar driver about to depart from Jackie's house. He recognised him immediately as the new face in the planning department. Ben Hurst looked up as he heard the honk and parked his car on the other side of the road from the private developer. "Fancy meeting you here," he said after getting out of his car and crossing the road to where Rivers was sitting.

"I could say the same about you," said Rivers. "What are you doing here?"

"I'm doing a bit of digging about the corruption in the planning department," the young man replied. "I thought Ms Quesling might be able to furnish me with some information. You know, tie down when it was that Jerry Vincent's name was deleted from that planning application."

Rivers whistled. "I admire your dedication to your work," he said, "but you do realise you're dealing with a murderer here?" He thought for a while. There was no earthly reason why he should not release that information. After all, Rivers himself had only just come by that information after extensive conversations with Debra.

"Gosh," said Ben.

"I was coming to confront her with the information I had," he said. "We have an eye witness who saw her lure Rob Corcoran out of his house on the night of his murder."

"Gosh," repeated Ben. He seemed quite excited about being

caught up in this criminal investigation. "Are you alone?" he asked.

Rivers looked at him in surprise. "Why do you ask?"

"Well, Ms Quesling is about to leave for the airport. It was all I could do to persuade to spend five minutes answering my questions."

"I've called the police but they're not here yet. I was going to ring to find out where they were."

He called Francesca on his mobile. "Where are you?" he asked.

"I've just located Gary. We'll be on our way in five minutes," said Francesca.

"Hurry," said Rivers. "She's about to leave for the airport."

"We'll be there as quick as we can," said Francesca, "but – in the meantime – can you stall her?"

"I'll do my best," said Rivers. He put his mobile back in his pocket.

Ben looked thoughtful. "So this must mean she was a party to the corruption in the planning department," he said.

"Yes," said Rivers, "and she was a former lover of Rob Corcoran's who found herself dumped rather publicly when his three lovers all met up in the Dog and Partridge pub accidentally a couple of days before he was killed. Two motives for murder. Now, if you don't mind, I've got to try and stall her until the police arrive."

Ben nodded. "I'll help you."

Rivers was not quite sure whether this enthusiastic amateur would help or hinder him in his attempt to stall Jackie Quesling. He decided to make no comment and let Ben do his own thing. Meanwhile, he drove up Jackie's driveway and parked across it so there was no way Jackie could drive past him and get into the main road. Ben, for his part, reversed along the main road and then drove into Jackie's driveway – parking himself behind Rivers. "Leave this to me," said Rivers. "I'll take it from here." Ben nodded and sat in the driver's seat of his car to await developments. A good ten minutes passed by and then Jackie Quesling emerged from the house carrying a suitcase. She looked at Rivers' car and sighed. He was still sitting in the driver's seat.

"Get out of the way," she shouted at him. "I have to get to the airport."

He got out of his car and moved towards her. She recognised him for the first time. "I think not," he said.

"Mr Rivers," she said. "What a pleasant surprise. And so soon after our last meeting."

"Yes," he said. "There are one or two things emanating from that that I want to discuss with you."

"The girl you were with when you came to my florist's was that girl who shared a flat with Sue Plummer, wasn't she?" Rivers remained silent. "She's only half there, Mr Rivers," Jackie continued. "You don't want to believe anything she tells you. She was besotted with Sue Plummer, too."

"Who said she told me anything?" said Rivers.

"Well, it's obvious. You wouldn't be shepherding someone like that around unless she was pretending to have information for you."

"I resent the phrase 'someone like that', Ms Quesling," said Rivers. "She's a brave, plucky girl. Worth ten of someone like you."

"Nice as it is to have this discussion with you," said Jackie – becoming a little exasperated as the seconds ticked away. "I do have a plane to catch. I need you to let me out."

"And I'm not going to," he said. "I have called the police. They'll be here soon. You'll be arrested on suspicion of having murdered Rob Corcoran."

"Rob Corcoran?" Jackie sounded surprised. She had anticipated that the girl had seen something on the night of Sue Plummer's death. After all, she had been her tenant.

"Yes. I have an eye witness who saw you luring Rob out of his home that night prior to his murder. You lured him out of the house to where a driver was waiting who ran him over in a stolen car."

"And this eye witness was that girl?" Rivers remained silent. "I think your silence speaks volumes. You could say 'no' if it wasn't her. Well, if you've got an eye witness to Rob's murder, they'll be able to tell you I had nothing to do with it."

"How so?"

"I was as surprised as anyone when this maniac driver came round the corner and ran him over."

"Then why didn't you tell anyone you were there? Why did you run away as fast as you could from the scene of the crime?"

"Much as I'd like to discuss this with you in the dark on my gravel path, I really don't have the time or inclination. As I said, I have a plane to catch so I need to get to the airport."

"And would you be running away from your home now if you felt you could convince everyone of your innocence?"

"You can't prove a thing, Mr Rivers. I'm ashamed to say that I thought it would look bad if I were to admit to the police that I had persuaded Rob to come out of his house prior to his killing – and that I ran away after he had been run over. I panicked. I'm not proud of it but I never had the slightest intention of killing him. Damn it, I loved him."

"Until two days beforehand when you found out he also had two other lovers."

"Mr Rivers, please get out of my way."

"Or you'll call the police? I don't think so. You may have convinced yourself that you have a strong defence but your actions show that – at least earlier in the day – you thought your best chance of escaping a murder rap was running."

"All right," said Jackie Quesling sensing that she was not going to be able to persuade him to move his car. "Come inside. We'll discuss it. I'll try and convince you that I didn't kill Rob."

"Or Sue Plummer."

"What evidence have you got there?" She then opted for

silence, turning on her heels and returning inside her house. Rivers followed her. "Are you relying on that girl again or – this time – do you not have any evidence at all?"

"Tell me, then," said Rivers once they were inside, "what was it that was so important that you felt the need to drag Rob Corcoran out of his house?"

"I had something to show him in the car," she said.

"What?"

"Oh – I can't remember," she said.

"So important that you can't remember," sneered Rivers. "If I were you, I'd brush up on your recollection before you face a jury."

"Let me make you a cup of coffee," said Jackie.

"Oh. Given up on your attempt to get to the airport in time for your flight?"

"Conceding that I can't bulldoze my way past your car," said Jackie. "You didn't say what you wanted?"

"Nothing, really. Just a confession to the murders of Rob Corcoran and Sue Plummer would do."

"I can't give you that," said Jackie as she disappeared into the kitchen. Rivers moved towards her – trying to keep an eye on her as she attempted to make herself a cup of coffee. She moved over to a kitchen drawer. "Just getting a teaspoon," she said. When she turned round to face him again, she had a sharp knife in her hand. She advanced towards him, carrying it menacingly. "Your keys, Mr Rivers," she said.

How did I fall for that? he thought to himself. However, he reasoned she wouldn't be able to drive his car out of the gravel path, pack her bags and drive her car on to the main road without dropping the knife at some point.

"Don't be stupid, Ms Quesling," he said. "You're only getting yourself deeper in the mire."

"Your keys, Mr Rivers," she added.

He shrugged his shoulders. "Okay," he said. He took them

out of his pocket and held his hand out to offer them to him. Rather than take them, she raised the knife as if to lung forward and stab him. Seemingly, she had made the same calculation as him and realised she would have to stab him to get away.

● ● ● ● ●

It had taken Debra some time to get to Jackie's florist's shop. She had taken cabs from Rivers' Finchley flat to a tube station and from Hertford North railway station to the shop. As a result, she was beginning to run out of money by the time she arrived. She was lucky – Jackie's assistant was still clearing up after the day's work and smiled pleasantly as she entered the shop.

"We're closing," she said.

"That doesn't matter," said Debra. "I haven't come for flowers. I need to see Ms Quesling."

"She's not here."

"I appreciate that," said Debra, "but I was wondering if you could give me her home address?"

"I can't do that, I'm afraid," said the assistant. "We don't hand out home addresses. Why do you want to see her?"

"We have a mutual friend in common who has been killed. I felt guilty about not offering her my condolences when I was here this afternoon."

The first bit of the story was true, the assistant reasoned. She knew an ex boy-friend of Jackie's had been killed recently. She was still reluctant to give out the address, though. "It would be the same for anyone," she said soothingly.

Debra was good at adopting a crestfallen look – which she did now – but it cut no ice with the assistant. Debra was at a bit of a loss now. She could not immediately think of any other way she could find out Jackie's home address. Then a thought struck her. Sue had told her the three lovers of Rob Corcoran had come across each other in the Dog and Partridge pub. Perhaps there was someone there who knew where she lived or – even better – she might still be a regular drinker at the pub. She realised, though, that she would have to walk to the pub as she did not have enough money for another taxi. It took her about 25 minutes. The pub was quite quiet when she arrived and she was soon served with a coke by Jed Coulson. "You were in here the other day?" he said by way of making conversation.

Debra nodded. "With Philip Rivers," she said.

"Are you helping him out?" he asked.

"No, not really," said Debra. "I just wanted to contact someone who – I believe – drinks here. Jackie Quesling. She was a friend of Rob Corcoran's."

"Yes, I know," said Jed. "She's not what you might call a Dog and Partridge regular, though. She came in here a few times with Rob Corcoran but we haven't seen her since his funeral."

At this stage Colin Standen moved over from the other side of the bar. "I couldn't help overhear what you were saying," he said. "You wanted to know where Jackie Quesling lives."

"Yes," she said. "I saw her this afternoon. I ought to have passed on my condolences over Rob Corcoran's death. I feel a bit guilty about it."

"You want to go out and see her?"

"Yes, I'd like to."

Colin Standen swallowed his pint. "I could take you," he said.

"No, I wouldn't want to interrupt your evening. If you'll just tell me the address."

"It'd take you ages," he said. "You haven't got a car, I take it?"

"No," said Debra.

"I'll take you." He walked back to the other side of the bar where his sister, Felicity, was sitting. "I'm just going to take – ." He paused realising he did not know Debra's name.

"Debra."

"Debra to Jackie Quesling's house. I won't be long." Felicity nodded. Debra finished her coke and then followed Colin out of the pub. Once they were in his car, he turned to Debra. "You were in the pub this lunchtime, too, weren't you?" he asked.

"Yes, with Philip Rivers," she said.

"Any particular reason?"

"No," said Debra. She sensed that she should try to give away as little as possible. After all, Rivers had promised he would not reveal to anyone that she was the prime witness to Rob Corcoran's killing. She should therefore not be imparting any information herself.

They were driving now – along the main road out of Hertford.

"I don't buy that," said Colin Standen. "I bet you must at least be helping him with his enquiries."

Debra gave a little giggle. "I don't like the sound of that," she said. "It's what the police say when they're interviewing their main suspect."

"Oh. Don't get me wrong," said Colin. "I didn't mean to imply that you had anything to do with the murders he's investigating. I mean, in the sense that you were responsible for them."

"Good," said Debra. She was beginning to feel a little bit uncomfortable in his presence. After all, she had spent the last few days solely in the company of people she trusted – Rivers, Jo and Nikki. She did not know Colin Standen – except that Rivers had asked her whether he had been the driver of the car that had killed Paul Corcoran on the evening of his murder. She hadn't recognised him – but then she didn't think she would recognise whoever it had been. "Do you know Jackie Quesling well?" asked Debra.

"Why do you ask?"

"Just curious. I wondered how you knew where she lived."

"I've met her in the Dog and Partridge – just a casual acquaintanceship."

They were soon outside Jackie Quesling's house and spotted there were two cars parked in the driveway. Debra immediately recognised one of them as Rivers' car. "Thank you," she said.

"I'll get out now."

Colin Standen saw the two cars in the driveway and immediately turned to Debra. "You go on up to the house," he said. "I don't think I'll pay my respects at this time. I'd be interrupting something. For sure. Do you recognise those cars?"

Debra remained silent and then eventually said; "Thank you for the lift."

Colin could see a look of relief had come over Debra's face as they had driven up outside Jackie's house. One of the cars must have been familiar to her, he reasoned. It probably belonged to Philip Rivers. He drove off as soon as Debra had got out of the car.

• • ● • •

Ben Hurst had waited for Rivers and Jackie Quesling to get back inside the house before he had got out of his car. He tiptoed round the side of the house until he found a vantage point where there was a crack in the curtains and he could see what was going on inside. He could not hear anything that was being said, though. However, at one point he could see Jackie Quesling emerging into the sitting room carrying a knife with her. He decided there was no point in just being a spectator – Rivers was in trouble – but could not fathom out what to do. He decided to hurl himself against the window with as much force as possible in the hope of cracking the glass and gaining entry or at least disturbing Jackie Quesling's concentration.

Inside the house, both Rivers and Jackie Quesling heard the noise. For a slight second she was distracted from the knife with which she was threatening Rivers. He sensed this and leapt forward hitting her wrist with a karate chop which made her drop the knife. He picked it up. "Round one to me," he said, motioning her with the knife to sit down. She obeyed. There was nowhere for her to run. Standing facing her with the knife in his hand, he motioned behind his back to Ben to make his way to the kitchen where Rivers unlocked the door and let him in. "Now, Ms Quesling, let's have no more of this nonsense about you being not guilty," he said. "If you were innocent, you wouldn't threaten me with a knife."

"I was being held prisoner in my own house. You were blocking my exit. I thought it was the only thing I could do."

"Not the only," said Rivers. "You could have called the police."

"I was afraid of what you might do."

Rivers started a slow hand clap. "Please don't waste your breath with these fantasies," he said. "I don't want to hear them."

"It will be my defence if it comes to being tried over Rob Corcoran's death – that I did nothing to cause his killing."

"I'll be interested to hear that," he said. "I expect I'll be in court at the time. Anyhow, what's your excuse over Sue Plummer's killing? 'Well, I went there with the person who killed Rob Corcoran. I didn't think he – or she – was going to cause Sue Plummer any harm.'." He mocked her voice. "'I was as surprised as anyone when they drugged her causing her to become unconscious and then strung her up from the nearest light-fitting'. Do me a favour."

"You can't prove anything."

"I know that Sue Plummer was told you had killed Rob Corcoran a day or so before her death. She went to confront you about it. For some misguided reason, she must have given you some time to come clean about it and call the police. She was naive, to say the least. Instead, you plotted her killing with your accomplice. It needed two of you again this time – to haul the body up to the light-fitting. Tell me, who was your accomplice."

"To borrow a phrase from you, Mr Rivers, do me a favour," she said. "If I tell you that, I'm admitting my part in the killing."

At that juncture, the doorbell rang. Rivers motioned to Ben Hurst to open it. The private detective was surprised at the identity of the visitor. "Debra," he said.

"I wanted to be here when Jackie Quesling was arrested," she said. She walked over to where she was sitting. "You killed my Sue," she said. Rivers had put the knife on the table beside him – out of reach of Jackie Quesling but within her reach. "You killed my Sue," she said, moving to pick it up. Rivers, however, sensed she was going to make a move for it and – quick as a flash – picked it up again. "No, Debra," he said. "That's not the way forward. We can let the law take its course now."

"If it ever arrives," said Jackie Quesling.

The strains of a siren could be heard from not too far away. Rivers breathed a sigh of relief. "I think it has," he said. With a couple of minutes, he had opened Jackie's front door again to let Francesca and Gary Clarke in – accompanied by two police constables. "You took your time," he said to Francesca.

"We were called in by the new chief constable for an update on the case," she said. "Luckily I know him well and – when I said the update would delay the arrest of the chief suspect – he let us go. What's the score?"

"I think there's enough evidence for you to arrest Jackie on suspicion of murder. I've told her we've got an eye witness who puts her in the frame at the time of Rob's murder, that this eye witness then told Sue Plummer that she had seen the murderer and gave her a description of her and that Sue went to confront her about it."

"We'll arrest her on suspicion," said Francesca, "and then question her down at the police station." She made her way over to where Jackie Quesling was sitting and cautioned her before handing her over to the two police constables.

As Jackie passed Debra, she stopped. "You must be the witness they've got," she said. "It's the only way to make sense of it. I hope you reflect on this. Everybody's been talking about an accomplice. Nobody knows who it is. If I did have an accomplice, just think. He or she is still out there."

"Ms Quesling," said Francesca sternly.

"Is still out there and benefits if the sole witness is silenced. Reflect on that."

"That's enough, Ms Quesling," said Francesca. "Take her away." The two police constables did as they had been bid. Debra, for her part, was visibly shaking.

Gary Clarke moved over her and patted her arm. "It's all right," he said. "I'll make sure you're all right." Then he added: "And I'm sorry."

Francesca smiled. "Nice one, Gary," she said. "Philip," she added, "join me down at the police station and we'll discuss where we go from here."

● ● ● ● ●

"I shouldn't have let her out of my sight," Nikki told Jo as she telephoned him to say that Debra had gone missing.

"It's not your fault," he replied. "By all accounts she was desperate to be there when Sue Plummer's killer was arrested. That's where she'll be and she won't come to any harm. Rivers is there, Francesca is there. She'll be all right." As he spoke, he could hear a car drawing up outside his block of flats. He looked out of the window. "That's them now," he said.

"Phew," said Nikki.

"I'll just go down and let them in," said Jo. "I'll get Rivers to call you later. Bye."

"'Bye," said Nikki replacing the receiver at her end.

Jo ushered Rivers and Debra into the flat. He could see that Debra was tense about something. "What's up?" he asked.

"Jackie Quesling threatened her," said Rivers.

"Jackie Quesling? But Francesca just phoned me to say she was being taken into custody."

"She reminded her that her accomplice was still at large and would most likely try to silence her."

"Ouch," said Jo. "Don't worry, Debra, whoever it is would be

337

foolish to try. It would reflect badly on Jackie if anything were to happen to you."

"She didn't seem to think so," said Debra.

"Well, she's desperate. Don't worry about her."

"I will worry about her," Debra stressed, "but she…." Her voice tailed off as she began to stifle a tear. "I feel I should do all I can to put her away," she said with a flourish.

"Great," said Rivers. "Does that mean?"

"That I'll testify? Yes, I will," she said.

"That's good," said Rivers. "That'll be a great help to Francesca in compiling the case against her."

"Even that Detective Constable Clarke was nice to me today," said Debra. "He said he was sorry for what he had done to me."

"And so he should be," said Jo. "Everybody believes that."

"So let's just recap on what we've got," said Rivers. "You saw Jackie Quesling lure Rob Corcoran out of his house on the night of the murder."

"I didn't know she was Jackie Quesling then," said Debra. "I just described her to Sue – and she realised who it was immediately."

Rivers nodded. "Someone else was driving the car but you didn't get a look to see who it was," he said.

"That's right," she relied. "Whoever it was looked thickset. That's all I can say."

"You then told Sue Plummer what you'd seen and she went to confront Jackie Quesling about it – to try and persuade her to give herself in?"

"Yes."

"Twenty-four hours later Sue was also dead – killed just before she was about to go to the police and name Jackie Quesling as Rob Corcoran's killer."

"Yes," said Debra – the memory of Sue's death coming back to her now. She stifled another tear. Jo put his hand on her arm.

"Right," said Rivers. "I'd better get this information off to Francesca. You'll be okay now, will you?"

"She's in good hands," said Jo.

After Rivers had left to go to the police station, Jo took the opportunity to ask Debra how she had got to Jackie Quesling's that evening. "It's a long way," he said.

"Yes," she replied. "I only just got there in time to see Jackie Quesling being taken away. "I was lucky. I went by cab to the tube and then pitched up at Hertford North. I took another cab to Jackie's shop but her assistant wouldn't tell me where she lived."

"I'm not surprised," said Jo. "I wouldn't do that if somebody turned up at our office asking for your home address."

Debra listened to what he had to say. It made sense, she thought. "I thought then how on earth was I going to find out where she lived. Then I remembered she used to go to the Dog and Partridge when she was with Rob Corcoran. I thought somebody there might know so I walked to the pub."

"Gee. Your determination does you credit. You'll make a fine detective one of these days."

Debra blushed. "I don't want to be a detective. I'm happy just to help in the office," she said.

"So did anybody know her address at the Dog and Partridge?"

"Yes," she said. "A guy we'd met earlier in the day when Mr Rivers was taking me to see the various suspects."

"Who?"

"His name is Colin Standen."

"How did he know where Jackie Quesling lived?" pondered Jo. "She's a bit out of his league."

"She's a murderer," said Debra, irritated that Jo seemed to be praising her. "You can't get much lower than that."

"Yes, I know," said Jo distractedly. "I was thinking of the time before she committed murder. Oh, never mind." When you're in a hole in a conversation with someone, he thought, the time comes when you have to stop digging.

"I don't know how he got her address," she said, "but he did. He said they knew each other from the pub. He even gave me a lift to her home."

"He what?"

"Gave me a lift. I had no money left. If he hadn't, I wouldn't have been able to get there."

"Yes," said Jo. "You know you shouldn't accept lifts from strange men – I mean people you don't know."

"But he and Mr Rivers were chatting earlier in the day. He just seemed kind."

"He's not," said Jo abruptly. "And he and Rivers were only chatting in the context of him being a possible suspect in the murder case. Debra, for goodness sake be careful if he approaches you again. In fact, call me immediately."

"All right."

It was obvious to Jo that she did not share his worries about Colin Standen, "What did he do when you got to Jackie Quesling's?"

"Well, I think he wanted to come in with me," she said, "but he had second thoughts when he saw from the cars there were other people there. I identified one of them as Mr Rivers'. I don't think he wanted to become involved."

"To be seen to be involved," said Jo thinking aloud. "Be careful," he added.

"All right, I won't accept another lift from him," she said. "Is that better?"

Jo nodded. "Sorry if I alarmed you," he added.

"You haven't. I did think at one stage I was out of my comfort zone when I was in the car with him – but then I'm only in my comfort zone with you, Nikki and Mr Rivers," she paused for a moment for thought. "And Francesca," she added.

"You can trust Francesca," said Jo, "and you may have quite a bit to do with her now you've agreed to give evidence. She'll want to take you through things before the court case."

"That's all right," said Debra. "Jo," she said so furtively he knew she was about to ask him a favour. "You know I always say that wine makes me squiffy?"

"Yes."

"Well, could I have a glass now? It's been a long day now and I don't really mind if it makes me squiffy."

Jo smiled. "I reckon you've earned one." She was right, he thought a few minutes later, it not only made her squiffy but sent her to sleep on the settee in the living room. Jo took advantage of her lapse into sleep to telephone Francesca. She was not responding – possibly she was still involved in questioning Jackie Quesling – so he left a message on her voicemail to let her know that Colin Standen had been angling to get to speak to Jackie earlier in the evening. "Make of it what you will," he said enigmatically.

• • • • •

"All quiet on the western front?" asked Rivers as he approached Francesca at the police station.

"Jackie Quesling is in the interview room with Gary waiting for me to start proceedings," she replied. "I was waiting for news from you."

"Well, it's good," said Rivers. "Debra is willing to testify."

"Great," said Francesca. "Wait until I break the news to Jackie. She won't be so cocky about her defence now."

"I would wait until you break the news to her," said Rivers.

"Why?"

"If you tell her you've got her bang to rights, she's likely to clam up. You can hold her in custody. You can charge her. You'll probably get a conviction. But you'll never find out who her accomplice was. She's not going to tell you. She'll just tell you that Debra is mistaken in what she saw. She was never part of a conspiracy to kill Rob – let alone Sue. She had just wanted to show Rob something she had in her car. Why did she run off

341

after he was run over – and not see if she could do anything for him? He was obviously dead and she'll concoct some story about how she thought she might be able to get a glimpse of the real killer if she chased after him. She might or might not get the jury to believe her – my money says they probably won't. But you'll still be no nearer getting to her accomplice."

"I see," said Francesca.

"Whereas if you pretend you haven't got enough evidence to hold her, you send her home and somehow the accomplice will contact her because he or she wants to know how much the police know. You could bug the house."

"I'm not sure I could get clearance for that," said Francesca.

"Well, I could bug the house."

"An illegal bug would probably not be admissible in court," warned Francesca. "No, I'll try and get official sanction for it. I'm sure the Chief Constable would back me up."

"Right and – in the meantime – I might just keep a watching brief on the house."

"Jackie Quesling would recognise you."

"She won't see me. I'll be across the road. Let me know when you let her go."

Francesca glanced at her watch. "It'll probably be tomorrow morning. She's all tooled up with a solicitor and we're running into dangerous territory carrying on the interview into the night."

"Yes," said Rivers wryly. "That's the sort of thing only Gary Clarke would do."

"He's a reformed man," said Francesca. "You saw the way he tried to reassure Debra at Jackie's cottage."

"I'm not sure Debra would like the experience of being reassured by him," protested Rivers.

"He's doing his best."

"All right," said Rivers. "Actually she did say that even Gary Clarke was being nice to her. It was one of the factors, I think, in allowing the police to question her and agreeing to give evidence. You know, Jackie Quesling dismissed her as being only half there. She is quite clever underneath it all."

"That's a bit patronising."

"I don't mean to me. I'm quite a fan of hers – especially after seeing what she can do with a frying pan. I've offered her a job in my agency."

"So you're expanding, then?"

"Only an admin job. I figured out we were losing a few clients because we don't have a full time presence in the office."

"You don't have to convince me you're doing it because of a profit motive. I'd be quite impressed if you said you were doing it just to help her out."

Rivers smiled. "I'd better be going," he said. "Jo and Debra are going to be round at Jo's flat in Hertford."

"I've got the address," said Francesca.

"I just thought you might need to get a statement from Debra before you interviewed Jackie Quesling tomorrow morning."

"There's no hurry. I won't need it by tomorrow if I'm going to release her because of a lack of evidence."

Rivers thought for a moment. "You do run the risk of her absconding," he said. "She was going to the airport tonight when I stopped her."

"We'll have an alert out for her. She won't get away. It'll look worse for her if she decides to flee – and then gets caught."

Rivers nodded and made his way out of the police station. Francesca went over to the interview room where Jackie, her solicitor and Gary Clarke were patiently waiting. "I'm sorry to keep you," she said to Jackie and her solicitor. "There are one or two developments I've had to deal with," she said. She turned to address Jackie by herself. "You have been arrested under suspicion of the murder of Rob Corcoran. I intend to continue questioning you in the morning when things have become clearer. In the meantime, we will hold you overnight in a cell. Shall we say until ten o'clock tomorrow morning?"

Jackie shot a sidelong glance at her solicitor who shook her head as if to indicate there was no point in protesting. Francesca called for a police constable to take her to her cell. When she and her solicitor had gone, Gary turned to her. "Developments?"

"There have been developments – but they can wait. I intend to release her on police bail tomorrow in the hope that she leads us to her accomplice."

"The developments don't help you in holding her, then?"

"Oh, they would do. Your friend, Debra, is willing to testify. She told Rivers – in a roundabout way – that he had you to thank for that."

"Me?" Gary seemed surprised.

"Yes, the kindness you showed her at Jackie Quesling's house," said Francesca, "but don't get too big headed about it."

• • ● • •

"Help me up with my suitcase," said Miranda as she pressed the buzzer to her flat.

"Be with you in a moment," replied Aaron. He walked downstairs to where Miranda was standing. "I wasn't expecting you back so soon," he said. "I thought you were planning to stay a couple of weeks."

"I couldn't settle," she said. "I wanted to know what was going on around here."

"I haven't heard anything," said Aaron. "There was an item on the local news tonight, though, saying police were questioning somebody over the murder of Rob Corcoran. Didn't say who it was, mind you."

"Or whether it was a man or a woman?"

"No," said Aaron. "We'll find out in time – if they charge them."

"I guess so." By now she was in the hallway of the flat. She took her suitcase into the main bedroom. "I'll unpack later," she said. She turned to Aaron and kissed him. "I missed you," she said. "It was wrong of me to go away – especially so soon after we'd patched things up. I'm sorry."

"That's all right." He kept his arms round her waist even after the kiss was over. "I'm glad you're back," he said.

"I couldn't settle," she said. "I thought I could get away from it in Scotland but – I don't know – I kept thinking about it."

"Why?"

"Rob's death was quite a shock," she said. "And I thought that if I stayed away people would become more suspicious of me. That private detective agency kept on harping on about how I had no alibi for the time of Rob's death. They thought I'd done it – and I felt the longer I stayed away the more their suspicions would grow."

"You never have explained – even to me – where you were between leaving Jackie Quesling's house and coming back home," said Aaron. "Perhaps now's the time."

"I would if I could."

"What do you mean?"

"I just went for a drive to think about things. I don't really know where I was. The other girls were talking about taking some revenge on Rob. I wasn't sure that was the road I wanted to go down."

"It's still not enough to get the private detective agency off your back," said Aaron.

"And you?"

"Me?" He gave a half laugh. "I could never conceive of you doing anything to harm Rob. I just worry that all this concern you're showing for him means that your feelings for him haven't yet been buried."

She looked at him in the eye. "Don't worry on that score," she said. "It's just a shock to find someone you know being so brutally murdered."

Aaron squeezed her and kissed her again. "Okay," he said. "I can accept that."

"Well," she said pouring herself a drink, "it's time I found out what was happening." She picked up the portable landline phone and made for the bedroom. "I'll ring Jackie," she added. "If anyone knows what's going on, she will." Jackie's mobile number went on to voicemail, though. Miranda decided against leaving a message. She tried her landline – again to no avail. It made her think. Could Jackie be the person that Aaron had been talking about – helping the police with their enquiries?

• • ● • •

"I'm sorry to trouble you so late in the evening, Rory," said Francesca.

"Don't worry," the new Chief Constable replied. "I'm beginning to find this is what this job is all about."

Hmmm, thought Francesca. He sounded a bit grumpy. Was it worth pursuing her request for a telephone tap? She decided there was no point in backing down now – having made the telephone call. "I need permission to tap someone's telephone," she began

"And you want authorisation for it?"

"Yes, please. "The suspect we're interviewing, Jackie Quesling. I believe if I release her on bail she could lead us to her accomplice."

"Have you got enough evidence to charge her?"

"I think so," said Francesca. "I have an eye witness ready to go on the record but I plan to keep that up my sleeve at the moment in the hope of trapping the accomplice."

"Bit risky," said Rory. "There will probably be a defence challenge to you using the evidence from the telephone tap."

"I'm aware of that but I think if I know the name of the accomplice I'll be able to get them through other means."

"Interview?"

"That's one of them," she said. "Another is a forensics search of the stolen car, maybe. Fingerprinting of Sue Plummer's home. We could even push our witness to identify the driver of the car."

"A lot of ifs and buts and maybes, then?"

"It's all we've got. If I charge her now, she's going to plead not guilty. I'll never get the name of the accomplice out of her because her contention will be she wasn't involved in a murder."

"I'm not minded to tell you not to proceed. I know a judge who lives locally who is a strong supporter of the police force. I'll try him. I'll call you back."

"Thank you, Rory." She replaced her receiver and prepared herself to wait for his return call. She reflected on it. She had felt a strong desire to revert to calling him "sir" instead of "Rory" as a result of his elevated position. She had resisted it but she wondered how he felt. She did not have to wait long for the Chief Constable to call her back.

"Request granted," he said.

"Great," replied Francesca.

"Report to Judge Mellor's chambers at St Alban's Crown Court at nine o'clock tomorrow morning and he'll grant you the authorisation."

"Excellent."

"You'll have to make your case out to him," said Rory. "He won't just sign it willy-nilly."

"No, of course not. I'm confident I can do that."

"So am I." She could sense him smiling at the other end of the telephone. "Oh, and one other thing," he said. "Don't mention the fact that you have an eye witness lined up which you haven't told the suspect about. It won't help your case."

"No, sir."

"Another thing – I said you would want authorisation to bug the house as well. I was thinking in the meantime before I called the judge that Jackie Quesling might receive a visit from her accomplice rather than a telephone call."

"Good thinking, sir."

"Thanks for the complement. I rather think it was my ability to do that that might have helped me get the Chief Constable's job."

"Yes, sir."

"Now I must get some sleep – and you should, too. Good luck tomorrow morning."

"Thank you, s – Rory." She realised she had earlier slipped into the deferential without thinking about it.

"It is still okay to call me Rory, Francesca," he said before replacing the receiver.

● ● ● ● ●

"Hi, Jo," said Rivers. "They're going to release Jackie Quesling tomorrow morning."

"Oh, no. What more do they want?"

"Don't worry," said Rivers. "They've got enough evidence – especially now Debra has agreed to become a witness. It's just that they want to catch her accomplice and they think this is the best way of doing it."

"She's not going to land him in it."

"Probably not – but whoever it is will want to know how close she is to being charged over the murder."

"Yes, I see."

"They're going to try and bug her phone and home. It occurs to me, though, that Jackie might suspect that's what they're going to do. That's why I'll be going up there tomorrow morning."

"What can you do?"

"At least see the comings and goings and – if she really is worried about the place being bugged – I could loiter around in the garden trying to pick up on any conversations they have if they go outside."

"That won't be easy."

"There's a terrace out back where they'll probably sit and

have some coffee. There's a derelict outhouse next to it. I could hide myself in there. I doubt whether it will be locked,"

"I'm not sure you'll be able to hear much. And, if she's that paranoid, they'll probably wander around the garden,"

"Maybe," reflected Rivers. "I was thinking – could you come up, too?"

"Yes but what do you want me to do?"

"It's just in case she turns anyone away at the door. You could follow them. See what they do next."

"Bit of a flimsy plan," said Jo. "If it's Colin Standen, he'll just go to the pub."

"I'd still like to go double-handed."

"Okay."

· · ● · ·

Francesca was beaming when she arrived at the office the next morning at just after eleven o'clock. She waived a piece of paper at Gary. "Here I have it," she said. "The authorisation. I've just been round to Jackie's house and watched them bugging the phone and house. Let's call her into the interviewing room and put our plan into action."

Gary smiled. "And what are we going to do after we release her?"

"Listen in," said Francesca. "We can do that from here. No need to arrest anyone on the spot. We've got an all ports alert on Jackie Quesling if she tries to escape but she won't. She's far too confident of her own ability to get off. We can pick her up later on this afternoon or evening. Anyhow, let's go down to the interview room. I'll ask one of the constables to escort Jackie from her cell."

"She's not there," said Gary. "She's already in the interview room. Her brief arrived earlier this morning and they're in there sitting waiting for us."

"Let's go," said Francesca. She and Gary then traipsed off to the interview room where Francesca mumbled an apology for keeping Jackie waiting before sitting down opposite her and her solicitor. Gary followed suit. "Jackie Quesling, I have to tell you I am releasing you on police bail on the understanding that you report to this station daily at five o'clock in the afternoon," said Francesca. "These are stringent bail conditions that have been introduced because we believe you are an impending flight risk. We know you were on the verge of leaving the country when you were arrested on suspicion of murdering Rob Corcoran yesterday evening."

"But I'm no longer arrested on suspicion of murdering Rob?"

"You're free to go. You can collect your things from the custody sergeant."

"Thank you."

"Don't thank me, Ms Quesling. I feel sure we'll be meeting up again in the near future."

"Not if I can help it." Jackie smiled but her solicitor gave her a reproachful look.

"I would advise you not to leave the Hertford area for the time being."

"I'm not going to have very much chance of doing that if I've got to report here every day," said Jackie. "How long do these bail conditions last for?"

"As long as is necessary," said Francesca. "We will keep the situation under review."

"So your little witness didn't come off?" Francesca remained resolutely silent. "Either that or you decided not to rely on her. Very wise. I would have hated to have seen her being torn apart in the witness box."

Gary moved as if he was about to say something but Francesca restrained him. "Good day, Ms Quesling," she said. Enjoy your short-lived freedom, she thought to herself.

Once outside, Jackie turned to her solicitor. "Were you expecting that?" she asked her.

"I have to confess I wasn't."

"You thought?"

"That you would be charged with murder after further interrogation and then brought before the courts to be remanded in custody."

"Yes." Jackie looked thoughtful.

"It could be that their witness has suddenly withdrawn her statement or refused to testify in any court proceedings."

"Yes." Jackie was still in reflective mood. "On the other hand…. "No, she thought. Don't say anything – not even to your own solicitor. Jackie was beginning to think perhaps it was a trap – that the police thought they could flush out more evidence against her if she was outside their control than if she was in a police cell. She collected what little belongings she had arrived with the previous evening from the custody sergeant and went on her way, telling her solicitor she would retain her in case she needed her again in the future.

Meanwhile, Francesca and Gary went back to their office. A young man in a suit whom neither Gary nor Francesca recognised was waiting for them.

"I'm from the press office," he said extending his hand to Francesca. "Stuart Beavers. I understand you rang our office and said you had some important information you wanted to put out."

Francesca smiled. She thought Beavers to be an appropriate name for someone who busied himself all day writing press releases for the police force. She decided not to mention it to the young man, though, feeling sure he had been the butt of such jokes often in the past. "Yes," she said. "We've just had to release our main suspect in the Rob Corcoran and Sue Plummer murder cases. If you're up to speed on it we had arrested her on suspicion of murdering Rob Corcoran but not the other case."

"We put out a press release yesterday saying a 39-year-old woman was helping police with their enquiries."

Just enough information, thought Francesca, for those close to the case to realise it was likely to be Jackie Quesling. The other two potential suspects were older and younger respectively –Miranda Headley was 32 and Trish Corcoran 53, "Well, I want you to put out another release saying the 39-year-old woman has been released without charge," said Francesca, "As quickly as possible. You can say police are continuing their investigations."

"Right."

"Oh – and can you make a special effort to get local radio and TV to cover it? We want people connected with the case to find out about this development as soon as possible."

"Yes," said the young press officer slightly bemused. "Normally police are reluctant to admit that they've had to release someone without charge," he added. "They think it smacks of failure."

"Yes," said Francesca, "but then we're not normal." She gave him a fixed smile.

• • ● • •

By chance Debra was listening to her radio that morning while doing some washing. She hadn't started her work with the Rivers detective agency yet and had given in her notice at the local school. It came as quite a shock to her – a 39-year-old woman had been released by police without charge after being arrested on suspicion of murdering Hertford planning official Rob Corcoran. That was Jackie Quesling, she thought to herself, and Jackie Quesling had murdered her Sue. Why? was her first thought. She had agreed with Philip Rivers that she would give evidence against in public the previous evening. Rivers had seemed happy that this would seal her fate. She rang him on his mobile. There was no reply. A voice told her that the number could not be reached at the present time. It offered her no facility to leave a message for him. Undaunted, she then rang Jo on his mobile.

"Yes?" said a voice that seemed distracted on the other end of the telephone.

"Jo," she said. "Have you heard? They've released the woman who killed Sue?"

"Yes, I heard," said Jo. "But don't worry – it's only temporary while they get more evidence."

"They've got more evidence," she said. "Me. But nobody's come to take my statement."

"They will come, Debra. Be patient. They're just a bit busy at the present moment."

"Yes, releasing the real killer." She put the receiver down forcefully and started to cry. They can't do it, she said to herself. They can't let her get away with it.

Meanwhile, Jo reflected he hadn't handled Debra's call as well as he should have done. He should have moved to reassure her by telling her it was a ruse to catch Jackie's accomplice. To be fair, he thought, she hadn't made it easy for him but he could see how the bald news that Jackie Quesling had been released without charge would upset her. He rang her back immediately. Debra looked at the name on her mobile telephone as it rang and saw it was Jo. She immediately moved to kill the call. No, she thought, he wasn't being helpful. She decided to ring Francesca Manners at the police station instead.

"We've a call for you," Francesca was told after Debra had contacted the main switchboard number. "It's a Debra Paget."

Francesca was busy setting up the equipment to monitor Jackie's telephone and home. "Can you tell her I'm a bit busy and that I'll ring her back?"

The officer on the switchboard acquiesced but then came back to Francesca. "She's being a bit persistent," he said. "She wants to speak to Gary Clarke if she can't speak to you."

Francesca looked at Gary. "It's Debra," she said. m"She wants to speak to one of us. Even you will do," she added, smiling.

"Be better if it was you, Francesca," said Gary. "You've

got more clout and – until yesterday – you were a more sympathetic figure."

"Okay," said Francesca. "Put her through," she said to the officer. "Debra," she said when the call was finally put through to her. "What can I do for you?"

"I hear Jackie Quesling has been released," she said.

"For the time being," she said.

"Why?"

Francesca was debating in her head what she should tell Debra. Normally, she would not give out details of a police investigation in this situation but she appreciated Debra was an especially vulnerable person and a key element of their case against Jackie Quesling. She decided to be honest and not stonewall Debra. "We think by releasing her we might find out who her accomplice was," she said.

"Oh," said Debra. The answer surprised her – putting a new element into the equation. "You know I am willing to give evidence now?" she said.

"Of course. I know you told Philip Rivers that."

"But nobody's come to take a statement from me," she said. "It just feels as though you're ignoring you."

"No, we're not," said Francesca, "someone will come to take a statement from you."

"Someone?"

"I will come and take a statement from you but it will just have to wait for a bit. I'm just listening in to a wiretap on Jackie Quesling's phone at the moment to see if she says anything to anyone to identify her accomplice. We will get around to you soon, I promise."

"Okay." Debra sounded far from convinced, Francesca thought, but she could not see how she could do any more to reassure her that everything was going to be all right.

"I mean what I say," said Francesca. "You are an important part of her case against Jackie Quesling and we will be taking a statement from you in the very near future. Is that okay?"

"I suppose so," said Debra. She put the telephone down and noted that Jo had rung her twice during her conversation with Francesca. She ignored him. There was one way of bringing Jackie Quesling to justice, she thought. Get a confession out of her. If her house was being bugged, Francesca would hear it on the other end of the line. She could do that, she felt sure. She knew where Jackie Quesling lived. She had been there before. It would not take her long to get there. She slipped into the kitchen and took a sharp knife from the cutlery draw. She may have to threaten Jackie to get that confession, she reasoned, but she would get it. She wouldn't kill her. That was against her nature but the knife would help her put pressure on Jackie to confess.

CHAPTER TWELVE

Jackie Quesling sighed as she finally entered the driveway at her home. As soon as she stepped through the door of her house, she shut it behind her and leant back against it in relief. At least she was free. She went straight to the kitchen to make herself a cup of tea and a snack. Once sitting down on the settee with her drink and food, she began to examine her options. Flight? No, she reasoned. The police would probably have covered all ports and airports with a warning to look out for her. She was slightly surprised that the police had not insisted on her surrendering her passport but she reasoned that may be because they thought they had that aspect covered – that she would be unable to leave the country. There was one option, though. Jerry Vincent. He could arrange for a private plane to take her out of the country but she did not know where he was or how to contact him. Besides, she would look guilty if she tried to flee and that did not appeal to her. She still felt she had a reasonable chance of mounting a defence – saying that she never meant to kill Rob Corcoran by luring him out of the house. It was just coincidence that the car had run him over. That brought her to the tricky question of why she had been released. Had the police's star witness turned out to be a damp squib. If it was that girl who was friendly with Sue Plummer, it was quite possible that could be the case, she reasoned. She was not exactly reliable. Or had the police released her in the hope of finding more incriminating evidence against her and an accomplice? That was quite likely, she thought. The only way she could combat that was by being extremely careful about what information she did reveal about herself while she was free.

As she sat down with her meal, she switched the radio on. She soon heard the news story about the 39-year-old woman being released from police custody without charge after being questioned over the murder of Rob Corcoran. Ah well, that would mean all her friends and associates would know she was free. She reckoned she could expect one or two of them to contact her in the near future – especially if they had been following the saga since her arrest the previous day. She was not disappointed. The door-bell soon rang.

"Douglas," she said as she opened the door. "And what can I do for you?"

"I thought I'd come and see how you were," said the suspended head of the planning department in Hertford.

"No, you didn't."

"I'm sorry?"

"You didn't come to find out how I was? You came to discuss what I'd told the police about planning matters. Anyhow, come in." She put her fingers to her lips as if to motion him to silence. "It's such a lovely day, I think we should sit out in the garden," she said. She tried to signal to him that she thought her telephone was bugged by mimicking putting a telephone to her ear and then doing an impersonation of someone avidly listening to a call.

"Fine," said Douglas Roulay.

Meanwhile, back at police headquarters, Francesca emitted a swear word. "She's realised she's being bugged," she said. "That means we're not going to pick up any information through the bug. I think you'd better get down there, Gary."

"We won't be able to pick up anything else through being there," he said.

"We'll see all the comings and goings," said Francesca. "If she sends someone away or there's an altercation on the doorstep, you'll pick it up."

"We'll still be able to pick up a few titbits from the bug," said Gary. "For instance, we know Roulay and Jackie Quesling are going to discuss planning matters. Speaks of them being in cahoots over the planning application. He's the authority and she's the applicant. They shouldn't really need to talk about them."

"You're right," said Francesca, "but I can pick that all up from here. No, I want you to take Ryan Johnson and go down there. Park away from the house. Don't alert Jackie Quesling to the fact you're there. But keep an eye on the comings and goings."

"Okay," said Gary. As he got up to go, a voice came from the bug on Jackie's house. "Lemonade ready. I'll bring it out." Francesca grimaced as Gary departed. Once outside the house, Jackie turned to Roulay who was hovering by some garden chairs and a table on the patio just by the back door. She motioned towards two more garden chairs at the bottom of the garden. "Let's sit down there," she said.

"You think you're being bugged," said Roulay.

"Precisely."

Meanwhile, in the derelict shed in Jackie's garden it was Rivers' turn to curse. He could see Jackie and Roulay through a hole in the door of the derelict and dilapidated shed. There was no way he was going to be able to hear anything that was going on if they sat at the bottom of the garden.

"So what did you really come about?" asked Jackie.

"I wanted to know what you'd told the police – what you were questioned about."

"I think the radio news stories have pretty accurately described what I was questioned about. I was arrested on suspicion of the murder of Rob Corcoran."

"But you didn't do it, did you, Jackie?"

"Thanks for that vote of confidence, Douglas. I'm shocked that you have to ask."

"Sorry," he said. "That young woman detective questioned me twice about the murders but I think I must be in the clear now.

She hasn't come back again. You must be, too. They've released you."

"I wouldn't place too much weight on that idea," said Jackie. "I think that bug shows they've only released me in the hope of finding out something more about the murders."

"You're sure you're being bugged?"

"As sure as I am that the Pope's a Catholic."

"Right," he said. "So did they talk to you about planning matters?"

"They wanted to know when Jerry Vincent's name was excised from that planning application. That, I'm sure they felt, would pinpoint whether you were the only person who could have done it. I didn't give them any information that could lead them to the conclusion that you were the only person that could have done it."

"Thanks," said Roulay.

"Is that it?" said Jackie. "Only I've had a trying 24 hours and I could do with some rest."

"Of course."

"Just one more thing before you go," said Jackie. "Do you know how to contact Jerry Vincent?"

"Why would you need to get hold of him?"

"I might need his services."

"To help you get out of the country?" My God, thought Roulay, she really did do it. Jackie remained silent. "I'm afraid not," he said. "I haven't seen or heard from him since we didn't have that meal together and he departed these shores." Jackie nodded and bade her guest farewell.

Rivers, watching from the derelict shed, immediately rang Jo on his mobile. "Question him as he leaves," he said. "Ask him what they talked about – only take him away from the house. I don't want Jackie to hear you."

"That's going to be a bit difficult if she comes to see him off. He's parked in her driveway."

"You'll think of something."

Jo did. Jackie didn't stand on the doorstep to bid farewell to Roulay for any length of time – leaving Jo time to drive his car to block the exit from Jackie's house. As an irritated Roulay was about to pip his horn, Jo motioned him to get out – showing him his card at the same time.

"What do you want?" he asked.

"I want to know what you've been discussing with Ms Quesling."

"None of your business."

"I think it is. I'm helping the police with their investigation into the murders of Rob Corcoran and Sue Plummer. Your visit to Ms Quesling immediately after her release from police custody makes me suspicious she and you might have been partners in these crimes."

"That's ludicrous."

"I'm sure the police won't come to that conclusion."

Roulay thought for a moment. "Look," he said, changing tack, "I do think I'll be able to help you."

"Yes?"

"Before I do, though, I want to know whether – if I help you over the murders – will that help me if I face any charges as a result of the planning enquiries."

"There are no enquiries into planning matters being pursued by the police at present," said Jo. "It's purely a council-run thing,"

"I'd still like to know whether it will stand me in good stead."

"I'm not the police so I can't really tell but – put it this way – it certainly won't harm your interests."

Roulay seemed reassured even though Jo had really given him nothing to pin his hopes on. "Jackie said something interesting to me at the end of our conversation. She asked me if I knew Jerry Vincent's address – you're familiar with who he is?" Jo nodded. "She thought he might be able to help her flee the country. An innocent person wouldn't ask that. I'd be prepared to give evidence to that effect."

"Thank you," said Jo.

"Now would you let me go?"

"Perhaps you'd better come clean about the planning matter?" said Jo,

"I'm sorry?"

"Well, you wanted the police to be lenient with you over that. Best if you tell them what you did."

"I will tell them," he said.

"Well," said Jo, looking about him as a car carrying Detective Constables Clarke and Johnson suddenly arrived on the scene. "It looks as though you'll get your chance sooner than you think." He turned to the two detectives. "Mr Roulay here wants to confess to his role in planning corruption. He says he has some information about Jackie Quesling's involvement in the murders of Rob Corcoran and Sue Plummer. He wonders if by imparting this information, you'll go easy on the corruption."

"Can't promise anything," said Gary, "but let's put it this way – if he helps us out with the murders, it certainly won't be held against him."

"Precisely what I said," said Jo.

• • • • •

As Debra arrived at Jackie Quesling's house, she could see a group of people standing outside it – they included Jo and Detective Constable Clarke whom she remembered from her interrogation. Another man, who seemed friendly to Jo and Gary Clarke was helping a fourth man into a car. The two of them drove off. Gary reached into his pocket and took out his mobile phone. Jo went over to his car which was parked on the other side of the road and opened the door and sat in the driving seat. Debra felt it offered her a chance to walk past them unnoticed and go up the driveway to Jackie's house. She was just about to knock on the door when she heard a noise behind her.

It was Jo running towards her with a finger to his lips motioning her to be silent. She stopped what she was doing and let him approach her.

"We can't talk here," he whispered to her and led her back down the driveway. Once they were out of earshot of the house he turned to her. "What do you think you're doing?" he asked.

"I've come to get a confession from Jackie Quesling to Sue's murder," she said – almost in a matter of fact voice as if nobody should query this.

"Why?"

"Why?" asked Debra sounding incredulous. "Because she killed Sue and nobody seems to give a damn."

By this time Gary had joined them having completed his telephone call. "That's just not true," he said. "Why do you think we're here?" he asked.

"I don't know," said Debra. "All I do know is I told Mr Rivers yesterday that I was willing to give evidence and he said the police would be coming round to take a statement but nobody has bothered to contact me."

"It may seem like that to you but we're here trying to get more evidence to incriminate her," said Jo.

"And to find out who her accomplice was," added Gary. "You want him to be punished as well, don't you?"

"Of course I do."

"Look," said Gary. "Your evidence will be crucial when we go to court but it won't be enough on its own. Jackie is going to defend herself by saying that her luring of Rob out of his home was not connected to the hit and run – that she was just as surprised as anyone else when the car drove down the road and knocked him over so we need more evidence to counteract that. We've already got some. We've just spoken to the head of the planning department whom my colleague took away to the police station."

"I know. I saw that," said Debra.

"Yes," said Gary. "He told us that Jackie was contemplating trying to get in touch with Jerry Vincent, the property developer, to ask him to arrange for a private plane to allow her to flee the country. Now, if she was really innocent, she wouldn't do that. We only let her go this morning so we could try and gain some more evidence against her and find out who her accomplice was. Please believe me. I said I would do everything in my power to look after your interests and bring Sue's killers to justice. I meant that."

Debra thought for a moment. She looked at Jo. "They will be coming round to take your statement," he said to reassure her.

"We would have taken it yesterday if we were going to charge Jackie and bring her before the magistrates' court today," said Gary. "When we decided to release her, it meant that it wasn't quite so urgent to have the statement and that we should make collecting more information against Jackie Quesling our priority."

Debra lay back against Jo's car. She was thinking about what Gary had said. She was inclined to believe him. After all, he had been so friendly to her and apologised the previous day. She suddenly felt a huge desire to sneeze and opened her handbag to get a tissue. As she did, Jo saw the knife at the top of the bag. "What's that?" said Jo.

"It's a knife," said Debra.

"Were you planning to use it?"

"I'm not sure," she said defensively. "I wanted to get a confession from Jackie. I thought it might help."

"Might help get you into trouble," said Gary. "If you used that against Jackie Quesling, I would have to turn from nice Gary to nasty Gary again. You wouldn't want that, would you?"

"No," said Debra quietly.

"I would have had to have charged you over attacking Jackie. It could have been a murder charge if you had killed her."

"She deserves to die."

"You might think that," said Jo. "We all might think that

– but what right have we got to start taking people's lives? We become no better than the Jackie Quesling's of this world if we do that. And you don't deserve to go to prison either."

"I suppose,"said Debra.

"There's no supposing about it,"said Jo moving towards her. "Now give me that knife so there'll be no danger of you using it." He was standing right in front of her now and she let him take it from her handbag and put it in his pocket."Now just sit and await developments" he added."I'm hoping that someone will come who will give us some useful information."

"We've got the inside of Jackie's house bugged and the telephone tapped," said Gary. Normally he would not have given out such information about police procedure but he felt it necessary to do so to build on the relationship of trust he believed that had been established with Debra."I think it's best you go home now and leave us to it."

"No," said Debra. "I want to see what happens. I promise I won't get in your way."

Gary looked at Jo who nodded."We've disarmed her,"he said. "She won't cause us any problems now."

"All right,"he said."You can stay."

"Thanks,"said Debra.

"But stay inside the car," Gary added. "That way we can be sure you do as you have said you will."

Debra nodded and walked over to the passenger side of Jo's car and sat in the front seat.

● ● ● ● ●

Jackie Quesling sat down on the settee after she had bidden farewell to Douglas Roulay. He had not been that supportive, she thought. He was only worried about the impact the planning enquiries could have on him. She did regret having hinted to him that she would have been happy to arrange to flee the UK through Jerry Vincent but then she couldn't see him co-operating with the authorities and passing that information on. She poured herself a gin and tonic and began to slowly sip it. After a few moments, she became aware of what sounded like a commotion outside. Commotion might be putting too strong an emphasis on it, she thought. Someone talking just outside her front door. She got up from the settee and made her way to the door when the telephone rang.

"Is that you Jackie?" said a female voice on the other end of the line.

"Yes."

"It's Miranda Headley here. I wanted to catch up with the gossip. What's been happening?"

The word "gossip" seemed to trivialise what had been happening over the past few days, thought Jackie, and she sought to convey her view to Miranda. "I'm not sure this is the best method of communicating for us," she said – referring to the telephone.

"I've been hearing on the news that police are questioning someone over the murder of Paul Corcoran," said Miranda – not heeding her friend's warning.

"Yes – and have released them," said Jackie.

"Oh. Do you have any idea who it was?"

"A very good idea," said Jackie.

"Who?"

"Me." She thought to herself that she could do no harm by revealing facts that were already known to a large number of people on the phone – which she suspected was being bugged.

"You?" Miranda sounded taken aback. "How did they....?"

"Come to that conclusion?" said Jackie, quickly intervening in the conversation. "I'm not going to make the police's case for them, Miranda. Suffice it to say they have released me on police bail. Let's just say that I didn't have an alibi for the period when Rob was killed."

"Nor did I," said Miranda.

"I know. You'll probably be hauled in next," said Jackie in a matter of fact voice. To be truthful, she rather resented Miranda's flippant approach to the murder investigation – and her talk of gossip. It smacked of seeming that she did not take the matter seriously.

"You don't think so, do you?"

"No. I think they're convinced that I did it."

"That must be an awful position for you to be in," said Miranda. "How are you coping?"

"Well enough, when I'm left on my own," said Jackie – trying to give her erstwhile friend a heavy hint.

Miranda cottoned on to the fact that her call was not welcome at this time. "Well," she said, "I'd better be getting along. Maybe I should call round for a natter sometime soon?"

"Give me a ring in a couple of days." Jackie replaced the receiver and went back to her gin and tonic.

Meanwhile, listening in to the call had been Francesca who – by now – had been joined by Detective Constable Ryan Johnson. They had both been involved in taking a statement from Douglas Roulay. "What did you make of that?" Francesca asked her fellow officer.

"Not a lot. Bit school-girlish – that Miranda woman," he added.

"Exactly," said Francesca. "It didn't sound to me like a conversation between two co-conspirators. Not in any way."

"Probably not, ma'am." He seemed to be less sure than she was.

"So it's not Roulay and we don't believe it was Miranda Headley. Not that we ever thought the co-conspirator was a woman. I'll just keep Gary up to speed with what's been happening." She rang her fellow officer's mobile number. "Gary, what's going on over there?"

"Not a lot," he replied. "You'll have talked to Roulay. All we've had here is an attempt by young Debra Paget to burst in and drag a confession out of Jackie Quesling."

"Did she succeed?"

"No, we stopped her before she managed to get to the door."

"We?"

"Jo, Rivers' sidekick is with me. We're mob handed down here. Jo and I are waiting outside. Rivers is hiding out in a derelict shed in the garden. We've got her covered from all angles."

"Good. I'll stay here," said Francesca, "and keep listening. Give Jo my regards."

Gary shut down his mobile phone. "She sends her regards," he said to Jo as the two braced themselves for a long wait.

• • • • •

Gary had gone down to the local shops to buy burgers for himself, Jo and Debra by the time the next arrival turned up at Jackie's house. The car turned into the driveway and a man stepped from it.

"It's Colin Standen," Jo whispered to Debra.

"The man who gave me a lift here," said Debra.

"This could be interesting," said Jo. "I wish I could listen in to what they're saying." Jo noticed Colin missed his footing as he stepped from the car – but he soon righted himself. Ah well, he thought, we could at least do him for drunken driving if nothing else happened. Colin knocked loudly on the door.

"Coming," said a voice from inside. Jackie opened the door. "You," she said as if surprised to see him.

"There's one or two things I'd like to talk over with you."

"Wait a minute," she replied. She went into the room by the left of the door which she used as a study and came back with some notepaper and a pen. "We may be being bugged," she wrote on the notepaper. "Go into the garden."

Colin looked as if he did not believe her but it soon became obvious she wasn't going to speak to him until she got him into the garden so he decided to hold his tongue for the time being.

"Would you like a drink?" she asked him.

"I'd like a beer."

"Sorry," said Jackie. "I don't stretch to that. I can give you a glass of wine, some gin, some vodka?"

"I'll have a vodka and tonic." With that, he walked through the sitting room and sat down on one of the garden chairs on the patio just outside the kitchen. He waited for Jackie to join him with the drinks. He didn't sip daintily from his glass – almost downing the vodka and tonic in one after she had given it to him. "I wanted to ask you something," he began.

"I can guess what," she said.

"When we first planned this," he said, "I stood a good chance of sharing in Trish Corcoran's fortunes."

Rivers was straining to hear from the derelict shed. At least it was easier than if they had gone to sit in the two chairs at the bottom of the garden. He could pick up the odd word or two but not whole sentences. He could see their body language, though. Jackie looked apprehensive, he thought. Colin was bullish, though.

"I'll now get diddly squat," he said. "She's not interested in me so I've committed a murder, two murders, for no gain."

"I don't think we should be having this conversation," Jackie said firmly.

"Why not?"

"People could overhear us."

Colin shook his head. "Even if you are being bugged, it's a long way from the phone and the house. Nobody's going to hear out here."

"You can't be too sure," said Jackie, fidgeting as he showed no signs of moving or shutting up about what he had been discussing.

"Well, if it makes it easier for you, we could go down to the bottom of the garden." He got up from his seat and strode purposefully to the two seats by the fence at the foot of the garden. "I'm not earning a penny from this," he continued, "but you – you've got all the money coming from the building f your new house through this planning scam."

"I wouldn't quite call it that."

"I was talking to a builder friend of mine and he reckoned you could get up to £1million by selling the new house you plan to build. It probably won't cost you much more than £100,000 to £150,000 to build. That's a clear profit of more than £800,000."

"I wouldn't start counting my chickens if you don't mind." She lay heavy emphasis on the "my".

"Why not?"

"There is an investigation to see whether the planning application was granted through corrupt means. They could rescind it."

"Or they could not. Let's at least establish a principle here. I should be entitled to some of that money."

"And if I say no?"

"I have killed twice."

"Come off it, Colin, you're not going to kill me," she said confidently. "Besides, I've killed twice, too. What does that prove?"

"I am not going to leave here empty handed," he said as he tried to calculate what he should do next. "I reckon I should be entitled to half the money you make on the house. I've put in half the risk after all."

"That's all very well, Colin, but when do you think I can pay you that money? Not until I've built the house and sold it – and the chances of that happening are looking slimmer by the minute. The planning investigation is bound to raise queries about the application. They may well reverse their decision to approve it. I could also go to prison over that – regardless of anything else. Your best bet is just to lie low, forget all about what we've done and hope it will all blow over."

Colin nodded. "So I get nothing at the end of the day?"

"Look, it's not my fault that Trish Corcoran wouldn't have you as her lover," said Jackie. "That's what brought you into this in the first place. You thought you could lead the life of Reilly on the proceeds from Rob's estate. I never promised you a penny. You wanted to be part of it."

"You sought me out to help you. You knew how desperate I was for money. You, in effect, hired me to carry out the killing that night in the Dog and Partridge after Rob's private life had been exposed to all and sundry. I'm not sure – did you kill him because you were a spurned lover or because he was on the verge of exposing the corruption over your planning application? It doesn't matter, I suppose,"he said reflectively. "All I want now is wages for what I have done. It's not an unreasonable demand."

"It's not unreasonable, I grant you, Colin, but there is no money. I could very soon be going to prison for Rob and Sue's murders. I won't have any money to pay you then."

"You've been released."

"Oh, yes, I've been released so they can build up more information and possibly catch my accomplice – which your comments are making easier for them if they are overhearing what you've said. I hope they aren't. As I said, that's why we're having this conversation at the bottom of the garden. They're probably bugging my house and phone."

Colin looked on edge."You're a danger to me," he said after taking the opportunity to think for a moment. "You're the only one who knows of my role in all this."

Jackie looked apprehensive. She was worried about where this turn in the conversation would lead them. "But I'm not going to reveal anything about your role," she said. "To do so would be to admit my guilt."

"There is another way of ensuring you don't blab,"he said.

"Don't be stupid, Colin. The cops will be all over you if you try to get rid of me." She began to get up off her seat and glanced towards the house to try and determine if she could make a run for it if Colin turned nastier.

"I don't buy your story about being bugged."He got up off his seat and moved towards her. "If you're out of the equation, so am I – in the police's eyes. Sit down, Jackie."

"Colin, no," she shrieked as he put his left hand on her shoulder and brought his right up so it was poised to punch her.

"Stop!" yelled a voice behind him. Rivers had been continuing his watch from the disused shed and thought it about time he should intervene. Colin turned for a moment to see where the noise was coming from. It was enough of a split second to allow Jackie to run towards the house. Colin turned to look after her and decided to give chase. Rivers, though, was catching up on him and jumped on his back, sending him flying. As he struggled to recover his composure, Rivers responded with three telling punches to his face – knocking him unconscious in the process. He quickly brought his mobile telephone from his pocket and called Jo. "I think Jackie is trying to flee," he said. "I've got Colin Standen in the garden. He's unconscious but I could do with some help in restraining him if he comes round."

"Right," said Jo. He switched the car's engine on and turned round in the road so he was blocking Jackie Quesling's driveway again. As he did so, he saw Jackie emerging from the front door – car keys in her hand. She was attempting to flee – that much was obvious – but it was also apparent that she had not had any time to pack. Jo felt he did not have to do much else. Jackie could not get out of the driveway and would have to come to a halt before she could turn into the road. Gary would have ample opportunity to arrest her then. What he had not bargained for, though, was Debra's reaction. On seeing Jackie emerging from the house and making her way to her car, she had flung herself out of Jo's car. She ran up the driveway and flung herself at the departing Jackie – the sheer force of her body, albeit tiny, being enough to knock Jackie over. As Jackie struggled to get up, Debra sat on her and started punching her in the face. "You killed my Sue," she shouted. "You killed my Sue."

Within a few moments, she felt a restraining hand on her

shoulder. "That's enough, tiger," said Gary. "We'll take it from here." Debra stopped and got off Jackie. She struggled over to the side of the driveway and sat down – tears streaming from her face. Jo came over to comfort her. Her red eyes looked into his. "She killed my Sue," she sobbed.

"I know," said Jo soothingly, "and now she's going to pay for it."

Gary, meanwhile, was cautioning Jackie who – by now had blood streaming from her face. "I've been hurt," she said interrupting his caution.

"Yes, I know," said Gary. "It's what happens when you mess with people's emotions by killing their best friends." He then continued with his caution and called an ambulance on his mobile phone. "I'd better accompany her to hospital. I'll get Francesca to get me some plods to help out."

Suddenly, they were interrupted by a cry from the garden. "Would somebody help me out?" came a distant voice. "I can't keep knocking this guy unconscious." Jo obliged – leaving Jackie with Gary and Debra.

"Keep her away from me," said Jackie firmly.

"I was thinking of leaving you alone with her," said Gary. "She seems to be better at my job than I am."

"You win," said Rivers as Jo approached him in the back garden. "You said Colin Standen was involved in the murders,"

Jo looked at the bedraggled figure lying on the floor by Rivers' feet. Colin was slowly coming to. "I think we have another candidate for the hospital," he said. He and Rivers then took an arm each and dragged Colin round to the front of the house where a police car had just arrived to reinforce Gary. Two constables took Jackie and Colin from their respective captors and escorted them to the ambulance after they had been handcuffed. "Room for another one?" Gary asked the ambulance staff when they were ready to depart. "Only I haven't got my car."

As he sat at the back door of the ambulance, he turned to Debra and said: "I'll be back to get your statement later. I promise."

Debra dried her eyes and looked after the departing ambulance.

• • • • •

"These are on me," said Francesca as she made her way into the Dog and Partridge where Rivers and Jo had been celebrating with Debra for a little while. She was accompanied by Gary. "Well done, lads and lass," she said. "The Chief Constable's pretty pleased with us."

"Have they confessed?" asked Rivers.

"They're not likely to," said Francesca, "but the evidence of the arrest and what you overheard in the garden will be enough to send them down." She went to the bar and ordered another round of drinks. Jo declined – saying he would have to drive home at the end of the day. Debra warned a second drink might make her squiffy but still ordered one. "More good news," said Francesca. "I've been told by the Chief Constable that there's a permanent vacancy in my team and I won't have to put up with trainees anymore." She stole a sideways glance at Gary as she spoke. "There'll have to be a board to interview all the applicants," she said, "but I've suggested the position would be just right for you if you want it, Gary."

Gary blushed. "I don't know what to say," he said.

"Thank God," said Rivers. "Then don't say anything."

"Just yes would do," said Francesca,

Gary nodded. "All right, yes," he said. "Thanks, Francesca."

Francesca smiled. "And I see you've got the etiquette of working for me right," she added. "Now all you've got to do is persuade Ryan Johnson to adopt it – if he works with us again."

"Will do," said Gary.

"And you," said Francesca turning to Debra. "The Chief Constable was impressed when Gary described the way you had tackled Jackie when you realised she could escape."

Debra blushed. "She wouldn't really have done," she said. "Jo's car was blocking the exit."

"Hmm, that's as maybe," said Francesca, "but for some unknown reason Gary forgot to mention that in his report." It was the junior officer's turn to look sheepish.

"I've got an idea," said Rivers. "Let's go and get a meal at that Italian across the road. It's where it all started."

The five of them trooped over to the restaurant and took a table near the door – in fact the same one Rivers and Jo had taken several weeks previously. It wasn't long into the meal before Rivers – facing the window and looking out into the street – spoke to Jo who was opposite him. "Don't look now, but there's a couple having an argument in the alleyway next to the pub.," he said.

"I'm not falling for that," said Jo.

Gary turned to look out into the street. "Rivers is right," he said. "There is."

"I think we should ignore them, though," said Rivers.

POSTSCRIPT

Debra saw it through right to the end. She had asked Rivers for leave to attend the trial of Jackie Quesling and Colin Standen but he had insisted on her taking the trial in as part of her work. She didn't feel quite right about that but Nikki had told her never to look a gift horse in the mouth. She wasn't quite sure what that meant but it seemed to suggest that she should take up Rivers' offer. So she did. Jackie had defended herself on the grounds that her luring of Rob Corcoran out of his house had nothing to do with the subsequent hit and run – as had been predicted she would. However, she found it difficult to answer Douglas Roulay's suggestion that she had talked about trying to flee the country – and Rivers' testimony that he had overheard Colin Standen mention they had been involved in two murders. Colin Standen's admission, again overheard by Rivers – appeared to have sunk any chance he had of getting off the murder charges. The jury had deliberated for five hours but in the end brought in a verdict of guilty to both the charges made against each of them. Both were sentenced to life imprisonment.

Debra was praised in the judge's summing up for her efforts to try and capture Jackie as she sought to flee, Gary, for his part, again failed to mention that Jackie's escape had been blocked by Jo. Jo, who was also in court at that time, wondered how different it would have been if they had not found her knife in time.

As Debra made her way from the court, she stifled a tear. Jo went up to her to comfort her. "Can I do anything for you?" he asked.

"I just want to go to where they scattered Sue's ashes and tell her what happened," she added. Jo nodded. He knew the spot.

It was in a field overlooking a common in Hertford. He stood back while Debra seemed to be saying something – probably to Sue, he surmised. When she had finished telling her former friend about what had happened, he took her back to the flat they were sharing. He offered her a drink. "No," she said. "I'm in control now. I don't need a drink. It makes me squiffy."

$$\bullet \ \bullet \ \bullet \ \bullet \ \bullet$$

It was another hot, sunny day on the Caribbean Island where Roger Bunting, also known as Jerry Vincent, had taken up residence. As he sat on the patio sipping his rum punch, he turned to his colleague. "So what brought you here?" he asked.

"Tax evasion," came the reply. "And you?"

"I had to flee the UK. I'd been bribing officials to put through housing planning applications for me – one of those involved was so worried about it she organised a hit on the person who was raking it up. Stupid, if you ask me. I had my ways of making sure no-one told on me."

He picked up the paper on the poolside table. "The person who organised the hit has been sent down for life, it says today. My two 'persuaders' – if you get my drift – have also been sent down for seven years for an attempted kidnapping. Their skills will be missed. They were very effective. Could persuade anyone to drop anything."

"I suppose you need people like that in your line of business," said the other man.

"Yes," he said. "Still do. You know the sad part of all this is I had to vacate a lovely home I had in the heart of the countryside. Almost a stately home, had to leave the sale of it to somebody else. Just heard that it's gone for £1.8million. Can't have the money sent to me because people will find out where I am."

"Do you want to get hold of the money?" asked the other man. "Only I know a couple of 'persuaders' who could do that for you."

Bunting, or Vincent, or whoever he was smiled. "You're not just here for tax evasion purposes, are you?" he said.

"Best not to go down that road," warned the other man.

"No, dear boy, I don't mean to pry."

"Good. Do you want me to get them to get the money for you? They can persuade your man to go and get the cash and then pick it up from him. For a small fee."

"I would be ever so grateful," said Bunting. "I'll leave the bloke with £300,000 for his expenses. Generous to a fault I am. He doesn't deserve the £1.8 million. Got off with a suspended sentence from the planning fraud. I think he did a deal with the police – nailing the woman who organised the hit in exchange for them pleading for leniency. Don't hurt him, though. That won't necessary."

"Certainly not. Who do you think I am?"

Bunting chuckled. "Now that's a road I don't want to go down," he said.

"Just as well."

"You know – both the planning officials I bribed got away with suspended sentences for helping the police. The other guy told the police about the extent of my operation – so far as he knew about it."

"Do you want him dealt with?"

"No point," said Bunting. "That would just be vindictive. I only bring in 'persuaders' when there's something to be gained from their interference."

"Wise move."

"Another rum punch?" The other man nodded.

• • • • •

Jo turned to Rivers one night when he was visiting his and Nikki's flat. It was a kind of farewell meal for the flat as Rivers and Nikki had completed the purchase of a house in Hertford.

"I've decided to stay," he said.

"With the agency?" asked Rivers.

"Yes."

"You're not as worried as you were about the racism, then?"

"No. There are always going to be some racists out there. I met my fill of them the first three weeks I was here," said Jo. "But there are other people. Good people. Francesca, Debra and even Gary. I would miss them if I pulled out."

"I'm glad you're staying," said Rivers. "You know, we should make use of your surname so we could have you as an equal partner on our business card."

"No," said Jo. "I'll just be Jo. I like it that way."

Also by Richard Garner

RICHARD GARNER

BEST SERVED
COLD

A thriller of revenge and corruption

Journalist Roy Faulkner is the prime suspect in a murder inquiry
when Kate Williams, the fellow journalist he accompanied to
a night club appeared to disappear from the face of the earth.
Worse still, he finds the detective who is investigating the case
harbours a long-standing grudge against him dating back to
their teenage years in a rock band. As evidence piles up against
Roy, he is charged with the murder of Kate. Private investigator
Philip Rivers faces a battle against time to find out what really
happened before Roy is found guilty.

£8.99   ISBN: 978 1 910074 13 8

Also by Richard Garner

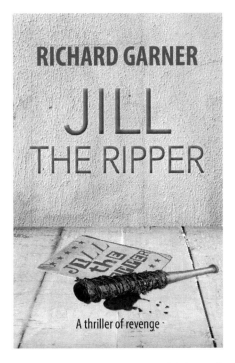

A small revolutionary feminist group publishes a leaflet urging revenge attacks against men for what its author perceives to be the glorification of Jack the Ripper. Soon afterwards, the bodies of two men are found mutilated on derelict waste ground. The police begin to investigate whether there is a connection between the members of the group and the murders, but find few leads.

Private investigator Philip Rivers is called in to help by the parents of their son, who they believe could be the killer's next victim, as he shares a flat with a member of the group. Rivers decides the best way to protect him is to find the killer

£8.99   ISBN: 978 1 910074 19 0